FROM THE DEAD

7/20/13

Hudson Class of 1993 —

Never give up!

[signature]

FROM THE DEAD

A NOVEL

JOHN HERRICK

SegueBlue

PUBLISHED BY SEGUE BLUE

Copyright © 2010 by John Herrick

All Rights Reserved
Published in the United States by Segue Blue, St. Louis, MO.
www.segueblue.com

Book design and layout by Jonathan Gullery
Author photograph by Pamela Rempe

Library of Congress Control Number: 2009939829

ISBN-13: 978-0-9821470-1-6
ISBN-10: 0-9821470-1-5

Publisher's Cataloging-in-Publication

Herrick, John, 1975-
    From the dead : a novel / by John Herrick.
    p. cm.
    LCCN 2009939829
    ISBN-13: 978-0-9821470-1-6
    ISBN-10: 0-9821470-1-5

1. Man-woman relationships—Fiction. 2. Fathers and
sons—Fiction. 3. Redemption—Fiction. 4. Life and
death, Power over—Fiction. 5. Ohio—Fiction. I. Title.

PS3608.E774Fro 2010
813'.6   QBI09-600209

PRINTED IN THE UNITED STATES OF AMERICA

For my brother Mike,
who shared the vision and held me accountable.

ACKNOWLEDGMENTS

Thanks to all who played a part behind the scenes.

My family: More than anyone else, they shared in the celebrations—and listened to my ugly rants. I love you all.

My early draft readers: Heather Manning, Melissa McLean and Pam Rempe.

Elsa Dixon, my editor.

My encouragers: Kathy Wakeman, Elizabeth Behling, Bobby Schroeder, Marnie Thompson, Lisa Fendler, Gigi Stanton, Terry Shields.

This novel would still exist on my to-do list if not for Aisha Ford. God used her to get my butt in gear at the strategic time.

Years ago, Phil Lewis provided my first opportunity to write for radio at then-station WCBW in St. Louis. I've never forgotten.

And to each person I've undoubtedly failed to mention here. You know who you are.

PART ONE

PREACHER'S SON

CHAPTER 1

JADA Ferrari lit the collection of miniature candles along the coffee table. Darkness evaporated from the living room.

As Jada leaned forward, Jesse Barlow admired the curvature of her figure, the way her brunette hair fell in curls past her shoulder blades.

"I just bought these today," said Jada, who brushed her hand above the flames and sent the aroma of jasmine wafting through the air. Ever the center of attention, she sat on the edge of the sofa beside Cameron and Gavin, friends from an apartment downstairs, as Gavin lit the round of joints.

The scene, once common, had grown less frequent in recent months. Nowadays, Jada, a burgeoning film director's assistant, sought company with people who could further her career.

Jesse's career, on the other hand, begged resuscitation.

From the recliner at the far end of the room, Jesse, distant and disengaged, stared out the window at the crisp glow of a streetlight two stories below. At the chirp of an activated car alarm, Jesse leaned toward the sound in time to see a male silhouette emerge from the shadows and wander into the apartment building next door.

An anonymous man. Los Angeles is filled with them.

Then again, everyone is anonymous to *someone*. And

everyone has an anonymous side, a shadow within, a guarded corner where secrets hide.

Gavin passed a joint to Jada. With a puff, she held her breath, coughed a few times, then fell back against the cushions and hung limber, as though she'd craved this all day.

Cameron grinned. "Next time, you buy."

Spoken like a low-level accountant.

Jada waved her joint toward Jesse in a hypnotic-like motion. "Are you gonna keep staring out the window or get in on the act?"

Years ago, he wouldn't have hesitated. Never an addict or heavy user, Jesse enjoyed a recreational hit when the urge mounted within. But the pleasure had long passed. He'd grown tired of breathing the strange air, the subtle loss of control.

He wished his guests would leave but knew it would be a few hours. Soon the music would start—Beck's *Odelay*, no doubt—followed by a raid on his refrigerator. Gavin and Cameron would argue whether "Loser" or "Where It's At" was the singer's breakthrough single.

Oh, what the hell. "All right, hand one over." And with that, Jesse reached out his thumb and forefinger.

"There you go." Jada beamed as she passed Jesse a joint. "You never have fun anymore. Gotta live a little!" She turned to her couch mates. "Right, losers?"

Lightheaded, Gavin giggled.

With the joint in his fingers, Jesse sank into the recliner once again. He yielded to the sharp herbal fumes that crept like a current through his veins and loosened his brain. The effect seemed immediate, his body no longer conditioned to the stuff. He focused on the array of candles as their flames increased in clarity and the jasmine grew richer.

Gavin exhaled a deep cloud and leered at oblivion, a pensive look on his face like a stoned Socrates. He waved his joint in front of his face, as if in afterthought. "You know, those Rastafari guys say this stuff helps you get close to God."

God, thought Jesse. The God who never seemed to give him answers to a lifetime of questions. And as Jesse sat, present yet isolated, those questions resurfaced in a torrent.

Why did she have to die?

Why did I leave them behind?

Jesse leaned back further against the black leather cushion and clenched his jaw.

I'm a preacher's son, he thought.

So how did my life get so fucked up?

CHAPTER 2

THE screech of an alarm clock pierced the 3:30 a.m. silence. Jada, groggy from the night before, groaned as she felt around the pre-dawn darkness for the button to make the ringing stop. Not one to snooze, she sat up in a heap as Jesse rolled over and mumbled.

"Is Barry scheduling sunrise meetings now?" Jesse asked.

Barry Richert. *The* Barry Richert, as Jada reminded everyone who would listen. Barry Richert, whose unexpected success arrived two years ago with a low-budget film that became a sleeper hit. These days, the man received hundreds of screenplays a week.

"A location shoot in Malibu. Call time is seven, but he needs me there an hour early."

Her commute from their Sherman Oaks apartment would require less than an hour, but Jesse knew Jada would spend much longer perfecting her image in the bathroom. She pressed her fingers against her head, which must have continued to pulsate from the prior evening's get-together.

"Go back to sleep, babe." She stroked his chest once and climbed out of bed. Jesse leaned on an elbow and eyed the silhouette of his girlfriend, clad in a slinky black negligee, as she tiptoed across the crowded bedroom and turned on the bathroom light.

Through the cracked door, Jesse heard the sputter of a

shower. Then he buried his head in the pillow and dozed off. He had come to dread the sunrise in recent months.

"A polarizing filter will help reduce glare," Jesse explained. "Kind of like wearing a pair of shades at the beach." From a display rack on the sales floor, he peered out the window while, for the sixth time, he rattled off the benefits of camera filters to a newbie.

"What about this one?" asked the customer, who grabbed a transparent red filter from the rack and held it toward the overhead light. "It looks like half a pair of 3-D glasses."

"More or less. It can be used to cover up skin blemishes. Heavy acne, that sort of thing," Jesse said.

The customer chuckled in a series of mother-hen clucks. She tucked a lock of silvering chestnut hair behind her ear and said, "That would come in handy for my daughter-in-law. The latest one, that is. Spent thousands on a boob job but can't get rid of that acne along her neckline. Spends half her life in the tanning booth to cover it up. That reminds me: Can any of these filter things hide my son's inheritance from her?"

"Sorry, ma'am."

LensPerfection sat on Ventura Boulevard near the Van Nuys intersection. Crammed within a dense stretch of bricked retail, the photography shop shared its walls with a Java Cup coffee shop on one side and an incense store on the other. Jesse found humor in the string of palm trees that loomed outside, whose lazy branches lapped sunlight in strategic array but, in the end, sat unnoticed by passersby. With their perfect spacing, the trunks appeared victims of a transplant, carted to the side of a busy street to project an image of California perfection.

Jesse smirked. Even the trees were cosmetic.

Once he'd satisfied all his customer's questions, Jesse led her to the checkout counter with a handful of filters he doubted she'd ever use.

By eleven thirty in the morning, LensPerfection attracted its usual surge of foot traffic from those who took an early lunch hour. Most were browsers. A portrait studio sat toward the back and lured the occasional actor-to-be, who arrived with a designer coffee or vitamin water in hand, ready to schedule a shoot for the head shot that would make him famous.

Jesse's head shots were free. After several years of part-time employment, the owner allowed the extra perk and arranged Jesse's schedule around his bottom-rung work on film and television shoots. But the shoots had become sparse and, for two years straight, Jesse had not met the minimal hours required to secure medical coverage through his union. At this point, however, benefits were the least of his concerns.

Jesse's wavy, dark-blond hair, chiseled jaw line, and tall, fit form caught frequent second glances from both genders. But for Hollywood's cameras, handsome didn't seem to cut it, not when perfection stood next in line.

Jesse felt a vibration in his pocket. When he flipped his cell phone open and discovered a new text message from Maddy, his agent, his hopes surged. She had gotten word of a possible audition, a small supporting role in a feature film, and had pursued the prospect for weeks. Although it consisted of five lines, it represented an opportunity to expand his resume and connect with its director and principals. Jesse needed the gig.

And the audition was scheduled.

Emotional attachments are dangerous; better to take the news in stride, but this audition could mark the official end of his dry spell and justify years of waiting in L.A.

Jesse returned his attention to the store and the hum of its electric doorbell. A customer, a man around forty years old, entered and hung his sunglasses on his shirt opening. Dressed in starched khakis and a perfect haircut, the man looked more like a mid-level executive who had stopped by on his way to a round of golf. Jesse wondered what a corporate job with steady hours must be like.

"Can I help you?"

"I tossed a roll of film in the drop-off bin yesterday." Jesse reached for the basket of completed photo packets on the rear counter. "Name?"

"Glen Merseal," he replied.

As Jesse flipped through packets, Glen fingered through some eight-by-tens stacked beside the cash register. When Jesse returned, Glen couldn't seem to pull himself away from a photo of a homeless man. In the photo, the subject leaned against a railing and gazed at the ocean, his face afire beneath a midday sun. With his fishing rod extended in search of a victim, the homeless man's face spoke of mystery. Jesse couldn't determine whether the subject appeared content or forlorn; perhaps the man struggled between the two.

Jesse began to ring out the order.

Glen tapped the edge of the photo with his finger and said, "This guy's expression intrigues me. The photographer captured his, what? His aura?"

"Oh, it's not a professional photo." Jesse chuckled. "It's just a sample photo to illustrate the paper quality."

"Do you know who took the picture?"

Jesse shoved a hand into his pocket. "I did." When Glen's eyebrows rose a bit, Jesse added, "I shot that photo at the Santa Monica Pier. I've seen that man from time to time. Guy's name is Marshall. He must catch dinner there. Life on the beach, huh?"

"Did you take photography classes?"

"A high school class way back, but nothing else. I dabble in it here and there, flip through books to pick up tips. Trust me, I'm no professional."

"That's amazing." Glen glanced at the photo again, but this time he held it up to the light. He extended his hand. "What's your name?"

"Jesse. Nice to meet you."

As they shook hands, Glen reached for his wallet and removed a business card.

"My kid's got a birthday coming up. We're giving her a little party in a couple of weeks at a park nearby. Would you be interested in taking some action shots?"

"You're making a professional out of me, is that it?"

Glen nodded.

"Sure," Jesse said. "Who couldn't use the extra cash?"

If only film and television jobs were this easy to obtain.

"Great! We'll figure out the details letter. Number's on the card."

As the customer walked away, Jesse peered down at the business card. Was it possible Glen might work in the legal department at a studio?

No such luck. Glen was a franchise owner in a fast-food chain.

CHAPTER 3

JESSE arrived home around six that night. No purse or keys on the breakfast-bar ledge above the kitchen counter, which meant Jada hadn't yet come home. He tried to recall her schedule today: Dinner plans with Barry Richert and a studio executive? Ink a deal to direct an adaptation of that recent book lauded by critics? He couldn't keep track of her life. By virtue of her job, Jada subjected herself to Barry's continual beck and call. Then again, Jesse was thankful to have the apartment to himself for the moment; nowadays her presence alone could trigger tension.

His eyes sensitive from the fluorescent lights at the shop, Jesse slid onto the black leather sofa in the living room and went limp for a few minutes. He ran his hand through his hair. Was he getting tired quicker? Though subtle, he had noticed a difference.

He stared at the jasmine candles on the coffee table, the ones from the previous night, his sinuses acute to the sharp scent. *What is it with women and candles?* he wondered. Jada wasn't the kind of woman to leave them at random spots around the apartment, however, so he counted his blessings. Subtle yet aggressive, she was the type to lay the bait and wait for someone to notice and respond with a compliment. And Jesse was grateful she chose a scent other than vanilla. Then again, Jada herself was anything but vanilla.

In its entirety, the apartment décor could be credited to Jada. The glass-top coffee table on a slab of generic gray stone, jazz wall prints fit for a coffee house, muted chrome lamps—everything possessed a contemporary nonchalance, as if an interior decorator stopped by on periodic visits and left behind articles much like you'd forget a ballpoint pen. Every element reflected Jada's personality. It was a far cry from the more traditional embellishments he found in his northern Ohio hometown. But to her credit, Jada had managed to frame a few of his photographs and put them on the bookshelves. Jesse held no strong opinions in the matter, though on occasion he felt like a stranger in his own home.

And, of course, the lease was in her name.

He grabbed his cell phone from his pocket and read Maddy's text message again. Countless months had passed since he'd heard good news; he had to savor this audition prospect. Most of Jesse's media work was as an extra, a random individual who walked down background corridors or pointed at superheroes that clung to the sides of buildings. Seldom did Jesse learn whether he appeared in the final cut until the film opened in theaters.

But he had never carried a line of dialogue. If successful, this audition would be a game changer. A small role, yet even award-winning celebrities had their minor moments early on: Richard Dreyfuss offered to call the police in *The Graduate*; Jodie Foster lent her voice to an animated Charlie Brown.

On the other hand, his confidence had taken a severe blow the last two years. It's said you shouldn't become an actor if you can't handle rejection. But while the initial rejections are heartbreaking, soon those rejections become routine, to which you grow impervious, like skin numbed by an ice cube. Jesse had always taken rejection in stride. Today, however, with his gears rusty, Jesse fought internal doubts about whether he could win this role. The way he saw it, the odds didn't fare well for him.

No. Forget the doubt, he thought. *It's been too long. This has to work out.* He didn't want to think about the alternative: another failure, another embarrassment, another step toward a terminated dream.

Jada didn't understand. Despite her industry savvy, she— Jesse heard keys jingle outside. Speak of the devil.

She entered in a flourish. Without a greeting, Jada unleashed as soon as she spotted him on the couch.

"Can you believe the guy in the next building parked his crappy car in front of our doorway again? I had to walk halfway up the block to get here. My Beemer is worth more than that guy's gas pedal! What the fuck's the matter with him?"

A delicate body figure with a cast-iron tongue. Polished and professional on the job, though. Not an off-color word from her on the set. She knew who fed her and how to perform for an audience of her own.

Jada left her purse and keys on the breakfast bar, then plopped down on the sofa beside Jesse and kicked off her shoes. As Jesse massaged her knee, she drew her legs underneath her and tugged at a bracelet. "I hate location shoots," she said.

That's right, she spent today in Malibu. "That bad, huh?"

"Once the police got the street blocked off and we started rolling, it went fine. A side street off the 101. We shot a couple of short scenes in the morning to minimize our days outside the studio lot." In a single motion, her eyes lit up and she engaged her hands in a near pantomime. "Oh, then it got to be noon and the real fun started. You know those people who wander by and decide they want to make their screen debut? Someone peeks behind a building across the street? We got one of those."

"A side street in Malibu isn't what you'd call a high foot-traffic area."

"I don't know what this guy was thinking, but he's coy. Starts out on the 101, just walks by. Maybe a tourist who just had lunch."

"How far away were you from 101?"

"A couple of blocks, but he wanders up the sidewalk. No crime. He inches closer till he's a few feet away from the action." She leaned forward and spread her fingers toward Jesse. "Amanda Galley's starring in this thing, okay? So she's hang-ing out, flirting with the crew like she does. This tourist guy waddles up and makes a remark to her, thinks he's gonna score with this A-lister. Well, I don't know what he said to her; the story versions change depending on who you talk to. But he got assaulted with a shoe, and—"

"A shoe? How?"

"He got hit in the head with a shoe."

"Whose shoe?"

"Amanda's! She's in costume, some riches-to-rags character, loses all her money and collects seashells by the seashore in her high heels. Anyway, she pulls off her shoe and hits the guy right in the middle of his forehead. *Disaster.* The guy doesn't know what hit him. He starts to scream when a trickle of blood runs down his nasty face. So now the police wander over to check it out, the guy says he's gonna sue, all this shit. Because he got nicked in the head by Amanda Galley's pink shoe. She'll prob-ably show up on the news tonight. What a moron."

"Amanda or the guy?"

"Both of them. Have you ever worked with her?"

"No."

"Prima donna. And if you think about it, she's never had a big hit." In a huff Jada fell back against the sofa and drew her brunette hair to rest on her shoulders. Jesse found her olive, Mediterranean skin tone exotic.

Jada had had dreams of her own at one point. She grew up in Reno, Nevada, with her own mother as her biggest fan since infancy. As a preschooler, the talented Jada entered a long list of beauty pageants, where she performed a tap-dance routine with a cane and top hat, choreographed by her mom, a former dancer in Vegas. By first grade, Jada had appeared in a handful of local commercials and, when she was eight, landed a role on television: *Bailey's Gang*, a hip, educational program that started as a local Reno show and graduated to syndication during the mid 1980s. Jesse had heard the rundown countless times. Jada played one of a dozen Tree House Kids on the song-and-sketch show which was, in actuality, a rip-off of better-known predecessors—an admission Jada allowed because she considered herself the show's answer to Annette Funicello.

After five years on the air, controversy raged when a reporter photographed Bailey handing a beer to a Tree House Kid. The show entered hiatus and never recovered. Jada's acting career screeched to a halt, but still existed in the deep recesses of her subconscious. She seemed to long for those golden days and, due perhaps to unresolved childhood issues, seemed to remain a little girl at heart. When they first moved in together, Jesse discovered a secret stash of videotapes in Jada's closet—her favorite *Bailey's Gang* episodes. Jesse found the stash adorable, but when he took his discovery a step further and joked about her collection, Jada actually cried.

Jesse got up and headed for the kitchen. "I'll get you a beer, how's that?"

"No, I'll just have a glass of wine at dinner. Did you work at the shop today?"

"Yeah, a full day. Wasn't as eventful as yours, though."

"Nobody tried to steal a roll of film? No armed robbery?"

"Not quite," he called from the kitchen. "A customer hired me to shoot pictures at his kid's birthday party. A little extra cash."

Expressionless, Jada examined her manicured nails. "Gee, exciting stuff. I can see why you like it there."

Bottle of Budweiser in hand, Jesse walked back into the room and took a swig. He settled back on the sofa, rested his elbows on his knees as Jada moved closer. She ran her hand along his back.

"I heard from Maddy today," Jesse said as he picked at the bottle label. "She scheduled me for an audition."

"Which project?"

"*Taking Sides*. It's a bit part."

"The new Mark Shea project? Why would you want that?"

"I need the gig. What's wrong with it?"

"He's lost his vision. His last three films tanked. He cast a sinking star in the lead role. You want to associate yourself with that? How many times have I explained this to you?"

"Look, it's not like I have a choice. I don't work for Barry Richert, who picks his projects."

"How many others are up for the part?"

"Four or five. Maddy doesn't have many specifics on it; she just knows they want someone tall."

"Well, you should have a decent shot at it." A quick pause before Jada swung her head around to face him eye to eye.

"What else is going on? You've got those lines in your fore-head—the ones you get when you're worried."

For a moment, Jesse traced his finger along the permanent crease line of his khaki pants, where the fabric had lightened a shade. He shrugged.

"Do you ever feel like you've lost your edge?" he asked.

"Like what, risk-taking?"

He waved at her reply. "More like your momentum—that bold side of you that drives you to face the odds."

"Have you forgotten who you sleep next to?" Jada searched his eyes, but furrowed her eyebrows when Jesse remained stone-faced. To her, he must have looked like he studied the ether that hovered over the coffee table. In truth, Jesse knew she didn't have a clue what motivated him. Nor did she care, as long as his motivation existed. "You aren't *afraid* of that audition, are you?" she asked.

"After as many as I've been on? Granted, not lately—"

"Because if you *are* scared," she continued, "you need figure out a way to hide it. Or else you'll never get that role." She chuckled to herself. Jada shook her head, then plopped back against the sofa and crossed her arms. "Don't you want to be an actor anymore?"

"Now *you've* forgotten who you sleep next to. Why would you even ask that?"

"Things change."

Great, now she's in challenge mode. Jesse clenched his jaw, threw his hands on his head in frustration. "Dammit, Jada! Nothing's changed!" After a deep breath, he let his hands fall to his sides. Why did he try to talk to her about this? Of all people, she would be the last to understand unless the struggle was her own. "Forget it."

For the first time in L.A., Jesse felt alone.

Weary, he turned to Jada and looked into her eyes. With a gentle rub to her back, he said, "Sorry, babe. It's nothing. Jitters."

But he could pinpoint the suspicion in her autumn eyes. When it came to fear detection, the woman had radar. Jesse leaned in and planted a kiss on her lips.

He'd always adored her Italian lips.

CHAPTER 4

THE next morning, Jesse grabbed the handful of film rolls from the overnight drop-off bin and carried them to the room behind the checkout counter, which housed a small processing lab.

A far cry from his high-school photography class, the room contained the same fluorescent light that filled the retail area. A mini-lab machine sat against a wall, where he deposited the rolls of film, cartridge and all. The machine would handle the rest.

Unlike his film development in high school, minimal human intervention occurred here: no need to remove strands of film under the glow of an ominous red light, no gloved hands to immerse film in toxic chemicals. While in the past he'd handled development with the same tender care he'd given to the shot itself, nowadays he treated the development phase like an afterthought rather than an art.

He removed a set of prints the machine had spit out during its last run. In his days at the store, he had seen a vast array of human behavior immortalized in photographs—some to his detriment, seared in his memory with regret. But this set of prints, a family gathering at a lake in a rural, wooded area, made him grin. Jesse flipped through the shots.

A proud young boy and his father posed with a silver fish, its length almost that of the boy's arm. A mother, dressed in a brick-and-charcoal-colored flannel shirt, humored the amateur photographer with a stare that implied, "I dare you: Take one step closer with that camera." Another photo showed the full family of four enveloped in a hug, where the boy giggled as his younger sister attempted to grab his nose. This last photo spurred similar memories of Jesse and his sister, Eden.

Jesse started to put the family photo down but took another look. Intrigued, Jesse stared at the father, who tried to kiss both kids at once.

When viewed through a camera lens, fatherhood didn't seem an intimidation.

After he matched the processed photos with their negatives, Jesse assembled the final package and brought it to the pickup bin on the sales floor. At ten thirty, ready for business, he unlocked the front door to a waiting crowd of nobody. Jesse maneuvered across the retail floor, wound around displays of cameras and how-to books, slid between narrow rows of shelving. He approached a row of sterling wedding frames and dusted them as he pondered the prior night's conversation with Jada.

Jesse had resided in California for eleven years. When he mulled this over, the banality of his status quo struck him. At twenty-nine years old, Jesse anchored his hope on an upcoming audition.

Don't you want to be an actor anymore? Jada had asked.

Jesse and Jada met at a Java Cup location a few months after he moved to the L.A. area. Invincible at a haughty eighteen years old, Jesse had made a swift departure from his home in Hudson, Ohio. At that point, Jada herself had lived in the L.A. area for a year already. Both starved for fame, both felt as though they flailed against its odds as if in deep water, and they became friends quickly. Their fear and vulnerability cemented their bond. They confided their dreams. At the time, Jada's personality represented everything Jesse wished he could be—an image contrary to that of his Midwestern roots, a previous life he had managed to escape. Jada thought she'd discovered someone as independent and driven as she herself was. And Jesse the actor played the part well.

A year later, the two friends moved into an apartment near Hollywood and Vine—a shoddy location after dark, but mere steps from the Capitol Records building, a shrine of industry power. The pair sought opportunities with a vengeance and exhibited sheer confidence, while in the evenings they returned home to dinners of seasoned oriental noodles at ten cents a package. At that time, Jesse and Jada made a pact: If one succeeded before the other, they would remain roommates to help the pair's less fortunate half in their quest for fame. For all Jada's flaws, she never reneged on her promise.

For the next ten years, Jesse and Jada gelled in a comfortable understanding, a shallow lifestyle speckled with self-centeredness and minimal thought to its consequences. Their focus centered on creature comforts and a dependence on credit cards.

Now Jada, with her steady career at thirty-one years old, paid the bulk of their monthly bills. And her elevated taste had, in turn, elevated their expenses. Convicted at heart, Jesse wished he could contribute an equal share. He wasn't raised to live this way, to meet a partner less than halfway. If anything, Jada was the gold digger of the two.

Life had unfolded contrary to Jesse's plan. By his estimation, he should have nabbed a handful of speaking roles by now.

Jesse felt the precursor of a headache settle in, one so slight he forgot to give it a second thought.

As customers trickled in, Jesse made his rounds, greeted

those who arrived and offered assistance to those who searched the shelves. The store's core clientele consisted of professional photographers and serious hobbyists, most of which arrived during the day. By contrast, portrait-studio patrons gravitated toward early evening appointments.

Jesse approached a balding man in wire-rimmed glasses, who examined a shelf of chemicals.

"May I help you, sir?" Jesse asked.

"Do you still carry a generic version of potassium bromide? It looks like the shelf is empty," the man answered. "Chemicals are chemicals—no sense in paying Hart-Bauer Corporation extra cash."

Potassium bromide is a powdery substance. After photographers dissolve the substance in water, they combine it with other chemicals to create developer and intensifier solutions. The same potassium bromide is also used as an anti-seizure treatment for domestic pets. Jesse marveled at the contrast: One substance could be used for exposure or suppression.

The things nature could hide.

To ensure a customer hadn't scooted the bottles into obscurity, Jesse peered into the recesses of the shelf but still found it empty. "Let me check the storage room. I'll be back."

The man nodded. Jesse headed through the door marked "Private" and into the shop's rear hallway. In the back of the building toward the right, Jesse walked into the storage room and flipped the light switch. A large ventilation grate loomed overhead. The room reeked of chemicals, a sharp collection of odors reminiscent of a science lab. The type of nervous scent that elicited apprehension in an untrained passerby, one who lacked knowledge behind what he smelled, yet sensed intangible danger that lurked somewhere within.

Two of the overhead bulbs had burned out—a task each employee pledged to fix and had, in turn, neglected. As a result, dabs of darkness overshadowed one side of the room where shelves of chemicals sat. Jesse considered a flashlight but decided against it. This wouldn't take long.

As he entered the shadows, he squinted at the assortment and found the small bottles of potassium bromide. Jesse removed a white plain-labeled bottle from the shelf and turned on his heel to leave the room.

Then the drip occurred.

He felt it hit his hand.

The plastic bottle hit the floor. Lightheaded, Jesse slid down the edge of the shelving unit to the floor, where he sat for a moment. Had the chemicals caused a reaction? He doubted it; after all, he'd worked in this shop for years. But what else could it be? Perhaps a temporary allergic reaction. This hadn't happened before.

Jesse shook the wooziness from his head and looked at his hand to see what had dripped. Whatever it was, it was red. He furrowed his eyebrows and gazed up at the shelves: All of the containers stood upright, squadrons of chemical soldiers. Nothing had tipped over—and stranger yet, nothing had dripped from them.

With his unstained hand, Jesse, still in a haze, rubbed his face. His hand came down smeared in scarlet. When he touched his nose again with the back of his hand, he discovered another droplet.

A nosebleed.

Odd, Jesse thought. By no means did a nosebleed pose reason for concern, but it would make more sense in a high-humidity climate. Southern California had been kind to him.

It had to be a reaction. Maybe the ventilation needed examination. Jesse would let his boss know when he arrived after
lunch.

For now, the man with the glasses needed his product.

Bottle in hand, Jesse made a slow rise to his feet. As his
lightheadedness subsided, he took a deep breath and exhaled.

Then he shut off the light and walked out.

CHAPTER 5

OUTSIDE his apartment building sat a large patch of gravel where grass had failed to grow. The patch accommodated three cars and, on a first-come basis, apartment residents parked there to avoid the scratches experienced by those who parallel parked overnight. When he eyed an available gravel spot, Jesse grinned at his luck and pulled his midnight-blue Honda Accord into it.

Aside from the occasional vehicle break-in, his neighborhood was safe. But nearby, if you continued northbound along Van Nuys Boulevard, the status soon deteriorated. On one occasion after dark, Jesse had ventured too far, taken a wrong turn, and questioned his safety in two of the most frightening minutes of his life. Soon after his arrival in California, Jesse marveled at how community conditions could change in a moment. What a difference between neighborhoods that sat five minutes apart.

Jesse made his way on foot toward his apartment building. Two stories high and laced with ivy, it featured pale yellow stucco and Spanish roof tiles that looked like adobe arches. Each level housed two apartments with front doors that faced each other. A similar building sat beside his own. Across the street, matching four-room houses sat nestled in a small, white-collar neighborhood, where the front yards lacked trees.

"Hey, Barlow! Kiss my horsey ass, you cocksucker!"

Jesse snickered. It was never just hello with this guy. "Can I help you?"

Jesse turned on his heels to find Gavin, his downstairs neighbor, who wore a green track suit and had slowed to a trot along the sidewalk. Based on the speed at which he panted, Gavin, a compulsive evening jogger, had fed his habit for the night. As the final hour of daylight lingered, a streetlight high-lighted streaks of perspiration, salty badges of achievement that glimmered across Gavin's face. Even from a few feet away, his track suit smelled like a dishrag.

"Got myself a gig!" Gavin said.

Jesse had crossed paths with Gavin, another struggling actor, at a television taping years ago. When the downstairs apartment became vacant, Jesse passed the address along to Gavin. Within weeks, the friends enjoyed their respective advantages of rent control.

"Quite a resume enhancement," Gavin continued. "I'm playing a character."

"Are you playing an idiot?"

"Whatever. You know that new themed shopping village that opened up around the corner from Hollywood Boulevard? The one that signed the deal with Sony to show its movie trail-ers around the place, where its afternoon-cartoon characters wander around in costume?"

"You're in one of the movie trailers?"

Gavin's breathing returned to its normal rate. "No, man! I'm Clickety Clack!"

"What's that?"

"That cartoon show, *Farmyard Frenzy*. There's a film ver-sion coming soon. Ever see the show?"

Jesse didn't follow. "The one with the pig named Bacon Bitz?"

"Yeah! I'm Clickety Clack, the horse that walks around on his hind legs and makes that clopping noise. I get to wear that costume at the shopping village."

Jesse rolled his eyes. "Did your agent arrange that for you?"

"Don't joke. It's just to pay the bills. They're gonna put me in a Clickety Clack costume that plays clopping sound effects out of a tiny speaker crammed up its ass. Sounds like a tin can bouncing down a sidewalk."

In an odd way, Jesse found the concept pitiful. If Jesse himself were to resort to such a stint, he'd refuse to admit it to anyone. "Could be fun—if you enjoy that sort of thing."

"Sure, you wave hello to the tourists. Pose for the cameras with the kids," Gavin replied. "That's nothing compared to what Mosley just landed, though."

"Did he get hired as Pitt's double?"

"No, it's better: The dude got a supporting role in a new TV show. He met the producer's assistant at a party in October, and she recommended Mosley to her boss." Gavin stepped back and rested his hands on his hips. He stared as if Jesse were a choice between two curious brands of lager. "Why doesn't your girlfriend hook you up with her boss?"

"She took my head shot to him, but I'm five-foot-eleven. Barry thought I was too tall. Said it screws up his camera shot."

"That sucks. Do you get that a lot?"

"Depends on the film," Jesse replied. Sometimes, especially when he stood among actors of the five-foot-seven variety, Jesse felt like a giant in his industry, as if he were a prom date for Judy Garland in *The Wizard of Oz*, one who loomed like a Munchkin scientist's cloning experiment gone bad.

Jesse basked in the comfort of this early March evening. "I have an audition tomorrow, though."

"Dialogue?"

Jesse beamed as a rush of encouragement electrified his arteries. "Yeah, a few lines."

"Way to go, big guy!" Gavin exclaimed. "About time, isn't it! What do you think your chances are?"

"My agent thinks I've got a decent shot at it. You know how these things go—nothing's a lock. Funny thing, they're looking for someone tall—for once, my five-eleven frame seems customized for the part. Maddy said it's the part of a basketball-player ex-boyfriend."

"It's no Clickety Clack mascot, but if *film* is what you're looking for." Gavin grinned. "That's cool. Good luck with it. Let me know how it pans out, okay? Gotta head in."

And with that, Gavin trotted to his apartment door while Jesse sauntered toward the stairs.

Jesse's confidence began to mount a comeback. Maybe the self-doubt would fizzle by morning.

He grabbed hold of the railing, the same black-metal décor he'd seen along cafeteria edifices, and climbed the narrow concrete steps to the second floor.

When Jesse shut the door, he detected the tang of marijuana. Jada had lit up again—a stash left over from earlier that week. Beyond his recent disaffection for smoking green substances, Jesse now decided that, yes, he had begun to detest the odor.

When he swept his sight across the living room, Jesse found it empty: just the light of a table lamp. He followed the scent through the living room and into the screened sunroom at the rear of the apartment, where Jada sat on a plastic chair. She had drawn one leg against her body to rest her joint-laden hand, limp at the wrist, on her knee. As she stared out into the evening, she seemed lost in a trance.

At first, she appeared distracted by the night air. Then Jesse realized she was something else: tranquil.

Jada seldom seemed at peace. Perhaps she found religion in the herb after all.

"Don't you want a light on?" he said.

"I like the dark." Her other leg rested on the opposite chair. With glazed eyes, Jada stroked his arm, then scooted the other chair toward him with her foot. She held out the joint. "Here you go, babe."

Jesse waved it off. Instead, he reached beneath her hair to massage her neck—but his caress seemed foreign to him and, for a split second, he felt like an intruder.

Jada had become a stranger to him.

Without a sound, he withdrew his hand with a tenderness that had, at one time, been passionate but now seemed shallow.

Together they sat in silence and listened to the steady hum of traffic as it rushed along Van Nuys one block away.

"Hear that?" she murmured. "Don't you love the sound of L.A.? It's intoxicating." She paused for a beat. "Everyone has somewhere to go." She tilted her head back, exhaled a stream of silk. The flow crawled like a seductive ghost.

Jada laid the joint aside, half finished. She drew her other leg onto her chair and, childlike, cradled both legs against herself. Jesse watched as she turned in her seat, a pensive expression on her face, and stared into his eyes. "All right, Green Eyes, tell me what's going on."

"Huh?"

"You're not the same. It's like you're no longer the Jesse I know."

He grabbed his camera, which he'd left on the plastic table between them, and fidgeted with its buttons. In a halfhearted effort, he forced a smile and snapped a picture of her. She nodded in faint humor and returned her gaze to the night sky.

Jesse reached out and brushed his fingers along her fingertips. "I don't know what you mean."

"You were outgoing way back when we first met. But now …" She shrugged her shoulders. "You're never in the mood to mingle. It's like you built a life here and just, I don't know— gave up."

"We went through this the other day, didn't we?" He found it difficult to argue with her while she was stoned. She looked so vulnerable yet could exhibit astounding recall the next morning. Even when subdued, she could be spiteful. But still, Jesse understood why she behaved the way she did: Jada had her personal issues.

Then again, so did he.

Jada pursed her lips, rolled her tongue against the inside of her cheek. She avoided his eyes. "When did you become your father?" she asked.

Patience intact, Jesse chose to ignore the question. "You're a little under the influence right now. Why don't we quit this argument before we say something we'll regret in the morning—because we both know you won't forget."

Yet her words jabbed further. "Speaking of your father, when will I get to meet him?"

"Yeah, I don't think so."

Jada perked up in her chair, her usual position before she

increased the friction. "We've known each other for eleven years. Isn't it about time?"

Jesse said nothing. He watched her eyes narrow, their pointed depths akin to a missile prepared for launch. The corner of her mouth turned upward. She must have enjoyed this. And times like this reminded Jesse of the love-hate relationship he and Jada shared. How could he be attracted to this woman, yet not bring himself to trust her?

Then again, he knew Jada had no use for trust.

"Come on," she pressed. "What, you don't think the preacher man would approve of me?"

Jesse clenched his jaw and made a slow rise to his feet. "Don't worry, he wouldn't approve of me either. By the way, in case you've forgotten, he and I haven't seen each other in those eleven years. I don't think his son's sex life is his primary concern."

Although Jesse had made the occasional phone call to his father, the last time Jesse had seen the man face-to-face was the night before Jesse left home. On that night, Jesse had explained to his dad that he planned to leave in the morning and revealed he'd made the arrangements weeks before. Jesse was eighteen at the time and, in his own rebellious fashion, had escalated the discussion to a heated argument.

Jesse never revealed the whole story to his father. The guilt weighed too heavy within. But when it came to the departure, Jesse assumed his father blamed himself.

Dad, if only you knew.

Jada resumed her joint. "So nothing's wrong; there's just a side to you I never knew existed after these years together. That's what you're telling me?"

"I have my secrets." Jesse walked away. "Do us both a favor and let it go, okay?"

From the living room, he heard Jada shout. "By the way, your sister called."

Great. More tension, as if the air weren't thick enough.

Jesse and his sister remained close after he moved to the coast. Jada knew Jesse confided in his sister regarding certain aspects of his and Jada's relationship—he could see the resentment in Jada's eyes. But he needed to confide in someone he could trust, and though he trusted Jada with his romantic needs, he didn't trust her with his soul. The implant-to-L.A. Jesse matched well with Jada; the true Jesse did not.

CHAPTER 6

"JESSE Barlow, we're ready for you."

Script in hand, Jesse, dressed for the role in a basketball jersey and long, shiny shorts, followed the staffer into the audition room. His stomach felt as if jelly jostled inside, back and forth, an invisible high tide. For him, the greatest challenge lay in the preliminaries—the hours and minutes that preceded an audition—when nervousness settled in, confined until the appointed time.

When Jesse entered the room, he noticed its blandness: Unlike an actual film set, this room appeared stripped down, with a less-expensive video camera pointed in his direction. He stood in front of the camera, his back to a bare, white wall. A hot overhead light, aimed at him, baked his skin. As he scanned the area before him, he found a folding table covered with a white tablecloth, where Mark Shea, the director, sat. In a hushed tone, Mark conferred with his assistant, perhaps Jesse's age, who took notes on a palm device. Two other people, a man and a woman, filled out the other half of the table.

The simplicity of the setting, however, worked in Jesse's favor, as it allowed his creative wires to emerge to the forefront and amplify the scene, to conjure imaginary props and visualize an environment that was not otherwise present. In essence, Jesse entered a world of his own.

A man of styled salt-and-pepper hair, the goateed Mark

wore khaki pants and a casual striped shirt with its sleeves rolled up. The assistant handed Jesse's form to Mark, who clucked his tongue while he advanced down each line with his pen.

Mark gazed at Jesse. "Jesse Barlow?"

"Yes."

"I'm Mark Shea. As your agent informed you, this film is called *Taking Sides*. Today you'll read for a supporting role: a professional basketball player, Rod Meacham, the ex-lover of the lead. The setting is a news conference. Lots of commotion between questions; cameras flash around the room. My assistant will read the lines of the other character in the scene. Do you have any questions before we begin?"

"No sir." Jesse held the script below eye level, about twelve inches from his face.

"And ... action!"

With a deep inhale from his diaphragm, Jesse started to read the dialogue. "I was not aware, and did not become aware until Monday afternoon, that Felicity Hugo has a husband."

"Mr. Meacham," Mark's assistant called out with a journalist's finesse, "can you confirm that you were an acquaintance of Ms. Hugo's prior to the alleged incident?"

Jesse's eyes felt hot under the lighting, his stomach in motion again. He shook his head to clear his thoughts, and then continued. "No, I never met the woman."

"Hold on," Mark said. "You're doing fine, but keep in mind this film will be a comedy, so an air of humor will surround this character."

Jesse nodded. To lighten his interpretation, he cocked his head back and swaggered like an egocentric ball player. He thrust forth a confident smirk. "No, I never met the woman."

"But Mr. Meacham, sources say they found your credit

card in Ms. Hugo's Denver hotel room. How do you respond to that?"

"I don't know. Maybe she stole the thing."

"And the money clip engraved with your name?"

"Psycho woman."

"Mr. Meacham?"

"No further comment." With this, Jesse completed the scene.

"Pretty good," Mark Shea said as he wrote a few notes on Jesse's evaluation sheet. "We'll be just a few moments."

Aware that the audition had gone well, Jesse suppressed a smile, attempted to remain calm. He kept his arms uncrossed to avoid negative body language. As Jesse stood there, he reminded himself not to bounce on the backs of his heels, a nervous habit Jada had pointed out. At the rear of the room, the doorway threshold reflected a glare from the overhead light, which Jesse used as a focal point while he waited. Maybe it would keep him from looking desperate by staring at his evaluators—or worse, from revealing a lack of confidence by focusing on his toes with his head tilted down.

To stand in front of a group of people as they whisper about you—Jesse found this to be the most peculiar aspect of an audition. In what other circumstance would you seek to be discussed and gauged in secret? But by Jesse's own admission, at his first audition years ago, such lull time had proven quite awkward, akin to standing before a group of strangers in his boxer shorts. What do you do with your hands while you stand alone, scrutinized like a specimen under a microscope?

But he adored this line of work—when the line moved. Jesse fell in love with drama as a teenager, but that passion didn't emerge right away. His height and physical aptitude led to membership on his high-school basketball team. Invigorated by the energy exertion and swift competition of the sport, Jesse proved a decent player. But the rush from the games couldn't compare to the personal revelation that surfaced when he discovered theater. On a whim, he auditioned for a fall play his sophomore year and secured a supporting role. From that point on, he participated in the fall and spring plays, which occurred, for the most part, during basketball's off-season.

As expected, Jesse's teammates didn't understand. The jocks seldom interacted with the creative types, and Jesse's interest in stage productions suffered verbal jabs. Yet he persevered in his craft, enthralled by the ability to climb into another character, to become someone else for periods of time. Although film versions existed for many of those plays, Jesse never rented them until the school production completed its run. While his cast mates watched the films to study their characters, Jesse wanted to adopt his role as his own, to create something visible from the unseen.

Unknown to those outside his family, Jesse possessed an innate ability to empathize with the pain of others. As a boy, Jesse would spot random individuals, such as a woman who sat alone on a park bench or a man who had entered his final years of life, and imagine how it must feel to wake up in the morning to their isolation. This tenderness helped fuel his interpretation of characters.

During his junior year, he played the role of Willy Loman in *Death of a Salesman*. And with the depth of human experience embodied by that character—the battle of despair and the ache of failure—the deal was sealed. Jesse Barlow would pursue a career in acting.

But this present wait, which couldn't have lasted beyond

a minute, bordered on eternity for Jesse. He sneaked a glance at Mark Shea and his crew, but they continued to whisper and shuffle papers.

At last, Mark nodded to his assistant and leaned toward Jesse. "I have to tell you, you look good to us. Your interpretation of the character was dead-on accurate. You're the exact height and build we need. Now granted, this part is only a few lines long, but for the film, we also need to take some shots of this actor playing in a basketball game."

He's already talking about the film shoot, Jesse thought. A positive sign—a strong one. Jesse's heart rate jumped a notch.

"Because the part is small, we won't invest in basketball training," Mark continued. "Do you have experience with the game? Nothing superior; just the basics. Enough to look like you know what you're doing?"

This started to sound even better.

"Sure. I played on a high-school team."

Again Mark nodded, as if his question were a formality and he had known its answer in advance.

Jesse grinned. His eyes grew feverish. Across his brow, perspiration beaded, not in anxiety but in raw relief: a golden triumph after years of defeat.

Could he have a lock on this role?

"Good deal," Mark said. "We have a couple more prospects to see, but we'll notify your agent of our decision by the end of the week."

CHAPTER 7

MARK Shea's decision arrived sooner. It came by five forty-five that afternoon.

And it wasn't good.

On his way home, Jesse's car idled with its stop-and-go companions, all engulfed in a soup of rush-hour traffic on Interstate 405. How he cherished the carpool lane when he could utilize it!

With the window rolled down, exhaust fumes funneled into his vehicle, accompanied by their heavy odor. Jesse leaned back in his seat and rubbed his eyes with one hand on the wheel. An old Toad the Wet Sprocket CD played on the stereo. When he felt the buzz of his cell phone in his pocket, he turned the music off and answered.

"I heard back from Shea's people."

The connection was shoddy, which muted Maddy's voice on the other end. Nervous, Jesse tapped his left foot on the floor with eager anticipation. He struggled to increase the phone's volume without missing a beat. He didn't want to be presumptuous, but if Maddy had received word so soon, he figured it must be a solid sign.

"Mark promised a decision before the weekend," Jesse replied. "Was it good news?"

Maddy's pause told Jesse all he needed to know. Sometimes, in an instant, your gut plunges into your belly and, try as you may to think your instinct faulty, you just can't convince yourself.

At this moment, Jesse wished his instinct worthless.

If only.

"It's a no-go," Maddy said.

He shook himself from a trance and realized the car in front of him had advanced. To catch up with the car was simple; to search for a response to Maddy wasn't. He moved his lips but couldn't locate his voice.

Jesse rested his head against his fingertips and asked, "Did Mark say anything? Did I do something wrong? From the way he talked, it sounded like I'd nailed the part."

"Absolutely. Mark was impressed."

"Then what happened?"

"He said your eyes are too wide."

Jesse grunted, his forehead a crinkle of confusion. "What does that mean?"

"Well, not owlish huge, just ... wide."

"Was it an aesthetic thing? Like that adage, 'The eyes are the window of the soul'?"

"No," Maddy replied. "It was pure preference. They didn't feel you looked the part; there's nothing more to read into it."

At least they were courteous about it, Jesse thought. He'd heard stories of industry people who made cutting comments about an actor's physical attributes. Now that he'd received such a remark firsthand, it sounded too ridiculous to be credible, yet it was true.

Jesse sighed. "So they found someone with better ... *eyes.*"

"It's a subjective business; you've learned that. Don't get discouraged over this. We'll keep plugging away, and I'll let you know when another project pops up. In the meantime, you're still networking as well?"

"Of course."

"Then we'll continue to move forward together. Lots of opportunities out there."

And with that, their conversation ended. The traffic accelerated from a sporadic crawl to perpetual motion as Jesse stared ahead in his own oblivion. His heart sank. His stomach grew acidic with nausea. That weighty sense of darkness, which had lurked for months in the background of his mind, crept closer to the forefront.

Stricken, Jesse felt reality finger its way into his fibers. After eleven years, today he wondered if he had lost this battle, and depression began to emerge as a formidable opponent. Jesse wanted to shed a tear but felt too exhausted to do so.

Surrounded by vehicles, he wanted one thing: to disappear.

CHAPTER 8

A S Jesse had expected upon arrival, Los Angeles shared little in common with his Midwestern hometown. But one similarity between the two struck Jesse as eerie: L.A. traffic on Sunday mornings seemed sparse. And at nine o'clock, this Sunday morning in mid March followed suit.

He lived in the second-largest metropolitan area in the country. *Could it be this simple for millions of people to hide?* Once Friday hit, many industry executives, he knew, escaped to homes elsewhere—some to outlying areas in California, others as far as Nevada. Less wealthy individuals must hole up in bed or in their own vicinities as he himself did, Jesse figured. But come Monday, lives would converge in a mix of destiny and pollution once again.

"What possessed you to go to the beach today?" Jada asked while she chewed on a stick of gum.

"Seemed like a good time to think for a change. When was the last time we went there to relax?"

Therein lay another anomaly: How many people, like Jesse, dreamed of living minutes from the ocean? Jesse had lived near one for years, yet he could count on one hand his number of annual visits to that ocean and have three fingers to spare.

Jada popped in a CD and reclined on the passenger side. Soon the car filled with the eclectic sounds of Joy Wilson, an indie artist whose music Barry Richert had featured in his last film. From the driver's seat, Jesse studied the lanes around him on Interstate 405, where he could picture tinny blue ghosts in a drag race through eons among unsuspecting humans. And in this city, Jesse doubted anyone would care.

He cocked his head and asked, "Have you ever thought about how shallow this whole scene is?"

"What scene? The 405?"

"No, the industry. All the promises made, promises broken. The notion that it's acceptable to be full of shit. It's even anticipated ahead of time."

Jada chuckled. "That's the club we joined. It's the way the game is played. What's wrong with that?"

"But isn't there a point when someone reaches the end of their rope? I mean, not everyone succeeds here—most people don't. Where do they go? Where do they end up?"

"I don't know," Jada sighed. "Jesse, I don't give a fuck."

"They must go somewhere."

"Maybe they sell chiseled art under those little pup tents at Venice Beach."

"I'm serious."

As Jesse veered onto Interstate 10, Jada turned down the stereo's volume and pivoted toward him.

"You know what your problem is? You're too damn honest. Always have been."

"Is that supposed to be a compliment?"

"It's not a bad quality. Look at your upbringing in Ohio: You're a white-bread boy from Bob Evansville. Hollywood doesn't come natural to you." She shrugged her shoulders, no big deal. "I grew up around bullshit. All those beauty pageants. And Reno? Tsk."

Jesse glanced in Jada's direction but said nothing.

"I'll admit I got lucky working for Barry," Jada continued. "But hey, you've stayed afloat this long; just stay afloat longer than anyone else."

After he turned left off of Santa Monica Boulevard, Jesse made his way down Ocean Avenue. As he drove parallel to the beach, mere feet between the road and the sand, he noticed a familiar sheet of horizon that peeked through trees and small buildings. Something about the view spoke of freedom to Jesse, a sense of pleasant foreboding: Here at eye level sat a massive stretch of sky, of infinite blue azure, like a giant come to earth. It fostered within Jesse a feeling of weightlessness, a horizontal vertigo. The universe was within his grasp.

Jesse turned onto Colorado Avenue and into the public parking lot.

With the temperature in the upper seventies, a tad aggressive for this time of year, they found the beach crowded—which, of course, Jada pointed out the moment her cherry-red painted toenails touched the ivory sand. She preferred to drive further north to a wealthier, less populated area, but today Jesse needed to watch the passersby, to connect with their carefree contentment.

Once they located an open patch of beach, Jesse and Jada spread their blankets on the granular surface and lay down. Side by side, they basked behind sunglasses in the shimmering sun. Jada propped her head against her beach bag and immersed herself in a script for the following day.

Jesse inhaled the fresh, salted air. As he peered up at the Santa Monica Pier that stretched overhead, he watched visitors stroll past souvenir shops and street performers, the snack rotunda and carnival rides—and the ancient Ferris wheel which, when afire with neon light in the evenings, appeared forever cursed with a burned-out bulb tube.

Jesse savored the warmth as it penetrated his skin and caked a layer of crusted sand upon his feet. A light breeze danced about, which tickled Jesse's hair and neck. He gazed at the water as it hurled back and forth. From the corner of his eye, a flash of motion lured his attention to a father and son, who frolicked on the shore. The toddler, dressed in tiny, fluorescent-green board shorts, giggled and hopped in circles along the shoreline. His father grasped him by his pudgy underarms. He lifted him a foot above the surface, then set him back on the wet sand, which sent the child splashing into a fit of laughter.

Transfixed by the father-child relationship that unfolded before him, a subtle smile quivered at the edge of Jesse's mouth.

Jesse nudged Jada. "Look at that," he said, then pointed to the pair at play.

Jada remained engrossed in her reading. She peered over her sunglasses for a split second without so much as a tilt of the head, then returned to her script. "What about them?"

"That kid looks just like his dad, don't you think?"

Indifferent, Jada peered up again, then back down. "You're right, same features head to toe—but the kid'll outgrow *his* chubby ass."

Intrigued, Jesse looked past the outward, physical qualities to study their actions and reactions: gentle hands that touched the boy's head; the father's arms around his son, which communicated affection and protection at the same time. The scene formed an indelible imprint on Jesse's heart, a photograph within his soul.

"I wonder how that dad felt the day his son was born," Jesse said. "Maybe he felt anxiety leading up to the day, but then a sense of relief." Jesse longed to know the answers; his heart reached out for them. "The moment when that guy looked at his kid and said, 'This is my son. This kid is a part of me.' It must've blown him away."

Jada ignored them. Typical Jada: What was there to see? A man and his kid playing at the beach. Big deal. Jesse sniffed at how two people could perceive the same thing in opposite ways.

Jesse turned to her and asked, "Haven't you changed your mind about having kids someday?"

She sighed. "No, I haven't. How many times do you intend to bring this up?"

"We'll be in our forties before we know it. Don't you think you'll look back and wish we'd made a different decision?"

"Look, you know I haven't budged on this since the day we met. Besides, what would I do with a kid? Even I have enough sense to know I'd screw that deal up."

Taken aback by the decisiveness in her reply, Jesse returned his gaze to the little toddler, who now picked up random shells and showed the prizes to his father.

Jada put down the script. Shallow creases wiggled along her forehead. "You always said you didn't want kids either. We talked about that early on: no long-term anything—no baby, no marriage. We both wanted our careers, remember?"

"Sure." Jesse shrugged, an attempt at passivity. "But back then I was what, nineteen? Twenty? The thought of fatherhood freaked me out at the time: the demands, the responsibility— another human being depending on you to come through for him."

"And it no longer scares you? Scares the hell out of me."

"I guess I've gotten used to the idea as I've grown older. It doesn't bother me as much. It's normal to start to question your life choices, right?"

"What choices? I *like* my life. How are we supposed to juggle a kid with our lifestyle?" She jostled her hair and read-justed her sunglasses. "Maybe kids fit your personality, but not mine. What's got you thinking about this out of the blue, anyway?"

"Random thoughts, that's all." He shrugged it off. "Second chances at—"

Jada interrupted him. "What the ..." She yanked her sun-glasses off and stared closer at his face. "You're bleeding."

"Huh?"

"Your nose, it's—wait."

Jada reached behind to her beach bag and found a tissue. Jesse dabbed at his nose, and then laid back. Another faint trickle. He felt his belly tighten with apprehension but waved it off.

"Are you okay?" Jada asked.

"Probably the sun."

Jada nodded. "I used to get those nosebleeds in Nevada. It was the dry climate." She put her sunglasses back on. "Is it easing up?"

"It's fine. Be right back." As he walked away, he could sense Jada's eyes on him.

Jesse disappeared into a restroom beneath the Pier to nurse the nosebleed. It seemed to take longer to quit than the last time.

For several months, Jesse had noticed occasional, random bruises that remained unexplained. When Jada pointed them out, he couldn't remember if he had bumped against a shelf or counter at the store.

Now he wondered if the symptoms were related. But then again, these were common things that happened to everyone. Best not to consider it while in an emotional valley, Jesse figured.

CHAPTER 9

WHEN they arrived home late that afternoon, Jesse offered to cook dinner. After a quick shower, he padded barefoot into the kitchen in a T-shirt and shorts. By no means was he a gourmet, but he had learned his way around a handful of simple, ten-minute recipes. Given Jada's preference for low-calorie meals, he opted for a pot of spaghetti, which now simmered on the stove in a pool of minced garlic, oregano and olive oil as a light sauce substitute.

He heard Jada finish her shower around the corner. He had to admit, he felt disappointed that she wouldn't budge on the prospect of kids. Granted, he had no reason to expect her to change, but the way she'd reminded him had sounded callous. It had landed a stone-cold blow to his gut, given his own reconsideration.

Shake it off, Jesse.

He stirred the spaghetti. As the scent of the entrée wafted through the kitchen, he closed his eyes and breathed the tempting aroma. Jesse placed the finishing touches on a salad and walked it to the dining room table, where he set out a pair of wine glasses. Jada had already had a glass while Jesse showered, but he was sure she'd want another. He turned off the stove and carried the entrée to the table.

With his back turned, he didn't see Jada when she strode into the room. Barefoot and dressed in her mauve terrycloth robe, she fingered her damp hair. She tiptoed from behind, slipped her arms around his waist, and rested her head against the back of his neck.

Jesse eased around in her arms and admired the glimpse of natural beauty before him, an image of fresh allure. He placed his arms around her waist and drew her against himself as she slid her palms down to his buttocks. She smiled. Her eyes danced.

"My favorite chef," she whispered.

He lingered and returned her gaze. "Would you like a glass of Chardonnay?"

"I want you to fuck me." She giggled in a subdued, sensuous manner all her own.

She possessed a magnetic draw. The woman was adept with her body and always won.

Jesse leaned in. He brushed his lips along her neckline and traced it with kisses on the way up. She turned her face; Jesse felt her relax in the flow of the moment. Through a gap between the edges of her robe, her flesh still glistened moist along the top of her chest. Her hair smelled of orchids and invigorated Jesse's senses. He removed his shirt, ran his fingers through her hair and down to her waist as he guided her backward to the living room, against the sofa.

Jada grew breathless as he laid kisses on her mouth, her earlobes, down to her shoulders. He glided his hands down her sides and into the opening beneath the knot of the robe—she wore nothing underneath. With agile fingers Jesse loosened the knot; her robe fell to the floor in silence. Jesse stepped out of his shorts and started at her belly. As he ran his hands upward, he traveled the surface of her feverish, Mediterranean skin. Jada's hands descended from the top of his head down to his waist as he worked his way along her belly. Then he retraced the territory with his lips, feathered her thighs with his fingertips as Jada let out a muted sigh of delight.

Jesse in the lead, he glided her around the sofa and laid her on the cushions with care. Jada grasped Jesse's backside as he hovered over her. His brow dampened; beads of perspiration fell down her belly and below her waist. Their flesh stuck to the leather surface, which released a series of subtle cracks and purrs in response to their motion.

Jesse began to descend further with his mouth when she broke his stride with a soft voice.

"Wait—hold on …"

Jesse paused, his lips still parted, and glanced up to see her face. "What is it?" he asked, then resumed his navigation.

"Stop," she said, then winced at the halt. "We don't have a condom."

He grimaced for a split second.

"Now?" he murmured.

"Go grab one from your drawer. You don't want to be a daddy today, do you?"

Startled, Jesse froze. A chill raced up his spine. His mind backtracked, and then returned in a fast-forward to the moment at hand. He shook his head.

"No … no, you're right," he said. "I … yeah, let me go grab one."

Jesse wrenched himself from the sofa, then padded into the bedroom and opened a condom packet from the dresser drawer. When he returned, he found Jada motionless, her back curved in a slight, delicate arch, her eyes shut, her lips parted. Jesse resumed position overhead.

He didn't pour her Chardonnay until an hour later.

_____

That night, Jesse lay awake in bed, his head propped against the pillow, eyes wide open. This was the second night in a row insomnia had crept in.

A glance at the clock revealed it was past three o'clock. Moonlight skulked through the window and slashed the foot of the bed with its oblong glow. Jada had fallen captive to slumber hours ago; her chest now rose and fell in hypnotic fashion. Jesse picked up a trace of the homemade facial mask slathered over her face—mixed scents of tomato, cucumber and oatmeal—an all-natural defiance to the natural aging process. And Jada didn't stop with her own remedy: She had convinced Jesse to wear suntan lotion each night to achieve the same goal through the vitamins in the lotion. But at the moment, it was a random ingredient in Jada's concoction that elicited his hunger pangs.

Jesse now admitted the obvious: A fruitless career served as a mere corner piece of his emotional puzzle. Curled on her side, Jada faced him as she breathed in steady rhythm as Jesse stared down at her.

The sex was good. The sex had always been good. Jada had accumulated a repertoire of experience by the time they met. In sharp contrast, Jesse had had much less practice. Their relationship had struck him as exotic, a far stretch from the type of girl he'd dated back home. He had allowed Jada to experiment within reason and didn't feel compelled to argue—she paid the bulk of the bills, after all. It was pleasurable, exciting. But to be honest, he felt dark during their intimacy: a subtle shadow, a nicotine stain on the edge of his heart.

So what was wrong?

Jesse paused. And then it hit him.

Affection. He missed the affection.

With Jada, that quality felt absent. And for her, it wasn't an issue. But Jesse had grown to desire something greater. He craved the opportunity to love. He sought the chance to pour himself upon another in mutual abandonment, where satisfaction remained intact longer than a few hours.

Jesse shut his eyes.

So they enjoyed an endless spiral of sex. That didn't sound like a raw deal, did it? Maybe the rest was overrated.

And with his past, he didn't deserve more anyway. His mistakes crawled to the forefront of his memory, silent screams of condemnation. The pressure closed in on him.

He had chosen this fate.

Forget it, Jesse. Tuck the emotions away.

CHAPTER 10

JESSE had never found clowns funny.

Dressed in a firecracker-red wig and green, puff-buttoned jumpsuit, Elmer the Clown, with his plastered smile, posed beside a pair of second graders at the birthday party. No sooner had Jesse snapped the photo when Elmer squirted the kids with his flower lapel, which sent them off with squeals of delight.

As arranged at the camera shop with Glen Merseal, Jesse roamed the public park in pursuit of spontaneous action shots. When Glen mentioned the birthday party, Jesse had pictured ten kids and a game of musical chairs. As it turned out, the party was a joint effort to celebrate the birthdays of two cousins born a week apart. A deluge of kids, what appeared to be a classroom's worth of them, had infested the place. Jesse hadn't been around this many children since his own childhood and wasn't used to today's chaos. He jumped at the shriek of a girl as a boy chased her around the monkey bars. More than once a kid raced past Jesse on foot and almost knocked the camera out of his hand. What madness—but he enjoyed it.

The families had reserved a pavilion, and the scent of barbecue lured Jesse to where some adults grilled lunch on this Saturday afternoon. Jesse got into position, and the parents waved their cooking utensils at his camera.

Point and click.

A mother leaned over to tie her toddler daughter's shoe.

Point and click.

A husband and wife sneaked a kiss behind the grill.

Point and click.

A dad embraced his children around the shoulders.

Point and click.

Life communicated a different tune from behind the lens of a camera. With the naked eye, you see concrete reality, actions without motives—the melody of a song. But behind the camera, Jesse discovered that song's tender bass line—the undercurrent, the heartbeat of a relationship.

Whether the subject was live or inanimate, Jesse found himself enthralled by his advantage as a photographer: He captured life as he wished it could be.

"Are you hungry?" Glen asked as he approached. He clapped a hand on Jesse's back.

Jesse scanned the array of kids that scrambled around a jungle gym. "Which one's yours?"

"That's the birthday girl right there, in the purple T-shirt." Glen pointed to a scrawny child who scuttled across the monkey bars. Glen removed his sunglasses and tucked them into his shirt. "I never imagined myself as a dad."

"A wild man in your day, huh?"

With a chuckle, Glen waved his hand at the notion. "I wouldn't say that. No more than usual, at least. But to provide for a family—I just couldn't picture it."

"You must've changed your mind, though."

"It was an exciting time, all the way to the day my oldest kid was born." Glen paused, then snorted. "Then we brought her home. I woke up the next morning and thought, 'What do I do with this little person? I don't have a clue how to be a dad!'"

Jesse nodded.

"And sure enough, I've made my share of mistakes along the way," Glen continued. He winked at his daughter, who sauntered toward him now. "But I wouldn't trade fatherhood for anything."

Maybe fatherhood wasn't such a stretch after all.

Jesse lined up his camera shot and had to smile at the scene before him, in which the girl tugged at her dad's shirt.

CHAPTER 11

THE birthday party was supposed to last until evening. But when relatives tired sooner than expected, the group opted to catch a movie instead. So Jesse's Saturday night was available after all. Jada had looked forward to an evening of rest, which meant she planned to vegetate in front of the television and indulge in her guilty pleasure: an old Cary Grant film.

But it appeared she'd changed her plans.

When he returned home late that afternoon, he found Jada in the bathroom, where she put the finishing touches on her makeup. Draped in a slinky black dress, she looked gorgeous.

With a look of surprise, she paused with her eyeliner. "You're home early. I thought they'd keep you till after dinner."

"They got sick of each other and wrapped up their shindig," he replied, then tried to recall whether his memory of her free evening was wrong. "You're headed out?"

She nodded and returned to her eyes.

"No Cary Grant after all?"

"Huh?" She began her lipstick, a shade of smoky maroon. After a beat, she replied, "Oh, I'm heading to the Acoustica."

"Clubbing?"

"Barry gave me a to-do. He wants me to check out the band that's scheduled to play tonight. Soundtrack potential---a favor to a friend."

"Sorry, I must have forgotten."

"No, it was a last-minute task."

"You're going alone?"

"Why not? It's business."

"Tell you what, I'll hop in the shower and go with you. It'll give both of us something to do."

"Sure … sure, of course you should come. But I doubt the band's impressive; Barry would have gone himself if he thought they were viable."

"Well, they must be decent if he told you to check them out anyway."

"I suppose."

Jesse glanced at his watch. "Gimme fifteen minutes."

"Fine." Jada snapped her lipstick shut.

The Acoustica pulsated within. A small, retro outfit tucked away in Pasadena, it catered to an artsy crowd with its plush, mock-velvet furniture. The club's cozy atmosphere was a well-kept secret on its block.

When they walked in that evening just past six, Jesse felt the sound vibrations reverberate against his jaw. The jazz-fusion band, in the midst of its first set, was a quartet. The lead singer tackled bass guitar and vocals, and at present snaked his way around a modern scat-rap mix.

Jada appeared more preoccupied with the décor than with the band. She tossed a quick glance in the singer's direction before she settled on a stool at the bar. After she ordered vermouth, Jada scanned the room and crossed her legs. From the stool beside her, Jesse followed the twists and turns of the rubbery vocals that emanated from the platform. He placed a hand on his girlfriend's knee and ordered a Heineken for himself. As he listened, Jesse couldn't understand Barry Richert's interest in this particular band; but then again, Barry was the one with the track record.

"Jada?"

His voice elevated over the music, the man sported a broad smile and dark brown hair that had begun to gray along the edges. Whiffs of Armani cologne permeated the air. He wore casual attire. Expensive casual attire—the kind that goes well with both jeans and khaki pants. The kind that downplays its cost, but whose buttons reveal how much the customer forked over for it.

Jesse turned to the stranger. So did Jada.

"Dale! What are you doing here?" She laid a hand on Jesse's shoulder. "Have you met Jesse?"

Dale's mouth rounded as if he were about to say more, then extended his hand. "I don't think so. Dale Lugar."

Jesse and Dale shook hands.

"I didn't expect to see you here," Jada continued. "It's such a tiny place."

"I've been known to stop by for a drink. Never been here on a Saturday night; figured I might as well try it out. I've never seen *you* here, though."

"Barry wanted me to check out the band for a film. The— wait, I just had a brain fart: What's their name?"

Before Jesse could answer, Dale chimed in. "Final Fuse." Another grin. Dale looked like a man who carried a perpetual inside joke and hid it behind a cloak of intellectualism. A man who, when caught by surprise, possessed enough self-control to steady his response. Cool under pressure.

"Dale was a medical consultant on a film a few months ago," Jada said.

That explained his composure. The guy was a doctor.

"Chiropractor?" Jesse quipped, just for the hell of it. Doctors seemed to hate the joke. Jada shot him a look that articulated she didn't share the humor, either. She had a sixth sense for money and influence, and this guy reeked of it. Jada didn't make enemies with such people.

Dale chuckled. "No. Plastic surgeon."

Jada laughed and touched Dale's arm. Jesse snorted to himself. Typical Jada, who flirted with anyone who might prove exciting.

"Good to see you again," Dale said to Jada. Then he turned to Jesse and added, "Nice to meet you." Jesse and Dale shook hands again before Dale sauntered off.

"He's not really a plastic surgeon," Jada said. "Last time I saw him, he was in the middle of a divorce. His wife waited till she got her plastic surgery paid for before she told him she intended to file. He was crushed."

Okay, maybe Jesse misjudged the guy. Different as Jesse and Jada were, Jada had become a part of Jesse's life, and he couldn't stand the idea of losing her.

An hour later, Jesse had his fill of the throbbing music and wandered to a patio outside, where a group of smokers congregated. When he eyed Dale, who stood alone, Jesse strolled up to him.

Dale took another drag from his cigarette. "A doctor who smokes," he admitted.

"My illusions are shattered." Jesse stared out at the horizon as it faded amid nightfall. "What kind of medicine do you practice?"

"Cardiology. I have an office in Sherman Oaks."

"A *cardiologist* who smokes."

"Yeah, you'd be surprised. My ex-wife loved to mention the inconsistency. She was a yoga nut."

"Sorry about your divorce. Jada mentioned it."

"My ex got everything but the Maserati." He extinguished the cigarette while the final cloud seeped through his lips. "What can I say? Shallow women suit me."

The smoker group returned inside, which left Jesse and Dale by themselves. Aside from the music, muted through closed glass doors, the evening was calm. Dale flicked a lingering ash from the railing.

"You and Jada have been together how long?"

"About ten years. We were friends back then, and it evolved." As he pondered his own reply, Jesse grew perplexed. "Come to think of it, I don't remember our first actual date."

"And you're a …"

"An actor."

"Anything I might've seen?"

Jesse hated that question. The answer forced him to face the reality of a typical week. "I work as an extra right now. Projects here and there, but not a big role yet. Jada never mentioned it?"

"I wouldn't take it personally. She never mentioned a relationship, that's all."

"I guess she wouldn't talk about it at work."

Dale stepped back and tilted his head to scan Jesse's face. "You're not from around here," he observed. "Born and raised, I mean."

Jesse sniffed. In the awkward silence, he could tell Dale was ready to head inside.

This guy is a doctor, right? Maybe he can make sense of my symptoms.

"Are you familiar with other areas of medicine besides cardiology?"

"A working knowledge. Why do you ask?"

Jesse squirmed inside; he didn't want to go into detail. On the other hand, he did want peace of mind in the matter, a sense that all was okay.

"Look," Jesse said, "this isn't a big deal. But Jada doesn't know anything about it, and you might be aware of how … reactionary she can be."

Dale chuckled. "Yeah, I've noticed." Jesse slid his hand into his pocket, which must have come across to Dale as a nervous gesture. Dale's expression straightened. "Have you experienced symptoms?"

"Oh … it's nothing major, just … you know, common things."

"Like what?"

Why did I tell this to a stranger? Now Jesse felt ridiculous to have brought up the issue. "I get exhausted for no reason at all …" He paused.

"Is that all? It could be stress. I wouldn't worry about it."

"No, there's more," Jesse said. "Nosebleeds—they come for no reason. And it's hard to get them to stop."

"It can take ten minutes sometimes."

"Five, ten minutes. Often it's more like a half hour, even longer."

"And Jada's never noticed this?"

"Given our mixed schedules, we're not around each other much. A couple of evenings a week, tops. She's seen one nose-bleed happen."

Dale nodded. "What else?"

"If I nick myself, like my finger, it can take that long for the bleeding to stop. Bruises in a couple of odd places, but I could've bumped against something. Once, my heart started to race, but it returned to normal after around twenty seconds—that was scary, but again, it only happened once. That could be stress too, right?"

"It could depend on the activity you were engaged in at the moment."

"I don't remember."

"How long have these symptoms occurred?"

"A few months. I never had a problem with them before."

Dale turned away. He stroked his chin and paced, back and forth, across the patio. When he returned to Jesse, he shook his head. "The out-of-the-blue appearance of your symptoms intrigues me; it may or may not be a coincidence. Have you seen a doctor about this? Just to rule out any possibilities?"

Jesse snorted, crossed his arms. "No, I haven't." Impatient with himself for his concerns—and because he'd drawn someone else into the matter—Jesse shrugged it off. "It's nothing. Those symptoms happen to everyone at one point or another. I'm sure it's stress from trying to pay the bills and jumpstart a career. I've never been an addict, but I've fooled around with pot here and there," he said. "I'm tired and have finally managed to get myself fucked up, that's all."

Dale's eyes penetrated Jesse's, a concentrated look that seemed to search for nonverbal clues. Jesse recognized the gesture—his father owned one himself.

"Look," Jesse continued, "never mind. I'm heading back inside. Don't mention this to Jada, all right?"

"Your call."

"Thanks for your help."

Jesse opened the glass doors and returned inside, where the music had started to sound like confusion.

CHAPTER 12

JADA couldn't sit still. The whole drive home, her foot tapped. She seemed stressed out, although the reason eluded Jesse.

When they walked through the front door, Jada tossed her purse and keys on the counter and made a beeline for the bathroom, where she opened the medicine cabinet. Curious, Jesse followed her in and caught her as she reached for the painkillers. Several years ago, Jada had her wisdom teeth removed and got a prescription for the ache. As it turned out, a bottle of ibuprofen had suited her fine. But rather than discard the unused painkillers, she saved them for special occasions—one pill to help her mellow out when she grew nervous, which was rare. The bottle remained half full.

Jesse knew better than to mention the pills. Maybe she had found that evening's jazz fusion as annoying as he had.

"Well, that was fun," she said, her voice rigid as a copper pipe.

Jesse turned his head and pretended not to notice as she returned the bottle to the cabinet. "I take it you enjoyed yourself?"

One pat to his butt, and she flipped off the light. "Sure."

Jada sauntered over to the sofa, where she fell into it, kicked off her shoes, and curled her legs underneath her. It looked like the painkiller buzz had started take effect already.

"So what did you and Dale talk about?" she asked.

"Huh?"

She smoothed the cushion beside her. Jesse took the hint and sat down.

"Tonight," she replied. When Jesse failed to give an immediate answer, she leaned closer. She peered into his eyes; Jesse found a gentle tease in hers. She said, "I saw you on the patio together. Did you have fun? You were out there long enough."

"Just shooting the breeze."

"Did you pick up some cardiology tips from him?"

"I learned he has a Maserati."

Tongue in cheek, she grinned. "I already knew that."

Jada leaned her head back as Jesse initiated foreplay. At last, she murmured, "What do you know—I'm getting laid tonight after all."

Jesse stopped. "What?"

"We both thought you'd work tonight."

"Right." He'd forgotten about the birthday party earlier that day.

Jada closed her eyes. "Kiss me here …"

————————

They lay naked beneath the sheets that night. Hours earlier, Jesse's cloud of depression had emerged again, and once they reached the bed, he had lost the urge to pursue intimacy further. An argument ensued—as if the circumstance weren't humiliating enough for him—which left them to fall asleep embittered and distant.

Halfway through the night, Jesse grew restless and stirred in his sleep. Groggy, Jada grunted, then patted around the bed with eyes shut. When she squinted at Jesse, she watched her partner rustle beside her as he struggled through a difficult dream. But his quiet moans and sighs didn't indicate fright—rather, a peculiar tenderness, a cautious concern.

"Babe …" she whispered. No response. She tapped him to no avail.

A chill formed in the air, and Jada pulled the satin sheet closer against her skin. Despite her attempt to return to sleep, Jesse's body shifts jolted her awake. At last, she reached over and grazed his hair with feather-light strokes. Jesse calmed. She continued for a few moments until he murmured in his sleep.

"Caitlyn …"

Jada halted in mid stroke. As she withdrew her hand, she stared at Jesse.

She didn't flinch. Didn't blink. She just stared at him, the gleam in her eyes sharp as a pair of precision razors.

Caitlyn.

As she pierced him with her eyes, she lay and watched to see what happened next. But his stirring didn't resume. Jesse continued to lay motionless. Soothed.

Jada's lips compressed until they all but disappeared. With a huff, she turned over and drew the sheet over her head.

———

Jesse sensed he'd had a troubled dream the night before but couldn't recall the subject. Not that this was unusual; he remembered few dreams nowadays. Had Jada stroked his hair, or was that part of the dream too?

Jada continued to sleep. Since it was Sunday morning, Jesse figured she'd want to sleep in. No appointments today. Besides, he couldn't shake the sense of tension, or at least something off-kilter, in the atmosphere.

From his seat at the dining-room table, Jesse heard Jada stir in the bedroom when she awoke. Without getting up, he peered around the corner and caught sight of her through a portion of the bedroom doorway. She held her hand against her head as though to combat a headache.

He watched her as she discovered the other side of the bed empty. She fingered the imprint of Jesse's body, still carved into the sheet, a ghostly reminder of his presence. When she rose, Jesse resumed his breakfast.

On her way out of the bedroom, Jada bit her lip. Her face looked a tad too flushed. To Jesse, she appeared bothered.

Though Jesse didn't ask, Jada gave him a status report anyway. "I didn't fall asleep till dawn. You shifted around last night," she said.

Jesse shrugged but said nothing.

With the aroma of brewed coffee in the air, Jesse watched as Jada padded into the kitchen toward the bistro-style pot. Jesse continued to munch on his organic oat cereal while he perused one of the scripts Jada had left on the table.

He had hoped the prior day's birthday party would help shake the relentless cloud of depression that continued to weigh on his shoulders, but it hadn't. And he didn't feel like talking this morning. Too embarrassed from having let her down in bed the prior night, he couldn't look her in the eyes. Such a problem had never occurred between them before.

Jada poured herself a cup of dark roast and topped it with a splash of soy milk. As she stirred, she eyed Jesse and took a seat across the table. "Script any good?"

Jesse swallowed another bite. "Did Barry sign on with it?"

"No."

"It's awful."

She forced a smile. "That's why it ended up on the table and not in my portfolio."

"Straight to the recycle bin, huh?"

"That's quite a comment from someone who won't go out of his way to recycle. You're full of surprises."

"Who knows? Maybe I've turned over a new leaf."

"Nothing wrong with trying something new." She sipped her coffee and shot him a grin.

He could tell Jada wanted answers, probably about his lack of performance. Humiliated enough, he wasn't about to take her bait.

Jesse set the script aside and took another bite.

Her jaw clenched, Jada inhaled the steam from her coffee. After Jesse headed for a refill, he returned to the table and studied his finger as he circled the rim of his cup.

"Preoccupied last night?" Jada asked.

"I wasn't in the mood, that's all."

"You initiated the whole thing to begin with. Was it because I wanted to be on top?"

"I'm sure that didn't help."

"I'll always end up on top one way or another—in everything."

"What are you talking about?"

"Never mind." Despite her pause, Jesse could tell she was ready to prod further. Jada continued, "Maybe we should try something different, spice it up for once."

"You mean with sex?"

"Yeah," she replied.

"Like what?" Disinterested, he didn't know how else to respond. When it came to intimacy, Jesse was more conservative than she was, but he seldom encountered an issue when he indulged her.

"I don't know," Jada said. "Maybe a threesome."

Alarmed, Jesse dropped his spoon. He glared at Jada. Determined to maintain his self-control after this unwarranted insult, he tried to hide his shock behind a neutral tone of voice.

"Are you kidding?" he said, his words clipped.

"Just one time, for a little variety. Kind of like—oh, I don't know—to treat ourselves."

"*A treat?* I don't see how that's a treat." Composed, Jesse channeled his anger to the cereal bowl as he slid it aside.

Thick as honey, tension hung in the air. Now both their jaws were clenched.

Jesse broke the silence. "Are you saying you're dissatisfied with me?"

"Of course not. Don't take it personally."

"How do I *not* take your idea personally?" Jesse felt his face turn shades of maroon. Was that a stifled grin on her face? She seemed to find satisfaction in his anger. Jesse stood before he would lose his temper. He shook his head in disbelief. Even for Jada, her suggestion crossed the line. His voice a notch louder, he added, "This is ridiculous. What are you thinking?!"

She kept silent, just watched.

He raged on. "And you're thinking the third person would be *who*?"

"Well, it's my idea," she said with a shrug of her shoulders, "so it's only fair to have another guy, right?"

Incredulous, his cheeks grew hot. "Unbelievable! What the hell is supposed to run through my mind while another guy fucks my girlfriend?"

"So you're into monogamy now?"

"Are you *high* right now? You don't make any sense!"

"So you're saying there's no one else?" she said.

"What?"

"You heard me."

"Of course not!" Jesse wasn't perfect, but he had remained faithful to Jada throughout their relationship.

Her voice was hushed yet venomous. Jada leaned forward, pressed her palms against the tabletop. "Then who the fuck is Caitlyn?"

"Who? Why are you asking me this?"

"Your dream. You had a bad dream last night and said her name."

"Wait, you're telling me this is all about a *dream*?! You're holding me accountable for my *dreams*?!"

"They come from all that subconscious crap, right? You must know a Caitlyn or be thinking about a Caitlyn!"

"How many times have you flirted with any producer you think could give your career a boost? You can never swallow what you dish out!" Jesse could feel his ears turn scarlet. He took a deep breath, then held up his hands and exhaled. "I'm not doing this right now. I don't need this shit so early in the day."

Jesse stormed out of the room. Jada got up for a refill.

CHAPTER 13

HE felt miniscule compared to the expanse of the ocean. Small.

Insignificant.

Atypical of southern California, the overcast sky featured ashen overtones today. From a window, one would think it a winter afternoon. The beach was desolate and, at the moment, belonged to Jesse alone.

Jesse loved Malibu. The oceanfront community didn't feel as commercialized like Santa Monica down the road. He loved to cruise northward along the two-lane Pacific Coast Highway as it wound through the area. The road ran parallel to a series of high hills, rolling plumes of greenery where white mansions sat nestled. While Malibu's cost of living was much higher than that of Sherman Oaks, walking the shoreline was free and Jesse escaped here to contemplate, to dream.

Jesse pondered his previous argument with Jada. Her words had dealt him a severe blow. In spite of her blunt accusation and lack of tact—both characteristic of Jada—to hear that she considered their intimacy less than satisfactory had sunken straight to the bottom of his soul. The last thing a man wanted to hear from his partner was that she was bored and he was the cause.

He had clung to her for so long that he'd forgotten why. It wasn't habit per se, nor could he attribute it to genuine love. But in recent days, as the prospects of life caved in around him, he needed her—she was the one constant factor in his life. Perhaps that made no difference to Jada, but he appreciated the security. Did that make him feel like a failure? Yes. Did it tarnish his sense of masculinity? Absolutely. Although unspoken, in this honest moment he had to admit it was true.

The breaking waves welcomed him. Jesse removed his shoes and socks. Camera in hand, he wandered barefoot across the fine, ivory sand and walked to where the water's edge ebbed and flowed. When it retreated back to sea, the savory water abandoned its bubbling, salty foam to reveal smooth, damp sand that begged for a fresh layer of footprints. Jesse halted. He closed his eyes to savor the chilled Atlantic water as it massaged the tops of his feet and hurled sand granules between his toes. He listened to the hypnotic undulation of the breakers and the squawks of seagulls that cried ownership of the scene.

Serene. That's the word he would use to describe this ambience. This is why he had come.

When he opened his eyes, he absorbed the sight once more, then took a photograph of serenity. While the sky above reflected how he felt inside, the steady motion before him communicated what he *sought* to feel inside. The ocean seemed to hold a spiritual quality: untamed yet predictable. Larger than life. Jesse's father, in preacher fashion, said God could be seen in nature. So where was God in times like this? Where was God as Jesse's future unraveled and he tried to hang on by his fingernails?

Jesse had to think of something. He couldn't lean on Jada for validation. It made him feel like a loser.

He held up the camera again, waited for a large breaker to mount in the distance, and clicked.

"Are you a professional?"

Apathetic, Jesse glanced at the figure that approached him. Grasping a camera made him appear an expert, while busting his ass for eleven years in front of the camera said nothing?

"Just taking a few shots," Jesse replied.

Jesse estimated the young guy to be in his mid twenties. His sandy-brown hair tousled by the light breeze, the guy looked like someone who had broken many girls' hearts in between tennis matches. He finished a cigarette, then made his way to Jesse's paradise to share in the vast view. Dressed in high-end, brand-name gear and a two-hundred-dollar watch, Jesse figured the guy lived in Malibu. He didn't see a parked car nearby, so the visitor must have strolled from a few minutes down shore.

"You live around here?" the guy asked, a hint of an accent in his voice—British or Australian. The females must croon over him, Jesse figured.

"Sherman Oaks."

The guy nodded. "I live around the corner. Tell you what, I'm addicted to sushi." With his thumb, the guy gestured south. "Especially the stuff they have at the hole-in-the-wall down the road. Ever been there?"

"No."

"It's a little dive on stilts—a bar-and-grill type with a sushi counter. Gotta make my appearance there every couple of days to feed my passion. If I hadn't just come from there, I'd insist on leading you over to it," the guy joked.

Jesse wanted his solitude back.

The intruder extended his hand. "I'm Adam."

"Jesse."

"So if you're not a photographer, what are you?"

Your first guess is correct, buddy. "An actor."

Adam's eyebrows rose. "Really?" He stepped back and gave

Jesse a once-over glance. "Makes sense though; you've got the build for it. Have you been in anything recent?" His tone wasn't judgmental like many with whom Jesse crossed paths in L.A. This guy didn't come across as threatened by a competitor; rather, he seemed curious, easy to talk to. By nature, however, Jesse remained guarded.

Jesse wasn't in the mood to fend off a stranger, so he decided to let the guy feel welcome for a few minutes. Jesse offered a polite smile. "An *unemployed* actor," he clarified. "Thanks for the compliment. Meanwhile, I work a part-time job but have today off. What do you do for a living?"

Jesse watched as Adam fought to hide a smug grin and shrugged. "I guess I take it day by day, enjoy life. Smell the sushi."

"Don't you work?"

"I'd be awful at it. I'm not really a nine-to-five kind of person. I dabble in production with some friends, tried to put together a couple of reality-TV shows. They never took off, though."

"Doesn't that make it hard to pay the bills?"

Adam withdrew into an air of genuine humility, as if he seldom shared the next piece of information with strangers. "Well, not if you're Mick Lewis's son."

Unbelievable. Known for his successful summer blockbusters, Mick Lewis directed action films with major budgets. In the late 1980s, Mick married Regan Cooper, an Australian actress who starred in his first film. They divorced ten years later.

"Mick Lewis?" Jesse chuckled, then pivoted in Adam's direction. More hospitable now, Jesse was eager to hear details about the good life. "Yeah, I guess I wouldn't worry about a job either. Lucky you. Is Regan Cooper your mom?"

Adam answered with a nod, which also explained his accent. Once again, he scanned Jesse. "No films in the pipeline, you said?"

Jesse shook his head.

Adam studied a seagull that stomped nearby. Before he caught himself, he rubbed his finger along his own bicep, which seemed an absentminded habit. Jesse thought he saw Adam take another quick glance from the corner of his eye. It was obvious Adam weighed his words.

"Listen," Adam said, "my dad's got films lined up. He's given a career start to some of my buddies. I could probably talk him into arranging a bit part for you—just a few lines, shouting at an enemy invader or something."

Jesse didn't expect this, and he never would have asked a stranger for such a thing. He'd heard Mick was a well-liked director; maybe his kid followed suit.

Speechless, Jesse searched for a response. "That's—wow. It's hard to believe you'd do that for someone you just met."

Adam pursed his lips. "Yeah ... sure, but I thought, you know, maybe something a little more ... if you're up to it."

"Like what?"

"Something more involved, if you know what I mean."

That's the way it often worked, through mutual back scratches. Not a problem.

"I doubt there's much I could do; but sure, whatever it takes. My roommate works for a director."

Adam slid his hands into his pockets. He pursed his lips as if Jesse had misunderstood the meaning. "It's ... well, it's not exactly a professional request. More like a personal one ..."

"A personal one," Jesse repeated. What was the reason

behind Adam's loss for words? Adam seemed to search for something in Jesse's face.

"A favor," Adam said, slower.

"Of course. Name it."

"No, I mean a *favor*."

Jesse paused. He tried to grasp what Adam meant by his
inflection.

Then it hit him.

Though no one was around, Jesse couldn't help but speak
in a hushed tone. "Are you talking about—you mean, like a
sexual favor?"

Adam stared at him. The absence of a reply spoke volumes.

Jesse's back grew rigid. Now the stranger's spontaneous
conversation made sense; Jesse's mind had been so focused on
his own life, he hadn't recognized Adam's words as a means to
try gauge his sexual orientation. He wanted to lash out at Adam
but contained it instead. Jesse attempted to maintain a neutral
demeanor. After all, Adam knew people in the industry and
could, with a phone call, ruin Jesse's future chances of success.

Jesse couldn't face him. So he stared into the distance. "I
couldn't do that."

"It wouldn't be the first time it's happened around here."

Jesse had heard of such scenarios but had never involved
himself in one, nor had anyone he knew. Some people would
jump at the opportunity. Granted, Jesse was desperate, but at
least he had an agent who worked on his behalf.

"Remember Michael Casey?" Adam continued.

Michael Casey was a young Hollywood heartthrob around
Jesse's age. News media credited Mick Lewis with the actor's
discovery after he cast him in a small role.

"What about him?"

"How do you think he got discovered?" Adam hinted.

Skeptical, Jesse snorted. "No." In a tug-of-war between his own honesty and the temptation to open a career door, Jesse hesitated, shook his head slowly. "No, that's not an option for me."

"Look, you don't need to do anything except stand there. Besides, you'd be safe; it's only oral, and I'm the one who would go down. Nobody will find out. Trust me, my dad would kill me if he knew." He pulled a piece of paper from his pocket and scribbled. "Here's my cell number. Think about it. Five minutes, and your career takes off. Small price to pay for your big break."

He handed the paper to Jesse and then continued his stroll along the beach. From the corner of his eye, Jesse followed Adam Lewis until his figure disappeared into obscurity. Adam never once looked back—this must be ordinary to him, Jesse concluded.

Jesse's belly churned. He shoved the paper into his pocket for the next trashcan he found.

CHAPTER 14

THE following afternoon, Jesse finished a customer's transaction at LensPerfection and bid her good-bye. With the lunch-hour rush long gone, the store grew dormant. He approached another customer to offer assistance, but the customer declined.

Jesse's cell phone vibrated.

As he rounded back to the checkout counter, he answered his phone in the nick of time before voice mail interfered.

"This is Maddy. Do you have a minute to talk?" She sounded concerned.

"I'm at work, but it's a ghost town in here." Jesse didn't concern himself with his reply. He wanted to hear what Maddy had to say.

Maddy paused. "I've always been direct with you, haven't I?"

"Of course. What's wrong?"

"There's no easy way to say this, so here's the deal: We've opted to release you as a client."

In an instant, Jesse's mouth filled with marbles and his tongue rested heavy. His life continued to worsen. Desperate, he lacked a backup plan.

Maddy filled the awkward silence. "The agency needs to trim its client roster so we can focus our attention in a more strategic manner. You're not alone; we've released 20 percent of our clients."

Broken, Jesse tried to think on his feet. "What can I do to avoid this?"

"I don't have a choice; I had to examine my roster and make objective cuts. I wish I could keep you, but I've have a hard time placing you for projects. As you know, your last audition was the first in two years, and I—"

"Couldn't we give it another month?"

Maddy listened. Throughout their professional partnership, she had listened and understood. But today that era had come to a halt.

"I'd keep you on board if I could." She paused. "Others may not recognize your talent, Jesse, but I believe in you. We've partnered together for a long time, and you've been a pleasure to work with. You're not a prima donna. You're patient, kindhearted. I wish I could partner with more clients like you. But in the end, that's just not enough." Jesse could almost hear her tongue in cheek as she said, "When you win your Academy Award, I'll cheer for you from the seats."

Even tender remarks could puncture a wounded spirit.

"Thanks," he mumbled.

"Good-bye, Jesse."

He didn't head straight home that evening. Though hungry, he had no desire to eat. He cruised westbound along Ventura Boulevard until he tired and headed back. Well past sunset, he passed the series of manicured palm trees that poked through shadows.

He had fought his tears for the remainder of his shift. But once he climbed in his car, they poured forth. And under the guise of night, those tears were his alone, revealed only by the illumination of streetlights that raced past him. The tears were overdue, stifled for many months. He didn't want his emotions to flow, but deep down, Jesse was tenderhearted.

Still, he had no other choice but to press forward—even if he had no idea how to do so.

Jada would never see the tears. Nor would anyone else.

It had taken Jesse years to secure an agent in Maddy. Now that she was out of the picture, the horizon appeared bleak. His chances of locating a role just grew slimmer—if that were possible.

And then, while he turned left onto Van Nuys and headed home, it hit him: He might have another option.

When he left for work earlier that morning, he realized he'd miscalculated his laundry schedule and had worn yesterday's jeans a second day to bridge the time gap. But maybe that wasn't such a bad thing …

He dried his eyes with his sleeve and cleared his voice to hide any evidence of his emotional valley. With one hand on the wheel, Jesse dug through his pocket in search of his trump card. Had he gotten rid of it? Coins, mints, cell phone …

There it was.

He removed the crumpled piece of paper and smoothed it against the dashboard. As he drove, he angled the paper and tried to decipher the digits beneath the streetlights. He hated to do this, but after eleven years in L.A., he'd grown sick of failure.

Five minutes. Was it such a horrible trade?

Five minutes for a career breakthrough. He possessed the talent to carry him in the long run; he simply needed an open door. Wasn't that worth five minutes?

The call wasn't easy. Jesse stalled for time: He tapped his

fingers on the steering wheel, calculated how many minutes until he arrived home, counted car dealerships along the way. At last, he tightened his jaw and grabbed his cell phone.

He dialed the number. It rang numerous times, and Jesse grew relieved when an answer didn't appear forthcoming. Ready to flip his phone shut, he heard a voice on the other end.

"This is Adam."

Jesse winced. Anger bubbled in the pit of his stomach—not anger at Adam Lewis, but anger at himself because he had stooped so low. Jesse bit his lip and moved forward.

"It's Jesse." No response. "From yesterday in Malibu—the beach." He gritted his teeth. "The offer."

"Oh yeah, I remember. I take it you've thought about it?" Adam shouted over music that blared in the background. A group of people with raised voices walked past him in laugher. The call was impersonal. "Can you hold on a sec? I'll find a quiet spot."

As the music grew muted on Adam's end, Jesse pulled in front of his own apartment building and turned off the engine. He remained in the car and listened.

"You still there?" Adam said.

"The answer's yes."

"You mean we have a deal?"

"I'll do it. But I want to clarify: Your dad has a role available, right? This isn't a situation where we go through with this, and then I get put on a waiting list?"

"He has a role he needs to fill. Don't worry, I don't offer to do this often."

"Why me?"

"Tall, blond—"

Jesse didn't want to hear this after all. "Never mind. I understand."

"So we're set?"

"Like I said, I'll do it. Not a public place though."

"It won't be."

And they made arrangements. They would meet at Adam's house. They figured a time when Jesse wasn't scheduled to work; when the Lewis family's housekeeper wouldn't be in the house; when Mick Lewis would be out of town, with no chance of unplanned interruptions.

In a matter of days, Jesse's career could surge.

His mind was relieved.

His stomach was queasy.

CHAPTER 15

O N Saturday afternoon, Jesse parked his car in the garage at Hollywood & Highland Center, bought a latte at a Java Cup, and roamed down Hollywood Boulevard. Jesse's sister, Eden, had asked him for a memorabilia trinket, so he'd headed out to the largest tourist area he knew. Jada had said she wanted to shop for clothes that day—alone.

He didn't miss the days when he and Jada lived in an apartment down the street. He didn't miss the automobile congestion or foot traffic or the smog that thickened nearby.

As he headed down the sidewalk, he observed the usual platter of American hors d'oeuvres: Starving-artist locals. An individual dressed in a fusion of Goth and drag. Pale-skinned visitors in fluorescent T-shirts at street corners who huddled around caricature maps of narrow streets and ballooned buildings. Jesse passed themed museums crammed into retail-shop-sized allocations; he peered into dives that sold key chains, miniature Oscar statuettes, and rolls of camera film. And most of the employees had a dream.

First, Jesse ducked into a shop to purchase a "Best Sister" Oscar statuette for Eden. Then he made his way further, along the Walk of Fame, where he tread upon terrazzo tiles of pink stars against a charcoal background, stamped with bronze seals to represent the celebrity's media sector. Jesse walked past Elton John's star, defaced by a worn decal applied by a passerby.

He arrived at Grauman's Chinese Theatre, where he scanned the series of handprints and footprints embedded in concrete slabs at the Theatre's forefront. The uneven imprints rippled under the soles of his feet as he walked on them. While some were recent, others had existed for decades. Jada dreamed of a star on the Walk of Fame; but in Jesse's view, the concrete prints represented living individuals who had applied their hands and feet to the ground as they had to their careers. For Jesse, these prints provided evidence that, yes, dreams indeed come to fruition.

Jesse noticed the horse mascot, which walked upright on its hind legs in the Theatre's far corner, near the entrance. Unless he was mistaken, the costumed character was Clickety Clack.

It couldn't be him, Jesse mused.

As he sneaked up behind the horse, which clipped along and waved to kids in strollers, Jesse heard the sound of tin-can hoofs reminiscent of the character's name.

"Gavin, is that you?"

Clickety Clack spun on its hind hoofs and spread its front legs apart like arms, a toothy smile stitched upon its furry face. As the character tilted its head back, Jesse caught a glimpse up the horse's nostrils, the location of two black-screened peepholes.

Gavin grunted. "Rescue me, man. This sucks. I'm burning up inside this costume."

"I thought you worked at the shopping place."

With his front hoof, Gavin gestured toward the massive theater beside him. "The movie version opens next week. They've got me out here promoting it. I've already gotten kicked in the gonads by a teenager. Fun and games for me." With a tone of sarcasm, he added, "If I do a good job, they'll promote me to the popcorn costume."

"I don't know about that promotion. You make a convincing horse."

"Yeah, well, it smells like ass in here."

"Clever, but your pun is inaccurate."

"I'll work on it. Anyway, this beats working in a wax museum down the street. I had a job in one of those in a former life. Like being surrounded by dead people. Felt like a morgue in there, cold as it was. Avoid it if you can."

"I'll keep that in mind."

"How'd your audition go?"

"It didn't pan out," Jesse replied. "My agent just dropped me."

Gavin clucked his tongue and leaned on his other hind hoof, which caused another clack to issue forth from the speaker inside the horse's derriere. "To be honest, I expect mine to give me a phone call of abandonment before the end of the year. Any possible leads to cover you in the meantime?"

Hesitant, Jesse feigned interest in a man who stood at a corner and handed out game-show tickets. "Yeah, I've lined one up—almost. One technicality to work out, but it sounds promising."

"In that case, congratulations! You've gotta celebrate the little things."

If only. Jesse hoped word would never get around regarding the specifics. He wanted to bolt before Gavin probed for more details—or asked Jesse to hook him up with a similar so-called opportunity. "Listen, I don't mean to brush you off, but I'd better run. Look out for those abusive teenagers you mentioned; it would be a shame to see you submit a workers' comp claim."

"I wouldn't worry about that. The next surly looking kid gets a rubber-horseshoe print across his pimpled face."

Jesse jingled his keys as he approached the door to his apartment, though he didn't need them after all. Before he reached the door, he watched it open from the other side. But Jada didn't walk out. Dr. Dale did.

Focused on his own car keys, Dale failed to notice Jesse until they were face-to-face in the corridor. Unable to hide a double-take when he laid eyes on Jesse, Dale regained his composure. "Jesse! Good to see you again! I needed to pick up a script from Jada." He waved the roll of paper in his hand.

"You're advising another project?"

"You got it." Dale's face was flushed, as if he had stopped by after a three-mile treadmill run. Then again, Dale was a smoker. That ruddy effect must not have required a lot of exertion.

"See you around, Dale."

"Later." He headed off, but stopped at the top of the stairs and snapped his fingers. "Oh, I almost forgot: Remember our talk the other night—the symptoms you've experienced?"

Jesse's eyes darted to the apartment door, but then he relaxed. If Jada were within earshot, she would have graced them with her presence by now. "Yeah, sorry about that. After I got it off my chest, I realized how ridiculous it sounded to be so concerned about it."

"I'm glad you mentioned it. Your symptoms aren't disconcerting at face value. But when I considered how close together they occurred, combined with their abrupt onset, it made me think." Dale leaned against the banister. "So I did some research. Bear in mind, you haven't had any tests run, and this isn't an official diagnosis. But the symptoms could point to a blood disorder."

Jesse sucked air but guarded against a visible reaction. "So I should be worried?"

"No, I wouldn't say so. Like I said, this is based solely on research and not tests, so it could be a coincidence. And even if it were a blood disorder, like a type of anemia, it may not be cause for concern. Anemias vary according to which type of blood cell is affected, as well as how those blood cells behave, such as overproduction or underproduction. Again, you'd want tests. In most cases, these tend to be treatable conditions. If it's not severe—and I'd be surprised if it were—it might mean a dietary supplement and a minor change in your daily activity."

"I *feel* fine, just tire easily on occasion. You think it's minor?"

"My thoughts aren't concrete. The more I researched, the more your symptoms seemed to point to a condition called Baer's Disease. It sounds bad but it's much like a form of anemia and is treatable. It's uncommon, but a possibility. Symptoms show up for no reason—the same sort you described. They don't appear to be much of a threat, and they don't need to be."

"So I can forget about it?"

"I didn't say that. Left untreated, the condition worsens. Catch it sooner rather than later, then your options improve and you can get it under control. In the meantime, don't make a blood donation—that could be fatal with this condition, as you might imagine." When Jesse winced, Dale waved it off. "Don't worry about it. They always ask you those things before you try to donate. Beyond that, I recommend you see your doctor and have some tests ordered."

"See my doctor? I don't have health coverage, Dale—I'm a starving artist with a part-time job."

"You're not on Jada's plan either?"

"We're not married and never took steps to pursue coverage. It didn't seem like a big deal. I'm only twenty-nine."

"I hear you. A lot of young guys try to go without health coverage. It works out fine, unless something goes wrong. If I were in that line of medicine, I'd help you out on a pro-bono basis. Unfortunately, however, you're talking to a cardiologist here. And one who smokes, so what do I know, right? Just think about it."

"I will. Thanks for your help. You're Jada's friend and don't really know me, so I appreciate it."

Dale shrugged. While he examined the soles of his shoes, he said, "I'm a doctor; curiosity gets the best of me." He checked his watch. "I need to head to the hospital, so I'll see you around."

Jesse pictured the medical bills that could pile up—and all to prove what was, in all likelihood, a minor nuisance. Didn't Dale himself say this could be a coincidence? Jesse knew someone who had surgery once, and six months after, bills continued to appear in the mailbox—three hundred dollars here, seven hundred dollars there. Without medical coverage, those bills would have scrubbed the guy's finances clean.

Fuck it. Jesse didn't survive in L.A. through worry or by cowering at every detail that tried to force him into retreat. He'd come here to find freedom.

Medical tests would hassle his finances. His symptoms were common and a coincidence.

Jesse listened to the engine of Dale's Maserati as it sped around the corner and out of range.

When a bricklayer builds a wall, he begins at ground level and works his way up. At first, the wall isn't impressive. But as he stacks layer upon layer, eventually he requires a ladder because the wall towers over his head, obstructs his view, and closes him in.

With all his recent downturns, Jesse related to a bricklayer, one who woke up each morning and faced the same cold, rough wall and its chipped, jagged surface. The bricklayer must become impatient. Yes, albeit metaphorical, he and the bricklayer faced similar circumstances, except for one difference: Jesse didn't feel like he'd laid his own bricks, and he sure as hell hadn't selected the color.

Jesse gripped his keys and felt their rigid edges dig into his palm.

Surely Jada had her own secrets. What was one more secret kept from her?

CHAPTER 16

O N the lifestyle ladder, Jesse thought he understood where he resided—until he drove deeper into the hills of Malibu. On countless occasions he'd seen the homes, but never from such close proximity. And so today, as he wound his way up the road to Mick Lewis's home, Jesse gained new appreciation for how a clean, well-maintained Honda can feel like a rust-mobile in these surroundings.

The houses were enormous so far, yet he continued to ascend the hill. He could only imagine what lay ahead. If he paid more attention, he was confident he would hear his ears pop due to the change in altitude. Technically, film directors were not full-time employees. Like Jesse, these people were part-timers, but compared to his job at LensPerfection, he preferred the media-mogul interpretation of part-time. Then again, many of these people had been in his shoes eons ago.

With the directions Adam Lewis had given him over the phone, Jesse reached his destination. As he inched closer, past an electronic security gate, the home emerged into view in slow motion, like a whale that bobbed through the surface of Alaskan waters. Cream-colored, the house's architecture, like neighboring mansions far below, encompassed a unique design but exuded eloquence worthy of Hollywood's golden era. He could picture this home occupied by Mary Pickford, or better yet, Bogart and Bacall. Given alternative circumstances, he would have been thrilled to have access for a tour.

The sensation of having wandered out of his element exacerbated his nerves. He had been nauseous since last night in anticipation of today, a quiver at his loss of self-respect. As he drove through the security gates to the top of Adam's driveway and shut off the engine, he wanted to turn around and return home.

Once he stepped out of his car, he gazed out toward the rear of the house and couldn't believe his eyes as he surveyed the view below: Matchbox cars rolled along the Pacific Coast Highway against an artist's breathless rendition of the Pacific. Now early April, the air prickled warmer against his skin and amplified his nervous goose bumps.

While he scanned the greenery and Spanish patio décor, Adam greeted him.

"You made it. The directions were clear?"

"It's quite a drive. Nowhere to go but up," Jesse stuttered. He tried to relax but failed.

"Come on in." Adam smiled and waved him through a side door, as if he were an out-of-town guest or a friend who'd stopped by after classes.

Weak in the knees, Jesse followed him into the house, which opened into a spacious living room, two-stories high with lofty, vaulted ceilings and a glass-windowed wall. On one end of the room hung a flat-screen television that seemed ample enough to satisfy a small auditorium at a movie theater. Plush, white-leather furniture donned the room, complemented by thick Oriental rugs on polished hardwood floors. The place smelled of pine. Jesse would have savored the ambience if his legs didn't resemble the flimsiness of thin aluminum sheeting.

"Glass of wine?" Adam offered.

Maybe the alcohol would help Jesse forget why he was here. "Thanks."

"Have a seat. Make yourself comfortable."

Adam left to fetch the drinks. Not a sound could be heard in the house, save the trickle of a waterfall which came from an unseen source. Jesse examined the banister that crossed overhead and seemed to lead to a bedroom; although he heard no voices in the house, out of paranoia he expected to find an onlooker peek from around the corner. Watch him. Survey him.

No voyeurs in the house, though. He and Adam were alone.

It's not sex if it's oral—that's what Jada always said. According to her rules, Jesse wouldn't cheat on her. Besides, all he'd do is stand there; aside from his own physical presence, he could remain passive as the act unfolded.

Jesse attempted to sit down but bolted upright again, fearful he would vomit if he sat still. Instead, he leaned against the sectional sofa and feigned comfort as Adam handed him a glass of red wine. Against the natural light of the windows, the liquid reminded Jesse of a stained-glass-window plate from his father's church back home.

"To dreams," said Adam.

Jesse lifted his glass, the contents of which sloshed around from the shudder of his hand. He wondered how many others had walked into this particular room with the same purpose as his. Unable to discard a mental picture of a naked person on the expensive rug under his feet, he wanted to search for evidence of similar activity. Had he gotten dizzy in the last few minutes?

Don't think about it. Just get it over with.

"Bette Davis adored this room." Adam gestured upward with his glass.

"She used to visit?"

"She owned it. Decades ago, long before she died. She lived here briefly, before she moved to a place with more privacy."

Privacy? From down below, the public would need a pair of binoculars to spot a human being through the windowed wall up here. And Jesse found that a relief.

"You're nervous," Adam observed.

"Yeah," Jesse said, his voice hushed—it was all he could muster.

"You don't like secrets."

"I already have secrets."

Jesse pretended to take a sip but swallowed a gulp of his wine. Adam continued to watch him, but Jesse couldn't look him in the eyes. Instead Jesse opted to memorize the tiny bubbles around the perimeter of his wine as he swished the glass. In the awkwardness of the moment, the room grew hollow. What did Adam see? What traveled through his mind? His eyes weren't harsh; rather, they appeared soft and pensive. This brought no comfort to Jesse, however, who felt like a cheap porn video alone on a shelf.

Adam drained his last sip of wine. "Well, are you ready?"

Jesse's glass remained half full. He shrugged with supposed indifference, then knocked back the liquid in one gulp. Hesitant, he forced himself to take a step toward the influential person in front of him.

"Music?" Adam asked.

"No thanks." Jesse didn't want to introduce any songs that would taunt him at random moments in an elevator. He closed his eyes and tried to escape to a crevice in the back of his mind, an attempt interrupted by Adam's hands against his biceps. Jesse opened his eyes, already glossed over with suppressed tears, and focused on the banister again. He felt so vulnerable as this unfamiliar person swept his hands along his arms.

Jesse flinched.

"Relax," Adam whispered, then sank down beneath Jesse's range of vision.

Jesse thought of Jada and their last time of intimacy together. He shut his eyes once more and clenched his jaw. By instinct, he recoiled when Adam's hand made contact below the belly to reach for the button on Jesse's jeans.

Jesse cringed inside. He felt filthy. Mixing business with pleasure, or whatever this was.

All this to help his career. This wasn't who he really was.

The last sound Jesse could recall was the purr of his zipper as it lowered.

————————

His body tense, his stomach the consistency of melted butter, Jesse burst into the apartment but found himself alone. He didn't want to stand; he didn't want to sit. Restless, he ran into the bathroom and scrubbed his face with soap and water until it grew chapped. He rinsed with mouthwash even though his mouth hadn't been involved. He applied rubbing alcohol all below his waistline. Whatever measure of disinfectant that occurred to him, he tried it.

But he couldn't reach the point where he felt clean. Jesse couldn't escape the sense of guilt that chafed against his conscience: He had betrayed himself, allowed himself to be treated like raw meat by a stranger for the sake of a job. And the more he focused on it, the closer he felt to hyperventilation.

He craved a second chance but his options had vanished. He'd made his choice.

Even if this resulted in the opportunity of a lifetime, the

memory of today would linger in the cavities of his mind. He was too honest to deny its existence and fearful of its discovery.

The pungent scent of rubbing alcohol loosened his stomach further. With a splash of cologne, he managed to find relief.

Jesse needed to relax. In the kitchen, he opened a can of beer and leaned against the sink. Within a minute of the first swallow, the wooziness of the drink settled in and started to medicate his brain. An image of the afternoon flashed in his memory—of Adam on his knees in the longest minute of Jesse's life.

No, Jesse thought to himself in defiance of the memory that taunted him. *Stop!*

Though Jesse had kept silent back in Malibu, those were the words he had wanted to shout.

No! Stop!

Now it was too late.

Jesse took another swig of beer. He tried to calm himself but failed. His stomach somersaulted. Then its contents climbed.

He darted back into the bathroom, just in time to kneel on the floor and vomit into the toilet. While he maneuvered into a crossed-leg position, he rested his elbows against the cold porcelain. Then he vomited again.

If only he could purge the dark shadows that way.

CHAPTER 17

TWO weeks passed after the incident with Adam. Jesse had climbed out of the depths of that afternoon and had become optimistic that things might turn around. Perhaps he could move on. He hoped the rumor of his mistake would never reach Jada's ears. The industry was large, but grapevine networks, he'd discovered, could rival a subway system in both complexity and speed.

Mick had scheduled casting for last week. Adam had promised to call him with an update, but the week came and went without acknowledgment. Now Jesse felt agitated. Sure, waiting was part of the game, but then again, he and Adam hadn't played by the traditional rules.

With the store void of customers, Jesse decided to give Adam a call. He fished the phone number out of his wallet—the same piece of paper that had instigated the mess. He hadn't programmed the number into his phone's address book. He didn't want a reminder of how he'd obtained it.

When he flipped open his phone, he dialed the number and waited until Adam answered.

"Hey there, it's Jesse."

"I'm sorry I haven't gotten in touch. It's been busy."

Where? At the sushi counter?

"Not a big deal," Jesse lied. "I wanted to follow up on your dad's film, though—our arrangement."

Adam hesitated with a response, and Jesse's shoulders went limp.

"Yeah, about that. Listen, we ran into a snag," Adam said.

"A snag?"

"I owed a friend, and he called it in." Adam paused. "He got the role."

Jesse bit his lip.

"I had no idea he would call in the favor," Adam continued, "but he got wind of the part and phoned me the night before Dad scheduled the auditions. I couldn't get you involved at that point."

"What other roles are coming down the pike?"

"Nothing. Sorry about that; I wish I had something for ya."

"What's the next step? Where do we go from here?"

"I wasn't looking for a relationship."

"Not that. I mean, what happens next with your dad?"

"Um … nothing. There's nothing else available."

"So I wait and call in the favor like your friend. Is that what you're saying?"

"No, that other guy was a part-time lawyer. We go way back, and I owed him after he got me out of a DUI charge. You can't expect me to keep a running tally, can you?"

"Then you're saying I'm screwed?"

"Look, how long have you been in the entertainment business?"

"Eleven years."

"Then you know there aren't any guarantees."

"I'd say a guarantee was implied when you had your mouth on me."

Jesse flipped the phone shut and banged it on the counter.

He should have known. He'd crossed a line. Now he wanted to climb into a sinkhole.

Who have I become?

He could sense the guilt eat away at the back of his mind. In his heart, Jesse felt he deserved the treatment Adam had handed him.

CHAPTER 18

HOW long was he supposed to hang on to this cliff? How much longer did he plan to claw his way toward nothing? Jesse wanted to give up.

Engrossed by the Pacific water ahead, he hoped Adam Lewis wouldn't wander by. Alone, Jesse sat cross-legged in the sand. His eyes, once vibrant with ambition and dreams, now felt hollow. He couldn't do this much longer. This wasn't a matter of missed opportunity or being played for a fool. This was a fight for his destiny, his soul's desire. He'd invested everything he had in anticipation of future success. And the ominous notion that he'd reached the final tool in his arsenal sent shivers through him.

What do you do when your spirit is broken?

He heard the waves call to him. What he wouldn't give to disappear.

Camera by his side, he had planned to take some therapeutic shots but didn't feel motivated. So he sat.

Jesse pondered his past, from where he had come. He hadn't appreciated his Ohio home until now. Though he'd come to California to discover himself, he had discovered a stranger instead. The people who knew him dwelt in Ohio.

And here? Welcome to the charade. He had fooled himself.

He wished he could return home and make amends. But by now he was too ashamed.

Jesse's cell phone chirped in his pocket. He didn't care who called and didn't want to talk, but out of habit, he grabbed the phone anyway. When he checked the caller ID, he discovered the first positive development in weeks: his sister Eden's name on the display. Despite his efforts to forget his past, Eden represented its final, albeit welcome, thread.

"How's my little sister?"

"Where are you? I hear waves."

Today, he would've paid in diamonds to hear the sound of her voice. "Malibu. Are you at work?"

"Heading home," she replied. "How'd the audition go? That Mick Lewis part you mentioned."

"It didn't work out." He'd forgotten that in his former certainty, he had mentioned that role to her. And he didn't want to go into further detail—not with anyone. In an attempt to change the subject, he asked, "How's Dad?"

"He's the same—you know Dad." Eden paused. "Why don't you come visit him?"

Jesse just shook his head and snickered, minus the humor. "I don't see that happening. After eleven years?"

"He'd want to see you."

"I call him every once in a while."

"But it's not the same as seeing you in person. He misses you."

"Can we change the subject?"

"How's Jada?"

"She's … Jada." He fingered circles in the sand and said little. Eyes heavy, he closed them beneath the weight of his inner shroud.

Throughout the years, whenever he'd talked to Eden, he had dominated their conversation with the latest news about his projects, his girlfriend and acquaintances, the clubs he'd frequented. From the way he'd spoken, Jesse had painted pictures of warm, glistening sunshine and a lifestyle of perpetual motion. But in recent weeks, even he could sense the vibrant detail had vanished. By now Eden must have wondered if something was wrong.

On the other end of the line, Eden waited. Jesse offered only wind and water in response.

"Are you okay?" Eden asked.

Jesse palmed the sand to erase the concentric circles he had engraved there.

Now you see it, now you don't.

In a moment. Gone.

He lifted his head again.

"No," he replied. "No, I'm just not."

CHAPTER 19

AFTER Jada veered off of Interstate 405 in her crimson BMW, she sped onto Ronald Reagan Freeway that Saturday night. The swerve snapped Jesse's head backward and pinned it against the headrest.

"I could've driven and avoided breaking my neck," he quipped.

Humorless, Jada didn't break her concentration. She shook her head but didn't need to say a word.

No, they wouldn't dare take his car to where they headed tonight. After all, someone might see Jada climb out of a car worth a mere half of its original—and affordable— retail value.

She extinguished her cigarette in the ashtray, where she left it to smolder in ferocious defeat.

By day, Jesse marveled at the high hills of foliage and bare, clay-colored land that sat in royal loftiness overhead. Even now, under the cover of night, he caught their silhouettes, which surrounded the freeway. He and Jada whizzed through Simi Valley on their way to Heights, a nightclub located on the bluffs above. When she'd heard a rumor that a group of trendy young actors frequented the venue on Saturday nights, Jada had jumped to follow suit and network with them. From Jesse's perspective, her actions had to be considered borderline stalking, but he had grown accustomed to her erratic behavior by now. Beyond the connections, she craved the air of importance that accompanied her mental Rolodex.

"Do me a favor," she said. "If we catch them there, let me do the talking. Go refresh my drink, okay?"

Jesse continued to stare out the window into the night.

"And don't stick with beer like you usually do," Jada continued. "If you see what they're drinking from a distance, try to mimic it." She smacked the steering wheel. "Oh, whatever you do, don't mention to anyone here that you're an extra who works part-time in a camera shop, okay? I don't need to look like a loser tonight."

"Do you ever listen to the way your words sound when you—"

"I think Dale's going to be there, by the way."

Jesse drummed his fingers against his leg.

"Why is that guy a sudden fixture in our lives?"

"Come on, we went through this already," Jada sighed. "He's a friend from work. Why are you so touchy about it?"

"You didn't mention why he keeps showing up in odd places. I ran into him at the apartment when he picked up a script the other day."

"He enjoys advising films rather than practicing medicine."

"Oh, of course."

He wasn't in the mood to argue. Unknown to Jada, he hadn't gotten out of bed after she left the apartment that morning. He didn't want to. As sunlight poured into the room, he buried himself under the sheets. The hours passed, and when he checked the clock, it was four in the afternoon. That scared the hell out of him and urged him out of bed before Jada could find out.

Jada checked her lipstick in the rearview mirror. "And try to act like you haven't been fucked up in the head the past few weeks, okay?"

What a fool he was. This woman didn't love him. And without her, he had nothing left.

Jada continued to talk, but Jesse zoned out and retreated into himself.

———————

Jada left her BMW with the valet at the front of the building. Together, she and Jesse walked through Heights's lobby and into a large room filled with patrons. On occasion, the club rented its facilities to wedding parties as a reception site, with the ceremony held on the patio outside, which overlooked the valley and its scores of traffic.

In one corner of the room, a light flashed behind a DJ, whose music throbbed throughout the venue and screamed into Jesse's ears.

Jada leaned over and shouted, "See anyone familiar?"

Jesse scanned the room. He wanted no part of the crowd tonight but determined to mask it.

When he failed to spot a celebrity presence, he shook his head.

"I'll see what I can find out," Jada said. "Go get me a martini."

Despite its size, the room had a snug ambience. A series of semi-transparent curtains adorned the walls. Their fabric dropped down to serve as partitions between otherwise open, cozy chambers of white sofas, where small groups of patrons huddled. The furniture and curtains sat awash in overhead ivory light. At the center of the room sat a dance floor packed with people in motion, free at last from the chains of whatever job had pegged them down all week.

Jesse made his way to the bar and ordered a martini for Jada and something strong for himself. When he considered the emotional sewage he'd waded through lately, he wondered if liquor might prove downright dangerous for him. But he didn't care; his heart ached inside and he wanted the pain to go away.

Dale headed toward the bar and leaned a few feet away from Jesse to place his own order.

Jesse turned away. He couldn't shake his suspicions about that guy and his manicured hands. Why did he sense that Dale had intruded into his world and usurped his privacy?

That guy had a confidence that oozed from one who held the upper hand.

That guy had to know something Jesse didn't.

Dale had yet to notice Jesse's presence tonight. Maybe he'd already had a couple of drinks. Maybe he'd taken a hit on something beforehand.

Jesse scurried away with the drinks and found Jada mingling with an assortment of model wannabes.

Within an hour, the dancing deteriorated to a trashier degree. With no one impressive around, Jada acted as though she'd abandoned concern for her own image. Jesse and Jada laid their drinks on a table. They headed for the dance floor, where they ground together to the slow, eerie shrill of a Euro techno-pop singer. Overhead, the lights shifted to an enigmatic blue, reminiscent of a cold January twilight. With the help of his first drink and Jada's carnal movement against him, Jesse abandoned himself to his own beguiling nirvana.

Several hours—and several drinks—later, Jesse felt the

alcohol stir in his head while he struggled for dominance. Not quite drunk, he decided to lay off the liquor and step outside to absorb the one a.m. air. Around him, conversation whirred, but he couldn't focus on it.

Though lightheaded, his heart and soul remained heavy. As he glared up at an isolated, full moon, the distance overwhelmed him. He wanted to climb up there, to crawl into a crater and freeze.

Where's Jada? He'd lost track of her a while ago. And now, he couldn't stand the loneliness that held him captive.

Jesse headed indoors to examine the euphoric crowd but couldn't locate her. He waded through clusters of people but found himself surrounded by strange faces.

Next he moved toward the sofas along the perimeter, poked his head inside each partitioned section, but still his quest remained unsuccessful. One by one, he found each section occupied by groups in conversation or flirtation, their voices raised above the pulsations of music.

When he reached the last sofa section, he couldn't utter a word.

All he could do was watch.

Two sofas faced each other. A group of women huddled on one while they inspected the dance-floor crowd with expressions that rendered judgment.

On the other sofa sat Jada.

And Dale.

They didn't notice him, nor did they hear his approach amid the music. Jesse could see the back of Dale's head; Jada faced Jesse, but her eyes remained shut. She had to be two hues shy of drunk by now.

Jesse felt betrayed as he watched Dale deposit kisses along Jada's cheeks and neckline.

The sharp, internal pain resembled a fist to Jesse's gut. His eyes began to water, but he forced the sensation into retreat.

One final rejection. He had, at last, reached the bottom.

He had given himself to her. Eleven years of his life—vanished.

Jesse stumbled in his beeline toward the exit. He rushed through the lobby and out the front doors, where a pair of taxis idled on standby for drunken passengers who needed a ride home. He hopped into the first cab.

"Where to?" asked the driver.

Back to Sherman Oaks.

Beyond that, Jesse didn't have a clue.

———

Jesse stumbled into the ink blackness of his apartment and turned on a small lamp in the corner. The living room brightened to an oppressive dimness.

He needed to think.

No—on second thought, the last thing he needed was to think. He didn't need more fucking silence.

He turned on the stereo and let it blare whatever CD happened to be inside. From the speakers, The Goo Goo Dolls performed "Better Days." *How's that for irony,* thought Jesse.

He sat on the sofa but couldn't remain still. At this point, with his head numbed by alcohol, he felt overpowered by despair. He wanted to shout, but felt so weak and distant from the rest of humanity, he didn't think he would be heard.

He'd reached the point of giving up.

And with nowhere to go.

Head in his hands, he sobbed alone in the room's

semi-darkness. Agony, a one-inch blade, twisted in his heart. He sought forgiveness. He craved deliverance.

Then he remembered: the painkillers.

Energy drained, he wobbled toward the bathroom and fumbled through the medicine chest to retrieve Jada's half bottle of painkillers. One snap of the lid and he peered down into the orange bottle, salivated at the dusty white tablets.

Make the pain go away.

Better days.

The stereo's vibration rattled the bathroom mirror as he shook the pills into the palm of his hand. Agitated by his shaking, sweaty hand, the pills rustled and left a powdery residue on the surface of his skin.

Jesse's face blushed with heat. He swallowed the pills in one clean sweep, and then slid along the wall to the bathroom floor beside the porcelain tub. There Jesse shut his eyes, bobbed his head—and waited for escape in the darkness of the bathroom.

Several minutes passed before regret, which manifested through violent pains in his abdomen, settled in. Arms crossed over his chest, he cradled himself.

The pain sharpened. Jesse rocked back and forth, not in comfort but in anguish, while he convulsed on the floor in terror. As he writhed in torture, he crouched low into fetal position. In a torrent, sodium-laden tears burst from his eyes and pattered on the floor.

Defeated, his face streaked with tears of torment ... of rejection ... of a life that crept toward its final minutes, Jesse opened his mouth wide to scream but couldn't locate his voice.

Eden ...

Dad ...

Caitlyn ...

Now he had made the ultimate mistake, and he was terrified.

Terrified and alone. With no way out.

He couldn't cry out. All he could do was mouth the words, and send a mental plea. The final words before his world went black.

God, I'm sinking.

Oh God, please help me.

CHAPTER 20

IN the heat of the moment, she had opened her eyes halfway. Jesse wasn't around. He and Jada had gotten separated at some point tonight. He hadn't been himself the last few weeks. And he still hadn't admitted what the fuck swirled around in his head.

She had pushed away from Dale and looked for Jesse throughout Heights. She'd searched the club from end to end. No sign of Jesse.

Back and forth, she had retraced the room four times. Next she had checked the patio and the balcony outside. She hadn't found him in the lobby, and the man who had walked out of the restroom had sworn no one else was in there.

"Are you positive?"

"Lady, it's empty. Get sober. Maybe he left."

Had Jesse seen her with Dale?

Jada had run out to the lobby and described Jesse to some employees, asked if they had seen him.

The valet had spoken up. "Yeah, I saw the guy. Got into a cab a while ago. Real upset. Gotta be drunk, or at least close to it."

At that point, Jada had decided to start with the apartment and work her way from there.

"Get me my car."

She discovered the apartment's front door unlocked. When she burst into the living room, she noticed a single lamp lit in the corner. An odd buzz sounded in the air; with a glance across the room, she noted the stereo as its source—a CD had reached its end. The evidence suggested Jesse had to be there. But aside from the buzz, the apartment was noiseless.

"Jesse?" she called out.

No answer.

She entered the bedroom and turned on the light, but he wasn't in there. The bed hadn't been ruffled. She peered around the room and found everything in its place. His wallet and keys hadn't been returned to the dresser for the night. Nothing disturbed or touched since they had left earlier that evening.

Her skin prickled with goose bumps, which tore their way up her arm.

"Jesse?"

The air dripped of his presence.

Jada stopped and listened again. Nothing.

She peered toward the dark bathroom, where the medicine cabinet appeared to be open. Its mirror surface glinted from the bedroom light. Jada darted to the bathroom and flipped the light switch.

She screamed when she saw him.

His face was ashen. His tear stains had formed a crisscrossed mess across his cheeks.

"Jesse!"

In a panic, she slapped him on the cheek, screamed at him.

"What's wrong?!"

She lifted one of his eyelids, then jumped backward when she saw his eyes had rolled back toward the tops of their sockets.

"Jesse! No! Jesse, come back! *Jesse!*"

She ran back into the bedroom and yanked the phone from its cradle to dial 911.

CHAPTER 21

THEIR faces stoic, the paramedics rushed into position and prepared the defibrillator.

They warned Jada in advance: This didn't look promising.

Paddles ready, one paramedic shouted.

"Clear!"

Her mouth covered with her hand, Jada stared as the electric current jolted Jesse's body into a lurch. The sound of the heart monitor grew long and steady.

"We're losing him! Ready—clear!"

Again Jesse's body lurched.

He could barely open his eyes; the light in the room appeared harsh through the slits as he squinted. His vision was blurry, but he heard two voices echo around him.

Then Jesse drifted back into unconsciousness.

CHAPTER 22

EXHAUSTED, he awoke for the third time in this hospital room. Jesse had been awake for about five minutes now, but he had been in this room since yesterday. That he knew. The rest was fuzzy. He couldn't recall much from the last few days, but he felt well rested. Besides this hospital room, his last memory involved himself crumpled on his bathroom floor.

He felt relieved to be alive.

As the physical effects and immediate regret of his suicide attempt settled in him that dark night, he didn't think he would get a second chance. He was sure he had died that night.

In spite of his willingness that night to end his life, today—after he'd survived the foolish mistake—he determined he would cling to his life no matter what.

He didn't know how, but his life would change. Amendments would begin. So would the apologies and restitutions toward the people he loved. Somehow. So help him God.

Yes, he felt relieved to be alive.

And unlike previous tears of sorrow, the tear that formed in the corner of his eye today was one of gratitude. Jesse was thankful for survival. The droplet fell without a sound.

Jesse fingered the sheets, caught a glimpse of dusk in the crack between the window curtains. A plastic pitcher of water sat on the table beside the bed; a nurse had come and gone. Jesse put his hand on his chest and felt the gentle thumps of his heart. He sat up straighter in the bed, studied the sterile atmosphere, and listened to the silence.

He heard nothing.

This was what time sounded like.

This was what it sounded like to be alive.

With a quiet knock on the door, Jada poked her head in the room. Peace arose within him; a good-bye was forthcoming, which Jesse welcomed. If he could survive his recent tragedy, he could face life one day at a time.

Jada took a seat beside the bed and stared at him for a full minute without a word. Then she spoke, her voice soft, almost in a whisper.

"Look … I can't do this anymore."

"I know," he whispered back. "Neither can I."

They both sat in the stillness.

Then Jesse asked, "How am I alive right now? Did you find me?"

"Yes."

"Thanks."

Jada nodded. "Are you feeling better? I got so worried. Despite our recent arguments, if you hadn't survived—" She cut herself short. They lingered longer, listened to each other's breathing. Mutual, though unspoken, understanding seemed to emanate between them. Both seemed to realize their relationship had reached its end. And so Jesse didn't find Jada's next words surprising: "I've asked Dale to move in with me. We've been seeing each other for months."

To most bystanders, the remark would have sounded cruel. Jesse, however, didn't even flinch. He didn't know what his next step would be, but he made a solid decision: He wouldn't live as a stranger anymore.

"They weren't going to release you," Jada said. "They wanted to put you under psychiatric evaluation. But I explained to them you'd never shown irrational behavior before—that you've had a few rough weeks lately. Then I told them your mother died—that did the trick. So you shouldn't have a problem getting out of here."

Jesse folded his hands in his lap, examined the plastic ID bracelet around his wrist.

Jada reached out to place her hand on his arm, her tone gentle and, in a manner uncharacteristic for her, genuine. "You don't belong here. Not in L.A."

She patted his arm and rose from her seat. When she opened the door, she looked back at him and spoke her final words.

"Jesse, go home."

Then she walked out.

Jesse stared straight ahead as her words soaked into him. He bit his lip.

Home.

Yeah, he wanted that.

PART TWO

FROM THE DEAD

CHAPTER 23

EN route, Jesse had spent the second night in St. Louis, departed at seven in the morning, and continued eastbound on Interstate 70. Two hours ago, he'd caught Interstate 71 in Columbus, Ohio, and headed north. On the passenger seat, he'd kept his camera to document his journey with every pit stop along the way. With each photo, Jesse captured his emotions, symbolized by flawed landmarks like decrepit buildings of yesteryear and old, paint-chipped billboards.

He had wasted little time leaving California. Jada wanted him out; she had given him cash—Dale's cash, more likely—for Jesse's half of the furniture and other apartment possessions. She wasn't home when he left. He wrote her a note and departed before the morning rush began. Would he miss his eleven-year hub? To his surprise, he couldn't locate an inkling of sentiment toward Jada.

That was two days ago. Now he neared the end of his three-day trek home, the longest leg of the trip.

Jesse marveled at his circumstances. On his way to his hometown, yet he had lunged into the unknown. He had no idea how his family and friends would respond, or for that matter, what he would do once he arrived. He didn't know anything. But unlike his life in L.A. where the unknown was a cultural norm for many, here in Ohio the lifestyle struck him as more predictable and constant.

At this point, Jesse needed to clear his head. One advantage: He didn't perceive a threat of lung cancer when he breathed the Midwestern air. No more dirty haze.

At a bit past five p.m., traffic proved light on the freeway compared to what he'd grown used to. As he made his way along the interstate, he counted a mere two lanes on each side of the road: one for driving, one for passing. A far cry from the chaotic labyrinth of the 405 out west.

The first difference he noted along the roads, besides the traffic reduction, was the expanse of greenery and the occasional farm house. Someone lived in each of these homes. These residents knew nothing of the inner workings of Hollywood. But these people had roots.

It was so quiet here.

And he could travel sixty miles per hour. When had he last experienced this during the work week?

Why am I here?

It was too late to turn around. Then again, he had no desire to backtrack. An invisible pull drew him northward. Perhaps he didn't know what would come, but he had come home. He could sort the rest of it out later.

He downed the last gulp of coffee.

After he turned off Highway 8, he followed Streetsboro Road until he reached Route 91. Here he hung a left—straight into the heart of Hudson, his hometown. Located between the cities of Cleveland and Akron, Jesse had always described Hudson as larger than a small town but smaller than a suburb.

Like most roads in the community, a single lane occupied each side of the road. The town square, which spanned about three small blocks, rested in the center of the community. For a few blocks, maps referred to Route 91 as Main Street. On his left stretched a tiny retail row populated with mom-and-pop shops; on his right, the town green with its gazebo and historic clock tower. An all-brick structure, the clock tower appeared no taller than a three-story building and served as the punch line for countless jokes among teenagers, who threatened to paint it black.

To Jesse, Hudson served up a slice of Americana; its century homes and resistance to modernization befitted an ode from Norman Rockwell. In the middle of rush hour, he could count the number vehicles that preceded him for the next mile.

He continued north to pass over the Ohio Turnpike, the muted rumble of which brought a whirr to the otherwise calm environment. His sister, Eden, lived off of Route 91 near the northern edge of town. She did not expect company; he hadn't informed her of his trip, nor had he mentioned his latest struggle before he'd left California.

No one here knew of his suicide attempt, nor would he tell anyone. This marked a fresh beginning, and Jesse determined to leave his memories in the past.

A lost soul had returned home.

Shit—his father. He'd have to face him too.

Take it in stride. One day at a time.

Jesse pulled into Eden's driveway and found the garage door open, her car parked inside. Her single-story house, quaint and of partial brick, had occupied this spot for decades—Jesse remembered it from his youth. He had driven past it on countless occasions, but not once had he pictured his sister living here in years to come.

As he walked to the front porch, his stomach fluttered. He

knew Eden to be nonjudgmental, but the humility of admitting his dreams had failed hit him hard.

Small flower beds, which bordered Eden's porch on its left and right, had started to bloom in vibrant colors for the spring. After he rang the doorbell, he turned and listened to the moderate flow of cars that rolled along the road. He wondered if he'd gone to school with any of the drivers. Then he glanced at his own car as it sat on the driveway: a California license plate. That would send ripples of speculation around the block.

He heard footsteps tap inside, which sent his heart in a race with newfound anticipation: He hadn't seen his sister in several years, not since her last visit to the coast.

Eden opened the door halfway, then peeked around it to scope out her visitor. When she saw who stood on the other side, she swung the door wide open.

"Jesse, you're—home!"

Unsure what to say, Jesse nodded and reciprocated her grin.

Eden planted her arms around her big brother and squeezed him hard.

He remained silent but held her close and savored the moment. How many years had it been since someone had embraced him with authentic love? He felt a warm, moist spot on his shoulder, where a tear had escaped from Eden's eye.

But she didn't cry. Instead, she wiped the corner of her eye, sniffled, and stepped back to take a look. As Eden gazed at him—at his face, his hands, his clothes—Jesse could tell she sought indicators of well-being. When she focused on his face again, she looked like she had located a clue in his eyes but couldn't decipher its meaning. Jesse assumed she must have felt too stunned by his visit to ask.

"You didn't tell me you were coming home. How long ago did you leave?"

"Day before yesterday."

Jesse waited for a reply, and before long, Eden caught herself staring at him. "I'm sorry," she said, "you caught me by surprise, that's all. Come on in."

Before she followed him into the house, she peered at his car filled with boxes and clothes on hangers—the same imagery from the day he had left town when Eden was fifteen years old.

An enthusiastic Eden showed him around her home, which featured notable feminine décor in both of its bedrooms. The living room, its walls accented with soft shades of burgundy, hosted an array of cherry-finished furniture. A plush, ivory-colored sofa beckoned Jesse to curl up in its cushions and take a nap after his drive. When Eden concluded her guided tour, she led Jesse to the kitchen table, where she poured a glass of diet cola for each of them.

"Are you hungry?" she asked. "I just got home from work, so I haven't cooked dinner. But there's food in the fridge."

"No thanks, I'm fine."

His sister—all grown up. This was the first time he'd witnessed Eden in her own environment. He had missed out on the minor changes in her life while gone. Now twenty-six years old, Eden was thin and possessed a natural beauty. She wore minimal makeup and didn't require any. She could pulverize Jesse with the honesty in her brown eyes. Her hair, a light honey brown, curled at her shoulders. Eden was the sort of girl whose personality and features had gone underappreciated until high school.

"How's Jada?"

"It's over."

"I'm sorry. Are you okay with it?"

Jesse shrugged. "Our relationship had become strained toward the end; we were both ready to part ways. I guess when you cling to something long enough, it's hard to let go until you need to."

Eden paused. "Have you seen Caitlyn since you've been back?" Though Eden had begged Jesse to keep in touch with Caitlyn when he headed to California, Jesse had refused.

"No, I drove straight here." Eager to change the subject, Jesse grinned, then shook his head. "When did you grow up, kid? We lost too much time."

She snickered. "I should have visited more often. After I finished college, I got so consumed with work."

Eden had lived her life right—the quintessential minister's daughter. An honor-roll student. Once she earned her degree in social work, she took a job with a private adoption agency, one operated by a Catholic charity. She still worked there, where she placed infants with families.

From the corner of his eye, when he took a sip of his drink, Jesse caught Eden steal a glance at him, but he pretended not to notice.

Nervous, Jesse hoped Eden didn't realize more went on inside him than his breakup with Jada. Her social-worker instincts tended to kick in when she talked to people. Daily she dealt with unmarried mothers who found themselves alone. She talked them through fears and concerns; in a matter of minutes, she could recognize when someone sorted through hurt or confusion. And Jesse struggled with both.

Eden's palms hit the table. Once again, vibrancy returned to her eyes. "Where are you staying?"

"I haven't thought that far ahead."

"In that case, stay here! You can crash in the extra bedroom. Won't that be fun?"

"I don't want to get in your way. I intended to figure something out on my own."

"Are you kidding? The room will sit there unused if you don't move in. And you can stay as long as you need."

Already Ohio's cultural difference struck him. "Okay, thanks."

"On one condition."

"Which is?"

She leaned forward and locked eyes with his. "Go see Caitlyn."

"I will." In jest, he lifted his glass. "Here's to the Barlow kids."

"To little sisters who come to the rescue with housing arrangements." She giggled as she clinked her glass with his.

They heard the front door creak open, followed by the jingle of keys. Eden looked at the clock.

"Oh, I forgot!" she said.

A tall, slender guy, who Jesse recognized immediately, walked into the kitchen.

"Blake?"

Hands on his hips, the guy's upper lip curled in the corner in apparent shock. "Jesse?"

The two shook hands and clapped each other on the back. Jesse and Blake were the same age and had played together on the high-school basketball team. They lost touch once Jesse departed. Then again, Jesse had lost touch with everyone except Eden and, to a minimal extent, his father.

"The movie star! What are you doing in town?"

Tongue in cheek, Jesse countered, "What are *you* doing letting yourself into my sister's house?"

Eden wrapped her arms around Blake. "We've been dating for five months."

Self-absorbed in L.A., the last few months in particular, Jesse had asked Eden precious little about her own life.

Jesse turned to Eden, gestured to Blake with his thumb, and quipped, "You could do better."

"Ha." She stood on her tiptoes and laid a kiss on Blake's chin.

Jesse shook his head at the sight of his old friend and asked, "Where do you work nowadays?"

"I'm a nutritionist. I own a shop on Main Street—herbs and other health-nut stuff. You should stop by; we'll catch up."

"Definitely."

Eden interrupted them. "I forgot Blake had promised to come over for dinner. Why don't we go out instead?"

"Sounds good to me," Blake said. He nudged Jesse. "How about you?"

"I'm exhausted. I drove in from St. Louis today, so I'll scrounge up a bite to eat, empty out my car, and go to bed early. You two have fun, though."

"Before we go—" Eden began, then ran into the next room. When she returned, she handed him a spare key. "This is for the house. Clean linens are in the bedroom closet, in case we get back late."

Eden and Blake headed out the door, while Jesse closed it behind them. Eden poked her head back inside. With a jab to his ribs in a playful manner, she whispered, "Go see Caitlyn. You promised."

"Yes ma'am."

"*Tomorrow.*"

"Tomorrow," he promised.

"I'm glad you came home, Jesse."

CHAPTER 24

WHEN he awoke the next morning, he still felt exhausted from the journey home. But as the sunlight spilled into the bedroom, Jesse sensed fresh vigor and, in stark contrast to the past month, the desire to climb out of bed. Today marked a new beginning; his life would undergo a change, albeit a tough one. He had let several people down, but he determined to make it right.

After he settled on a box of granola cereal in the pantry, he poured himself a bowl and sat at the table, where Eden had left a page of printed driving directions. Typical Eden: She had gone online and located Caitlyn's address already.

According to the directions, Caitlyn lived in the same vicinity as she had in high school: near Canton, almost a thirty-minute drive. Here in Ohio, this had been far enough to prevent rumors from traveling to his father. But compared to L.A., such a commute was pocket change.

Perhaps she would be home from work around five thirty that afternoon.

All day Jesse's belly felt numb, gripped with apprehension in anticipation of facing Caitlyn. While he remained positive about the reunion, a part of him was scared and considered bolting, but to where? He had nothing left to return to on the coast—not that he harbored a desire to revisit what had proven to him a world of smoke and mirrors—and he had nowhere else to go here.

He vowed never to run again.

So he continued forward. Southbound on Highway 8 beneath an overcast sky, he checked the clock, which read 5:25. Unless she worked far from her house, she should be home by the time he arrived.

Jesse found the neighborhood without a hitch and wound through it until he reached her street. She lived in an older section of town, its homes smaller than their more recent counterparts. Along the sidewalks he noted a significant presence of retired couples, who had likely dwelt there since the 1960s, raised a family, and emptied their nests. When Jesse had scanned addresses painted on mailboxes and located Caitlyn's house, he pulled to the curb in front. He ignored his labored breathing, the thumps of his heart. Instead, he took a deep inhale to calm himself.

On his way up the driveway to the petite house, he tried to appear normal. A neighbor, distracted by the out-of-state plates on Jesse's Accord, stared from a distance as Jesse approached. Jesse waved to the woman, who returned the gesture and resumed her gardening.

His own world had imploded. What could he possibly have to offer Caitlyn?

For starters, he could show up.

Caitlyn's house featured snow-white siding, accented by black shutters and black shingles. To Jesse, the home looked gentle, undisturbed. From its stature, it didn't appear Caitlyn earned a sizable salary. Her lawn had been shaven recently; in the breeze, Jesse detected the scent of an early spring mowing.

It was now late April, and the last of the evening flurries had disappeared three weeks ago.

He hesitated a final time. Now or never, he figured. So he pressed his finger to the backlit doorbell and waited for destiny to unfold before his eyes. He tried to picture Caitlyn's initial reaction: Surprise? Anger? Indifference? He deserved the anger and he knew it.

He caught a whiff of perennial flowers, among them a patch of violets, Caitlyn's favorite.

Who would answer the door? Would she? Or perhaps a boyfriend—what would Jesse do if another man emerged?

His answer arrived in moments, and nothing could have prepared him for the sight of his high-school sweetheart.

He'd never forgotten her.

Her face registered shock before she steadied herself. As Jesse glimpsed her eyes, he saw them recoil a step, the reaction of a wounded soul. She bit her lip.

He felt an unexpected pang—Caitlyn's pain. And he had caused it. They had parted ways so he could pursue his dreams. He was the reason she had, no doubt, cried alone.

"Hi," he whispered.

Emotionless, she stared at him in a manner factual yet unrevealing. Jesse had no idea what went through her mind; for that matter, he doubted Caitlyn herself knew. Jesse felt enshrouded in a murky cloak, the shadowy sense of a trespasser. He no longer belonged in her presence.

Yet undeserving as he felt, he forced himself to look into her eyes. "Can I come in?"

Her stare spoke of indecision. Or was it apprehension?

"Please," he whispered again, the knowing tone of one to whom she had once bound her soul.

Without a word, her eyes softened as she allowed him in.

The front door opened into a living room with a meager collection of furniture, respectable yet apparent hand-me-downs. But overall the room appeared kempt and comfortable. A fireplace sat at one end, an arm's length from a coffee table and plaid sofa, with the front window behind them.

As he grew more awkward by the heartbeat, Jesse sat on the sofa before he could think of a question to ask. Caitlyn continued to stand and watch him, arms crossed, to wait for him to say something. But he couldn't find the words. Although he had rehearsed different things to say to her, those words were mere threads in the fabric of what he wanted to express.

Caitlyn broke the silence at last. "I don't know if this is a good idea."

"Cait, please …"

He watched her jaw stiffen, but then she sat beside him. She seemed caught between fret and uncertainty. Hard as he tried, Jesse couldn't get a read on her.

Then it hit him: Was she afraid she could get hurt all over again?

He tried to connect with her sapphire eyes. He stared at her porcelain skin, her wintry blond hair—almost white in its shade—which drifted a couple of inches past her shoulder blades. Despite her silence, the woman exuded strength. Whatever he had to say, she wanted him to speak first.

Say something, Jesse. Anything.

"No cat, huh?" he said.

"Drew can't have them around. He's allergic to them."

Jesse's heart sank again. She had a husband.

In an attempt to break the ice, Jesse continued, "But you

always had a cat. How does he deal with it when you two visit your parents?"

"I haven't seen my parents in years."

Jesse nodded. This he understood.

When he peered down at her hand, he noticed she didn't wear a wedding band. No husband after all. "Are you in a relationship?" Immediately he wanted to kick himself for his bluntness.

But she didn't appear offended. Rather, she looked remorseful as she buried her face in her hands.

"Sorry," Jesse said. "I figured Drew is—"

"Drew is my son."

Jesse nodded, unsure whether to step with caution or change the subject altogether. But he was eager to know. "Well," he said, "I'm sure Drew has a terrific dad. I'm happy for you, Cait."

Her shoulders sank. She wouldn't look Jesse in the eye. "He's never met his dad," she said, her voice muffled by her hands.

"Why not?"

At last, she relented. Her eyes met his. "He's yours," she whispered.

Jesse cocked his ear forward. Had he missed a detail? "He's … what?"

Her arms fell to her lap. "I couldn't go through with the abortion. I couldn't make myself do it."

Shell-shocked, Jesse made a slow rise to his feet. Caitlyn reached for his hand, but Jesse pulled it away. He didn't know whether to feel angry or scared. "How am I supposed to respond to that?"

"Before you say a word, please let me explain," she said.

"You said you couldn't handle a baby!"

"You wanted to go to L.A.! We both thought an abortion would solve everything. But the closer I got, the less my heart allowed me to go through with it. By that time, you were already gone, and I didn't have your new phone number—"

"You didn't try to call Eden or my dad?"

"You wanted to keep the pregnancy a secret from them. Remember?"

Jesse crossed his arms over his chest and waited.

"I'm sorry," Caitlyn said. "I know it doesn't eradicate what I did, but I made the best decision I could. Jess, please believe me." She rubbed her forehead as she started to sob. "If I'd told you about Drew, it would have disrupted your life, your dreams, all you wanted to build for yourself in L.A. It didn't seem fair to you: You didn't want to be tied here, and you said you couldn't handle fatherhood. Did you want the baby and not tell me?"

"No, but …" Jesse knew she was right. Indeed, when it came to his life apart from her, he had filled it with errors and regret. Nonetheless, he struggled with anger over today's revelation, so he pursed his lips and paced the room.

"Jess, you know me." Her eyes a plea, she peered up at him. "You know I'd never hurt you on purpose."

Confused, Jesse gazed into Caitlyn's face and saw the girl he'd once loved. She was right: He knew her heart. So he made his way back to the sofa and sat beside her.

Caitlyn rested her head on her hands. "I didn't try to mislead you."

He sighed, unsure what to think. "I know you didn't."

"Look at me," Caitlyn said. Their eyes met. Caitlyn's dripped with sincerity. "You don't need to do anything you don't want to do. I promise. This wasn't your choice. You don't need to provide. You can walk away if you want to, and Drew would never know you were here."

Jesse could tell her offer was an honest one. It wasn't an attempt to remove him from the picture. Rather, she offered him a place in it.

Eleven years ago, they had found themselves drowning in an unexpected predicament. His departure had been by mutual agreement, though he knew it must have rubbed her heart sore at the time.

Jesse glanced at Caitlyn, who massaged her temples. Regardless of her past choices, he knew she must be scared to let him in again.

Neither knew what to say; each had launched the other into a state of confusion.

As Jesse got up and walked over to the fireplace, Caitlyn caught a glimpse of her high-school sweetheart—the same person, just a tad older. And tanner.

The room felt so still, Jesse could hear himself breathe. He searched for something to say, something to ask, but what? They had each made their share of mistakes.

On the mantle sat an arrangement of pictures. Jesse picked one at random, took in the sight of Caitlyn and a friend in front of a museum.

And then another picture captured him.

As he leaned in, his eyes widened. Jesse reached out and retrieved the framed photo.

"Wow," he whispered as he stared at the young boy in the picture. He glanced over his shoulder and asked, "Is this him?"

Engrossed, Jesse couldn't remove himself from the photo.

Caitlyn joined Jesse at the mantle. He sensed a bond between Caitlyn and himself, a mutual knowledge of how he felt at this moment: the overwhelming sense of joy when a parent looks at a child and realizes that child is *your* child. Together, Jesse and Caitlyn gazed into the picture of Drew in a Cleveland Indians baseball cap, a duffel bag in hand on his first day of summer camp.

Drew was now ten years old.

"Yes," Caitlyn replied, her voice gentle. "It's him."

Blown away, Jesse stifled a chuckle of pride. "Light blond hair," he said under his breath, then glanced over at the boy's mother. "Just like his mom's."

Caitlyn smiled; her demeanor softened in the moment. "He's artistic."

"Like his dad …" Jesse whispered to himself.

While Jesse studied every detail in the photo—his first introduction to his son—Caitlyn examined Jesse's subtle reactions. In a subconscious manner, Jesse ran his finger along the edge of the frame; the corner of his mouth twitched with the delicacy of a feather.

Caitlyn returned her gaze to the picture. "He's been asking questions about his father lately."

"He has? Like what?"

"General things. What he was like, why he left." She chewed a fingernail. Her eyes darted from Drew to Jesse, then back to Drew again, the photo of her son without his father. "Maybe … maybe I can introduce you to him." Before Jesse could respond, she held up her hand to cut him off. "But we need to take it slow. I need to protect Drew."

With a nod, Jesse bit his lip in authenticity. "I understand."

For a few minutes longer, they looked at the picture without speaking. Jesse savored the moment. More than a decade had passed since they had shared such close proximity. Somehow, it didn't seem so long ago when they had felt secure in each other's presence.

Before he left the house, Jesse gave her his cell number.

When Caitlyn shut the door behind him, she leaned her head against the door frame. Then she moved to the window and gazed out the window at the only man she had ever loved— the one who walked back into her life less than an hour ago.

As Jesse approached his car, he felt at peace. For the first time in months, he felt as though he had done something right.

CHAPTER 25

THAT evening, Jesse walked into Eden's house stunned.
From the kitchen, Eden called out, "Jess, is that you? I'll
be there when the popcorn's done. I put *The Breakfast Club* into
the DVD player so we can hang out tonight."

The DVD player, by default, moved from its menu and
started to play the movie. On any other night, Jesse would have
looked forward to his favorite film. He headed into the living
room and plopped down on the sofa, where he stroked his chin
and replayed the Caitlyn scenario in his mind.

With a bag of popcorn in hand, Eden shook its contents
as she walked into the room. She settled in at the other end of
the sofa and crawled under a fleece throw. "What's up with you
tonight? You're so quiet. Did you see Caitlyn?"

Lost in thought, Jesse remained subdued. "Everything
changed today."

"You seem distracted. Didn't it go well?" Steam wafted from
the bag as she tore it open. She savored the first buttery bite.

"She had the baby."

"What?"

"Look, don't get worked up about this, but Caitlyn and I
… she got pregnant years ago. Back when I was ready to move
to California."

"How could—"

"I kept it a secret from you because I was scared Dad would

freak out. Cait was ready to start college, I was ready to leave Ohio. So we agreed on an abortion."

"You what?"

Jesse watched as shock registered on Eden's face, followed by the relief of a social worker who placed babies in adoptive homes. "She didn't go through with it. She said she couldn't, that she changed her mind after I was gone. But she couldn't contact me because she didn't have my new phone number, and I'd made her swear never to tell you or Dad. It wasn't her fault; she did nothing wrong. But she wanted the baby and has raised him all along."

Eden's arms went limp as she fell back against the sofa. "All by herself …"

Jesse nodded. "His name is Drew. I haven't met him yet; we'll ease into it. And we won't tell him the truth until later." Jesse glanced at his sister. "I know you want to ask questions, but my mind is running in circles and I don't have many answers for you. So why don't we try to salvage the evening since you went to the effort of the movie?"

From the way Eden sealed her lips, Jesse could tell she fought to restrain her questions. In her eyes he saw compassion. She held the bag out toward him, and he slid a piece of popcorn into his mouth. It was after seven, and he hadn't had a bite to eat since lunch. Not that he could consume much with an edgy stomach.

So they stared at the movie. They laughed less than usual as the group of teenagers, who sat bored in the school library, bickered back and forth on the TV screen. Soon the students delved into their lunches, and Judd Nelson watched as Molly Ringwald prepared her sushi with prom-queen delicacy.

Jesse turned to Eden. "Please don't tell Dad about Drew, okay?"

She sighed. "Not a word."

"I know you hate to keep secrets from him, but I'll tell him in my own time. The only reason you and Dad didn't hear about it already is because word doesn't travel from a half hour away. Cait's pregnancy wouldn't have started to show until months after she graduated, so by then, everybody that went to her school was off at college or had already moved away. For the most part, she and I used to hang out with each other alone anyway."

Eden took another piece of popcorn and seemed to grow deeper in thought as she examined its edges. "Since I can't tell Dad, can I just tell Blake so I'll have someone to confide in? You know him: He'll keep quiet about it."

Jesse nodded. He didn't want her to share the secret with anyone, but it didn't seem fair to have her bear the burden alone.

Eden crunched on the piece of popcorn. At last she brightened up. "So you have a son to meet."

As he became acclimated to the concept, Jesse smiled. "Like I said, we'll take it one step at a time for Drew's sake. Besides, we have to figure a plan. She caught me off guard about Drew, and I caught her off guard when I showed up at her doorstep."

"I know the feeling."

Jesse snickered before he changed the subject. "Tell me about your job. You must enjoy it if you stayed there this long."

Eden's faced beamed. "It's amazing to watch dreams come true for parents who can hardly wait to have children. I have my rough days, though. Some of the girls find themselves pregnant without supportive families. Some of the babies' fathers find out their girlfriends are pregnant, and they take off—"

Jesse pretended to keep half an eye on the movie, but he wanted to bury his face in shame. He fell into the category.

When she noticed Jesse's discomfort, Eden stopped. "I'm sorry for that remark. I didn't mean to insinuate—"

"I know. Don't worry about it. God knows I deserve worse."

Eden tilted her head, her face warm with care.

"At least you got a second chance."

CHAPTER 26

WHEN Jesse pulled into the church parking lot, he blinked out of reflex. He couldn't believe he was here. An era had reached its end. When he left for California, he planned never to come back. But as the years rolled by, the notion of his return lurked in the back of his mind and, after a while, he considered it inevitable. Eventually. But he hadn't given thought to this particular moment, nor had he planned what he would say. He expected it to be awkward. Yet from hundreds of miles away, he could banish it into the unforeseeable future.

But no longer: His day of reconciliation had arrived.

Frightened, Jesse reminded himself that such an emotion was ridiculous. After all, he'd come to see his father, not a cruel stranger. But facing his father didn't trouble him; rather, fear of the unknown did. What would come next?

Jesse decided to move forward. If he took each step as it came, the rest would fall in line.

So he climbed out of the car. Jesse marveled at how the trees in the church's lawn had changed. When he left town, they were five years old; by now they had doubled in size. The building, a sprawling, maize-colored structure with a chocolate-brown roof, looked the same as he remembered. A patch of tulips in bloom swayed along the building's perimeter, tickled by the hint of an otherwise imperceptible breeze.

And in a far corner, Jesse identified a window which he knew to be a replacement. Jesse grinned at the sight. One summer afternoon as a kid, he had broken that window when, by accident, he hit a baseball through it. His dad had forced him to spend the next two days pulling weeds out of this massive lawn. It marked the first of many incidents. Once Jesse reached his teenage years, he had developed a keen rebellious side—one that savored the challenge of pissing people off.

He and Eden had spent as much of their childhood at this church building as they had spent at their own house. Not long after they moved to Hudson, their father started the congregation with a handful of families. At first they met in a storefront, a former grocery store on Streetsboro Road, which the congregation rented, painted, populated with furniture, and called home. Within three years, the congregation multiplied in size and showed signs of sustained growth. The group required a larger campus to keep up with its rapid expansion in membership, so after several years of waiting and saving for a down payment, they built this current building near the southeastern corner of town. Jesse was thirteen years old at the time.

Five years later, he left.

Jesse noticed a motorcycle parked outside the front entrance. According to Eden, their father still drove one—he'd adored them for as long as Jesse could remember. And a mere eighty feet away, Jesse mused, his father sat in his office and didn't have a clue what he would encounter.

Jesse wiped his damp palms on his jeans. From his pocket, his cell phone chirped. *Not now.* He debated whether to answer, then opted against it. Soon another tone sounded to indicate the caller had left a voice message. Jesse would listen to it later.

As a minister's son, Jesse spent his youth in his father's

shadow, where Jesse suffered comparisons from outsiders and endured muttered public criticism when he rebelled. None of these were his dad's fault; his father had encouraged him to ignore the murmurings that occurred. Yet a teenaged Jesse blamed his father—he had to blame someone. All Jesse sought was freedom, an escape from the microscope of scrutiny, which seemed the one thing beyond his reach. To his astonishment, people seemed to wonder why he fled to the coast.

At first, he tried to sneak unnoticed into the church through a rear door, which he remembered to be left unlocked on days the maintenance man worked outside. But not today. Jesse would have to walk through the front office door in full view. He hoped to find everyone out to lunch.

Save a receptionist on the phone, the room was empty. He found an assistant pastor's door shut, perhaps due to a counseling session inside. When Jesse reached the receptionist's desk, he didn't recognize the woman, who hung up the phone and wrote a message. He wanted to walk past her, but she had noticed him when he walked through the front door. With a glance she revealed she didn't know Jesse from an average Joe, but her smile invited his approach. Instantly he felt less like a stranger.

"Hello. May I help you?" the receptionist asked.

"I'd like to see Pastor Chuck, please."

"Do you have an appointment, sir?"

"No. Is he busy?"

"Well," she replied, her best effort at a polite rejection, "unless it's urgent, he tries to schedule appointments when possible."

Though he understood her reply and figured the receptionist screened all unexpected visitors, Jesse felt like an object of the woman's scrutiny. "I'm … his son."

Once the receptionist recovered from the rapid blinks of her eyes, she, in all likelihood, scurried to assemble a suitable reply. How should you respond when your minister's son—a son everyone knows exists, one upon whom many have never laid sight—materializes before your eyes after more than a decade of disappearance? Jesse almost felt sorry for her.

"Oh, I ... you're ... Jesse, right? I don't think we've met. I'm Maureen." They shook hands and Maureen's smile returned. Her shock swallowed, she seemed delighted to meet him. "He's putting together some notes for a sermon, but he'll be thrilled to see you."

Jesse thanked her. Before she could rise to lead him, Jesse was halfway around her desk and on his way to the office. After all, he already knew which door was his father's. Jesse could indeed feel her stares, but then again, could he blame her?

With a quiet tap on the door, he cracked it open. His pulse on the rise and his hands in a sweat again, Jesse, who felt like an imposter, took a quiet step inside.

An unsuspecting Chuck Barlow, with his back turned to the door, stood in front of a bookshelf and paged through a Bible commentary. His New Testament bookshelf, Jesse recalled.

Without even a turn of his head, Chuck assumed his receptionist had walked in. "Maureen, did we hear from the folks in Solon?"

"Dad ..."

Jesse could only imagine the look on his father's face. From a posterior view, Jesse watched his father's shoulders go rigid. Chuck dropped the book on the shelf and spun around—elated.

"Jesse." Frozen in place, Chuck's mouth fell agape as he gazed at Jesse, in the flesh and not an illusion. Then he ran over to his son and embraced him taut with fervor.

Now it was Jesse's turn to freeze. Though Jesse returned a half hug, the gesture settled bittersweet in his stomach. After eleven years away from the man's physical presence, Jesse wasn't used to this. It felt like when he was fourteen, when he underwent a self-conscious phase and refused to hug his father and anyone else of the same gender.

Chuck stepped back and took another look at his son. Though Jesse wondered whether Chuck was familiar with his son's adult appearance, he assumed Chuck had seen him strut in the background in a handful of films.

"Why didn't you come back for a visit all this time? I've been worried sick about you!" But before Jesse could respond, his father waved off the rapid-fire, concerned-parent questions. "Have a seat!" he said as he settled behind his own desk. Jesse sat in a cushioned chair across from him.

Chuck himself was a tad overweight, but only by ten or twenty pounds. Though he'd started to bald toward the back of his head, his now-graying hair had once matched Jesse's shade of blond. A man familiar with current trends, Chuck dressed in a sport shirt and jeans. In fact, Jesse knew his father didn't even own a clerical collar and, on one occasion, had to borrow one from a friend, a Lutheran minister. Jesse's father fought the image of a stereotypical minister. Chuck hated pretense and performance; to Chuck, the importance lay in connecting with people, and he didn't believe God minded his Calvin Kleins. Or his motorcycle.

After years of distance, Jesse noticed a change in how Chuck acted around him, as if Chuck now treaded with caution. Still, though delighted to see his son, he was also a minister with an acute ability to read people, Jesse was aware. On second examination of his son's demeanor, Chuck squinted but didn't pry for information. As a dad, although he might have imagined what Jesse's life in L.A. involved, the dares and the detours, Jesse had relayed only minimal details to him.

"This is a surprise. A pleasant one," Chuck said. "I can't believe Eden didn't mention you were coming home. How long will you stay?"

Jesse shifted in his chair. "I'm *home*."

Chuck nodded for a second. "Permanently?"

"Yeah." Jesse peered down at his own hands, folded in his lap.

"Do you have a place to stay?"

"I'm crashing at Eden's for now."

"Your old room's available at my house. You can stay there till you get on your feet, if you're interested."

"Thanks, but I can't do that."

"Sure, I understand. So, are you working nearby?"

Jesse could see a longing in Chuck's eyes, years of hurt piled inside, yet his father's responses remained measured. Though Jesse pretended not to notice, he could imagine the pain he must have caused Chuck by putting distance between them. Yet to change gears today seemed unnatural, not to mention awkward, so Jesse maintained a distance and pressed a hand against the pang of regret that settled in his belly.

"Actually … look, this homecoming happened on the spur of the moment. I don't have a lot of professional skills after all the time I pursued acting. I … I need to earn some income in the meantime, just to get on my feet here. I realize you don't owe me a thing. I know I shouldn't ask, but if—"

"You can come to work here. As long as you need. We'd planned to find an assistant to help with maintenance anyway. April's almost over and the grounds will need more care."

"That's fine. I'll do anything."

"It may not be what you imagined when you asked, but I—"

"Hey, I'm familiar with the weed formations out there. I pulled so many of them years ago."

Chuck laughed. He shook his head at the sight of his son who sat before him.

At last, Jesse thought. After all these years, another weight removed from his shoulders.

"Show up here Monday morning, and we'll get you to work," Chuck said.

"Thanks." Unsure what should happen next, Jesse got up to leave when an object at the corner of the desk caught his attention. "Hey, is this the same Bible? The one you had when I left town?" Jesse asked. He picked up the thick book, its leather cover scuffed along the edges.

"Same one."

Jesse traced his finger along Chuck's name, engraved in the lower-right corner of the book's burgundy cover. Its spine rebound, the pages appeared worn from frequent use, discolored with age. True to memory, Jesse found the page margins filled with Chuck's handwritten comments that related to the verses. Stuffed between pages, random sheets contained additional notes.

Although he fingered through the book with care, a handful of sheets spilled out and fluttered to the floor. When Jesse bent to pick them up, one particular item caught his attention, its paper weight heavier than the others.

"You have my head shot in here?" Blown away, Jesse examined the photo and recognized it as his most recent.

His elbows now on the desk, Chuck rested his chin on his

hands and grinned, the proud father. "Eden gave it to me. She's done it for years."

Jesse had to admit, this revelation came as a surprise. He'd wondered if his dad had grown so accustomed to his son's absence that Jesse no longer came to mind. But with the discovery of his head shot, Jesse now knew his father cared about his career in L.A. And to think, all this time he'd assumed Chuck had felt ashamed of him.

Then a notion struck Jesse: Chuck didn't know his son would appear in his office, so this Bible must serve as permanent home for the head shot.

"You keep this in your Bible? Don't you have more important stuff to keep in there?"

With a shrug, his father replied, "It was the only way I could see you daily."

He had missed him? Touched, Jesse felt a ray of warmth in his chest, the newness of a spring dawn.

Jesse shook himself from a trance. He stared at the photo, the one whose home sat in the middle of the sacred text—he knew the reverence with which his father treated this book. Chuck wouldn't even set his Bible underneath a sheet of paper or set a coffee cup on this book. But here was Jesse's head shot stuffed inside. Jesse searched for a crease in the binding where the item once sat. "Sorry, I don't know what page it fell from."

"Psalm 37:4."

"Huh?"

"Psalm 37:4: 'Delight thyself also in the LORD; and he shall give thee the desires of thine heart.'"

"The old-school wording."

"King James. The dude rocked."

By his own admission, Jesse enjoyed this interchange of

cheesy minister humor, the kind to which Chuck had subjected him as a kid. But now Jesse had to ask: "So, is that verse true? Has God given you the desires of your heart?"

His father shrugged. "He brought you home, didn't He?"

Without a word, Jesse nodded and downplayed a smile. After he inserted the photo back into the proper chapter of Psalms, he stuffed the other orphaned sheets inside the front cover and returned the Bible to Chuck's desk.

As he headed toward the door, Jesse turned around. "Please don't make a big deal of my coming back—no announcements at church, okay?"

"Your choice."

On his way out of the church parking lot, Jesse felt content as he pondered the events of the last few days. After years of self-focus and months spent in agony over his regret of past mistakes, a part of him felt clean again. A small part, but progress nonetheless.

He remembered the voice message from an hour ago, the one that arrived on his way into the church. With one hand on the wheel, he retrieved his cell phone and checked the call log, which revealed an unknown number. Jesse dialed into his voice mail and listened to the message left by a female voice:

"Mr. Barlow, this is Oakside Mercy Hospital in Sherman Oaks. We tried to reach you at your home number, but a Ms. Ferrari provided us with this cell number. According to our records, you had a brief stay here recently. In the course of your treatment, the doctor ordered some blood work as a follow-up. The test results have arrived and we would like to have you come in to discuss them. Please call us at 818-555-4220. Thank you."

Like he could afford a hospital test. He'd just begged his father for a job! Now he's supposed to fly back to L.A. because a nurse freaked out about the aftermath of a suicide attempt?

Jesse deleted the message. As he slid the phone into his pocket, it rang again—another unknown number, this one from Ohio. Had Eden given his number to someone already?

It was Caitlyn.

Her mood sounded favorable as she got straight to the purpose of her call.

"Do you have dinner plans?" she asked.

CHAPTER 27

WHEN he arrived, he found her at a booth near the back of the restaurant.

Jesse walked past black-and-white faux-granite tabletops, past chrome-legged chairs and booths padded with red vinyl, some with small tears that exposed discolored foam underneath.

Back in high school, Jesse and Caitlyn had frequented Brick Oven, a local dive that specialized in pizza and deep-fried, quickie Italian cuisine.

He checked his watch tonight and, sure enough, they weren't supposed to meet for another ten minutes. And she'd arrived already. This had to be a good sign.

"You're early," she said. "I'm impressed."

"Seemed appropriate." He scanned the room, then returned his attention to her. "When will Drew get here?"

"I never said he would come tonight." She pursed her lips as her forehead rumpled with compassion. Her voice was tender. "I'm sorry, but I have to look out for him. We should talk a little first—when we *don't* have each other off guard."

"Yeah, you're right." He felt disappointed he wouldn't meet Drew but understood Caitlyn's perspective. "So how was work?" he asked. "You never told me what you do."

"I'm an office coordinator at an insurance company. One of its local branches."

"Exciting stuff?"

"I have some intriguing stories. But I'd have to kill you if I told you." She winked.

They continued their small talk as an earnest Faith Hill ballad drifted from the ceiling speakers. Jesse's nervousness dwindled as he noticed subtle mannerisms that defined the Caitlyn he remembered: the way she parted her lips when she listened to an answer, the crinkle of her nose as she made a clever remark, the dimple that appeared on her porcelain cheek when she smiled.

A waitress stopped by to take their order—a large pizza they would split—then brought their drinks.

Caitlyn took a sip of her iced tea. "So, I can thank Eden for getting us back in touch?"

"Actually, I've had you on my mind for quite a while."

She nodded. Never a demonstrative girl, her slow-motion blinks revealed her relief to hear his response.

Conversation proved awkward at first. Although they had once shared an intimate bond, both had grown since that time, and because they had not grown together, today they felt like strangers in the midst of déjà vu.

The two sat silent for a while, each left to their own thoughts. Jesse fidgeted with a pair of greasy, diner-style salt-and-pepper shakers, their aluminum tops dimpled from being dropped. As he focused on the miniature objects, Caitlyn studied the curves of his hair and his green eyes.

She used to stare into those eyes. Those eyes used to look deep into hers and speak volumes. As Caitlyn had once told Jesse, his eyes, with a single gaze, communicated intimacy and intensity, longing and frustration—signs of a restless soul.

When Jesse started to raise his head again, Caitlyn darted her glance away.

"Tell me about California," she said.

At this point, it was a chapter of his life he wanted to forget. Jesse shrugged and replied, "Not much to tell. People glamorize it, but it's just another state with its own set of qualities and quirks—a lot more people, an ocean within driving distance."

"I saw you in some movies."

"Background stuff; nothing impressive."

"A Clint Eastwood movie."

"He's a nice guy. Treats people well."

"Who were you friends with?"

"Some people who lived in the apartment below mine. I met one of them on a set. We hung out; I wouldn't call them *good* friends, though."

Here was Caitlyn, a person he knew, yet didn't know. Who was she now? In what ways had she changed? Caitlyn folded her hands, leaned forward. Yes, she must have wondered similar things about him, too.

Caitlyn took another sip of tea, seemed to stall for time before she asked her next question. "Did you have a girlfriend there?"

Now Jesse stalled for time as he wiped the condensation from his plastic tumbler. "Yeah. She was …" He snorted in bemusement.

"She was what?"

Jesse peered into her eyes. "She wasn't you."

With a tilt of her head to the side, delicate in motion, Caitlyn leaned in further.

Then the pizza arrived. They parted ways.

Between them, the aroma of steaming tomato, eggplant and green pepper wafted from the entrée. Caitlyn's favorite, Jesse remembered.

Jesse waited for Caitlyn to select her first slice, then he sprinkled red-pepper flakes onto a slice of his own. With his first bite, he savored the melted cheese and doughy deep-dish crust. When combined together, the roasted vegetables made his mouth water. He'd forgotten how much he adored this place.

Caitlyn finished her first slice. "Friday night," she said.

"Friday night?"

"I'll introduce you to Drew on Friday night."

CHAPTER 28

WHEN Friday evening arrived, Jesse didn't find himself as nervous as he'd anticipated. After reunions with several people of his past, the initial discomfort proved fleeting. That said, tonight he faced his most important introduction yet, which elicited a mix of flutters and thrills.

Through Caitlyn's front window, he caught a glimpse of two figures as he pulled into the driveway. Unaware of his arrival, the silhouettes moved out of the living room and beyond his line of vision.

Caitlyn answered the door when he knocked. They greeted each other. Before she let Jesse inside, Caitlyn leaned her head out the door and spoke in a low volume. "He's looking forward to tonight."

"Does he know? About us, that is?"

"I told him you're a friend," she said. "I want him to get to know you; we'll see how things go and decide how to progress. But he can't hear the truth tonight; it could be months before he's ready. I'm serious, Jess: Don't tell him."

Jesse nodded.

"Promise me," she said.

"I promise."

Jesse understood Caitlyn's concern. After all, she didn't know how long Jesse would stay in town this time. He was sure she would keep a keen eye on him, on his interaction with

Drew, every detail. Sure, he could tell she wanted him to have a chance, but he also knew she couldn't risk additional hurt for Drew if the situation were to fall apart. To be honest, Jesse wondered how long he could trust himself. How could he expect otherwise from Caitlyn?

Caitlyn chewed a fingernail. Then she poked her head back inside, where Drew could be heard rustling in the kitchen. When she turned back, Jesse locked on to her sapphire eyes.

"Okay," she said, "follow me."

As they made their way through the foyer, Jesse cast a glance at the pictures that sat on the mantle, the ones he'd seen before. Last time, Drew was a figure in a photograph. But in a matter of seconds …

His back turned, Drew sat at a small writing desk in the kitchen corner while he played on a computer. His shoulders jerked from side to side, his finger clicked on a mouse. Just like in his picture, his hair, short and cropped, was light blond like Caitlyn's.

"Drew," Caitlyn said, "time to get off the computer. Come meet Mom's friend."

"But I just started."

"Drew."

He huffed in the typical fashion of a ten year old, but closed the application on the computer and wandered over. Height wise, he reached Jesse's chest. Jesse looked closer and discovered he and Drew shared the same eye color.

Caitlyn waved her hand toward Jesse. "This is Jesse."

The boy stared up at his mother's friend. A smatter of faint freckles speckled his nose and cheeks. An air of innocence overshadowed Drew's face, his eyebrows raised in a combination of boredom and indifference. Yet at the same time, he seemed to evaluate Jesse's appearance, no doubt wondered why this other man had entered his mother's life.

Awestruck, Jesse marveled at the sight before him.

In an effort to appear calm, Jesse extended his hand. "Nice to meet you."

"Same here."

"I like your name."

"Thanks."

This was his little boy.

This little boy was a part of him.

As Caitlyn watched them interact, a smile flickered at the corner of her mouth.

Nothing could have prepared Jesse for what he saw. The simplicity of another human being—but Jesse had played a role in *this* human being's existence. Even today, he could recall the day of this little boy's conception.

Yet Jesse had no idea what to say next. The kid was shy, just stared at him.

"So, you're into computers?" Jesse asked. "What kind of stuff?"

Nonchalant, Drew looked over at the computer. "Oh, that? I was playing a game with someone."

"That sounds cool. A kid from school?"

"A kid from Ireland. It's a game site on the Internet. You play against kids from all over the world—they're not awake in Japan right now, though."

Caitlyn swept in. "He's addicted to the computer. Gaming, emailing. Aren't you, honey?" She ran her fingers through Drew's hair. He, in turn, ducked a few inches out of her reach.

"I've embarrassed him in front of our guest," she prodded.

Then she grabbed hold of him and, for extra measure, planted a kiss on the top of his head.

Drew pretended not to giggle as he squirmed out of her grasp. "Mom, stop."

"Come on," she said, "we'll grab a bite to eat at the park."

———————

This first week of May had brought temperatures in the upper sixties. By seven that evening, beneath a still-sunlit sky, Jesse could feel a hint of spring warmth on his face as he strolled through a community art-and-craft fair with Caitlyn and Drew.

The annual event, held in a nearby park, featured a series of tents under which local artists displayed and sold their creations. For Jesse, the scene drew to mind the craft stations lined up along Venice Beach, which formed a long barrier between sand and shops. Tonight, as Jesse, Caitlyn and Drew wove their way past homemade jewelry, paintings and leather-craft accessories, they poked their heads into each tent. Like most others in attendance, they browsed but didn't buy.

The trio munched on hot dogs and sodas as they watched kids chase each other around the grass. Peals of laughter erupted among families that had emerged for the event, relieved that the cold had indeed thawed for the season.

Drew caught sight of a Ferris wheel from afar. As they approached it, he saw more carnival rides and game booths.

Drew's jaw dropped. He swiveled around to his mother and shouted, "Mom, they have bungee-jumping! Can I try it out?"

Though not keen on the defiance of gravity, Jesse, eager to sample the parenting role, spoke up nonetheless. "Of course. Let's go."

When Caitlyn returned a look that could penetrate an ice cube, Jesse knew he'd given the wrong response.

"Or maybe you should ask your mom," Jesse offered in a recovery attempt.

Caitlyn looked at the miniature contraption with reservation. It was more like a safer, hybrid version of the real thing. A lone father watched as the structure flung his kid several feet from the ground. And with that, Jesse saw a decision solidify in Caitlyn's eyes. "Are you kidding? I wouldn't trust that thing!" she said.

Jesse, by his own admission, didn't blame her. If that father over there decided to go for a whirl on that oversized rubber band himself, Jesse wouldn't put it past the device to come snapping apart and send the guy airborne.

"Why don't you and Jesse try the scrambler instead?" Caitlyn suggested.

Yeah, in this case, Jesse put more trust in the tried and true. "Sounds good to me," Jesse replied. "Wanna go, big guy?"

"Sure. Mom, can you hold these?" He handed his dinner to Caitlyn, who watched as he and Jesse made their way to the ticket booth.

With a compartment to themselves under flashing neon lights, the ride attendant locked them in and left to secure other passengers.

"Do you and your mom come here every year?" asked Jesse.

"Sometimes." Given their introduction an hour ago, a shy Drew said little but seemed to enjoy his mom's friend. The boy continued to sneak an occasional look from the corner of his eye.

"I used to ride the scrambler all the time as a kid," Jesse said.

"Did they have black-and-white TV back then?"

"No. Why? Do I look that old?"

Drew shrugged. An innocent mistake, he now grinned at the humor in his own question. "How much older are you than me, anyway?"

"I'm your mom's age. So I'm only eighteen years older than you."

"That's like, almost two decades. Did they have cable back then?"

Jesse chuckled. "You're getting better. So what grade are you in?"

"Fourth."

"Like it?"

"It's okay. Homework sucks."

With the sound of a buzzer, the ride's tentacles and compartments whirred into motion and gained momentum. Shrieks and squeals ensued from nearby compartments as passengers dodged each other. Through shifts and spins, the ride jerked the father and son against each other in the cramped quarters. Drew giggled as Jesse exaggerated the force of momentum.

When the ride decelerated and came to a stop, Jesse and Drew stepped off to regain their balance and shake the dizziness from their heads. Drew retrieved his hot dog and soda from Caitlyn, and then took off toward a booth that caught his eye up ahead. "Mom, I'll see you when you catch up."

"Don't run into anybody on the way there!" When their son was beyond earshot, Caitlyn and Jesse sauntered along the pebble-embedded walking path. "Did he talk to you?" she asked.

"Not much. Of course, we just met."

"He'll come around."

The scent of funnel cakes filled the atmosphere at the park. Around the corner from a kettle-corn stand, they caught a whiff of warm butter and salt. By the time they caught up with Drew, he had finished his dinner and started to thumb his way through a rack of nature photographs, enlarged and housed in contemporary frames.

Intrigued by a color photograph of Niagara Falls, Drew lifted it from the rack. In the photo, the majestic semi-circle of water foamed and poured in a torrent. "Cool! Mom, we should go there some time. I want to take my own picture of it and frame it for my room."

Jesse looked over his son's shoulder. "I could show you how to take a good one. I play around with photography a little."

"Really?"

Even Caitlyn stepped back and crossed her arms in amusement.

"I worked in a photo shop in L.A.," Jesse explained.

"You lived in L.A.?" Drew's eyes widened. "Did you see anyone famous?"

"Sure. It's not as big a deal when you live there, though."

"Why not?"

"Well, it's normal to see people you recognize out there, so you get used to it. Kind of like getting used to snow over here— you see it so often, it seems common."

Drew nodded, once again engrossed in the picture. "Where is this place?"

"Niagara Falls," Caitlyn said. "It's gorgeous."

"Tell you what," Jesse said, "if your mom says it's okay, maybe we'll head out someday and look for some good shots for your room around here."

From behind, Caitlyn wrapped her arms around Drew. "Maybe. Right, my little guy?"

Jesse found Eden's car already parked in the garage when he arrived at the house after midnight. He expected to find her asleep as he tiptoed into the foyer. But no sooner had he clicked the door shut when Eden raced over to him dressed in baggy shorts and an oversized T-shirt—the little-sister garb in which she had always slept. Some things never change.

"How'd it go?" she asked. "You were out late enough! Were you with them this whole time?"

"Remind me, do you run on double-A batteries?" Jesse quipped.

"Come on!" She grabbed his arm and dragged him into the living room, where she pointed to the sofa. "Sit your butt down. You know I want to know all about how it went tonight!" She only came up to his chin, and he wanted to call her Squirt.

As Jesse shed his jacket, his sister, her face ecstatic, sat opposite him. She flicked her hand with a motion that ordered him to spill his guts.

"So where did you go? What did you do?"

"We went to a craft fair near Canton."

"And you met Drew?"

Jesse couldn't help a broad smile. "It was—it was surreal," he said, then settled back. His eyes sparkled with life as he recalled random details from the evening. "I took one look at him and—that little guy's a part of me. I mean, he has my eyes and ears, Caitlyn's hair and her chin. You can't help but love the kid."

"So, Caitlyn's comfortable with your getting to know him?"

"She seems to be. She's protective."

"That's understandable. I'm sure she's glad you're here again, but it will take time for her to realize you're here to stay."

As he thought through the events of that night and about

his newfound son, he gleamed. Then his smile began to wither as reality set in. "It's just … I don't know if I have what it takes to be his dad. How could I ever measure up?"

"What do you mean?"

"Well, I look at Drew and he looks a lot like me. But at the same time, we're two strangers. I have no idea how to relate to my own son."

"You were gone a long time. He's grown up without you in his life until now. But this is a new start. It'll work out."

Jesse stared at his shoelaces, one of which had come untied. "I sure hope so."

"Hey," Eden began. She leaned forward, gripped his ankle, and looked straight into his eyes. Her tone sincere, she said, "I guarantee Drew has wished for his dad. He needs you more than ever." She jiggled his ankle. "You can do this. I believe in you."

Here—this was Eden's defining characteristic, the one that astonished him more than the others. Eden had an inherent ability to see the best in people—especially when it came to her brother. She treated him with unconditional acceptance, as if he could never fall short. Throughout the years he spent in California, as long as he wasn't too ashamed, he could admit his shortcomings to his sister and trust she would remain nonjudgmental. To talk to Eden in their adulthood breathed fresh life into him. It made him believe he could accomplish anything.

How long had it been since Jesse had an influence like that within arm's length?

"If Drew doesn't know you're his dad, who does he think you are?"

"We told him I'm a friend."

"That's best for now," she said, ever the social worker. "The time will come."

CHAPTER 29

AFFIXED to the second-floor's exterior, the wooden sign read: "Naturally!" The business, sandwiched in townhouse fashion, shared its walls with a realtor's office on one side and a denim store on the other.

On Saturday afternoon, still on an emotional high from his prior evening with Caitlyn and Drew, Jesse walked into Blake's shop. A bell tinkled a greeting from above the doorway. If he caught the air at the correct angle when he breathed, Jesse swore he could still smell astringent. Back when Jesse last lived in Hudson, a sentimental mom-and-pop drugstore, complete with a vintage soda fountain, had occupied this retail spot, as it had for decades.

From a far corner, Blake emerged and called out, "Jesse Barlow, you've graced my humble shop with your presence!"

A customer turned around to witness the episode but soon returned her attention to a container of vitamin D. Jesse wondered if he knew her.

With his arms spread wide, Blake gestured around his domain. "What do you think? Piece of beauty, isn't it?"

Throughout the store sat rows of glass shelves filled with vitamins and herbal supplements, bags and jars of nonperishable, organic food products, and other items whose origins could be traced to one chemical-free shade of dirt or another.

"Self-employment," Blake said. "This is my castle."

"Nice. How long have you owned it?"

"Coupla years. Got my pharmaceutical degree and worked in the old drugstore before this."

Blake didn't mention Drew or Caitlyn, so Jesse assumed Eden had yet to tell him. Relieved, Jesse picked up a plastic jar of fish-oil tablets but returned it to the shelf even faster. He almost gagged at the pungent odor. "Why natural herbs and shit—I mean, stuff?"

Blake crossed his arms and examined a few expiration dates. "As a pharmacist, I saw too much. Too many people taking prescription drugs every time their legs itched, pumping chemicals into their kids to calm them down—I don't know, regardless of what the FDA says, my conscience feels better now that I've turned to natural products. Not all drugs are bad, but I figure this helps keep them to a minimum."

"But they say you can overdose on herbs," Jesse said.

"You can overdose on water, too. As long as you keep your regimen in balance, you're cool. It's a natural remedy: You're not forcing foreign garbage into your body that it's not meant to handle, so it'll react in a more natural way." Blake paused, then chuckled. "Plus you'll never fail a drug test—like Ryan Reeves from our basketball team. Remember that moron? Lives in Seattle now."

Jesse snickered in return. "Well, my future's filled with herbal experiences of my own: My dad gave me a job at the church—maintenance work, lawn care."

"Hey, it's cash, right?"

"At this point, I just want to earn a paycheck. I can look for more down the road. In the meantime, I have other things to sort out."

When Jesse heard the overhead bell tinkle again, he turned

to see a high-school-aged employee walk in for work. After a casual introduction by Blake, the teenager, Matt, headed over to the checkout counter.

With a squint toward the window, Blake scratched his chin. "When was the last time you shot some hoops?" he asked.

"Geez, not since we were on the team."

"Matt!" Blake called over his shoulder. ""I'm gonna be out of the office for a while." While he shouted to his employee, he shot Jesse a knowing look. "I've got some official business off-site."

———————

"Prepare to lose, Barlow!" Blake shouted.

With a dodge to Jesse, Blake attempted a three-pointer, but the ball deflected off the basketball rim and into Jesse's hands for the rebound.

The court, empty on the weekend except for the two of them, sat at the rear of Jesse's former elementary school. Along with other members of their basketball team, they had met here for games of pickup on countless occasions. Oftentimes they had shown up drunk on Saturday nights after a high-school party—Jesse had tried his best to hide his hangovers at church the mornings after.

Around the half court Jesse traveled before he pulled a quick move to garner a surprise two-pointer. "Here's to your hippie life of herbs."

"Nice moves on the court, Barlow. It's good to see you didn't lose your talent in L.A.—your inferior talent, that is."

"Keep talking, Number Two."

"Speaking of L.A., how'd you like living there?"

The question took Jesse by surprise. Gone only a week or so, he had all but forgotten about his former residence.

With a toss of the ball to Blake, who dribbled it down the center of the court, Jesse answered, "Warm and sunny. You can't beat that."

"Girlfriend?"

"Of course." Jesse wiped the sweat from his brow. "Eden didn't tell you?"

"She didn't talk much about it."

"Good. That means you don't have blackmail material."

After an unsuccessful block, Jesse watched Blake sail the ball through the hoop to bring the score to a tie. As he geared up to regain his lead, Jesse glanced over at Blake's dark-blue convertible in the parking lot.

"How long have you had the car?"

"A few years. Bought it new. Like it?"

"A beauty."

Blake heard his cell phone chirp from the corner of the court and ran over to answer. "Hello?" A pause. "I'm at the old stomping grounds—with Jesse Barlow ... Yeah, no joke, he's in town."

Jesse wondered who had called and had a hunch another reunion would result.

"The elementary school," Blake continued. "Okay, later." He snapped the phone shut and announced, "Randy's on his way over with Sanders. Like old times, huh? Everyone else from the team relocated after college."

So most of Jesse's schoolmates had departed and taken their engrafted roots with them.

A transient community in its latter years, Hudson had experienced an influx of white-collar executives who worked in the Cleveland suburbs. Nowadays, families tended to move into the area, stay less than ten years, and then transfer to positions in another state. Jesse found it humorous that when he compared his second-grade class's yearbook pictures with those of his senior class, 90 percent of the faces must have changed. Because his father ministered at a church he himself had founded, Jesse and Eden spent most of their childhood in this community and became exceptions to the rule. Even Blake had moved to town in his sophomore year.

When he caught sight of a duo that approached the court, Jesse cracked a smile.

"Barlow! Look at you, man!" A red-headed beanpole, Randy observed his old friend's tan through wire-rimmed glasses before he shook hands.

"You still live here?" Jesse replied. "Thought you couldn't wait to leave!"

"I took a job with an investment company downtown, and the rest is history. I live in Twinsburg now," Randy replied. He jerked his thumb northward to the adjacent community. "Married with two kids."

"Married his boss's daughter," Sanders chimed in. With Sanders's hair dark as charcoal, Jesse remembered him as the only guy in middle school who could grow full facial hair. His stocky build presented a stark contrast to that of Randy or Jesse.

"Do you have a wife too?" Jesse asked Sanders.

"*Had* a wife. We lived down in Dayton, three kids, but I returned here after the divorce. One day you're in high school, dating half the cheerleaders who line up for you—next thing you know, the glory disappears and you're living back here."

"You don't look like you've changed much."

Blasé, Sanders shrugged it off. "Ah, the usual stuff: a few gray hairs around the ears, little more of a belly, and a pain in my ass—but that's caused by my ex-wife, who insists on calling me every few months, trying to collect an extra check. Claims the child support got lost in the mail."

Jesse wondered how Caitlyn felt as she tried to raise a son without a trace of child support. Granted, he'd had no knowledge of his son; but to the average onlooker, would his situation look like Sanders's?

"So, Barlow, tell me more about that girlfriend of yours," Blake said.

"Good looking?" Sanders asked.

"Sure, she was gorgeous. A child star in some local TV show."

"Anyone I'd know?"

"Don't let her hear you suggest she's an unknown," Jesse said. "Her name is Jada."

"Sounds like a Hollywood name to me. Jada what?"

"Ferrari."

"Jada *Ferrari!*" Sanders remarked. "Sounds like a lady who feels most at home between satin sheets in the heat of passion." A faint smile inched across Sanders's face, his eyes now lost in the clouds above. "A woman with the name of a car. Does *she* go zero to sixty in four seconds?"

Jesse forgot how crude Sanders could be, even while sober. He opted to ignore the comment. "She isn't on screen anymore. She's an assistant to Barry Richert."

Randy snapped his fingers. "That's the director of—oh, the movie where the guy crashes through the stained-glass windows with a kitten under his arm."

"Right." The things people remember. And not always related to the plot.

"By the way, I saw you in a movie a few years ago, walking down a sidewalk."

"Been in anything else?" Sanders asked.

"Here and there," Jesse replied. "Gigs are kind of hard to come by. Lots of competition, even for the bottom rung."

More small talk, more fawning over the lifestyle Jesse had once prized but, in the end, found wanting. When people asked about L.A., they dreamed of glamour. How easy it seemed to gloss over the reality of a struggle toward accomplishment and simply focus on the rewards that Jesse never experienced. These acquaintances treated him as though he had plundered a gold mine.

At last, the reunion wound down when Randy checked his watch. "Gotta go," he said. "We were on our way to the auto shop. Sanders's engine is getting remounted and I'm his ride."

Sanders landed a playful punch on Jesse's arm. "We need to get together and hang out sometime, bro. Brotherhood of the bachelors."

"Later," Jesse replied without a commitment.

"I'd better head back to the store," Blake said as he watched Randy and Sanders turn onto a side street. "If I leave Mark at the counter too long, the teenagers tend to stop by and scrounge for ginseng samples."

Jesse grabbed the basketball and the duo walked to the car.

Blake patted him on the back. "Are you going to church tomorrow? It would make Eden happy."

"No, I don't think so." Jesse pursed his lips. "Maybe some other time."

As much as he had enjoyed these reconnections with individuals of his past, Jesse wasn't ready to show his face at a church service, despite his status as an employee there. He didn't want to get absorbed in a crowd of random people. He'd lived most of his childhood behind glass walls, feeling like a caged orangutan on display. In his mind's eye, he pictured glaring faces and could hear the whispers.

The preacher's son returned. There he is: the one standing alone.

Truth be told, it wasn't the risk of other people's judgment he dreaded. Rather, something in Jesse wouldn't *let* him show up at the building for a worship service. Coming home marked a step in the right direction, but he no longer *felt* at home. He was an outsider. He no longer belonged.

And he would be a hypocrite. After all, if anyone knew the mistakes he'd made in his life, he assumed he would be scorned. He called to mind ancient cultures, where people like Jesse were taken away and maybe even stoned. People like him were outcasts, pictures of shame.

The gleaming church people could bask in God's acceptance. But when he evaluated his own life, Jesse was sure he had lost God's acceptance years ago. Watching them worship would serve as a painful reminder of his spiritual solitude.

He didn't need these folks to remind him of his own faults. He was well aware.

CHAPTER 30

WHEN Jesse walked into Chuck's office two days later, he found his father already at work on the computer. From a small CD player on a bookshelf, the soft praise music of an acoustic guitar ushered forth and brought a soothing ambience to the air.

"Nowhere you'd rather be on a Monday morning, huh?" his dad jested.

"Sorry about yesterday."

"What happened yesterday?"

"I probably should've come to church."

Chuck dropped his fingers from the keyboard. "Hold on a minute," he said. He came around and sat on top of the desk. Chuck's eyes spoke of sincerity as he concentrated on his son. "Why are you apologizing?"

His father appeared confused. Jesse furrowed his eyebrows. "I figured it was kind of expected for me to show up." He paused. "Wasn't it?"

"No," his father replied as though he couldn't comprehend what Jesse had suggested. But he snapped out of it and patted Jesse's shoulder. "Come on, I want to reintroduce you to somebody."

With few people at the large building this early in the morning, they walked unnoticed through a series of halls. At the opposite end of the church, they turned into a corridor and knocked on an open door labeled: "Maintenance."

Beneath the fluorescent lighting that stretched above, a hefty man sat hunched over, his back to the door, while he attached a bit to an electric drill. When he heard the knock, the man spun around on his wheeled stool and peered through a pair of bifocals.

Chuck spoke first. "Your assistant showed up, the poor dude."

From where he sat, the maintenance man scrutinized Jesse through beady eyes before a glint appeared in them. Then a wave of surprise washed over the man's face. "Jesse, is that you?"

Had he not caught himself, Jesse would have done a double-take himself. "Mel?! You're still here?"

"Where'd you dig up this guy, Reverend?" Mel abandoned his wide view to meet Jesse and Chuck in the corridor.

Hands on his hips, Chuck said, "Don't ask me. The poor sap came searching for Mel, begging for the chance to work with our veteran staff member." Chuck winked. "You know me, always aiming to please."

A man Jesse had known since late childhood, Mel had aged a bit over the years, but the process had treated him favorably. His forehead boasted more crinkles but nothing severe. The last time Jesse saw him, the man had dark hair, which had now retreated to a frosty white. It must shine against a summer tan, Jesse figured.

"Look at you!" Mel let out his trademark high-pitched laugh. "I can't believe you're the surly little fella who hid in the bushes one day and shot me in the rear end with a paintball gun!"

Jesse snickered as he recalled similar memories. He had

caused this man more than his share of stress. But with the chunks of time Jesse had spent at this building each week, Mel had become the kid's prank buddy.

Mel shook his head. "Couldn't believe the innocent little preacher's kid could inflict such misery. I had a welt for days after that incident. Do you know how long it takes an old man to heal?"

"Oh, buck it up, Mel!" Chuck quipped. "You were only fifty years old at the most." On his way out the door, he added, "Can I trust this place not to implode once the two of you team up?"

"Depends on if Mel's figured out what he's doing yet," Jesse replied.

"Come on, buddy," said the maintenance man. He wrapped his arm around Jesse's shoulder and handed him a pair of pewter-gray coveralls. "I feel inspired by that paintball incident. I think I know the perfect spot to start your work today."

———————

Seated on the floor in a restroom, a rubber-gloved Jesse scrubbed the fourth toilet in a row of five. Mel had disappeared to tackle repair work outside. Located in the wing where Sunday school and evening classes were held, the restroom's vicinity was quiet during the day.

Engaged in what might be the most disgusting job available, Jesse had to grin. The task offered no resemblance to the life he'd lived the past eleven years, and for that reason alone he found it appealing. Granted, a maintenance job wasn't one he would circle in the want ads. Even without practical experience, he was confident he could locate a job that featured tasks less monotonous or mundane.

But amid the tile and porcelain, Jesse sensed that, somehow, what he did right now would help somebody else. As a boy, Jesse's dad had explained to him that, although many people described a church as a building, such a notion was inaccurate. The church, his father said, is composed of people—and those people could represent it in a positive manner or an embarrassing one. Every Christian was critical, the preacher had told him.

His father was a kindhearted soul—which is why it frustrated Jesse not to let go of the anger he'd kindled toward the man.

Jesse remembered the calls his dad received at home from a church member in distress, while other members pulled him aside after church to talk about an alarming doctor's report or a recent victory. Chuck had a way with people, a unique ability to discern where you dwelt on an emotional and mental level, and could relate to you at your point of need. Rather than act like a spiritual guru, Pastor Chuck responded to each individual like a friend, leaned in to ensure every syllable would be heard. Like Eden, Jesse never saw his father judge anyone; Chuck met them where they were at in their lives. And from that point, however high or low, Chuck would try to help that person.

Comfort. Understanding. Hope. That's what he ministered to people.

Maybe Chuck drew on the hurt he experienced when Jesse's mother died more than twenty years ago.

But Chuck didn't take credit for the help he brought, even when the community sought to bestow it on him. Throughout Jesse's childhood, his father had stressed the role of a minister; he'd ingrained it into Jesse's brain as he reminded his son over and over: "When people get helped, it doesn't boil down to me. It boils down to the person who greeted that individual at the door on their first visit; the person who vacuumed the floors earlier that week; the person who gave an extra ten bucks in the offering plate that covered the electric bill for that particular church service. *Those* people impacted the visitor before I ever got up to preach. That visitor decided whether they'll come back before they ever laid eyes on me," his father had said. "I have the privilege of serving as that person's minister, but you can trace it to those church members' acts of service."

There it was. That's why Jesse felt content to scrub a toilet today.

For the first time in many years, Jesse thought about someone besides himself.

He hadn't seen Caitlyn or Drew in three days, and now he missed them. At the thought of his son, Jesse couldn't help but smile. He sensed a rush in his veins. But however incredible his reunion with his son, it paled in comparison to the in-the-flesh miracle that occurred when he looked into the face of a child whose genes were half his own. Jesse felt awestruck.

Maybe he would stop by their home that evening.

CHAPTER 31

AFTER dinner that evening, Jesse decided to take his chances and show up at Caitlyn's house unexpected. When they had dated, she'd loved surprises. True, their hearts, once knit together, had grown apart; but if Caitlyn remained the same girl deep down, she might respond well to his overture. At the same time, he realized he would need to earn her trust, to convince Caitlyn that the Jesse who hadn't wanted a baby could make a permanent commitment to Drew's life.

As Jesse approached the house, he found Drew outside, where the boy shot a basketball at the hoop attached to the garage. Drew didn't run and dribble the ball; instead, he walked around with it, bounced it a couple of times before he took his shot. Based on the kid's lack of technique, it was clear Drew possessed limited experience.

Because the ball deflected from the rim with a loud shudder, Drew didn't hear Jesse approach. Jesse picked up the ball when it rolled down the driveway. Drew noticed a figure approach him, squinted in the post-dinner sunset and, at last, recognized Jesse.

"Hey, Drew-man." Jesse lobbed him the ball. "You're into basketball?"

Drew responded with a smile. "Not much. I try, but it makes me tired. So I don't do it often." Again he dribbled the ball, took a shot, and watched it deflect from the rim. Drew snatched the ball on rebound. "I'm not too good at it anyway."

"Here, let me give you a tip," Jesse held his hands out to catch the ball, which Drew tossed his way. Then Jesse took position opposite the basket. "Plant your feet and keep your head up, equal distance between your feet." Then he held the ball above his head. "Now, when you're ready to take your shot, try to keep your body in a straight line: your hand, your arm, elbow, knee, and foot. See?" he said as he demonstrated the technique.

Jesse handed the ball to his son, who then emulated the stance.

Drew made a stiff attempt to imitate Jesse. "Like this?"

"Good job. You're almost there: Your hands are in good shape, but see those elbows? If they point out sideways, it'll hurt the path of the ball. So point them toward the basket." He nodded as Drew followed directions. "Now lean your arm back a tad, so your elbows are angled to the hoop more than your wrists are. Yeah, there you go."

At the sound of a familiar male voice, Caitlyn wandered out of the house and across the lawn. She stopped at the edge of the driveway unnoticed since the guys, engrossed in their activity, didn't hear her approach. She watched but didn't interrupt their moment of bonding. Instead, Caitlyn crossed her arms casually to enjoy this image of her son, aided by his father for the first time in his life.

"Ready?" Drew asked.

"Go for it," Jesse urged.

The swish of a basketball as it sinks through a net: a quiet event—but in this setting, it sounded forth like a trumpet. Drew's face gleamed. Jesse let out a shout.

"You made it, Drew-man!"

After a congratulatory high-five, Jesse watched Drew pump his fist with wide-eyed excitement.

Then Drew turned around and discovered another witness. "Mom, wasn't that awesome?"

Caitlyn giggled. She approached Drew and hugged him close to her. "No other word to describe it. You've tried to figure that out for so long. Did Jesse give you some tips?"

Drew nodded. "How'd you know all that?" he asked Jesse. "Did you play?"

Nervous at the reminder of the past, Jesse twitched when he caught Caitlyn's gaze. Their eyes communicated, words abandoned. Jesse returned to Drew's question. "I played a bit in high school."

"Jesse's modest," Caitlyn piped in. "He was good at it."

"You two knew each other back then? Did you go to school together?"

"No ..." she said. Aware they had slipped up, Jesse locked eyes with Caitlyn again. Her gaze grew pointed, as if to instruct Jesse not to give an answer while she calculated damage control that was true, yet vague.

"Then how'd you see him play?"

"We met at one of his games when he played at my school." Before Drew could ask further questions, she faked a slap on her arm. "Honey, I think the mosquitoes are coming out. Why don't you go in and finish your homework?"

"Can I show Jesse my room?"

Caitlyn sighed. "Fine, go ahead. Make sure he doesn't stumble over anything on the floor." She followed a few steps behind, which allowed Jesse and Drew more time to connect.

But still she kept an eye on the nuances between the father and his son.

Inside his bedroom, Drew led Jesse through the highlights, which included a Scouting award he had earned a few years back, some action figures arranged on a small desk, and his backpack. And a picture of Drew and his mom. Not a father in sight.

They ended with a tour of the posters that hung on the wall. Thankful none of them depicted scenes from a movie, Jesse listened while Drew commented on what he liked about each one.

Finally, Caitlyn cut in. "All right, finish your homework. It's eight o'clock."

"Mom, not while Jesse's here!"

"Don't argue with me," Caitlyn responded with a firm tone.

Though he lacked eagerness for his homework, Drew relented. He zipped his backpack open at the desk and muttered as he retrieved a textbook. At first Jesse felt it awkward to behold their tug-of-war; then again, he figured, Drew and Caitlyn must have their share of headaches like any other parent and child.

Caitlyn and Jesse headed into the kitchen, where she asked, "Was I too tough on him?"

"With the homework? Didn't seem like it."

Caitlyn released a slow exhale. "Sometimes I have no idea where the balance is," she said.

"Are you serious? You're a good mom to him."

"Yeah, well, I have my doubts. Half the time, I make my best guess and then hope I don't regret it later."

Caitlyn started to rinse dishes in the sink and load them into the dishwasher. She shot Jesse a look of frustration. "I keep telling him to put these in the dishwasher when he's finished with them, but you know boys." She grinned.

"Want me to help?"

She shook her head and peered through the open window. "I started rinsing these before, but then I heard two voices in the driveway."

"I should have called first."

"I suppose I don't mind."

Jesse watched her a second as she tucked a lock of hair behind her ear. "Here, let me take care of that for you," he insisted. Jesse retrieved the plate from her and went to work while she wiped down the counter. He sneaked a glance at her again. She wore a black cable-knit top, which contrasted like salt and pepper with her fair skin and hair. A remnant of lipstick remained on her mouth. "Tired?" he asked.

"A long day. You?"

"Truth?"

She stopped and crossed her arms. "Truth."

"I scrubbed toilets today."

Caitlyn burst out with a laugh, and then waved it off. "Why? Did you cause undue harm?"

Jesse loved to see her laugh. He remembered that well. "I'm working for my dad for the time being. Maintenance at the church."

"I didn't know you're handy with tools."

"Do I *look* like Mr. Fix-it? At least I'll figure out what those gigantic wrenches are used for."

Caitlyn chuckled more. As he finished the last dish, she caught a second glimpse of Jesse's cheek, the same cheek against which she used to cuddle her head. Then she wiped around the sink and rinsed the dishrag.

Jesse wanted to linger here, to prolong this simple moment. He sensed a mutual desire in Caitlyn as well. A piece of Jesse still missed Caitlyn—and that piece took pleasure in her presence tonight. This person who stood beside him wasn't a blind date or a little-known acquaintance. They knew—or once knew—each other.

Caitlyn studied him again, the concentration in his face.

When he closed the dishwasher and pivoted toward her, she darted her face away.

"What you did for Drew tonight was sweet," she said.

"I wouldn't trade it for anything," Jesse replied, then added, "He mentioned he gets tired when he runs with the ball."

"Lately he's gotten worn out much sooner. It makes me wonder, but it doesn't happen often enough to have it checked out." She paused. "He's a lot like you. He's introspective, internalizes his emotions. Worries about his mom and won't let me convince him not to. He's approaching middle-school age, so the tiredness could be suppressed stress taking its toll."

Jesse turned and stared at Caitlyn's face, searched, tried to find something unspoken.

Caitlyn ran her fingers through her hair and looked away at a random point, as though she struggled with whether to speak. Then her eyes met his again. "He needs a male influence in his life. And I can't give him that." She wrung her hands. Her voice softened further. "I'll let you take him out for an afternoon, maybe a Sunday, but only if Drew is comfortable with the idea."

Warmth spread like an afterglow across Jesse's chest.

Caitlyn locked eyes with his. "But I'm trusting you with him. So help me, if you get him in one inch of trouble—"

Jesse reached out and touched her arm. "I'll take care of him." He leaned in. "I promise."

Caitlyn didn't brush his hand away from her arm. From her reaction, or lack thereof, to his touch, Jesse supposed she hadn't been touched by a man in years.

And this touch, the delicate stroke of his thumb on her bicep, just above her elbow—it wasn't sensual, but rather a hand of support. She had raised her son alone and must have forgotten how such a gesture felt. With his tranquil breathing and the calm composure in his hand, Jesse communicated compassion.

Indicators that, perhaps, he had changed.

Jesse admired the beauty of a smile that dimpled at the corner of her mouth.

And her eyes. Her engaging blue eyes.

Time spoke through her eyes.

CHAPTER 32

THE aroma of hickory emanated from the backyard patio. From one end of the grill, Jesse watched streams of pallid smoke drift upward. Blake, his arm wrapped around Eden's waist, hovered from the other side. Eden nestled her head against his chest as he drew her closer. Jesse grew amused as the couple flirted, giggled together, lost in shared secrets.

It was early Saturday evening.

"Ladies and gentlemen, your chef has returned!" Chuck called. He left the kitchen and slid the glass door shut behind him. As a church pastor, he had hosted countless guests at his house, which sat less than a mile from the church building. But tonight's dinner was a family affair.

In a swift motion, Eden craned her neck toward the entrées as Chuck forked the slabs of meat onto the iron grid. "What on earth are those things you picked up to barbecue?"

With a grin that seemed to suggest his mouth watered, Chuck patted his belly. "They're delicious. Pork steaks—haven't had them in so long."

"Sounds awful."

"Truth is, they remind me of my childhood."

Blake scrutinized the steaks. "Would that be the ragtime era?"

Chuck gave him a playful poke in the arm with the blunt edge of the barbecue utensil. "When I was a kid, my dad took me on a road trip." He monitored the juice that beaded on the meat's surface. "We went to a Cardinals game in St. Louis—Cards against the Cubs, eleven innings, Cards won five to four. After the game, we stopped in a local bar for dinner and noticed half the people ate pork steaks, the house specialty. So we tried 'em out—and it was love at first bite." Chuck flipped the steaks over to reveal the fat charred along the edges, but no harm done. "I seldom see them anywhere, but found them at the store today. Consider it an expansion of your borders."

Amusement in her face, Eden remained skeptical and turned toward her brother. "Hmm. What do you think of that?"

"Hey, you know me. I'm always ready to expand my borders."

Eden shook her head at Chuck. "If you make me sick on these things, I'll never forgive you," she joshed. Then she grabbed Blake by the arm and tugged him over to the glass-top patio table, where the pair set out plates and plasticware. Blake mimed a fork full of potato salad and waved it in front of Eden's face. She veered back in laughter and pecked him on the chin.

Jesse glanced over at them, then returned his attention to his father. "What's a party without the entertainment, huh?" Jesse borrowed the cooking utensil to move the lesser-cooked steaks to a hotter area on the grill.

Chuck eyed Eden and Blake as they traded jabs on their own side of the world. He snickered at the sight. "They're always having fun. I like it when my kids are happy."

"So he meets your approval?"

"Sure, he's a good guy. And he's sweet to her." Chuck brushed barbecue sauce onto the steaks, which crackled over the flames. "Those two are much like your mom and me when we started dating. We were even younger than they are."

"Do you think Eden loves him?"

"I think so. She didn't look for love, though."

"What do you mean?"

Chuck pursed his lips and added a final touch of sauce to the steaks, which Jesse turned over once again. "She never considered dating a priority. Not as a high-school kid—unfortunately, I didn't have the pleasure of interrogating any suitors. Even after college, she grew preoccupied with larger-purpose things, work and so forth. After Blake came to church five years ago, his life changed. A while after that, he and Eden became friends. Poor guy; she was oblivious to his crush on her—and I'm talking *years*."

"Sounds like Eden," Jesse chuckled.

"He tried to get her attention, showing up by coincidence at activities, striking up conversations with her. Everyone could detect his interest—except her. And when she finally realized Blake's crush, my daughter, in her typical strong-willed fashion, just kept her eye on him. She wanted to know how he operated when he didn't *know* she saw him."

"Played hard to get, huh?"

"That's an understatement. She had him going for months longer—he wondered what in the world he did wrong." Chuck gave Eden and Blake another glance. "She wanted to make sure he was trustworthy before she committed. She's seen a lot of personalities as a social worker; she doesn't want to enter a first date, much less a relationship, blindly."

Jesse thought back to Jada. "Can't say I blame her."

Together, he and his father shifted the pork steaks, smoky scented and crisped around the edges, to a platter and headed over to the table, where Chuck said grace over the meal.

After dinner, Blake ducked out early to run by the shop for

some inventory work. As the rest of them gathered the table settings, Chuck smacked Jesse's hand in jest.

"I'll take care of these," the minister said. "You two hang out." And with that, he disappeared into the kitchen with a stack of disposable plates and ware for the trash.

Jesse looked over at Eden. "You and Blake."

"He said you've been a gentleman about the whole dating-your-sister scenario."

"A *gentleman*?"

"My own paraphrase. He said you've taken it like a man. You'd better be nice to him."

Jesse feigned innocence. "Far be it from me to interrupt your personal bliss." In the initial taste of sunset, he listened to a dog bark in the distance—a large one, from the timbre of its voice. He pictured Jada trying to be kind to a Siberian Husky and getting trampled by the miniature horse as it lapped her face in gratitude. What had Jesse seen in her?

At the far corner of the yard, he noticed a football behind a bush, no doubt lost by the kid next door. Jesse headed over to retrieve it. "Remember when you used to tag along whenever the guys and I played? I was what, twelve years old?"

"How could I forget! I was only nine and, like, half your size. It was dangerous."

Jesse had a glint in his eye. "Please! It was only flag football."

"Yeah, until you bowled me over and tackled me to the ground!" She shook her head, the wounded soul. "One of your friends made it his ambition each game to try to give me a broken boob—if I'd had any back then!"

"Whatever, whiner," Jesse joked. Football in hand, he walked back toward her and bumped it against her elbow. "How about a game right now? You know, for old time's sake."

"No way, Barlow."

"Not up to the challenge?" he teased. "What's the matter?"

"You cheat. You made it *your* ambition to break my *arm*!" she bantered in return. "Plus you believe in wedgies as loser awards, and I want to save you the embarrassment. What if I turned the tables on you after all this time?"

Jesse taunted her further until Eden snatched the ball from his hand and raced to the opposite end of the lawn.

"Wait, now who's cheating?"

With a fist pump, Eden hooted and shouted, "Give it up for the girls!" She laughed. "First touchdown, and without a broken bone!"

She gave the ball a light punt and ran toward her big brother. When Jesse caught the ball and started to dart, Eden grabbed his ankle at the last moment in an effort to stop him. Though she clung with limited success, Jesse maintained his balance and dragged her, inch by inch, across the grass.

Chuck sauntered outside again. From the patio, he caught sight of his kids as they scuffled in hilarity in the lawn. His face impish, Chuck charged in with a shout, tackled both his kids in his arms, and tumbled over them.

At last, the three of them rolled apart, settled on their backs in the cool grass and its emerald hues of life. All three lay there in spontaneous mirth, their laughter so intense that tears of joy erupted from their eyes.

A family together.

Just like old times.

CHAPTER 33

ONE morning around eight thirty the following week, Jesse, seated among red and yellow tulips, added fresh soil to the flower garden in front of the church. The dirt, when brushed over his skin, tickled his senses with its rich scent of minerals. Albeit crisp this time of day, sunlight warmed his skin and soothed his cheeks. Unlike the perpetual, lazy shine of the California sun, Ohio sunlight seemed to possess a brisk quality that left him invigorated and signaled a fresh start. To think, mere weeks ago, he could have caught snow flurries on his tongue in this garden.

By his own admission, Jesse found it easier to relax amid the pace here. An occasional car passed along the street before him. But with most people at work or school, the environment lacked the constant activity of the culture from which he'd emerged—a city that never slept, filled with actors between gigs or who worked the night shift at a restaurant.

At the sound of the familiar motorcycle putting to a stop, Jesse's eyes darted straight to the parking lot. He shook his head in amusement as Chuck stripped off his helmet. Hard to believe: As far as Jesse had pushed the envelope as a young guy, he hadn't taken his dad's motorcycle out for a spin. And knowing Jesse back then, he wouldn't have fooled with a helmet.

As Chuck approached the building, Jesse heard a set of keys

clash in a tiny metallic chime as Chuck spun his key ring around his index finger. Jesse jerked his head toward the motorcycle.

"Do you ever wonder how many people would crucify you for being a preacher who rides a motorcycle?"

"Hey, don't knock it," Chuck played along. "I used to take you out on my old one." With a glance toward his ringing cell phone, Chuck chose to ignore the call. "So Mel assigned you the dirty work, huh?"

"Literally. But it's relaxing. Never had time to just fuck around with dirt back in L.A.—oh … sorry, I meant, 'dig around in the dirt.'"

Jesse winced and peered up at the preacher, who kept silent. In fact, to Jesse's surprise, Chuck hadn't winced or expressed the slightest ounce of anger. Without a doubt, the man didn't find humor in his son's verb selection—Chuck wasn't one to use offensive language—yet he seemed to let it pass in a non-judgmental fashion. Still, Jesse could see a wrinkle in his father's forehead that revealed Chuck indeed held an opinion.

Jesse dug in the dirt again. "I guess people might crucify *me* for swearing on church property, huh?"

Chuck compressed his lips, tilted his head in what seemed an indifferent manner. With a pat to Jesse's back, he replied, "Well, if they do, they've forgotten the life *they* used to live." Chuck rubbed a kink from the back of his own neck. "Still, it's probably a good idea to watch your words. Deal?"

"Yeah, okay."

Chuck slid his foot across a bare patch of soil and changed the subject. "I sure enjoyed the family dinner the other night."

"It's been a while."

"Apparently, poor Eden thinks you busted her rib during your scrimmage." The minister winked at his son.

"Daddy's delicate princess."

"I'd better get inside." Chuck checked his watch. "Later, dude." The preacher chuckled on his way into the building.

Jesse wiped away beads of perspiration that sprouted beneath his chin and returned to work. And a moment later, he felt a strange pooling sensation at the edge of his nostril, followed by a drop of blood that fell to the ground. Anxious and lightheaded, Jesse tilted his head back. Palms against the ground, he extended his arms behind him and reclined to stifle the bleeding.

It had to be due to this extended time in the sun and the chilly morning air. That's what Jesse decided to chalk it up to.

Had the door clinked shut?

Jesse took a quick look toward the entrance to make sure Chuck had made it inside.

Good—no sign of his father. No need to get him involved in this, whatever it was.

Unable to pinch his nose closed because of his soil-caked hands, he leaned back further and rested on his forearms. On average, these nosebleeds had taken twenty minutes to heal.

So he waited.

CHAPTER 34

THEY met at Brick Oven again. Just the two of them. Together they joked about the modest atmosphere and the high-school kids in booths around them. Neither Jesse nor Caitlyn had anything to hide—neither swam in cash at this point in their lives. Caitlyn enjoyed the restaurant's sentimental strings. And Jesse treasured his rediscovery of how it felt to spend time with the girl he'd once loved.

And perhaps still did.

Drew wasn't happy when told he couldn't come along, but Jesse promised to take him downtown one day that upcoming weekend.

They ordered the same pizza at the same table as before. They sat on the same sides of the booth, and caught glimpses of each other's familiar eyes.

"Drew talks about you constantly," Caitlyn said. "He's thrilled with Mom's new friend."

"Is *Mom* thrilled with her new friend?"

She pondered the question. "Mom's trying to process it."

Jesse treaded with caution. "Is that good or bad?"

Without a word, Caitlyn picked at her pizza crust. She seemed to avoid his face. "Why did you …" She wavered, as if unsure what to say next—or rather, to select the precise words. "I don't know, maybe I shouldn't ask."

"Ask what?" He leaned forward, his heart in search of hers.

At last, in a slow, delicate motion, Caitlyn raised her head and peered into Jesse's face. Her voice yearned for honesty.

"Why did you come back home?" When Jesse eased back in his seat, she held out her palms. "I'm sorry, I didn't mean for that to sound cruel. But after eleven years, I'm just … well, curious."

That, plus scared to death of another broken heart, Jesse figured. Though she seemed to feel less awkward about his reappearance, Jesse could tell her own doubts caused her concern.

"Don't apologize. It's a fair question."

"Did something happen?"

"A combination of things, I suppose." He stumbled around for an answer. Yes, he wanted to offer candor. Jesse owed her that much. But he couldn't mention the suicide attempt. "The situation got rough out there, not quite the picturesque outcome I'd imagined as a kid. Life happened. Then the reflection settled in: You reach a point in your life when you ask questions, evaluate where you've been and where you are—maybe even *who* you are. And I realized I'd failed out there, including ways unrelated to show business," he said. "There were mistakes …"

Jesse shook his head with regret. The words came forth slow and honest. Though he felt ashamed, a purity existed as time froze in place. Caitlyn nodded her encouragement.

Jesse pressed on. "I guess it was time for me to slow down, time to take inventory of what matters in life." He closed his eyes and escaped into the pain of the past before he reopened them. "Hard as I tried, I couldn't forget about the baby, though I never laid sight on it or even knew it was alive. Random thoughts came to mind: Was it a boy or girl? If it were alive, what color hair would it have? Would it be left- or right-handed? Would the kid walk on the sidewalk or on the street?" A beat passed before Jesse continued. "But most of all, I thought this: Would the child wonder about its dad?"

Caitlyn folded her gentle hands on the table. "He wondered about you often."

"Did he feel hurt?"

"No, not hurt. It was normal for him to be without a dad—that was all he'd known his whole life. He only wanted to understand." She stared at her hands as she rubbed her thumb against her palm. "He had many questions—a lot of why's: Why was his dad absent while other kids had their dads? Why couldn't his mom and dad stay together?"

Jesse felt a blade in his heart as he pictured Drew, a young boy, struggling with rejection. Regardless of whether it was all Drew had ever known, a kid should never experience such a thing in the first place. Oh, if Jesse could turn back time.

Caitlyn must have perceived his regret. She reached for his hand.

"He turned out fine," she said. "Whatever void he might have, you're filling it now."

Each of them ate another slice of pizza in silence.

Jesse watched a middle-aged couple across the aisle, who rose from their booth and headed to the front counter to pay their bill. He listened to the idle clang of a cash register. The man drew his wife close and laid a kiss against her temple.

Jesse returned his attention to the girl before him, who sipped her iced tea with subtle refinement, before he broke their silence. "I never really forgot about you, Cait."

Her cheeks deepened into a light blush, and she fluttered her hand in front of her face as if to hide the coloration. She held back her smile.

"You're special," he added. "You're an emerald."

Caitlyn's face sobered. Still mild-spoken, she asked, "Did you have a girlfriend in California?"

Taken aback, Jesse paused.

"Yes," he said. A vulnerable admission, one for which he could muster little more than a whisper.

Caitlyn deserved to know the truth. But Jesse knew it must be difficult for her to hear.

Caitlyn nodded as she processed it. Her eyes flitted from his eyes to her hands, and then returned to his eyes again. In her eyes, Jesse found a look of compassion, almost forgiveness. Her tone remained steady, kind, as though she knew the answer to the next question on her heart but needed to hear it herself. "And did you stay together with *her* long term?"

He sat amazed by her boldness, her strength, her quiet confidence. This was the girl with whom he had fallen in love. And now he found himself at a loss for words: What, in this present context, could justify his answer? He'd given Jada the relationship Caitlyn had sacrificed.

"Yes," he replied. "Yes, we … ten years …"

Caitlyn nodded again, then turned her head and focused on a spot on the wall. In the corner of her eye, the one furthest from Jesse—did he see a tear in formation? Caitlyn pretended to rub her temple with her fingertip, but Jesse noticed she had brushed away the tear.

"Cait …"

Jesse reached for her hand, but she withdrew it—not in anger, but with tender grace.

"Don't," she breathed. "It was long ago. *We* were long ago."

For Jesse, the ambience faded around him. The music from the overhead speakers drowned out. The people at other tables blurred, their conversations a muffled drone. Before him sat

Caitlyn, the girl he had, at a time long lost, vowed never to crush. Now look at her, pierced to the soul without cause.

And in that moment, Jesse comprehended what had happened during their time apart.

She had waited for him.

In her heart, despite the disappointment and upheaval, she had never stopped loving him.

This—*this*—was the girl he had left behind.

The ambience resurfaced around him. Between Jesse and Caitlyn, a magnetic pull seemed to facilitate an unspoken communication. Their silence spoke of mercy.

A ballad played above them, a flavored Dave Matthews Band beauty with which Jesse had often serenaded Caitlyn while in the car as teenagers. Tonight, Jesse hummed the tune to himself; its vibrations buzzed along his sealed lips.

When she heard the faint hum, Caitlyn giggled.

Jesse wasn't aware he could be heard until he noticed her reaction. Embarrassed at first, when he saw her awash in radiance, Jesse increased the volume for her to hear. Then he remembered why she seemed to enjoy it.

In former days, he'd started to sing this tune as a serenade. Then, by the second verse, he'd mimicked Dave Matthews's high-pitched, staccato voice, which never failed to ignite giggles in Caitlyn. After their quarrels, it was common for him to sing to her in this way, which broke the ice and healed the wounds between them.

He thrived when he saw her happy.

So tonight Jesse continued to sing quietly. And Caitlyn, her chin at rest on folded hands, leaned forward to listen.

She gleamed with delight.

And she giggled some more.

CHAPTER 35

JESSE preferred afternoon baseball games. But with his son beside him, Jesse lauded today's Sunday game as his all-time favorite.

Tied to a strict ticket budget, he and Drew sat in the uppermost tier, but Drew didn't appear to care. The kid seemed content as he munched on a foot-long hot dog.

With a win-loss record of 22-6 to date, the Cleveland team gelled early on to ignite its fans' hopes for the season. While it was yet May, most already considered the team a probable play-off contender. And Drew scoped out players as a federal agent might scour the files of a tax cheat.

Today the Indians played Seattle, whose fortunes had turned nasty soon after the season started. Seattle's current win-loss record had dwindled to 11-17.

As Drew focused on the Indians pitcher at the mound, Jesse scanned the human sea of navy blue and white. The line of lean bachelors in the row ahead had opted to shave their heads and paint them the team colors. A pair of pot-bellied fans, adorned in full quasi-Indian headdresses, sat several sections over. Jesse pitied the folks who sat behind them with a partial blockage of view. From this height, a single feather could obscure a player below.

The stadium, Progressive Field, had opened as Jacobs Field in 1994, when Jesse was a kid. Chuck made it a priority to take his son to a game, live in person, once a year. But for all the improved proximity offered by the new ballpark, Jesse still favored the timeless, grandiose layout of the old Cleveland Stadium, where he'd viewed his earliest games.

Odd enough, the last time Jesse stepped foot in the former stadium occurred not during the Indians' final season in 1993, but in 1994, when Chuck took Jesse and Eden there for a Billy Graham Crusade. Jesse recalled that warm June evening as the three of them walked through the gates with ease. The atmosphere distinguished itself from a routine baseball game; at the Crusade, Jesse had sensed a calm—albeit personally unexpected—fervor of anticipation.

Jesse remembered the stage's position at midfield that year, and the Thursday crowd that filled a full semi-circle at one end of the stadium by the time the program began. He thought back to when he heard the gray-haired preacher, held in utmost respect by Chuck, speak in a genteel Southern drawl. Jesse could still picture the scene that followed the sermon, when Reverend Graham gave an invitation to receive salvation— where a middle-school-aged Jesse, not much older than Drew, watched what appeared to him a thousand people descend the concrete stadium steps in a perpetual stream as the traditional hymn "Just As I Am" played. Some of those people wept, others remained stoic, as they spilled onto the field—the field where Jesse had seen players scramble to steal third base. At the time, Jesse had marveled as the field transformed into an ocean of changed lives.

Beyond experiences in his father's church, that night had made a strong spiritual impression on Jesse. Yet he couldn't remember when, prior to today, he had last thought back to that evening.

The cheer of the crowd jerked Jesse back to the game at hand. A Seattle hitter cost his team their third out and brought the game to the middle of the fourth inning.

Jesse looked down at Drew, who had borrowed his father's sunglasses for fun. Jesse finished his bratwurst and wiped his hand on a napkin. He signaled for the beer vendor, and the transaction completed as Jesse cast the cash along the row of fans and a beverage floated his way in exchange.

"You're drinking a beer?" Drew asked.

Wheels turned in Jesse's mind as he analyzed the situation. This was new to him; in a split second, he learned that kids notice everything.

"Yeah, just one," Jesse replied. "Wait—is your mom okay with that?" He'd promised Caitlyn not to get Drew into trouble.

"Give me a drink of it and I'll keep my mouth shut—then she won't find out."

"I'll take my chances." He hoped this was the kid's idea of a joke, but now Jesse wondered.

Drew shrugged. "I think she's okay with it."

The kid had nearly caused one of Jesse's aortas to rupture with that scare. Then again, he had chosen to embark on crash-course fatherhood.

Jesse pointed out a mustard drop at the corner of Drew's mouth, which Drew wiped away and ate before Jesse could find a napkin.

"Enjoying the game?" Jesse asked.

"Pretty cool."

"Do you pay much attention to baseball?"

"Oh yeah! My favorite player is Creed Harris—he's the Indians' second baseman. He's got a batting average of .412

so far this year. Nine home runs, thirty-four RBI's. The guy's awesome. They got him last year in a trade with Detroit."

"Impressive. How long since you saw your last game here?"

"Never."

Jesse tore his focus from the Indian at bat. Drew had given his answer in such a matter-of-fact tone that Jesse had to ask again. Every boy had been to a baseball game, or so he thought.

"Never?"

"Well, we don't live close to the stadium and I don't have a dad to take me," Drew said, as if it were a normal aspect of his life, nothing out of the ordinary. "I went to a minor league game in Akron with my friend and *his* dad, though."

That should never have had to occur. Jesse wanted to ask more about this but opted against it, unsure how sensitive Drew might be. Maybe Drew wouldn't want to discuss the issue.

Jesse returned his attention to the manicured field, where Seattle's first baseman, Lanny Ortega, attempted to catch a foul ball before he ran out of room at the barrier. Instead, the ball tumbled into a mob of grasping hands. With the next pitch, the batter struck out, which left Cleveland at 0-2 for the inning. A runner stood at first base, and another runner had stolen third base a few minutes ago.

By this point, the fans craved another run. To everyone's surprise, the Indians trailed by a score of 3-2 so far. They had loaded their bases twice before batters struck out and destroyed the momentum. Drew took another bite of his hot dog as Creed Harris, his apparent hero, stepped up to the plate.

Seattle pitcher Bruce Beckett, known to flirt with the edges of the strike zone, zipped the ball across the corner of the zone at ninety-six miles per hour. Strike one. Drew eased forward in caution, tapped his foot, and pounded a small fist against his knee.

Jesse didn't care about the excitement of the game. He marveled at his son's individual personality, the boy's readiness to cheer as the suspense unfolded before him. Jesse couldn't believe his sunglasses now sat on his son's head.

With a tap of his bat to home plate, Harris geared up for the second pitch and waited. The ball arrived and he fouled. Drew scratched his head and exhaled. "Come on," he murmured.

Next, Beckett delivered ball one, which Harris anticipated; Harris had held steady as the baseball zoomed past him. That intentional ball paved the way for an *unintentional* ball two, followed by a ball three that proved the pitcher's concentration waned.

A full count—and with two men on base.

Now the pitcher looked agitated. This was the sort of snag that had led to his team's less-than-desirable record.

The sound of a Native-American drum pounded from the loudspeakers, which sent reverberations through the stadium like a tamed electric current. Jesse felt it buzz on the concrete beneath his feet. The fans filled the stadium with an ominous growl.

Tension hung in the air. At the last moment, as if to prolong Beckett's anxiety, Harris stepped away from the plate. Beckett, in response, wiped sweat from his brow. Harris's capabilities were notorious in the enemy camp—including his reputation that he, in times of weak pitching, tended to chase balls to deliver a hit.

Drew bit his lip. Beckett wound up for the pitch. Jesse kept one eye on the game, the other eye on his son, eager to see how Drew might react to a combustion of victory.

Beckett released the pitch. The ball sped toward home plate. And Harris made contact.

Deep contact.

Some players report that they can sense when a ball is a home run as it sails halfway across the field. This ball soared like a laser into right field and into the stands. Harris noted the home run on his way to first base and hopped on his feet.

The crowd roared. A flurry of white team towels waved around the stadium as spectators jumped to their feet.

Both Jesse and Drew shot up and screamed with excitement, arms up in the air, as Creed Harris rounded the bases in a celebratory trot. His team had improved its score to a winning 5-3.

As Harris rounded third base and jogged to home plate, motion seemed to slow for Jesse as he glanced down at an ecstatic Drew.

Jesse stood dumbfounded.

So this is what my son looks like when he cheers.

When he slipped into the house that evening, Jesse removed his shoes at the door. He found Eden in the living room, curled up on the sofa. The television, which she had on mute, flickered from the other side of the room.

She looked up from the book on her lap. "How was the game?"

"We won, 8-3."

"Blake thinks they'll win the division this year. But it's so early in the season; I don't think he can tell."

"Male know-how."

"Whatever. Harris is strong at second base."

"Another home run and two more RBI's today. The guy had a .412 batting average when he headed into the game."

Eden looked impressed, then shot him a look of suspicion. "You follow baseball?"

"I have my sources."

"Speaking of your source, how's Drew?"

Jesse's eyes sparkled with excitement. "He had a blast. You should've seen his thrill when the home run occurred—he yelled his lungs out. And you wouldn't believe how much food the kid eats! Such a smart guy, too. He takes after his mom."

Eden checked the clock. "Did you just take him home?"

"I grabbed a bite to eat after I dropped him off, then went for a drive." He nodded toward the television. "Good TV show tonight?"

Based on her reaction, she'd forgotten she left it on. "No. I started to watch a reality show, but the bickering got on my nerves."

Jesse angled his head to peer over Eden's lap. "What are you reading? Oh—Bible?"

"I'm winding down before bed."

"I don't think I even know where mine is anymore," Jesse half joked.

Like their dad, Eden took reverential care of her book. As she continued to read, Jesse stared at its leather binding. Thin as tissue paper, the pages crackled when turned. A few days ago, unknown to Eden, he'd flipped through those pages, their text underlined in various places and Eden's margins speckled with handwritten notes about the pages' contents. Some people seemed appalled that someone would write in a Bible, but Jesse and Eden had watched their dad do just that all through their childhood. To them, it was commonplace.

Over the years, as Jesse had talked to her on the phone and watched Eden's lifestyle here at home lately, he could tell she had peace with God.

"Do you ever think about Mom?" he asked.

Eden looked up, furrowed her eyebrows. "Mom?"

"Yeah. Just in general."

She gazed at the ceiling for a moment, then pressed her lips together and nodded in peace. "From time to time."

"What kind of thoughts?"

Eden closed the book and rested her hands on top of it. "Even though I never knew her, I always knew what she looked like from pictures," she said. Eden gazed into the distance. Her smile grew warmer. Again, that peace of hers resurfaced. "So when I was a little girl and I'd fall off the monkey bars or skin my knees, I'd picture Mom wrapping her arms around me so tight and imagine how safe that would have felt." Although she didn't seem to notice, Eden drew one hand around to her other arm, a half hug.

She continued, "Then, of course, I wished she could have taken me to those mother-daughter events or explain sex to me—Dad was hilarious with that one. But even now, sometimes I stop and imagine what it would be like to go to lunch together, or to tell her about each little baby I place for adoption."

Eden paused, and Jesse could see her sink deep in thought. Yes, she must have spent much of her life pondering what might have been. A mere three years old at the time of their mother's death, Jesse, unlike his sister, enjoyed the benefit of a recollection—albeit a vague one—of his mother. As he'd clung to her memory, her face had grown clearer in his mind's eye. He sympathized with Eden's lack of even a hint of remembrance to hold dear.

"Do *you* think about Mom?" Eden asked.

The house was silent except for the rustle of a fan in another room.

"Oh, every once in a while." He pretended to shrug the notion off as if it didn't bother him. He scooted forward, his eyes intense with concentration, and tapped his fingertips together. "When you read your Bible, do you ever wonder why God allowed her to die?"

"For a while I did—years back. But I realized I could never figure out the answer, so I refused to spend my life trying. And when I was oh, maybe twelve, I started to look at it as Mom's love for me—like she sacrificed her life for me. Somehow that helped me cope with it." She squinted, perhaps to consider her words and judge them accurate. "Maybe that's why I love my job: I get to give mothers to babies."

Jesse digested what she said, then pointed out, "So you understand how Drew felt without a dad all these years."

"To an extent." Her smile made a full comeback and she perked up. "But here's the good news: You get to change that for him now. Even if Drew doesn't know you're his dad, you get to participate in his life and give him a gift no one else can give him: a second chance at a full family."

His voice almost inaudible, the revelation hit Jesse. "Like coming back from the dead ..."

Eden tilted her head, nodded. "Odd way to put it, but yeah—in a way." She inspected Jesse, who had now lost himself in concentration. Eden set her Bible on the coffee table and scooted closer. "You're okay, right?"

Jesse shook himself out of his trance. "Huh? Oh—yeah, I'm

fine." Rapidly in his mind, he retraced his steps from his Ohio departure to his suicide attempt, from his near-death rescue to his reunion with Drew and Caitlyn. Then he looked over at his sister and remarked, "You don't believe in coincidences."

"No, I don't," she replied with resolute confidence. "Life is too big, too filled with purpose for that."

A month ago, he might have argued with her opinion. But not anymore. The way he saw it, he now lived on borrowed time.

CHAPTER 36

LATE that Tuesday afternoon, Jesse crisscrossed the church's rear lawn in a riding mower. Even with the low humidity of the upper Midwest, the sun felt hot after an hour. Drops of perspiration trickled down his cheeks and crawled to his neck.

His last conversation with Eden brought perspective to his situation. No wonder Caitlyn shielded their son like she did.

With further reflection, Jesse imagined the rough times Caitlyn must have endured alone. Then, by contrast, he thought about his own status during one of those moments: A brief stint as an extra on *Love and Errors*, a dark romantic comedy. The day he and Jada moved into their Sherman Oaks apartment, the upgrade from Hollywood and Vine. And one Christmas Eve, courtesy of a credit card, he took Jada to an expensive French bistro in Pasadena, where they ate in a corner by candlelight.

What value he'd placed on things that now meant nothing, watercolor paintings that had faded with time.

All while Caitlyn and Drew struggled.

And to think, mere weeks ago, Jesse felt screwed because a film role had fallen through.

When he walked through the church building's back door, the air conditioning prickled his skin like the fresh chill of spring water. Around the corner, at the end of the corridor, he poked his head in Mel's office to say good-bye before he headed home.

Eyes drilled to a repair-in-progress, Mel beckoned with an absent wave behind his back. "Hold on a second!"

Already out the office door, Jesse backed up and poked his head back in as Mel reached inside a desk drawer.

"Technically, you report to me," Mel said, "so *technically,* I'm supposed to be the one to give this to you."

He fluttered a flimsy, letter-sized envelope, which Jesse took. Confused, Jesse gave it a perfunctory look. Through the envelope's window, Jesse's name appeared above Eden's street address.

"What's this?"

Mel snorted. "Your first paycheck, what else!"

With the recent developments in his life, Jesse had forgotten all about money.

Tired, Jesse walked out of the building and toward his car. But halfway there, he stopped. He grinned at the thought that dawned on him, and then slapped the unsealed envelope against his palm. Jesse jogged the rest of the way to his car.

If he hurried, he could get to a bank before it closed.

Jesse heard a basketball bounce across the street but didn't think to look for its source. He had walked all the way up Caitlyn's driveway when he heard footsteps approach behind him. Before he had a chance to turn around, Drew pounced on him from behind.

"Hey Jesse!" His skinny arms wrapped around Jesse's shoulders and met on the other side before Drew hopped off. At least the kid appeared excited to see him. And it made Jesse's whole day worth living. How many of these spontaneous gestures had he missed as his son grew up?

Drew panted rather heavily, Jesse noticed. Hadn't Drew mentioned he doesn't play basketball much because it made him tired? And Caitlyn had concerns as well. But then again, Drew's current panting was, in all likelihood, a side effect from his record-time bolt from the opposite side of the street.

"What's up, buddy!" Jesse patted the kid on the back. "How many more weeks of school?"

"Two; we're almost done. That's my friend Ryan over there."

Drew pointed toward the house across the street, where another kid bounced a basketball and watched with curiosity. When Jesse waved, the kid responded with a nod and went back to his free throws.

"Are you here to see my mom?" Drew asked.

"Yep." Jesse knuckled his son on the arm. "Better get back to your game over there, bud. Your friend is waiting."

"Oh, I forgot! Okay, see ya."

When they parted ways, Jesse knocked on the front door and Caitlyn let him in. She led him into the kitchen and offered him a beverage, but he declined. She poured him a glass of water anyway. Jesse settled at the table, where Caitlyn took a seat beside him.

"I don't intend to stay long," he said. His eyes felt a bit brighter in anticipation of what would occur. From his back pocket, he retrieved the envelope that had housed his paycheck. Now the envelope felt heavier. "I want to give you this."

Caitlyn took hold of the thick envelope. "What is it?"

"Open it."

Jesse had replaced the contents, wrapped them in a single sheet of paper, and sealed the envelope. When Caitlyn tore it open and unfolded the sheet, she tried to find her voice as she stared. In her hand dwelt a stack of unblemished twenty-dollar bills, seven hundred dollars in total. The bills were so new, a few still stuck together. Jesse could detect the scent of fresh ink.

Speechless, she looked up and found sincerity in Jesse's eyes. "I don't understand," she said.

"It's my first paycheck," he replied. "This is something I could have done all along, if I had known about Drew. I should have been there for you."

In obvious bewilderment, Caitlyn shook her head, her mouth in the shape of an O. Her eyes still fluttered at the sight of the cash. She tried to meet his eyes again but retreated; she appeared on the verge of weeping.

Jesse sensed her loss for words. Though he didn't want to cause her any discomfort, he reached over and clasped his hands over hers. "Look, I know this doesn't begin to make up for all the years I *didn't* do this. But I hope this is a step in the right direction." Caitlyn continued to stare at the envelope and run her finger along its edges. So Jesse continued to speak. "From now on, you'll get a portion of each check. If I hadn't racked up a good deal of debt in L.A., I'd give you the whole amount each time." He watched her lip quiver. "But I promise: You won't need to do this alone anymore."

She sniffled once. At last she looked back at Jesse. "I don't know what to say."

"Don't say anything." He peered deep into her eyes. "If you can say this is a step forward, that's all I need to know."

Caitlyn bit her lip. "Yes." As a full smile emerged, she added, "This is a good thing."

From her expression, Jesse discerned she'd needed this provision more than he'd realized.

After one more mesmerized glance at the envelope, she scooted out of the chair and walked over to her purse, where she placed the money inside. Grateful she understood the gesture and the heart intention behind it, Jesse folded his hands in his lap, content.

Caitlyn didn't sit down just yet, as if her knees felt weak or her heart trembled. She wandered over to the refrigerator to retrieve something, or perhaps to stall for time.

When Caitlyn grabbed the refrigerator handle, she uttered a response somewhere between a chuckle and a sob. "Oh, Drew." She rubbed at one spot, touched her fingertips together. "It's sticky—probably juice." Then, in mock disgust, she turned to Jesse and shook her head. "Boys."

Darting up from the table, Jesse wetted a dishrag and handed it to her.

"Thank you." She wiped the spot and handed the rag back to Jesse. "He's a sweet guy, though."

"Just like his dad, huh?" Jesse quipped.

"Don't push your luck."

He could see she enjoyed the humor.

Jesse's mind returned to the paycheck—and to something that hadn't occurred to him before. "Can I ask you a question?"

"You mean, why didn't I make Drew clean this? I should have."

"No, it's—why did you raise Drew alone? I mean, you could have broken your promise and told Eden you'd had a baby. She could have given you my number."

He followed her into the living room, where they sat together on the sofa. Through the window, they watched Drew and his friend take free-throw shots across the street.

"Even after Drew was born, I had a choice," Caitlyn said. "I could have given him up for adoption. But deep down, a part of me wanted to keep him. I backtracked; that was my decision, not yours." She ran her hand through her hair, then rested her cheek against her palm. "I didn't search for you because—well, I didn't want to force anything on you that you didn't want to be a part of. But I'll admit, I questioned whether I had done the right thing by not telling you." She massaged her wrist as small creases of contemplation formed along her brow. "Meanwhile, life rolls on. Before you know it, you're going on thirty years old and you're just used to it. So you stop questioning; you just … live."

She fascinated him. Between the two of them, Jesse knew she was the stronger individual.

He fidgeted with the band of his wristwatch. Though difficult to hear, how fresh her honesty poured forth.

"Don't worry about the past," she said. "We're alive and well. And if you decide to up and leave tomorrow, we'll still get along just as well." Caitlyn halted her speech, her smile apologetic. "I didn't mean that the way it sounded."

"Do I make you nervous?"

"A little." She tugged at her lower lip. "Look, you may have changed, and I believe you can."

"But you're not betting your life on it."

She leaned in. "Can you blame me?"

Jesse laid his hand on hers. He looked straight into her eyes. "I'll prove it to you."

She shrugged. "It'll take time."

Jesse nodded. "How much?"

"Please stop." She sighed, then clasped Jesse's hands together. "You were gone eleven years. It'll take a while to rebuild what you left behind—or build it to begin with. I mean, Drew, me, parenthood—this isn't a Hollywood job you come to, work for a few days, and then move on to another project and the rest of your life. This is a commitment—a long-term commitment."

"I can do that."

"I know you can." Compassion kindled in her eyes. "Now you need to follow through … over time."

CHAPTER 37

THE whir of the vacuum echoed in the empty church lobby as Jesse swept the floors the next morning. When Chuck walked up the hall and poked his head down each corridor along the way, Jesse shut down the vacuum.

"Have you seen Mel?" Chuck asked.

"It's Wednesday. He works afternoon and evening."

"Oh, that's right." Chuck started back down the hall before he stopped in his tracks and spun around again. "Hey, are you busy right now?"

"Sweeping the floor."

"That can wait. Anything ASAP?"

"No."

"Let's grab a late breakfast. Want to?"

After more than fifty years in business, the mom-and-pop restaurant occupied the same stand-alone building, on Route 91 near the heart of Hudson. Around nine thirty on this weekday morning, a handful of patrons sat scattered among the booths: retirees, businesspeople and those who enjoyed a random vacation day. Behind Jesse and Chuck, a real-estate agent met with clients who prepared to relocate to the area—from Minneapolis, based on what Jesse couldn't help but overhear from the cackling, over-eager agent.

Yes, life seemed to roll along. But Jesse recognized it as

a mirage, for his toughest hurdle would come when he told Chuck about Drew. But not today.

"This place hasn't changed at all," Jesse pointed out as he examined the dark-stained woodwork and aging light fixtures. Even in the middle of the day, the place seemed too dim. When Jesse was younger, Chuck had taken him here often, particularly after a season in which they had spent insufficient quality time together.

A silver-haired waitress approached their table—apparently en route to retirement—to take their order. "Preacher Chuck, my favorite bachelor!"

"Winnie," he replied.

With a wink, Winnie removed a pen and order pad from her apron. When she eyed the younger half of the pair, she stepped back. "I don't believe it: Jesse Barlow, is that you?"

Geez, now Jesse remembered her. She'd waited on them since he was a kid, back in the days when she died her hair an unfortunate shade of strawberry blond.

She asked Jesse questions about life on the west coast and why on earth he'd depart the beautiful ocean for this region's winters on ice. They bantered back and forth until Jesse's belly erupted with a loud groan. Winnie collected their orders—an omelet for Jesse, corned-beef hash and eggs with a side of bacon for Chuck—poured two cups of coffee, and disappeared toward the kitchen. Jesse stirred cream and half a sugar packet into his cup.

Chuck seemed surprised. "You always got pancakes—wouldn't touch an omelet to save your life! What happened?"

"Jada got me hooked on them," Jesse replied. "But she ordered hers with cholesterol-free eggs and filled with spinach and tomato. A health nut."

Chuck sipped his coffee. Jesse watched his father savor the scalding liquid as it trickled down his throat. Chuck said, "I don't think I ever talked to her on the phone. What's she like?"

Jesse shrugged. "L.A. girl. Pretty much fits the stereotype everyone imagines."

An awkward pause, with Jesse all too ready to forget Jada. His father must have noticed Jesse didn't want to delve deeper.

Chuck looked at his son like he wished he knew what to say, something that would allow him to connect with Jesse. A familiar expression, Jesse recognized it as the ache of a minister on behalf of a loved one. Strange how two people, despite shared flesh and blood, can become strangers, victims of time and distance.

"How long have you two been together?" Chuck asked, his eyes glued to Jesse's.

"*Were* together," Jesse corrected. "About ten years—friends first, though."

"All those years and I never met her," Chuck said, closer to an afterthought than an acknowledgment.

"You never came to California."

"Was I welcome?"

Though Chuck's tone communicated full sincerity, Jesse took offense.

Jesse traced the rim of the coffee cup with his finger. "Can we change the subject, please?"

Regret settled into Chuck's face. "I'm sorry, I didn't mean it that way."

Another uncomfortable pause. From the booth behind them, the real-estate agent—the cackler—excused herself and headed to the restroom. As soon as she walked out of earshot,

Jesse heard the married couple conspire to find a different relocation expert once they returned home.

Winnie returned with their breakfasts. Chuck prayed over the meal, and they started to eat. From across the table, Jesse picked up the scent of over-medium eggs and warm, greasy bacon fresh from the grill—two reasons he regretted letting Jada goad him into a healthier diet.

Jesse speared a fried redskin potato, the restaurant's answer to hash browns, as he soaked in the ambience some more. "Seems strange to hang out at this joint again. The guys and I used to skip classes in high school and come here."

A knowing glint in his eye, Chuck grinned. "You guys skipped classes in *middle* school and came here, too!"

Jesse exchanged a wider grin. Shocked, he fell back against the booth in disbelief. "How'd you know about that?"

"Are you kidding? I'm your dad—and a minister. I knew more about you back then than you realized." He crunched on a bite of bacon. "Besides, you're forgetting that day in seventh grade when I drove right past this place and saw you guys out front, trying to figure out how to hold a cigarette."

Jesse fought to swallow his mouthful of coffee before he burst out with a laugh. "Oh, that's right! Sanders finagled those cigarettes up at the gas station—the poor guy had a five o'clock shadow in seventh grade and the cashier never questioned his age." Jesse's eyes widened as he relived the long-gone memory. Then he gestured at his father with his fork. "You were so mad, you stopped the car, rounded us up, and took us back to school—even *recommended* a detention for us, as I recall."

"Let the punishment fit the crime, I figured," Chuck replied through a guffaw.

Jesse shook his head in wonder. "I gave you my share of headaches growing up, huh?"

"You were a strong-willed kid," Chuck agreed. "It proved a challenge at times, but I never wanted you to lose that quality. Thanked God for it." He paused, then delved into his hash. "That strong will of yours will save someone's life one day. I believe that; I've always sensed it about you."

Rapt, Jesse now absorbed his father's every word, though Chuck himself didn't notice. Jesse wondered if his own spirit of determination were a genetic quality, one which would manifest in Drew as the child grew older.

"Anyway," Chuck continued, "it came as no surprise you were as ... *vibrant* as you were. Your mom was much the same. A pistol."

"Are you sure I take after Mom? You like to have your share of fun too."

"Not nearly like she did. After we first married, we got into countless arguments because I was so nervous and she was so spontaneous. She loved life, your mom. She taught me to kick it up a notch. Said I should buy a motorcycle." He toasted Jesse with his coffee cup. "So I did—a few years after she died."

Jesse examined his father's eyes—eyes that communicated a loss, minus the helpless sorrow. "Do you miss her?"

Chuck blinked in slow motion. "Every day. She was my other half." He took another look at his son's intent expression. "Are you doing all right? I mean, is life okay, in general?"

"Sure." Jesse brushed off the question. He couldn't mention Drew and the near-abortion after all this time—he'd feel too ashamed at what his father might say, too fearful of the disappointment he pictured in his father's eyes. Jesse told himself he shouldn't care about Chuck's opinion, but he did care.

Jesse felt inadequate in his father's presence. The issue didn't reside in what Chuck *did*, but rather, in who he was. A frustrating quality, Jesse couldn't put his finger on it. Throughout Jesse's existence, Chuck had lived a clean life. Yet the man didn't exude self-righteousness; he didn't lord a religious aloofness over anyone, or even criticize Jesse. Maybe that was it. Deep down, did Jesse *want* his dad to say something to him? At this point in his life, Jesse possessed a profound regret for his own mistakes but couldn't find a sufficient way to repay the losses. Maybe Jesse wanted someone to scream at him, to provide a method of penance.

Winnie returned with the check and a coffee refill.

Jesse took another bite of his omelet.

CHAPTER 38

WHEN Jesse returned to the church building before noon, he focused his efforts on the front lobby and its surrounding hallways, in preparation for that evening's midweek worship service. He buffed the floors with the giant machine—the one with the spinning round brush—he'd seen over the years but had never handled.

Once he finished in the lobby, he stopped the machine. Then he glanced over at the doors which led to the worship auditorium.

He still hadn't attended a worship service since his return home. Now that he thought about it, he hadn't even stepped back inside the auditorium itself. Mel had cleaned it thus far. Jesse wandered over to a pair of walnut-colored doors and stepped through.

The room was pitch black except along the sides, where a series of elongated windows accented the walls. Daylight seeped through crevices in the closed blinds. Jesse could trace the vague figure of his hand in front of his face but couldn't quite see his fingers when he wiggled them. Along the back wall, he felt his way in search of the lighting panel. At last, he located it and bathed the room in a warm sepia glow. But as he scrutinized the room, one quality struck him: how cold and lifeless it seemed without people assembled inside. As Chuck had said, the church isn't a building but, rather, a group of people.

The congregation had remodeled the room since Jesse left home. He strolled along the aisles. Toward one corner of the room, he located the third row from the back—the area where, at sixteen years old, he and other classmates had hung out during services. From these seats, near another set of doors at the corner of the room, he and his buddies had sneaked outside during services for a smoke along the side of the building, an implied dare for a late arriver to catch them.

Anything to distance himself from his identity as the preacher's son.

Jesse took his time as he wandered up the center aisle across thin, tan carpeting, the industrial type. He made his way past rows of chairs, their frames the color of charcoal, their backs and seats padded with material the color of merlot. Large, fabric-covered rectangles hung along the khaki walls to help absorb sound. Overhead hung a series of track lighting, both general lights and spotlights aimed toward the main platform, which sat at the auditorium's forefront.

Jesse ran his fingers along the wood paneling of the platform before he climbed a trio of steps that led to the top. Speakers loomed overhead, pointed down toward the auditorium's chairs, and balanced an impressive set of feedback speakers that sat on the platform's floor for the band's benefit. On the platform, behind a series of microphones, a collection of instruments sat: a keyboard, drums encased in a plexiglass cubicle for sound absorption, electric and bass guitars, and a small set of percussion instruments. Chuck believed church should be a celebration. And Jesse had to admit, he loved it when the music got loud and sent the room into vibrations.

Jesse sat down on the platform, dead center, the position from which Chuck started his preaching—*started* being the key word, as his father tended to roam back and forth when he spoke. To Jesse's recall, Chuck took pleasure in walking down the platform's steps and interacting, like a good friend, with members who sat in the front rows.

Jesse peered out into the sea of chairs before him, which numbered close to one thousand, packed during worship services but empty in this serene moment. How intimidating, yet invigorating, the view had appeared to Eden and him when this building first opened. During the week, when the church was empty and they'd gotten bored, he and Eden used to jump off the platform to see who could land the farthest. A slew of similar memories, random and minute, now rushed through his mind.

Jesse could recall the day they broke ground where this room now sat.

"Soon this empty plot of land will be filled with people," Chuck had whispered to him at the time, his father's heart in a clear ache for random individuals, faces Chuck had yet to meet. "People who hurt, who seek answers in their lives. People who need what you have."

On his feet again, Jesse now sauntered over to his right, where he ran his finger along the wall that bordered the back of the platform area. At its far edge, he reached the baptistery. This was a large, tiled tub in which a minister immersed people in water during baptism, a symbolic gesture that illustrated a Christian's death to sin and new life of salvation. Jesse ran his hand along the sparkling teal tiles.

He was thirteen years old during his own baptism. One of the first to step into this tub, he had waited until a Sunday when the schedule showed an assistant minister would perform the ordinance—his wait an act of independence on Jesse's part, even at that age.

Although Jesse had seen others undergo baptisms, it proved a pleasant surprise to him when he himself stepped down into the waist-deep water: It felt cozy, like a warm bath. At nine years old, Jesse had become a Christian and affirmed the decision at his baptismal moment. As an assistant minister gripped Jesse's hand, he guided Jesse backward into the water, which engulfed Jesse with fresh abandonment, and pulled him up again. The immersion itself took about two seconds, but right away Jesse knew he'd underestimated its impact. As he emerged from underwater, broke through the surface, he felt the water sweep over his face and chest. Inside him, a sense of radiance seemed to dawn, an acute awareness that he had undergone a biblical ritual and had exhibited obedience to God. He found himself overcome by peace—a stark contrast to the frustration and confusion that developed in the following years. But on the day of his water baptism, he felt like he had begun afresh all over again. From young Jesse's perspective, that moment had belonged to God and him.

Jesse had sensed God's smile on him that day.

So when did everything change? When did Jesse start to retreat?

He couldn't pinpoint a particular day or event that triggered his withdrawal, but he knew the change had been gradual. Circumstances blended together as he entered high school. Jesse grew angry. And then came his relationship with Caitlyn, followed by confusion when they discovered she was pregnant.

Coaxed by the creak of a nearby water pipe, Jesse snapped out of his reminiscence.

He walked down the platform's stairs, headed down a side aisle of the auditorium, and turned off the lights.

CHAPTER 39

WIND, cooled by the temperature of the water, swept over the surface of Lake Erie. Jesse felt invigorated as its gusts rustled through his hair. Mid June proved balmy with minimal humidity and temperatures in the low eighties where he lived further south, but here in downtown Cleveland, as he overlooked the lake, the air brought to mind a Canadian summer.

Jesse and Drew sat side by side on a park bench a few feet from the lake, watched sailboats drift along and pedestrians gravitate after some downtown shopping. Distanced from the ocean, his perpetual west-coast tan in a fade, Jesse felt at home again. Before him, lazy waves danced along the endless horizon as he basked in the sun. He listened to the lapping water as it nudged against its concrete perimeter.

They had grabbed a to-go sack of burgers, fries and sodas—Drew reminded Jesse that in northern Ohio, people called the beverage "pop"—from a fast-food outlet down the street. When finished, they threw the trash away and Jesse reached into his backpack.

"All righty, ready to get some cool pictures for your room?" Jesse asked.

Drew bounced on the seat once before he caught himself in his outburst of childhood innocence.

Jesse hadn't used his camera since his journey home from

L.A., in those days following the suicide attempt. Eager to introduce his camera to a positive turn of events, he held it in front of his son.

"This is a digital camera," Jesse began, "but many people still like the natural side of a film-based camera. If they wanted to take shots of slow-moving objects on the water, they might load it with film that will advance at a speed of 200 since the camera's not mounted on a tripod. That way, the picture won't be affected as much."

Drew gave him a quizzical look, as if Jesse had just recited a page from Plato's journal. *Okay, so I'm not an expert parent.*

Jesse stifled a laugh and clarified his words. "For fast action, you'd use fast-speed film. For slow action, you'd use slower stuff. But this is digital, so we're safe."

"Gotcha."

They approached the barrier above the water. Jesse handed the camera to Drew, who, without hesitation, pointed it toward the closest sailboat and peered through the lens.

"You see that rectangle that shows what your picture will look like?" Jesse said. "Do you want to know how the pros line up their shots to make them look cooler?"

"Yeah."

Jesse pulled a pen from his pocket and drew a tic-tac-toe frame on the palm of his own hand. "It's called the law of thirds: You take that rectangle you looked at and, in your head, divide it into thirds, top to bottom and left to right, so it ends up looking like tic-tac toe." Jesse drew a dot at each of the four spots where the vertical and horizontal lines intersected—the four corners of a square in the middle of the frame. "These four points are where the thirds meet together. They're the strongest places in your picture. When you line up your shot, pick out the one thing that you want to be the main object in your picture, and try to position it at one of those four points. So if you wanted to take a picture of a sailboat, that would be the thing you'd put there. The boat is traveling right to left; so to make it look like the boat has made a lot of headway, place it toward the left; to make it look like it's on a journey, place it toward the right."

Drew responded with an exhale of confidence, one that lingered between understanding and the thrill of a kid in the company of an adult who made him feel significant. He aimed the camera to take a few practice shots of a boat, one with a green-and-yellow sail that flapped in the wind. As Drew pointed and clicked, Jesse could tell he'd gotten the hang of it. He showed Jesse his latest attempt.

"That's great! Move it a little further to the left—give the boat a chance to catch up to your focal point by the time you click the camera." Jesse checked the next shot. "You've got it, bud! We'll select the best one and blow it up to poster size for your room—a Drew original." He patted his son on the back.

As Drew took additional shots, Jesse tilted his head back and took a deep breath of the scent of rich water. Compared to the Pacific Ocean and its hectic, surfer-speckled waves, Lake Erie's two-foot waves looked like ripples of serenity. They glimmered beneath the sun.

Another scarlet drop fell. Jesse watched it land on the railing.

"Oh my gosh!" Drew said. "Are you okay? What's wrong with your nose?"

"I'm okay, bud."

Short of breath, Jesse feigned normalcy for Drew's sake. He didn't want him worried. But for a moment, Jesse felt as though he couldn't regain his breathing. His heart rate increased. He reached behind, stumbled backward a few feet to the bench, and sat down. Jesse tried to pretend this was all a simple inconvenience. On his brow, a sweat broke forth, but it dried and cooled him like rubbing alcohol in the lake-kissed breeze.

"Is that blood?"

"No big deal; just the humidity." Drew wouldn't know any better.

A minute later, Jesse's body returned to normal—his body, not his concerns. *Stress, that's all,* he convinced himself. This would not defeat him. Not during his time with his son.

Jesse took some deep breaths, relieved when the event ended. He inhaled through his nose deeply to prevent an escape of further drops. After another minute to relax, he noticed Drew, who still stared at him. Jesse decided to distract Drew's attention from what he'd just witnessed. Caitlyn couldn't hear about this.

He nudged his son. "So, what would you be doing on a Saturday if you weren't here?"

With a shrug, Drew said, "Not much. Maybe play on the computer."

"What about your friends from school? Wouldn't you hang out with them?"

"I don't really hang out with anyone."

"How about your friend Ryan across the street, the one I saw you shoot hoops with one day?"

"Ryan's parents are divorced. He visited his dad that night. He's only there maybe once a week."

Jesse flipped through his past chats with Drew. "You mentioned you went to a baseball game in Akron with a friend and his dad—how about that friend?"

"That was Ryan too." Drew fidgeted with the camera. In search of intriguing buttons he could push, Jesse figured. "Mostly I hang out with my mom."

"You and your mom get along pretty well, huh?"

"Yeah. Plus, I don't like to leave her alone much."

That sounded odd. "Why not?"

A soft-spoken Drew gazed at a wayward seagull that must have taken a wrong turn and ended up on the wrong shoreline. "I don't think she's too happy."

"What makes you say that?"

"A few years ago, I got home one day and thought I heard crying come from my mom's bedroom, but I couldn't tell for sure. So I walked over to her room real quiet and peeked in, and I saw her sitting on the floor against her bed. It was her—she was the one crying, but she tried not to make any noise."

Jesse leaned closer to capture each syllable. "Why did your mom cry?"

Although the incident had made an obvious impression on Drew's memory and caused him discomfort, he seemed open to talking about it. Maybe he needed someone to confide in.

"I don't know what was wrong," Drew replied. "I asked her, but she said it was nothing. Then she looked at me and smiled, but she still looked sad. I think she just tried to make me feel better about it."

Jesse didn't know what to say. He ached at the thought of Caitlyn weeping. "Does your mom cry a lot?"

"Not anymore."

"What did you do when you saw her crying that day?"

"I rubbed her shoulder to try to make her feel better. She asked me to sit down by her, so I did. Then she gave me a hug and kept holding on, real tight." Drew set the camera aside. "I don't ever want her to be sad like that again, so after that day I decided to stay with her as much as I can because I know that makes her feel better."

"Does she know that's why you don't leave her often?"

"No."

Jesse chewed on this a moment. "And you said she never told you why she cried that day, huh?"

Drew shook his head. "All she said was, 'I'm sorry you couldn't meet your dad. For some reason, I always believed you would.'"

Thunderstruck, his ache doubled on Caitlyn's behalf, Jesse covered his head with his hands. All these years, and he'd had no idea. If he'd known about Drew's birth, would Jesse have tried to take care of them? Jesse had no idea.

Then Jesse remembered Drew beside him. He looked over, relieved to find Drew hadn't noticed his reaction.

"Why do *you* think your dad wasn't around for you?" asked Jesse.

The boy's eyelashes fluttered once, his eyes moistened. He must have gone through hell all these years, but he held his composure. Not a tear escaped. "He would be here if he could. That's what Mom says, anyway."

Jesse yearned to tell Drew the truth here and now: His dad sat right beside him on this bench. Instead, he chose to respect Caitlyn's timetable.

Back on his feet, Drew took one more picture and halted. He examined the display on the camera. "It's full."

In a daze, Jesse came to. He dug into his backpack. "I've got another memory card for you." And then, for a moment, he stopped his search to gaze up at his son again. He watched Drew examine the camera and, in all likelihood, rearrange the settings to render it as challenging as a Rubik's Cube to recon-figure. But Jesse didn't care.

As he gazed closer, Jesse bit his lower lip to suppress a smile. His son had his nose.

CHAPTER 40

DRESSED in T-shirts and shorts, Jesse, Caitlyn and Drew spent the entire day downtown at The Flats for a Fourth-of-July celebration along the Cuyahoga River, where Drew had a blast. When the three of them returned to Caitlyn's house that evening, Drew darted to his bedroom.

"Mom, I'll be right back! I'm gonna get the bottle rockets you bought me!" Drew shouted on his way down the hall. Before long, he must have gotten distracted him in his room, because he didn't emerge.

Exhausted, Jesse and Caitlyn hauled themselves into the kitchen.

"Would you like some iced tea?" she asked.

When he took her up on the offer and thanked her, she told him she would meet him outside, so he wandered out to the patio alone. Underneath a deepening sky, Jesse settled into a plastic chair and marveled how, even past nine thirty at night, daylight still lingered. Jesse had never figured out if these summer daylight hours existed because Ohio sat further north than other states or due to its position within the time zone. But during the Ohio summers of his youth, he'd cherished the final glimmers of early July light until they faded into history around ten o'clock.

Soon Caitlyn made her way outside with two glasses of iced tea. She handed him a glass. "You won't believe this." With a touch to his arm as if to share a tidbit of inside humor, she said, "I stopped by Drew's room, and he's conked out on his bed. He must have lied down for a minute and fallen asleep."

"Busy day. I'm sure he's wiped out. One thing's clear: You and I no longer have the energy of a ten year old."

"Half the time I fake it to keep up with him." Caitlyn pulled a chair beside his and began to sip her lemon-jolted tea. Finally able to relax, she leaned back in her seat and drew one leg up against herself. "Do you think that makes me a bad mom?"

"Of course not."

Unintentionally, and ever so discreet, Jesse glanced over at Caitlyn's sun-kissed leg, not more than a shadow in these minutes before twilight. In times past, he used to caress her leg and, in a shared joke, would try to find the solitary freckle hidden inches above her knee.

Wait, what am I doing? Jesse shook himself out of the memory.

Then again, that freckle—it always made her chuckle when he searched for it.

Jesse leaned over and brushed his knuckle against the bottom of her calf in a featherlike motion. "The freckle, if I remember."

And sure enough, she responded with that same laugh he relished, just like she used to. "Still there."

"What did I name it?" Jesse scrunched his mouth in concentration and sifted through the lush soil of their mutual past.

Caitlyn rolled her eyes. "You named it *Judith*. Don't remind me!"

She giggled more, and this time he joined her. When the laughter died down, Jesse paused and recalled another detail.

"Wait, I gave it another name later on, didn't I?"

Yes, he had. And in truth, though he pretended otherwise, he had not forgotten. Now Caitlyn leaned her head back at the memory.

"Emma," she said and paused for a beat. With a smile, she turned toward him and stared into his eyes. She looked ready to blush. "You named her Emma, because you thought it sounded like the name of a princess."

Though he recalled the name earlier, he mocked his recall in a now-that-you-mention-it manner, his vowels drawn out. "Oh yeah, that's right. Why did I do that again?"

She leaned in closer. To Jesse, she seemed caught in a bittersweet rush. "You said *I'm* a princess, so my freckle needed a name worthy of a princess." They shared a gaze together. At last, the spontaneity passed and Caitlyn broke contact. She turned her head away. "What a schmooze," she teased.

From above, they heard the pop of a small firework, though they saw nothing.

"There they go." Jesse nodded toward the sky.

"Just kids. The park up the street holds its display at nine thirty. We can see them from here. What time is it?"

Jesse aimed his watch to catch a glint of moonlight. "It's 9:28."

The two sat in silence for a while and watched the sky deepen in its shade of blue. Together they listened to the whistles and snaps of neighborhood bottle rockets. Soon the scent of singed firework fibers teased the summer air.

Then the local park began its fireworks display a half mile away. In the distance, a series of cracks and pops delayed in its arrival as the speed of light rushed past the speed of sound. Above the trees, neon hues of red, green and white burst across the night sky in majestic form. Stars, circles and other patterns, in single colors and combinations, shot forth one after another—some in full force, while others failed in mid formation. As the sky filled with fire and withdrew to darkness between launches, Jesse peered over at Caitlyn. Her face shined in the intermittent glow as it reflected the lights above. She looked beautiful.

Eleven years ago today: July fourth marked the final time a pregnant Caitlyn had seen him. A few days later, Jesse departed.

He didn't need to mention such an anniversary. He knew she remembered well.

"I called you a couple of times," he said, his voice hushed.

"You did? When?"

He shrugged. "Back in California. I missed you most of my time there. When Jada and I hit rough patches, I'd take a drive in the car and dial your number."

"I don't remember that."

"That's where it ended—dialing the number. I wanted to get back in touch, but as soon as I heard you say hello, the sound of your voice—well, it reminded me that I'd given up on our relationship. I figured you were better off without me. So I hung up the phone and let you live your life in peace."

"I wish you would have talked to me."

A shower of red and white burst in the sky, followed by another deep boom.

"Was it tough for you? Wait, what am I asking? Of course it was tough."

Enveloped in the sporadic light, she said, "Things got worse. Once you left, everything started to tumble like dominoes. Ten weeks pregnant, I didn't know what to do. So when I decided to have the baby, I went to my parents. They didn't know about the pregnancy, of course—nothing showed yet."

"How'd they take it?"

She rested her hand against her temple. "They were furious. You remember how strict they were. But I didn't have anywhere else to turn. So I came home one night and got them together in the living room. I could barely get the words out, couldn't look at them, felt so ashamed facing them alone." She sighed. "I told them what had happened. They were shell-shocked. But really, can you blame them? My older sister had lived a perfect life and graduated from college, everything about our home looked ideal—white-picket fence, the whole deal. Then I disrupted it all. So Mom and Dad sat there without a word. Mom sobbed the whole time. After a few long, never-ending minutes, Dad looked me straight in the eye—I can't begin to describe the rage in his eyes—and he said in this weird, soft, monotonous tone, 'We didn't raise you this way.'"

Caitlyn's lip quivered, but she bit down and continued. "He said, 'How many times did I tell you to stay away from that Barlow kid?' I told him I was sorry, but he wouldn't listen. And that was the moment he stopped looking at me—it was the moment I was no longer his daughter. He simply said, 'I want you to pack your bags. I don't know where you're going to go, but I want you out—tonight.' I pleaded with him but he wouldn't listen. Mom was scared to death of him and didn't say a word."

Jesse reached out, but she pulled away.

"I'm sorry," Jesse said.

She waved her hand as if to brush away the need for consolation. "It's over. Besides, that would've happened whether you'd been here or not."

"Where did you go? That night, I mean."

"I stayed with my sister. She and her husband lived in an apartment further south. I lived there a few months until I realized I'd have to press through on my own. And by then, my sister and her husband were ready to have their place back to themselves." In apparent afterthought, Caitlyn reached for her iced tea. She took a sip; the ice had melted but had kept the tea chilled. "I went through a deluge of emotions during that time: confused, scared, hurt, betrayed, humiliated, you name it."

As a decade of repressed anger seemed to rise to the surface, tears seeped through her eyes. Jesse wanted to comfort her, but he felt the least worthy person to do so. He hated to see her in torment. If only he could wrap it around himself like a cloak, a personal purgatory.

She drew her other leg against her body and sat huddled in her chair. It became clear to Jesse that she was stronger than he ever realized.

"Anyway," she continued, "I got an inexpensive apartment and a data-entry job."

"You wanted to go to Duke and study psychology. You always made terrific grades."

"Yeah, well—priorities shift when you're a single mom. I didn't know what I was doing or how I was going to do it, but I knew I had to start somewhere. So I did." She scratched her knee. Jesse heard her fingernail as it bristled against her skin. "I couldn't sort through my perception of you: One day you were the only person I'd ever wanted to fall in love with, but the next day you were a cruel, selfish person who left and never looked back, never called … never seemed to care." She turned to Jesse in earnest. "I loved you with my whole heart, Jess. I know we talked about your move to L.A. I know that I encouraged you to pursue your dream, but it didn't stop the pain of losing you. You and me—that was *my* dream. So when I realized it was a lost cause—" Caitlyn tightened her lips, shook her head. "I tried so hard to hate you. I felt hurt and angry, did everything I could to despise you for not coming back."

Jesse nodded. "I can't blame you for that," he said, a mere whisper because he felt it was all the sound space he deserved to occupy.

"But here's what made it so frustrating: For whatever reason, a piece of me still loved you because I knew you *weren't* cruel or selfish—not in your heart." She paused. "You were scared."

Jesse gripped the arms of his chair.

She was right.

Scared to death. He'd never realized it before, but …

After all this time, he had never stepped back to ask *why* he took off. At first, he had tried to ignore his personal plight. Then feelings of guilt had resurfaced and consumed him, dominated his attention. Always faced with one distraction or another, he'd never sought an answer to *why*.

Stunned, he shook his head in awe. "You're right," he said and sifted through the revelation. "I know that doesn't begin to justify my self-centeredness, but life closed in and … I'd panicked when the pregnancy happened." He turned toward her. "How did you know that?"

"I knew you better than anyone. I knew your responses, how you react to situations that overwhelm you. And I knew, when you felt scared, you went into hiding—not literally, but in your own way. That's why you loved those high-school plays— you could hide behind the characters. But when you reach your limit, when there's nowhere to hide—you try to escape. So you ran to California to escape as far as you could. To escape from your dad's shadow, from your relationship with me—maybe even to escape yourself. Maybe you didn't like who you were." While her words hung in the tranquility of the air, the fireworks finished. Then she broke their silence, her voice in a search. "Is that why you came back home? Are you escaping something? Please tell me …"

Jesse remained silent, unable to attach words to what he wanted to say. He felt vulnerable and transparent. In her own tender way, Caitlyn, the girl he had loved, had now cut to his core. She had drawn to the surface who he truly was, forced him to confront himself in all his naked weakness. He was scared right now: nowhere to run, no mask to hide behind.

He was Jesse. She was Caitlyn. And in their moments of honesty, this was who they were together—they were at their best when together.

Caitlyn's eyes narrowed. She eased back. Neither angry nor offended, she seemed to understand his inner conflict. To change the subject, she chuckled and said, "Once Drew was born, I felt unprepared. I had no idea what to do with a baby. I only knew I wanted him."

"I'm glad you made that decision. I can't imagine him not here today."

Each of them stared at the sky, its hue in full darkness now, and counted stars. The smoky Fourth-of-July haze formed a screen across the stars and moon.

Touched, Jesse turned to Caitlyn and whispered. "Thank you, Cait."

She met his gaze. "For what?"

He scratched at his chair, then returned to her eyes again. "For believing in me," he said. "For believing the best."

By this time it was too dark to tell for sure, but Jesse thought he caught a flicker of a smile from her. His gaze lingered with hers a bit longer before she turned her attention back to the sky.

In the distance, several neighborhoods away, an isolated

firework popped, but it proved faulty, its yellow sparks sparse and lacking.

CHAPTER 41

"**D**ON'T you ever leave for lunch?" Jesse joked as he poked his head into Chuck's office. Bagged lunch in hand, he made his way inside.

Chuck peered up over his reading glasses. "I have a couple of hospital visits this afternoon, so I'll break away in a bit. Are you headed outside?"

"Yeah, just figured I'd check in on you."

"That's nice. Any particular reason?"

"No."

"What's for lunch?" Chuck gestured with his head to Jesse's plastic bag.

"PB and J—the meal of champions."

Chuck gave him a look of parental concern, one which a parent never seems to outgrow, no matter how old his kids are. "Are you sure you're eating enough? You've got cash, right?"

"Don't worry about it. You're forgetting I survived on the coast."

"Right." Chuck eyed his son. "So, how are you and Eden getting along sharing her place?"

The bag rattled as Jesse shifted it to his other hand. "You mean, have we managed to refrain from strangling each other? Sure thing! We take turns making dinner, plus she delights in having me as her personal maid to keep her house clean."

Chuck laughed. "It's good to see you two hang out together. I know she enjoys having you back."

Jesse watched as his father set his reading glasses aside. Chuck cleared the paperwork in front of him and rearranged a pile on one side of the desk. On the other side, a hardcover Bible commentary lay open, as did a Bible itself. Behind closed doors, the books served as evidence of what Jesse already knew: The minister that people saw in public operated with equal dedication in private. Despite the differences between Jesse and his father, Jesse respected the man's commitment to his beliefs. He admired Chuck's determination to weave those beliefs into his daily walk as he preached to his flock and encouraged those who, it seemed, wouldn't step through a church door. But to Jesse's surprise—and sometimes to Chuck's as well—some of those random acquaintances did indeed step through a church door eventually.

Yes, his father had caused himself headaches as a result of his own dedication. Jesse recalled when Chuck's faithfulness to his scruples had spurred problems with those who disagreed with what he preached or how he testified to God's goodness in his life. And, sad to say, sometimes those disagreements came from churchgoers with good intentions. Many forgot that, unlike Chuck, they had never walked in the shoes of a minister and lacked awareness of the considerations that came into play. Jesse could remember one such encounter, when an angry community alderman yelled at Chuck. The alderman's face looked as if blood boiled beneath the surface. After the encounter, Chuck tightened his jaw and went for a long, brisk walk around the church.

With regard to his critics, Chuck guarded his tongue and chose to avoid negative speech. Jesse remembered how he would hide and watch as his father escaped by himself to an empty field near their house. In such times, he'd see Chuck fall to his knees, lift his arms to heaven, and ask for guidance. Then his father, still alone, would start to worship in the field, just between God and him. Chuck always returned refreshed.

From across the desk, Jesse peered at Chuck's handwritten notes. "What are you working on?"

"I'm preparing for my sermon this weekend."

Since Chuck had always cooped himself up in his office to prepare his messages, Jesse had paid scant attention to his father's process. He'd seen Chuck preach but hadn't cared how it all came together. "Do you write them out word for word, and then memorize them?"

"Some ministers like to write them word for word. I'll jot down some notes beforehand, but I end up straying from them after the first ten minutes. It's God's church service; I figure He can take it in whatever direction He wants. When you get down to it, I'm just a guy who rides a motorcycle. Why God chose to use me as a preacher I'll never figure out."

"But how do you know God directs you?"

"Funny as it sounds, I don't think of myself as the one preaching. I look at myself as an empty vessel, and it feels like God speaks through me for an hour—God's words, something special He wants to share with the people in the room. The words seem to rise up, so I speak them. Later on, I don't always recall the details of what I said, but somehow God causes it to minister to somebody. That's what I love about it: God uses me as a tool to help people. But when I look in the Bible, I see that God doesn't to restrict that to preachers—He wants all of His people to carry inside them that sensitivity to His voice."

A knock on the door—Jesse forgot he'd left it open.

"Hi, Pastor Chuck. I didn't see Maureen outside, so she's probably out to lunch. But your door was open, and—"

"Come on in, Bethann."

"Oh, you have company! I'm sorry to interrupt. I came to pick up the paperwork for the youth trip. Do you happen to know where she left it?"

"Next to the fax machine, hidden from view. She said you might swing by," Chuck replied. He gestured to Jesse. "This is my son, Jesse."

With a warm smile, Bethann shook Jesse's hand. "Oh, how nice to finally meet you! I didn't know you live here."

"I lived in L.A. for a long time. Just came back three months ago."

"Bethann and her family moved here nine years ago," Chuck said.

Disinterested, Jesse feigned interest and nodded anyway. Jesse had met countless individuals who wanted to be personal friends with the minister; in response, Jesse had developed a habit whereby he disregarded them. After all, he had shared his father with them throughout his childhood.

Bethann was effervescent, a quality Jesse found genuine for some and a façade for others. Jesse tried to determine which of these he saw now.

"So tell me, do you plan to be a minister like your dad?"

Jesse detested that question. What was it with people? Who did they think they were? Why did they try to force their way into his life and expect him to live in his father's footsteps? He'd escaped this place to escape his father's shadow; yet no matter how many years passed, the issue continued to bubble up. Because he was the preacher's son, he'd felt shoved into a public spotlight, one where people seemed to feel an entitlement toward him, as if he were public property.

Jesse bit his lip—along with his tongue. Another irritation he endured as a preacher's son: Any outbursts of anger would reflect poorly on the preacher himself.

Chuck, with one look at his son's lips in compression, changed the subject. "We're content to let him become the next Marlon Brando instead. Thanks for taking the time to grab that paperwork."

"Not a problem." She offered Jesse a parting smile. "Nice to meet you."

Jesse painted himself a polite grin and gave her a two-finger wave. Bethann closed the door behind her.

Jesse still simmered beneath the surface.

"Sorry about that; she didn't mean to put you on the spot with the minister-to-be remark. People mean well." He examined his son, then added, "You know, you have me one-upped: I don't know firsthand how difficult it is to be a minister's kid."

Jesse pretended to shrug it off. "How do you know she's not faking it with all the God stuff—the happy face, the serving?"

"I've been her minister the whole time she and her family have lived here. I've watched her. I'm familiar with her spiritual growth. When you're the minister, you keep an eye out for wolves that try to penetrate the flock with harmful intentions."

"Isn't that a form of judging people?"

"It's a matter of protecting people. Nobody's perfect; any Christian who won't admit they have faults is lying to you. People who seek answers or seek to know God—they're welcome here no matter where they've been in life or what they've done. God never turned away the heart cries of people who sought Him. That's different from people who come to a church with the sole intention of causing disruption—I'll show them the door myself. As a minister, I'm a shepherd and I'll protect my sheep. Much like I protect my kids."

Jesse's jaw grew rigid. "So you're telling me if some prostitute or heroin addict who's still high walked into the church, they'd be welcome?"

"Absolutely."

"And the other people in the chairs are just waiting to say hello?"

"I hope so. If not, they need to stop and remember the way they used to be before they became a Christian."

"So you don't see a difference between right and wrong?"

"It's not a matter of right and wrong. It's about allowing people to change."

"So what do you think of me?" Jesse said.

"Truth?"

"Yeah."

"I think you're searching for something. I think you've decided to make a change somewhere in your life—exactly what, I don't know."

"You're telling me you never wondered what kind of life I lived in California?"

"Of course I did. But in the end, that's none of my business. Everyone walks through life their own way."

Jesse's guilt wrenched inside. "Geez!" he shouted. "Will you get angry at me *just once!* Stop being so fricking understanding all the time!"

"What do you want me to say?"

"Tell me I'm a screwup! Tell me I don't deserve to be in your family anymore! Tell me *something* that takes the guilt away!"

"Guilt? What guilt?"

"Never mind."

Still on his feet, Jesse fumed as tension hung thick as concrete in the air. He didn't know how these arguments began, but they had occurred often in the past.

Chuck appeared at a loss for words. "I don't think you're a screwup," he said at last.

"I wish you would."

"I don't see you that way. I remember where I came from before I was a minister, before I even met your mom—I was a teenager who got into a crowd I shouldn't have. Started smoking pot behind the factory where I worked in the summers—pot had just come on the scene at the time. Other details I'd be too embarrassed to go into." Chuck peered at his silent son. "I know the attraction in running wild. I've been there."

"You don't know anything about me. You don't know about my life—you don't even know about my last *six months!*"

Jesse wanted a remedy to take the stain away—the one that festered in him. When he searched for a way to erase it, to make up for his faults, he couldn't find one. Life had begun to improve with regard to Drew, Caitlyn and his family, but it wasn't enough. It didn't fulfill his yearning. Jesse wanted to be free. But the freedom he sought was internal, not external. He'd tried a physical escape to L.A., but to no avail. So he remained trapped.

"What are looking for from me, Jess?" Chuck said.

"I'm looking for a difference! You have no idea how I *detest* myself as a preacher's son! I hate that I'm considered open territory for anyone who's interested in my privacy. I hate that I've had to share you with anyone who asks! I hate that when I look at you, I see a part of me—because, and this might hurt you, but I don't want to be *you!* Do you realize I got *forced* into this?

You got a choice in the preacher thing; you chose to sacrifice your privacy. But I never got that choice! That's why I never visited: I didn't want the life you had to offer! Do you know what it's like to be fourteen years old and have adults scrutinize you, against your will, like they're entitled to it? Do you think I ever got a thank-you for it? I can't be the person *they* want me to be—I can't be you! I can't break away from it, but I can't reconcile it inside of me! And like it or not, when I see you, you symbolize the issue. When I see you, I'm reminded of my faults, of who I'll never become."

Angry, Jesse stormed out of the room. In the lobby, he passed Maureen—of course she had returned from lunch in time for the outbursts. She said nothing, but Jesse was sure she had heard plenty.

CHAPTER 42

HOURS later, still in a simmer from his argument with Chuck, Jesse clenched his jaw and grabbed a knife from its wooden block. He peeled an onion and, to vent his frustration, diced it with forceful chops. He picked up the scent of ground beef as it browned.

When Eden opened the door to the house, she heard the knife chops before she saw their source. Jesse's ears burned.

"What's for dinner?" Eden asked.

"Taco salad." With half the onion chopped, he used the blunt edge of the knife to slide the pieces into a large bowl of lettuce. Then he resumed with the other half of the onion.

Eden set her purse on the counter and took a seat. She crossed her arms and took in the sight of Jesse as he unleashed his anger on the innocent vegetable. "Are you okay?"

"Fine," he said in his irritated-guy grunt. His next verbal clue didn't arrive until he cut his finger by accident.

A minor cut, he shifted to the sink to wash it. Eden jumped up and headed over to him. When Jesse insisted he was okay, she finished the onion while he wrapped a clean paper towel around his finger and sat down at the table.

Elbow on the table, Jesse held his finger upward and applied pressure to the cut to aid the clotting. Besides his recent nosebleed symptoms, he had noticed cuts took longer to stop bleeding as well, so he waited.

The ground beef continued to snap and sizzle on the stove. The scent of black pepper and green chiles engulfed the kitchen. After she added the remaining ingredients to the salad bowl, Eden sat across from her brother. "What happened today? Why are you so ticked off?"

"It's nothing. I had a fight with Dad, that's all."

"Was it that bad?"

"No. I don't want to go into it."

"Maybe you should. Obviously, internalizing it hasn't helped." No response from Jesse, so Eden asked, "Why do you get so upset with Dad? It used to happen all the time. What did he do today?"

"It's not what he does—more like what he *doesn't* do. Look, it's confusing; I've never figured it out." Jesse took a deep breath. Lucky he hadn't sliced his hand, he figured a count to ten might serve him well at the moment. At last he said, "It's a constant frustration that doesn't go away."

"In you?" she clarified.

"Yeah," he admitted. "I feel a weird sense of guilt. And I can't escape it—it just lurks in me day and night. I end up so confused that I don't know what I feel or who I'm angry at: Dad or me."

"And this just started happening?"

"Are you kidding?" Jesse murmured. "It started when I was a kid—maybe fifteen." He stared at his finger, where blood had seeped through the layers of the paper towel. Jesse rewrapped the cut with the unstained portion of the towel. "I hate living in his shadow. If I imitate him, I'm a fake; if I act like myself, I make the preacher look bad. All I ever wanted was to break free," he said. "Geez, I just wanted to figure out who *I* am. That was the plan when I went to L.A. The acting didn't take off like

I'd hoped, but at least I was free to be myself—whatever that is."

Eden listened. Both of them were preacher's kids, but each had adapted in a manner that matched their respective personality. Eden hadn't found it problematic. Jesse, on the other hand, had sought unique opportunities to vent.

"You visited me out there," Jesse continued. "You know what I mean: The place is always full of *life*."

He watched her ponder this for a moment. Then she said, "I also remember you called it cosmetic over there, not to mention the pressure to project an image—kind of like a minister's kid in reverse."

"Sure it was cosmetic, but at least it was *active*." He bit the inside of his cheek, a nervous habit. "Maybe I have too much time to think here."

"To be honest, after all those visits, I never thought you seemed happy there."

"Things got dry the last couple of years. But before that, my life was in constant motion. Remember all the running around we did when you first visited? We had a blast."

"I'm not talking about external stuff. On the outside, yes, you seemed upbeat and at home. But I could sense sadness about you, the kind that dwelt deep down. I could see it in your eyes—a longing, a distanced look, the way you would gaze at the Hollywood hills. It's tough to hide your eyes, Jesse. It looked like dense smog settled into them, a heaviness that stood between you and the utopia you were seeking."

Jesse let out a soft, knowing laugh. "So many people there," he said, almost to himself. "How can someone be surrounded by people, by friends and a girlfriend, and yet feel so—alone?"

Eden allowed the comment to settle before she asked, "Have you talked to Jada lately?"

"No, I haven't." Jesse's finger had stopped bleeding. He headed to the wastebasket to toss the paper towel and wash his hands again. The meat for the taco salad looked ready. He tossed the salad, fixed two plates, and spooned the beef on top. After he brought two glasses of water and sat down again, Eden said grace over dinner and they started to eat.

"Don't take this the wrong way," she said. "But I saw the way you and Jada used to interact. I had the impression Jada was a distraction. A *welcome* distraction: It got your mind off other things."

Jesse relented. "Psychoanalysis from a social worker," he quipped. "And your diagnosis?"

Eden acknowledged his prods with a grin, yet kept her words sincere. "Maybe you felt a hole inside and tried to use Jada to fill it."

With a snicker, Jesse swallowed a bite. "I think we used each other."

A pause.

"Do you miss her?" Eden asked.

He mulled it over. "I thought I would. We'd been knotted together for years, kind of like a habit—a bad one, it turned out." He shrugged and chewed on a diced tomato. "Things got rocky toward the end. We started to coast; she became bored with the relationship. It crashed and burned. Finally, she broke it off and kicked me out of the apartment. Her name was the only one on the lease."

Eden furrowed her eyebrows, as if she sensed a missing detail. "So why did you turn back to Ohio?"

Jesse pursed his lips. "Why not? Where else would I go?

Besides, the thought of Cait haunted me, drew me home. Jada knew nothing about Cait or the pregnancy, but she could tell I kept secrets from her." He paused. "I'd gotten tired of it anyway, I suppose—tired of putting on a false front. I mean, even the palm trees are spaced apart perfectly. Remember? All along Ventura Boulevard." He speared a trio of kidney beans with his fork. "At this point, I even look forward to the first foot of snow here."

He heard Eden crunch on a taco chip. When she swallowed, she gestured toward him with her fork.

"I think the life's returned to your eyes since you came back—the life that seemed missing on the coast," she said.

He nodded. "Yeah, I missed having you around. And Cait's played a big part, too." His fork clinked against the plate as he set it down. "What a contrast between Caitlyn and Jada, huh?"

Eden feigned surprise. "Oh, you noticed?"

"Jada seemed exciting when she and I first met. She personified what I searched for: the exact opposite of what I'd come from. That's where it ended, though."

"What do you mean?"

"She had no depth. Not like Caitlyn. Look at Cait's compassion, her patience ..."

"Deep down, I believe Caitlyn saw those qualities in you, too."

"Yeah," Jesse said. "Maybe she did."

Late that night, as Jesse lay in bed, he squinted at a lone stream of moonlight that filtered through lace curtains into the otherwise pitch-black room. From the open window, a gentle breeze trickled in. He could hear the hypnotic tick of a clock, which emanated from another room and teased the silence.

His alarm clock taunted 1:41 a.m. Nowhere near sleep, Jesse got out of bed. He pulled on a T-shirt and shorts, shoes and socks. From the dresser a few steps away, he grabbed his keys and cell phone—*funny how we grab that along with our keys nowadays,* he thought—then slipped out of the house.

Beneath a starlit sky and a half moon, Jesse immersed himself in the stillness of the night. He walked down Route 91, which, by this time, lacked the hum of automobiles in the distance. When he arrived home at this hour after late film shoots in L.A., he used to rush down the street to reach his apartment. Only in the Midwestern suburbs could he walk alone in the ink of night and feel secure. While others slept, this present tranquility afforded him the chance to clear his head and gain perspective.

The air felt so fresh here. Unblemished by angry particles of smoggy tar. Pure.

He reflected on his argument with Chuck and the subsequent discussion with Eden. Regret settled in with regard to his father—not a regret of torment, but a reaction of love to a father who exuded love. Perhaps Jesse himself needed to change. Yes, he admitted to himself: After years of carefree—and, in the end, uncommitted—living, he had bypassed certain aspects of maturity. In the past, he merely needed to get by.

But no longer. Like a foreign piece to a mismatched puzzle, such an approach to life proved unfitting and unwelcome.

Life seemed different now, enhanced for the better. His perspective broadened. He had a child he vowed not to turn his back upon.

On his right, he turned into a neighborhood and walked down streets awash in a streetlamp cascade. Jesse felt his skin glow in the balmy July air. The moon, which cast fluorescent beams across the homes, also instigated shadows around the corners. Row after row, darkened house after darkened house, this community slept.

He reached into his pocket. Cell phone in hand, he flipped it open and dialed Chuck's phone number—his office number to avoid waking him. At the voice-mail cue, Jesse paused. He didn't have a speech prepared. No explanation to justify his behavior or his lack of regard.

Instead, he spoke from the simplicity of his heart.

"It's me," he said. "I'm sorry." How many arguments, what lack of appreciation and recognition of value, he sought to cover with that single phrase. "I'm just … I'm sorry."

He lowered his head, snapped the phone shut—and savored the wave that washed through his fibers. Another good decision stacked upon the others. Step by step.

As he took a deep breath, he stopped for a minute and took in another glimpse of the moon. He watched as it assumed the role of backlight for thin clouds that crept across it like paranormal fingers.

Tired at last, he turned around and headed back to Eden's house.

CHAPTER 43

"READY to go?" Jesse asked as he strolled into Blake's shop.

He caught Blake and Eden in the midst of flirtation at the counter.

Eden pecked Blake on the lips. "I'll meet you there," she said and headed out the door.

Blake admired his girlfriend as she left, then turned to Jesse. "Almost ready. I need to wrap up a few things up before I leave." He snatched a tiny container from the counter and tossed it to Jesse. "Here, take a bottle."

"What are these, pills?"

"Vitamins. It's a new brand. Just got a bunch of samples the other day." He thumped Jesse on the chest. "Have you taken your vitamin today, young man?"

Jesse rolled the container in his hand.

Blake proceeded to lock the door—he closed up shop at six o'clock on Friday evenings—and rang out the day's totals at the register. The shop was empty, his assistant gone.

"I hear you're seeing Caitlyn again," Blake said.

"I don't know if 'seeing' is the right word, but we've spent time together lately."

"Long time since that happened, huh?"

"That's for sure. She's much the same, though."

Blake stopped for a second. "I don't think I've seen her since she watched our games in high school."

Guarded, Jesse wasn't sure how much detail Blake knew, and he didn't want to open the floodgates.

Back at the counter, Blake noticed Jesse's hesitation and shut the cash register's tray. "Eden told me a couple of months ago, after you returned—about Caitlyn and Drew, that is. I hope that doesn't bother you."

"No, I'm not concerned about you," Jesse replied. But Eden had promised she would tell only Blake. "Does anyone else know?"

"Nobody else. She swore me to secrecy," Blake said. "But I wanted to let you know you have another person in your corner."

Jesse nodded. "So how serious are you and Eden? She wouldn't confide in you if she didn't see long-term potential. Is marriage inevitable?"

Blake shied away. "I'm sure it is, but not for at least another year. I'm ready to expand to a second shop; I want that established beforehand so Eden would have solid support." He ran his thumb up the palm of one hand. "I know marriage is a dream of hers."

"That's an understatement. She started planning her wedding when she was eight years old."

"I wouldn't doubt it," Blake snickered. "But I think it's deeper than that. For her, it represents more."

Jesse's approval of his sister's boyfriend continued to grow. "How so?"

"She and I haven't discussed the why behind the what," Blake replied. "But I believe it's because your mom died so young. I think Eden wants to be a wife and mom—the wife and mom she never got to have firsthand."

"It didn't seem to bother her as a kid. I asked her about it, and she seems to cope fine."

"She's a strong person. She manages it well. I'll bet it didn't surface until she was a teenager, and that's when you headed out of town. At that point, she only had to downplay it from you on the phone, plus a week whenever she'd visit you."

"I guess you're right." Jesse mulled it over. "All this time, she's held strong for me while she hurt inside."

"Don't worry about it. It wasn't quite like that," Blake said. "More like it's buried inside her, and it comes to the surface now and then. She's fine; it's just that there's an empty hole there." Blake gave the countertop a decisive tap with his fingertips. "And eventually that hole will be filled." He paused, then asked, "How *did* your mom die, anyway?"

Caught off guard, Jesse exhaled and tried to decide where to begin.

Blake stopped him. "Sorry, man. No need to answer. I didn't mean to pry; I'd wondered but didn't want to bring it up with Eden."

"It's not a big deal," Jesse replied in a matter-of-fact tone. "I was three years old back then. I don't remember much about Mom—just minor details, like her long hair, same color as Eden's. I remember her hugging me one day when I was a year old, maybe because there are so few memories to choose from and that one's branded in me." Jesse grinned. "I do remember her belly getting huge and my asking why, even though she'd told me several times already—I guess a kid can't fully comprehend it, so he keeps asking. When she told me a little brother or sister slept inside, it amazed me. I asked what kind of clothes it wore in there.

"One day, back when we lived in Albuquerque, my grandma picked me up from preschool, which struck me as odd because Mom always picked me up. I asked Grandma why she came to get me. She said Dad had to take Mom to the hospital to have the baby, so I would stay overnight at Grandma's house. Grandma and I played kid games all evening." Jesse paused as a shiver crawled up his spine. "Then a phone call came in the middle of the night. Grandma had one of those rotary phones, and its bell ringer pierced the silence in her house. I could hear her answer in her bedroom, but her voice sounded muffled from where I lay. Even as a kid, I thought she sounded excited, then a bit concerned. But I drifted off to sleep and forgot about the call.

"The next morning, Grandma seemed sad. Dad came by to pick me up—this was long before he was a preacher. I asked him where Mom and the baby were. Dad said the baby was at the hospital and that we were going to see her—'your baby sister, Eden.' He didn't say anything about Mom.

"When we got outside, I asked about Mom again." A film of tears glazed the surface of Jesse's eyes, but he blinked them away. He refused to shed anything in public. "Dad stopped walking. He seemed tired—not impatient with me, just … tired. He took me by the hand, and led me to Grandma's backyard. He sat me down on the back porch steps and knelt down to face me eye to eye. 'Mommy's in heaven.' Those were his exact words, sort of said them under his breath. 'Why?' I asked. Dad told me giving birth had been tough on Mom—and she had died. He tried to explain death to my 'kid brain.' I pictured her sitting on a cloud."

Embarrassed he'd even asked, Blake said, "I'm sorry. Don't tell me any more—I shouldn't have asked."

"No, I want to," Jesse said. "I haven't talked about it in so long, and it follows me everywhere I go." Jesse took a deep breath and continued. "Dad explained the situation to me when I got older. During the delivery, Mom experienced complications, so they needed to do an emergency C-section on her. She started to hemorrhage and lose blood fast. It happened in the mid 1980s, when they discovered some of the blood supplies tainted with HIV. Everyone was on high alert, and for a while, they didn't know which blood supplies were safe. Some doctors were scared to use the blood and made individual judgment calls. So when Mom started to lose her blood, the doctor hesitated to expose her to a transfusion. He believed she would make it through the emergency, but soon the situation got worse. When he finally decided the transfusion was necessary ..." Before his next words, Jesse seared his lips shut for a moment. "It was too late," he said. "They lost her."

In a trance, Jesse shook his head. His own nosebleeds had sparked memories of his mother's blood loss, which, in turn, had introduced a fresh aspect of heartache. Yet Jesse pressed on with his story. His face blushed from emotion. "Dad wasn't a Christian at the time, so he didn't know anything about prayer—said he didn't even *think* of praying.

"Dad told me that in the weeks after Mom's death, he spent a lot of time in solitude, withdrew from everyone except Eden and me. While he was alone, he says, he could sense God's hand on him, a touch of compassion. He could sense God's help as he balanced full-time work with single fatherhood. When Dad came through the ordeal, he says, he looked back at how God had protected and cared for him and his kids. *He wanted to know that God.* That's when he became a Christian. And not long after that, because he'd felt God's love and comfort through the storm of loss, he knew he wanted to become a minister. Says he wanted to help others to know that love."

To preserve his friend's dignity, Blake avoided eye contact with Jesse. But it proved unnecessary: Jesse, who absorbed himself in his story, had forgotten where he was and to whom he talked. His cheeks and nose felt hot from the sensation of restrained adrenaline.

Jesse stared at the floor in downcast concentration. He shook his head in disbelief. "What kind of God would allow such a thing to happen to two little kids? To allow a little girl to never meet her mother? I don't understand. It's not disrespect, just frustration. Confusion." He looked up at Blake again. "I had blind faith as a kid. But when I got older, these questions came to mind. And I don't have answers for them."

Blake shrugged in a resigned manner. "Neither do I. I wish I did, but I don't know what to say or where to begin."

"If I could come to terms with those questions, I think I could move on with my life."

Jesse paused.

"If God could speak," Jesse murmured.

––––––––––

That evening, after Jesse, Eden and Blake had eaten dinner at Blake's house, Jesse drove home alone.

As he reflected on his conversation with Blake a few hours before, his eyes watered. Weary from the emotional cleansing of the last several months, he tried to smother the thoughts and hold back the tears. Successful at first, his mind soon wandered back and those tears welled up once again. Vision blurred, he pulled over to the shoulder of the road, put the car in park, and shut off the engine. Then a dam broke loose inside him.

Anger. That's what he felt.

Anger toward the past. Anger toward God. Anger because he cried like a defeated soul.

His face crimson, he pounded the dashboard with ball of his palm.

Pound!

Anger released.

And again: *Pound!*

Pound, pound, pound!

Jesse screamed with fury and fire. Hot tears darted down his cheeks; their saline stung as they settled upon his lower lip.

"I don't understand this, God!" Jesse screamed. "I just need an answer!" He waited, then screamed again. "*Are You listening to me?!*"

Then he sank back in the seat, went limp, his hand at rest on his forehead. He rubbed his eyes dry.

He looked up but found his view of heaven blocked by the fuzzy beige interior of his car.

Vulnerable, Jesse settled down. His voice softened to a plea.

"If You can answer me, I think I'll be okay."

Jesse listened. He heard nothing. With its windows rolled up, the car felt muggy; Jesse's warm breath enhanced its temperature.

"Can You hear me?" Jesse whispered in desperation.

He waited. Then he asked again.

"Can You hear me?" Jesse craved a reply, a sign—*something*. But nothing came.

"Where are You, God …"

CHAPTER 44

IN Jesse's opinion, Brandywine Falls, a natural waterfall in Cuyahoga Valley National Park, was well worth the short drive required to get there. He craved the ambience of water today.

The walkway, made of wooden planks and railings, wound beside the Falls in a gradual descent. Though Jesse and Drew could hear the rush of water, its source was not yet within view. Surrounded by the lush foliage of the shallow woods, they strolled down the walkway, side by side, Jesse's camera in Drew's grip.

As they passed a grandmother who tried to control her brood of grandkids, Jesse turned to Drew. "Have you been here before, buddy?"

"No," Drew replied. The Falls represented one of those nearby natural attractions that falls victim to taken-for-granted status: If you're not careful, you might not get around to a visit until your latter years. As a father, Jesse determined to bring value to his son's life, even if it started with new experiences that other kids might consider ordinary.

"They have a bed and breakfast here," Jesse said. "That's sorta like a hotel, but more like a house."

Drew clucked his tongue, appeared content with Jesse's attention regardless of what they talked about.

The rush of water amplified, its sound akin to a hundred

bathtubs filling with maximum gusto. Its echo bounced among the leaves in nature's version of a relay race. Unseen birds chirped from camouflaged branches. Jesse picked up the strong scent of foliage around him.

"So, you told me there's a girl you kinda like," Jesse said with a poke to Drew's ribs. The kid smelled like cookies. "Does she have a name?"

His face in a blush, Drew tried to hide his laughter. "No."

"She doesn't have a name?"

"Her name is No."

"Clever."

"Maggie."

"Maggie. Hmm …" Jesse rubbed his chin and feigned contemplation. "Yeah, Maggie. I like the name Maggie."

"Good, 'cause I'd need to beat you up if you didn't," Drew joked. "Do you like the name Caitlyn?"

"Of course."

Three observation points, located at different heights, provided views of the Falls from different angles. As they reached the first point—the uppermost, from which you can look down upon the Falls—Drew raced toward the railing and snapped a wide-angle picture of the water as it poured forth in a forceful flow. After that, the kid leaned over the railing, took note of the distance to the bottom of the gorge, then spat down into it and counted the seconds until contact. Regardless of the decade, some aspects of childhood remain the same, Jesse mused.

Jesse considered this observation point his favorite. From this height, the waterfall's strength seemed muted, something you could harness. He imagined God hovering over a world where nothing escapes His view, where looming circumstances appear miniscule in the grand scheme of life. Jesse leaned over the railing beside his son, closed his eyes, and listened to the rolling water—much more contained than the Pacific, but more active than Lake Erie.

When a retired couple approached the railing, Drew held the camera out to the lady. "Excuse me, ma'am. Could you take a picture of us, please?"

The lady, in her early eighties by Jesse's estimation, appeared as though a face lift had made a cameo appearance in a past life. Jesse grimaced at the impression that this couple still enjoyed an active sex life. Horrified, he shook the thought from his head and swallowed the bile in his mouth.

With proud satisfaction, Jesse humored the scene before him, in which Drew explained to Sexy Grandma how to use the camera and mimicked Jesse's tutorial on shutter speed. She would shoot two people who stood still, Drew pointed out, so he'd go with a low speed if he were her.

The lady backed up into position. Then Drew bounded over to Jesse and wrapped his arm around his older buddy's waist, their backs to the railing and the Falls in the background.

One photo snap and Sexy Grandma returned the camera to Drew. "Are you brothers?" she asked.

Jesse swallowed. Eighteen years apart—and both young through this lady's eyes—he could understand how she might have drawn the conclusion.

Drew told her Jesse was a friend of his mom's, which elicited an aw-how-nice reply. Jesse and Drew thanked Sexy Grandma again before she and her boyfriend waved and sauntered off, hand in hand, in search of the next observation point and a fountain of youth. The image of the couple's love life re-emerged in Jesse's head.

"Geez, I hate to think of those two in the bedroom," Jesse muttered to no one in particular.

Drew glanced up. "Huh?"

Jesse gritted his teeth. He'd slipped with that comment, accustomed to former days when he joked with Gavin. In an attempt to recover, Jesse replied, "They probably hang posters of black-and-white movies. Can you imagine?" Relieved that Drew bought his explanation, Jesse hoped he hadn't caused long-term damage for the kid. He made a mental note to guard his future comments.

Before they headed further down the walkway, Jesse rested his arms against the railing. He took a last glimpse of the waterfall. From the corner of his eye, he noticed Drew lean closer toward him. Drew focused on Jesse's face as though he searched for clues.

Jesse chuckled and asked, "What are you doing, bud?"

"Looking for something," Drew replied, half absent.

"Looking for what?"

"You have eyes like mine."

Taken aback, Jesse said, "What? What do you mean?"

Drew shrugged. "When I was, like, four years old, I asked my mom what my dad looks like, and she said he has eyes like mine. So sometimes I look at people's eyes. Did you know both of us have green eyes?"

"Oh. Yeah, that's cool, huh?"

"Kinda cool." And that was all.

Jesse's heart started to beat again now that he realized Drew hadn't put two and two together. Had Drew drawn a conclusion, Caitlyn would have freaked out.

How do I measure up with this fatherhood thing? Jesse wondered.

They strolled further down the walkway, further into the gorge. As they walked, the rubber soles of their sneakers clomped on the wooden planks.

When they reached the second observation point, which unveiled the Falls once again, Drew hopped over to the banister to absorb the beauty at mid level. Much closer to them now, this same waterfall seemed larger, more ominous and intimidating than before. It reminded Jesse of his own finite vulnerability.

Drew snapped more pictures. "This one's my favorite so far," he said. "I want to take a good one for my mom."

"Seems more intense from this angle, doesn't it?"

Drew developed a glint in his eye, a hint of dominion as he stared at the rush of water. "I'd like to ride down it in a jet ski."

The things you can learn from an innocent kid, Jesse thought. What one sees as a formidable foe, another sees as an opportunity to conquer.

With his eyes still glued to the Falls, Drew's wistful smile faded. "What's it like to have a dad?" he asked.

Jesse bumped his knee against the railing, caught by surprise at the question. "Kind of like having a mom, I suppose. Except your dad is a guy." While Jesse had taken the concept for granted, how foreign it seemed to Drew. The kid truly wanted to know; Jesse had forgotten Drew's limited knowledge consisted of an outsider's observation and the kid's own imagination.

"What's *your* dad like?" Drew pressed. "Does he remember your birthday?"

"I'm sure he does. But we didn't talk to each other on my birthday. Didn't speak to him often. For a while, I didn't even visit him."

Drew looked up at Jesse. "How long?"

"Lots of years."

Nonchalant, Drew puffed his cheeks. "If I had a dad, I'd make sure I talked to him every day," he said. Jesse nodded. Maybe his son's emotions had dried up at some point in the past—when Drew discovered he needed to grow up before his time. "Does your dad love you?" asked Drew.

"Yes, he does." The things Jesse deemed commonplace, for which Drew seemed to have radar. "We didn't always under-stand each other, though."

"Are you interested in different things? He likes football and you like baseball?"

"I guess you could say we were interested in different things. Better to say we didn't see eye to eye on much."

"But he still wants to be your friend anyway?"

Jesse chuckled. "Yeah, he does." He scruffed the top of Drew's head. "He'll love me no matter what stupid choices I've made."

Drew scratched at a splinter on the railing, then said, "If I could pick a dad, I'd want him to be like you."

In that instant, Jesse's heart ached, a soaked towel wrenched by large hands. His joy motivated him to hug his son, but Jesse knew he couldn't. "What makes you say that?" Jesse asked instead.

"It's fun to hang out with you. When you take me places, it makes me feel good. No one else did that for me before," Drew said. "That's how I'd want my dad to treat me. And also you listen to me."

Of course; you're my son, Jesse thought. "Of course; you're my buddy."

"Plus you're nice to my mom. That makes her feel good."

"Your mom approves of me?"

"I think she likes you okay. Lately she's acted a lot happier than I've seen her in, well, I can't remember how long." Shoulders loose, Drew grew more relaxed as he spoke. He crossed his arms on the railing and rested his chin on them.

Jesse felt a bittersweet pang in his gut as he watched his son. "Takes some of the pressure off you when your mom's happy, huh?"

"Yeah." Drew pressed his lips together.

"Your mom loves you so much."

Drew furrowed his brow. He gave Jesse a fleeting glance. "Sometimes if I feel like I need my dad, I pretend you're my dad and it makes me feel better," Drew said. He looked up with innocent eyes. "Is that okay?"

Words couldn't express how impacted Jesse felt. He leaned down and gave his son a side hug. "That's fine, buddy," Jesse said. "You pretend all you want."

Jesse nudged Drew and, in unison, they pushed away from the railing.

Without another word, they continued down the walkway to the final observation point.

Father and son.

CHAPTER 45

ON the ride home, Jesse drove out of his way to further stretch his one-on-one time with Drew. They stopped at a gas station along Route 91 in Twinsburg, just north of Hudson, where Jesse pumped gas while Drew waited in the car.

"Jesse?"

From around the side of the pump peered Sanders, one of the high school pals with whom Jesse had reunited a few months back. Sanders had stopped by the Saturday Jesse and Blake had played their pickup basketball game. Jesse hadn't seen the guy since.

Arms crossed, dressed in worn jeans and a printed T-shirt, Sanders walked around the pump to make casual conversation. "Where are you coming from?" he asked.

"Brandywine Falls. First time since I came back home." Jesse wondered at this old pal. Married, kids and divorced so young? Jesse still found it hard to believe.

Over Jesse's shoulder, Sanders caught sight of Drew, who scrolled through previews of that afternoon's shots in the front passenger seat. Sanders nodded toward the car. "Who's that?"

Jesse pivoted on his heels, his adrenaline in a spike—he'd forgotten about Drew. To Jesse's relief, he found the boy occupied and out of earshot. Only Eden and Blake knew of Drew and of Jesse's reunion with Caitlyn. Jesse didn't want to offer details to anyone else; not even Drew knew the story yet. "Oh, that—I'm babysitting for someone's kid. Just for today," he said.

"Babysitting for *who*?"

"You don't know them. Someone I knew from the old days. I've kind of known the kid since he was born." To Jesse's relief, the gas pump clicked off. Desperate to change the subject, he said, "Gotta go."

"Listen, I'm getting together with some people tonight," Sanders said. "Having a few brewskies. Want to meet up? I mean, unless you're *babysitting*."

Jesse considered the offer. Since his fateful night in L.A., Jesse had managed without a drop of alcohol, aside from his beer at the Indians game, where Drew had questioned him about the beverage choice. Jesse felt snakebitten by the L.A. incident and veered away from the stuff ever since. The more he thought about it, he more he realized he'd felt quite content without the buzz.

On the other hand, Jesse detested the fear that had domi-nated his year: fear of failure, fear of fatherhood, fear of what people would think of him. He didn't want to add fear of alco-hol to the list.

To stall for time, Jesse returned the nozzle to the pump and twisted the cap back on the car. Then he glanced at the car window, where Drew continued to scroll. Jesse sensed an inkling of doubt.

Then again, he'd progressed so far. A few beers, no big deal. Jesse could feel the relaxation ooze through his bones already.

"Why not?" Jesse said. "Where should I meet you?"

———————

At one in the morning, the sky was overcast, the moon

invisible. As usual, the streets were empty. They had met at Sanders's apartment, less than a mile from Eden's house.

It was a wonder Jesse made it home in one piece. Not that Jesse realized it.

Drunk, he stumbled toward Eden's front porch. Along the way, he tripped over a step in the darkness and smacked his shoulder against her front door with a loud thump. Though he fumbled with his keys, he managed to find the correct one before he tried—unsuccessfully—to insert it into the keyhole. At last, he gave up, sat on the concrete, and giggled.

The porch light flipped on. Jesse squinted.

"It's the middle of the night," Eden hissed as she opened the door. "What are—" She knelt beside him. His clothes reeked of alcohol—and what smelled like a trace of marijuana. "Are you drunk?" she asked in a harsh, low voice. "Look at me," she said.

Head in his hands, Jesse laughed some more.

Though her eyes looked livid, Eden maintained her composure. With Jesse's stupor, lashing out would have accomplished nothing anyway. She grabbed him by the arm. "Come on."

At first he resisted, but then yielded when she tugged again. Eden led him into the living room, where he made it as far as the couch before he decided to settle there for the night.

Impatient, Eden grabbed his arms and shook him. "Drew wasn't with you, was he?" she demanded through clenched teeth.

Jesse told the truth: "No."

"Were you doing drugs too?"

"No," he said, again the truth.

As Jesse erupted in a series of spontaneous giggles, Eden looked closer at his face.

Between bursts of laughter, Jesse's face winced—back and

forth, humor and hurt, pleasure and pain. Overcome by the effects of the alcohol, sadness permeated his eyes, an agony of regret. Even while under the influence, Jesse wished he hadn't made this mistake.

He began to blather and struggled to construct a cohesive thought. "Painkillers would be bad right now," he said. "Hide the painkillers, Eden …" Then another wince of pain in his face.

"What? You don't make any sense." With another fierce look, Eden got up and flipped off the light. "Go to sleep."

––––––––––––––

His lapse the previous night hung heavy on both Jesse's mind and heart. He tallied all the people he'd let down in a matter of hours—Eden, as well as Caitlyn and Drew, although they were unaware of what happened. Jesse had also let himself down, but that was the least of his concerns.

His appetite ruined, he skipped lunch. As he sat on the floor of the worship auditorium and polished the woodwork along the platform, he vowed never to touch alcohol again. This wasn't a religious decision for him; rather, he acknowledged his contentment during the drink's absence and, well, it marked yet another piece that no longer fit into his life.

He heard a knock on one door, its volume stymied by the immensity of the room. When he lifted his head, he noticed Eden stood in the doorway. Furious, she made a beeline for him before he could get a word out.

"What's the matter with you?!" she shouted.

At her voice, the final remnant of a hangover-induced headache, which had killed him all morning, clanged along the periphery of his skull. By now, however, the pain felt much less prominent. "I apologize." He darted his eyes toward the doorway and hoped no one else could hear.

Eden lowered her voice. "You could have gotten yourself killed!" she hissed. "You have no idea how much I wanted to smack you last night! What if Drew had been in the car with you when you drove drunk?!"

Jesse held his palms out to stop her. "I'm sorry. Look, there's nothing you can say that I haven't already said to myself."

She stared at him, her face flushed, but he could tell she tried to determine his sincerity.

Eden shook her head, sat down on the platform steps, and took a deep breath. "Maybe I shouldn't have blown up at you. I'm not usually so abrupt, but you had me wide awake until sunrise, so now I'm worn out." She crossed her arms. "Wait, why am I apologizing to you? You're a guest in my house. You owe me an explanation."

And Jesse didn't disagree. He rested his forehead on his hand and cast his gaze toward the floor.

"So what happened?" she pressed.

"All the progress I'd made—I botched it up last night," he murmured. "Remember Sanders from high school? Guy with the jet-black hair? I ran into him yesterday; he invited me over for a few beers, casual. I was sick of all my fear, so I figured it wouldn't hurt. When I walked into his apartment, I hung out with a few people I'd never met. It started out with a beer around a ball game on TV, then more people showed up and things snowballed. By that point, I'd had a few drinks and gotten careless. I did stay away from the pot one of the guys brought, though."

"You mentioned that to me while you were drunk, but I'm

thankful to hear it's true. It explains why I smelled marijuana all over your clothes when I found you on my porch."

"The rest of the details are a bit fuzzy—I had a bit too much to drink, not that you didn't notice. Thank you for getting me inside, by the way."

"Yeah, not a problem," she muttered.

Because sarcastic replies from Eden were rare, this one pricked Jesse's heart. "I had a hunch the whole get-together would be bad news, but I went ahead anyway." Jesse hunched over a tad. "I don't think I fit into that crowd anymore. And you know what else? I don't think I *want* to fit into that scene anymore. If I were to say I enjoyed myself, it would be a lie. Once the drinking turned heavy, I sat alone on a chair in the corner of the room and watched everyone else have a deranged time—that much I remember. I just sat there and stared at them, realized I felt like ..."

"Sorrow?" Eden's face suggested her anger had thawed.

"No, I felt like a stranger. A stranger in a crowd of jumbled voices. I felt purposeless: the opposite of the joy I've come to know with Cait and Drew."

Jesse felt uncomfortable, and Eden must have picked up on it. She folded her hands together, rested her elbows on her knees. She bit her lip in concentration. "What else happened last night?"

"That's the whole story," Jesse said. "Actually, it's not a matter of what happened; more a matter of what *didn't* happen."

"Meaning what?"

"In my old life, I'd walked into many shabby situations, some of them worse than last night—too humiliating to mention." He flashed through mental images of nights smoking marijuana with Jada, his mistake with Adam Lewis, his suicide attempt. But Jesse kept these memories to himself. "A year ago, I would have considered recklessness normal, but my life has changed since then. And last night, I couldn't even *force* myself to enjoy it." Jesse paused. "I tried; I tried to relieve the stress and confusion and frustration, but I just can't do it anymore. Not that way."

"Why not?"

"Drew, Cait. You." With mounting fervency, he clenched his fists against his lap. "The whole time I was under the influence, one beer after the next, deeper and deeper, I tried to escape—it felt like a thick veil. The further I dove into it, the sadder and lower I got instead of getting free." He rubbed the polishing cloth against the shiny wooden surface. "Not long before I returned to Ohio, I started to go through a self-evaluation whenever I was under the influence: a guilty conscience, thoughts about Cait and the baby I thought we'd lost. But last night, even though my heart cried out on their behalf, I resisted it and paid the price."

Jesse felt horrible. In social work, Eden could detect an act when she saw it. But it wouldn't have taken a social worker to identify Jesse's regret as genuine.

Jesse turned toward his sister. "Last night, the sense that I'd let Cait and Drew down took a heavier toll: I'm an active part of their lives now. And it became real to me that every step I take, I'm responsible to them. Selfish missteps are a form of betrayal to them."

Eden eased, even smiled. "Don't underestimate your progress, despite the hiccup last night. I have hiccups myself—look at the way I barged in here today." She shrugged her shoulders. "Was your action inexcusable? No question. But I've seen so many cases where fathers showed no conscience whatsoever toward their kids, where missteps meant nothing to them."

Jesse's eyes became steel. "If Cait and Drew had known what I'd done, it would have hurt them deeply—especially Drew. What a disappointment. I won't do it again. I can't."

His sister patted him on the knee. "I know you won't." And her gesture let Jesse know she meant it.

Intrigued, Jesse scrutinized her. "You know what astounds me about you? You carry perpetual hope inside. You see the best in me—better than I see in myself." Of all his sister's qualities, this was the one he appreciated most. Regardless of where he'd lived, or what he'd done, or how he'd failed over the years, in the midst of his disillusionment he would talk to her, desperate for the hope that emanated from her. "When you look at me, you see my potential as a good father and brother, an asset, a success in life. But it's not just with me; you see that hope in pretty much everyone. And I don't understand it." He paused. "Why? Why would you see potential in such a hopeless situation?"

She spread her arms as if to wave the answer off as obvious. "That's what faith is: believing *before* you see it, knowing in your heart it's there, even if it's not evident to your eyes."

"You mean God."

"Yeah. Take the wind, for example: When you look outside, you can't see the wind; it's invisible to the eye. But you can't deny its reality because you can witness its effects: leaves rattle on the trees, a chilly breeze on your arms, or the jolt in your car when a gust of wind hits it on the highway. You know the wind is there. But to accept it existence, you need to be willing to look beyond what you see. That's what faith is—faith in someone's potential, faith in God. People with faith see with their hearts before they see with their eyes, and they believe."

"I understand faith," Jesse said. "I believe God exists. I even had faith in Jesus as a kid, but I started to question it later—not question whether Jesus ever lived or that He's a religious figure. But when I looked around and saw bad things happen, I wondered how someone could put their whole faith in Him. It just started to seem like religious mysticism to me. Don't you ever wonder if that's all it is? I mean, Jesus the religious figure and Jesus the human being, those are historical. But what about the miracle-working Jesus that Dad talks about? Or the Jesus that supposedly healed people? Doesn't that seem like a myth when you see people in pain?"

Eden didn't argue or grow irritable; she listened. Then she replied, "I wish I had all your answers; I don't. But I see the other angle of it, the wind angle: I see the effect of Jesus in people, and I can't deny it's there."

"Well, you and I were raised the same way. Where'd the difference come in?"

Eden thought for a moment. "You and I are accustomed to our quality of life: We take it as a given—and lose sight of the details before we realize it. But two years after you went to California, when I was still in high school, I went on a mission trip to Zimbabwe for a week one summer. A group of us high-school kids from church went with another organization that had established itself in that country, and we built a small shelter for kids who had lost their parents due to HIV. AIDS was rampant over there, the nation's economy had already experienced sky-high inflation, and those people were so poor. For the Christians in Zimbabwe, Jesus meant everything—He was all some of them had, and the others were just plain downtrodden. The people in that country hurt so bad, and the ones who would listen to us opened their hearts to the gospel." Eden had an intense longing in her eyes, as though she craved to see the people one more time. "They wanted to know there's hope." Eden's face flushed; she clenched a fist. She seemed to search for words to depict how she felt inside. "I believe in hope. I want people to know there's hope."

What she said incited nervousness in Jesse, yet he wanted to hear more. So he sat still. He weighed each word she spoke, absorbed every nuance.

As she recalled details from the past, Eden's lips tightened and her eyes danced. She continued, "What I said about believing God because you can see His effect—I saw it over in Zimbabwe. People walked up to us, curious about the building. Because English is prevalent there, we talked to people as we worked. A woman came up—this woman had lost her husband and a kid to AIDS, and now tried to raise the rest of her kids by herself. She was desperate for hope." Eden wiped a tear from her cheek. "I saw that woman give her life to Christ. I know that decision's not an emotional experience for everyone, but you should have seen her—the peace that overcame her, the tears that poured from her eyes. And she lived in such poverty, Jess. That woman had no money, but she had joy. Granted, I was a Christian before the trip, but that moment sealed it for me. I watched the gospel progress from words in a Bible to something alive: something that can get into someone and change who they are from the inside out—not from the head, like a lobotomy, but from the heart, like falling in love."

Another knock sounded at the rear of the auditorium and stunted their conversation. Blake walked up, wrapped his arm around Eden, and kissed her. "I had a hunch you'd stop by your dad's office since you had an adoption placement out this way," Blake said. He stopped. "Did I interrupt you two?"

"Just small talk," Eden said.

Blake peered closer. "Babe, are you crying? Are you okay?"

She laughed, and then sniffled by accident. A brush of her hand to her eyes and she said, "It's nothing. I'm just … thankful." She took Blake's hand and rubbed her thumb along his knuckles. "Just thankful."

"Have you eaten yet?" Blake asked. "Do you want to grab a late lunch?"

"Sure, I'll be right behind you." She nodded to Jesse. "Want to come along?"

Jesse declined, and Blake headed out the door.

When Blake was gone, Eden turned again to Jesse. "I have faith in you, Jess." She got up and grabbed her purse. "I think Caitlyn does, too."

Jesse mouthed his agreement without a sound.

Eden took one step away, then swiveled back around. "When was the last time you and Caitlyn took time by yourselves—not where it happened by accident, but where you *gave* her the time?"

"Not since we were eighteen. We've talked a lot since I've been back, but that's all."

"If you think about it, she's lived under stress for so many years. She could probably use some time together with you, just to hang out for the evening. I'd imagine she's missed you all along."

Eden waved good-bye and walked out of the auditorium.

Alone in the room, Jesse pondered what she'd said about Caitlyn. Eden had a point. During the process of getting to know Drew, he had managed to overlook Caitlyn. Jesse wondered what would make his former girlfriend gleam.

Then a smile emerged on his face.

CHAPTER 46

"I need to see so I can lock the door!" Caitlyn said as she closed the front door to her house. Jesse covered her eyes in jest.

On Friday just past six o'clock, the clear sky sparkled at full light. Jesse parted his fingers and allowed her to peek until she got her key into the lock, then closed his gates again. Caitlyn's giggles proved infectious, and Jesse laughed as he watched her bask in the attention.

"Okay, this way," he said. As he stood behind her, Jesse wrapped his free arm around her waist and they proceeded from her porch, step by step, down the concrete walkway. "So, how late can we stay out tonight?"

"Till whenever: Ryan's visiting his dad for the weekend and Drew's spending the night there. When can I look?"

"Almost there."

When they reached the driveway, Jesse uncovered her eyes to reveal a dark-blue convertible with its top down. It sparkled after a fresh wash and wax. The orange sun painted a sporty, reflective stain across the door on the driver's side.

She started to form a word, but abandoned it, which left her mouth in a small O. Now motionless, a wide-eyed Caitlyn stared at the vehicle. "Where did you get this?"

"I traded cars with Blake until tomorrow."

Her face drenched with delight, she cuddled back against Jesse. "You *know* I love convertibles!"

Jesse took Caitlyn by the hand, led her around to the passenger side to open the door for her. When he had her buckled in and situated, he bowed and closed the door, which prompted another look from her. Jesse got in the car and pulled out of the subdivision.

Southbound on Interstate 71, they sat in silence for a while. For Jesse, relaxation proved beneficial as stress fizzled, seeped through his nerves and out of his body. He and Caitlyn raced in the direction of Columbus, though they wouldn't travel quite that far.

Caitlyn sank into her seat and yielded to the wind that cascaded around her. "Wow, I haven't ridden in a convertible since—probably since you rented one for prom. Remember?"

"And the next day we drove it all the way to Niagara Falls."

"We're not going *that* far tonight, right?" she teased.

"If we were, then I'd say we're already lost since we're driving south."

Both wore sunglasses. Jesse, one hand on the wheel while he rested the other on the door, leaned his head back. Soon they reached a stretch of highway where population was sparse and cars were even more so. He glanced over at Caitlyn, who had melted into her seat, eyes closed and hair whipping in the wind. She wore stylish jeans and a salmon-colored top. Unnoticed by her, her navel peeked through the space between the two articles of clothing. A pleasant reminder, her navel—Jesse had loved to lay kisses there.

Beyond the threat of speed traps and radar, Jesse turned on the stereo, which he had stocked with CDs of artists he knew Caitlyn enjoyed. Within a few seconds, Toad the Wet Sprocket's

"Come Down" blasted through the speakers. And in the sonic landscape, Jesse and Caitlyn found themselves liberated.

After the first thirty minutes, they exited the freeway and headed down a local rural highway, where the speed limit dropped to forty miles per hour but neither stop sign nor traffic light impeded them. Dominated by farmland and undeveloped country, the area boasted a scant number of homes, plus a handful of billboards which sat low to the ground and peeled by the hour.

When she opened her eyes, Caitlyn removed her sunglasses, took a glimpse, and recognized the scene immediately. To compete with the music, she shouted, "Wait a minute! Are you taking me to—"

Jesse grinned.

She reciprocated his smile, then shook her head and sank back in her seat, a vision of contentment. She turned the stereo volume down. "I can't believe you still remember Caitlyn's View." Caitlyn's View was the nickname Jesse had given to an isolated clearing upon which they had stumbled as teenagers.

With feigned nonchalance, he replied, "The only place in northern Ohio fit for a princess—Princess Caitlyn, that is."

"That's right! I forgot all about that part." Her laughter resurfaced. "How sweet; he remembers my favorite place within a hundred-mile radius." She leaned over to give Jesse a playful hug as he drove. "Thank you."

With the music low, neither Jesse nor Caitlyn spoke for a bit. She watched in abandonment as tall grass and maturing corn stalks frolicked in the breeze. They passed barns painted brick red and aged farm houses with whitewashed edifices. After a quick shuffle, the CD player transitioned to Michelle Branch's "All You Wanted."

Her curiosity piqued, Caitlyn turned to Jesse, her eyes narrowed with playful suspicion. "Why are you taking me out here,
anyway? I mean, to remember all this, you must have given it a
lot of thought."

"I figured you could use some time to let loose and
unwind," he said. "I thought back to when we used to trek out
here on Sunday afternoons. You always seemed so free when we
got away from home for a few hours."

With yearning in her eyes, Caitlyn unearthed the memory.
"Yeah," she said. "I did feel free. The way we'd drive for miles,
wind blowing through my hair, not a soul around: For a while,
I never had to fit in, never had to care."

He took his eyes off the road for a moment to glance her
way. "Not as easy to let loose as you get older, huh?"

Caitlyn chortled. "What, is that a dare?" she teased.

Jesse played along. "You were fearless back then." Years
ago, during these drives, he'd spurred her on; she had, in turn,
emerged from her restrained nature.

"Oh, and I've lost my edge on this drive?"

"We're getting older. A couple of old farts in a convertible."

Her mouth agape, she replied, "Whatever, Barlow." She
unbuckled her seat belt. Jesse hadn't counted on that. "Eat my
dust, buddy."

And with that, she ripped the stereo volume to full blast.
Amid the blare of music, she eased her way to her feet and stood
on her seat, practically sat on its headrest. She steadied herself,
then looked toward the sky.

Caitlyn spread her arms sideways, stretched her fingers as
far as she could, and let the wind rush against her body like
a cleansing rain. She looked as though emancipation rose up
within her and charged her veins, as if she found herself caught

between laughter and tears. And it was then that Caitlyn let out a carefree yell, satisfying and sustained—a purifying shout which, for her, Jesse knew, symbolized all her heartache, all her unspoken hurt and pressure. For a brief moment, Caitlyn was a teenager again—those final teenage years she had lost to oblivion. Her smile spread and her face radiated as time slowed to a crawl just for her.

Even from his low vantage point, Jesse noticed a pair of tears that trickled from her eyes and dried in the wind.

And then Jesse knew: After all these years, once again, if only for a fleeting moment … Caitlyn was free.

Their journey ended along a dirt road—whether an intentional or unintentional road, they had yet to decipher. When they arrived at the clearing around 7:20 that evening, Jesse parked the car and turned off the engine. Awestruck at first, Caitlyn didn't move, until reality settled in that, yes, she had finally returned here. Slowly, childlike, as if she now experienced the ambience for the first time, she eased out of the car and made her way five yards ahead. Then she stopped. Jesse came alongside her and, together, they soaked in the sight.

Not a house in sight, nor had they ever spotted another human being during their visits. They couldn't determine if the property was public or private. Jesse had nicknamed it Caitlyn's View because it seemed like a place of their own, a shared secret.

Stretched before them, nature's expanse sat untouched by human hands. They stood at the edge of a cliff three stories high. Below them, a tranquil stream rippled, its chirp a treble whistle as it passed over smooth, oblong stones. Acres of yellow-green grass rolled before them as far as the eye could see.

And in the air, Jesse picked up the summer scent of moss and wildflowers.

Neither Jesse nor Caitlyn had returned here after Jesse left. Yet the scene remained the same.

They breathed pure air tinged with minerals of the soil beneath their feet.

Jesse jogged away and returned with a bouquet of wildflowers, freshly picked from the shallow woods nearby. When he handed them to Caitlyn, she clasped them in her hands, soaked in their hues of dusty purple, velvet red, and sunflower gold.

They gazed ahead and spotted the lone tree, bent at a slight angle in the eastern corner of their view. It appeared to have doubled in size since they last saw it. They peeked downstream and found the large boulder they remembered, its stratums colored with tones of pottery.

And Jesse watched as Caitlyn, rapt, immersed herself in the view—Caitlyn's View.

CHAPTER 47

AROUND nine thirty that night, as daylight faded and stars speckled the sky, Jesse and Caitlyn sat in the top-down convertible and listened to crickets chirp from the woods. They stared at the sky, far from the industrial haze that obstructed their view of the stars back home.

As nature purred, Jesse placed his hand on Caitlyn's, which rested upon her knee. They whispered in the night.

"I'm glad we got back in touch again," he said.

Caitlyn nodded. "It could have happened sooner."

"It never seemed an option, I suppose." He looked into the distant shadows, the rolling hills now blackened. "If I hadn't left," he paused to find the words, "would we still be together today?"

At first Caitlyn pondered the question. She peered down at his hand upon hers, ran her thumb along his. "I don't know. Maybe ..." Between them the question lingered.

The minutes ticked along. By now, they sat in complete darkness, save the moonlight, their faces lit by its incandescent fire.

Caitlyn seemed hesitant. "That girl you were with, the one in L.A.," she whispered. "What was her name? Did she keep you drawn there?"

"Jada?" He considered the question, then shrugged. He tapped the steering wheel. "She and I ran into problems last year. In my soul, I realized it could never grow beyond the status quo."

Jesse struggled to speak. His sincerity, his vulnerability, the earnestness in his tone seemed to comfort Caitlyn. In the recesses of his voice, an undeniable honesty existed, and as the layers peeled away, the old Jesse emerged, the one that had first drawn Caitlyn to him.

"I wouldn't let myself break free from my relationship with Jada. I don't know why: Fear of failure? Fear I'd end up alone? Maybe it truly was habit—perhaps staying with Jada had become an addiction … or maybe deep down, a part of me just gave up."

"Gave up?"

"Gave up. Lost heart. Settled … Somewhere along the line, I knew I would never have with Jada what I once had with you." Jesse felt the warmth of Caitlyn's hand in his. He grazed his fingers along hers. "The limited time you and I had together to develop our relationship—even that was deeper than I ever thought I'd find … or deserve."

They stared out at the beautiful nothing before them. Around them, insects hummed in unison, stopped for a while, then continued, their voices an aural glow. Jesse ran his hand along Caitlyn's arm in a soft caress.

She rested her head on his shoulder. "Do you remember that night in Niagara Falls?"

"I do," he whispered. He rested his head against hers. "That was the night we made love."

"It was my first time."

"Mine too." With a trace of embarrassment, Jesse said, "I'm sorry your first time had to be in a convertible."

"I wasn't offended," she replied. "We were eighteen. We

didn't plan to spend the night in Canada, had only sixty dollars between us—not enough for a hotel if we wanted gas for the trip home."

It was a night like this one: perfect stars glittered across a translucent sky; the air cool and breathable; an absence of foot traffic where their car sat. Neither Jesse nor Caitlyn had visited Niagara Falls before, and the area's small-town nuances fascinated them. Although they had expected a metropolitan area, instead they discovered a modest number of pedestrians who strolled past a smatter of hotels and buildings a few stories high. Within blocks, they found residential neighborhoods and kids who played catch without a second thought that a few blocks away sat a natural wonder, one for which tourists traveled from around the globe to see.

While there, Jesse and Caitlyn had found a small park in the vicinity. Though it had closed for the evening, somehow they had found their way in and forgotten to leave.

"We were lucky no one caught us," Caitlyn said.

"No one would have. They didn't expect us to be there."

"We whispered the whole time. Just like tonight."

On that evening in Canada, they had snuggled together in the back seat of the top-down convertible, wrapped together underneath a blanket, the one they had used for a picnic lunch while en route. By that time in the evening, the park had fallen silent, its shadows weightless and still.

They had felt so secure in each other's arms, as though the steeliest enemy couldn't compete with their embrace. They had lost themselves in the nuances: the heat of his palm as he stroked her thigh, and the invigoration that he sensed ripple up her spine when he kissed her. His moist, balmy breath as it swathed her shoulders, and the pleasant contrast of perspiration that cooled in the late-April air as they gasped for breath. Bound inside the blanket, they made love against a backdrop of Niagara's roar, which emanated from an unseen horizon.

Afterward, in a mutual loss of innocence, Jesse and Caitlyn had laid there for hours, unclothed inside the blanket. For them, the close proximity had reflected the intimacy of that spring evening. Both Jesse and Caitlyn left that experience changed: On that night, a bond had sealed between them. Though unplanned, their coming together had proven one of destiny.

They never made love again after that night.

That was the night Caitlyn conceived Drew.

And tonight, enveloped in the Ohio summer air, Jesse and Caitlyn found themselves in close proximity once again, together yet apart.

They gazed into the depths of each other's eyes and spoke without words and without pretense.

"That was the night I fell in love with you," he whispered. "But it happened *before* we were together in the park. It happened after dinner, as we walked past shops and listened to conversations—half of them in English, half in French. I could sense something in that moment—I knew I loved you. I wanted us to have a language of our own, one in which only the two of us were fluent."

"We had one. It was unspoken, but it was there, like a heartbeat." Caitlyn studied her fingertips, rubbed them together, and asked, "Jess, what's happening between us?"

Jesse cuddled against her head and whispered, "What do you *want* to happen between us?"

Caitlyn allowed the question to remain unanswered. Instead, she leaned into him further and he cradled her in his arms. They felt each other's heartbeats, inhaled each other's breaths.

After a while, Jesse turned the key forward in the ignition, on battery power but short of starting the engine. He reached for the stereo and turned it on at low volume. The last CD they had listened to began to spin: another Michelle Branch CD—Caitlyn's favorite. Jesse skipped to "It's You," and soon the gentle pluck of an acoustic guitar filled the atmosphere.

With a tender smile, he nodded to the car door. "Come on," he invited.

"What?" she said, as if lulled from her personal reverie.

"Trust me."

They left the car from their respective sides and met in front. With her hand in his, Jesse led her a few feet from the car, where the song could still be heard. He placed his hands on the small of her back. She placed one hand on his shoulder, the other against his chest. To think how their lives had changed since they had last done this.

Together they danced.

He rested his chin on the side of her head. He lay his every exhale on her hair.

History seemed to cycle around again. They found security in each other's touch.

And in this moment, Jesse found himself falling in love with her all over again.

CHAPTER 48

AFTER work several weeks later, in early September, Jesse pulled into Eden's driveway. The Ohio skies pelted the ground with a cold drizzle, its temperature too cool to stir a scent from the wet asphalt. In this hint of autumn, a blustery wind whipped around corners and licked the rain from Jesse's cheeks. In Eden's front yard, her large apple tree yielded to the wind and dropped unlucky yellow leaves to piles on the ground. Jesse made a mental note to rake them that weekend.

From his pocket, his cell phone rang as he got out of the car. He raced to the shelter of the front porch and answered. As he peered out at the ashen environment, Jesse recoiled.

But not because of his surroundings.

"Are you still in Ohio?"

At the sound of Jada's voice, a stunned Jesse didn't know whether to laugh or hang up without another word. He opted for a midpoint, to let her say whatever she could possibly have to say to him. Her connection sounded shabby and her voice swooshed in its volume, so Jesse pictured her stuck idle in traffic. Was she bored?

"It's been months," he said. "Why are you calling me?"

"A letter arrived for you at the apartment."

"For me? When?"

"I don't know, maybe June."

"Three months ago? And you figured today is the appropriate time to tell me?"

"The letter's from the hospital. It doesn't sound positive."

"How can you tell?"

"Well, you're not here, so I went ahead and opened it."

"You realize that's against the law, don't you?"

"Whatever. It says they contacted you by phone but you didn't return their calls. They have concerns about some medical tests they did while you were in the hospital after your brain fart that night."

"You have a way with words."

"By the way, Dale pulled some strings and got your medical bills waived. He's aligned with that hospital and convinced them to classify you as indigent."

"Tell him thanks." As much as he hated to think of the guy, Jesse had forgotten about bills and was grateful for the gesture. Dr. Dale probably felt guilty for destroying Jada's and his relationship.

"When he heard you'd gone home to Ohio, he thought it was the right decision on your part. He didn't want you distracted."

More like Dr. Dale didn't want a distraction to return to L.A., Jesse thought, but at this point, Jesse didn't care. He wanted nothing Jada had to offer. "What a guy."

"I showed the letter to him. He doesn't think you should fool around with this. He said it had to do with your blood, like the tests didn't look right, according to what the letter said. He thinks you should call them or get some tests done right away."

Jesse's mind filled with images of his recent—and more frequent—symptoms. "I'm sure it's no big deal." No way would he let Jada have the satisfaction of handing him medical advice.

"All right, here's the thing." Jada lowered her voice as if the CIA had bugged her apartment. "I'm not supposed to tell you this; I was supposed to convince you based on the letter. Dale swore me to secrecy because he could be in deep shit for doing this. But like I said, that letter concerned him, so after he got the hospital to waive the charges, he got access to your record somehow and checked it out." In her pause, Jesse could picture her spying over each shoulder to decide whether to listen to the tiny angel fairy or the tiny devil one. "They're convinced you've got some disease. A disease named after a bear, he told me."

"You mean Baer's Disease?"

"That's it. Seriously, get it checked out."

Jesse gritted his teeth and chose to cast it to the back of his mind. After all, wasn't Jada the embodiment of exaggeration? A paper cut could send the woman into a rant. And besides, his symptoms were commonplace. Plus, when he and Dale talked outside Jesse's apartment a while back, Dale had said he doubted Jesse's status was severe. Dale had mentioned it could mean minor changes in Jesse's diet and daily activity. Jesse knew Jada well enough to take her perception of the threat—however overblown—and dial it down a few degrees.

To change the subject, he said, "So I take it you and Dr. Dale are one happy couple?"

"Shit, Jesse. Apparently he's had second thoughts about his marriage. He's been fucking around on me. Moved out of the apartment three weeks ago."

What goes around, Jesse thought.

"Anyway, I'm finally out of traffic, ready to pull up to Barry's office. Gotta go. But listen to what I said before, about the tests."

Jesse started to say good-bye but didn't get the chance to

complete the gesture; Jada, who saw no reason to waste time with such a formality, clipped the conversation to an end with a disconnection.

CHAPTER 49

THE basketball clanged against the rim before it ricocheted and landed in Jesse's expectant hands.

"Next time!" Chuck said, a failed attempt at dignity after his own failed shot.

"Don't worry, there won't be one," Jesse prodded. With an eye on his opponent, he dribbled the ball casually along the edge of Chuck's driveway. One month since Jada's phone call, and Jesse felt fine. Not even a nosebleed in the last few weeks.

Chuck began to perspire despite the early October refrigeration. He unzipped his green windbreaker halfway and, hands on knees, prepared himself for Jesse's approach. The score was 15-6 with Chuck on the losing end.

Jesse switched hands and teased his father with a nod of haughtiness. "I figured you would've gotten better after a decade."

"I'm a preacher. I believe in miracles."

Jesse rounded his dad, managed to keep the ball in his own possession, and sprinted up the driveway with Chuck close behind. When Jesse leaped to make his two-point attempt, a mischievous Chuck tapped Jesse's elbow and the ball rolled out of his hands. Chuck grabbed the ball and made his way to the basket.

"Hey, whatever, old man!" Jesse shouted, his arms outspread in humorous dispute. "I haven't read the rule book line by line, but I think your maneuver qualifies as a foul!"

Out of breath, Chuck feigned an air of innocence. "What'd I do?"

Jesse grabbed the ball to take a penalty shot. "I'm gonna make a shot here, so take good notes." And with that, he sank the ball in a perfect swish through the net. His nose cold, Jesse stuck his hands in his pockets and allowed the ball to roll into the grass. He'd gotten used to the cooler climate, albeit a slow transition for him.

They laughed for a moment and allowed their hearts to return to their regular paces. Before them, their breath clouded in the evening air.

Chuck gave his son a playful slap on the back. He stalled another moment and then softened his voice. "I know it wasn't easy for you to live your life between glass walls as a minister's kid," he said. "After you left, I couldn't help but think I'd caused it." Chuck watched as Jesse, quiet but attentive, focused on a passing car. "I regret we weren't closer in touch all these years. And I don't know all the details going on in your heart …" Chuck lowered his head and examined a crack in the pavement. "But I want you to know I'm sorry for anything I did to drive you away." Chuck's eyes grew moist, and Jesse could tell Chuck held more emotions inside. "I'm so glad to have you home."

Jesse scrutinized the same pavement crack. "You didn't cause it, despite all I've said. It was me: I had to figure out who I was, and I couldn't do it in someone else's shadow. That's the best way to describe it." Jesse picked up the ball and gave it a halfhearted shot, then forgot about retrieving it. "Life's gotten clearer, though. Coming home was a positive thing."

They headed over to the front porch and sat on the step, side by side.

"I agree," Chuck said at last. "People seem to place expectations on you to live your life the way I have and follow the career I have." He tilted his head so it was eye level with his son. "I want you to know I've never expected you to be anything you're not designed to be. You need to be the man God created you to be and follow whatever burns inside your heart."

Jesse exhaled and watched his breath disperse before him. "I feel like I've really let you down. I know I always acted like I didn't care what you thought about me—and maybe even made a few comments to that effect, huh?"

His dad chuckled. "Yeah, a few."

"But the truth is …" Jesse stopped, bit his lip. "I really *did* care what you thought. And that's what made it so frustrating: that tug-of-war inside my bones."

"I think you turned out fine."

Jesse snorted. "My life's a mess. Los Angeles was supposed to be my cure-all, but I blew it. All I did was run away, and now, eleven years later, the inevitable still haunts me. I let down so many people when I left."

Chuck had a glint in his eye. With a nudge to his son's shoulder, he smiled. "Your heart is open. That's what counts. And as for coming to terms with the past—well, that's a process. Often it's not about the destination, but the journey—the growth that occurs along the way."

"I guess I figured if I just showed up again, my issues would disappear and everything would get sewn together overnight. Naive, huh?"

Chuck peered up at the dark sky. "What you have right now is a chance to retrace your steps, to start fresh. Rock bottom?

Yes. But at rock bottom, circumstances can only get better, as long as you don't give up. You have a fresh opportunity; how high you climb and what you *do* with this opportunity—well, it's up to you." Chuck paused. "So you have another decision on your hands. You made the decision to come home; now you face the decision of how you want to spend the rest of your life. No, you don't know what's up ahead, and you'll take risks based on what you can't see, but that's why we take life step by step."

They sat there for a while until Chuck responded to his son's silence.

"Is anything else going on?"

Jesse wavered, then admitted, "When I got to be a teenager, I was angry at God and angry at you. I looked at you and saw a hypocrite: How could you be a preacher for the God who took your wife, and then expect me to follow suit with your beliefs? I resented you for that."

Expressionless, Chuck listened and nodded. "I don't have answers to all the 'why' questions. There's so much I'll never understand this side of heaven. It's part of the walk of faith." As they delved deeper in conversation, Chuck's grimace revealed an ache for his son and the pain Jesse harbored. "This world isn't perfect," Chuck said. "It's not heaven, so it has some flaws. The horrible things that happen here don't always make sense, but they go with the territory. I don't blame God for your mom's death; the way I see it, that's just part of this fallen world, where we have weakness, disease, and so forth.

"I'll say this about God, though: I wasn't even a Christian when your mom died, but the love I felt during the ordeal— God's love—stretched beyond words. And I've sensed that love countless times. As I've gotten to know God better—not as a minister, but as an average Christian—I've gotten to know His nature. And I've come to the conclusion that the God who loves me, who loves my kids, who loved your mom—He's a good God. He blessed me with that amazing woman for years, and He's given her a home in heaven where there's no more bleeding, no more suffering, no more pain. At this moment, she sees things that I can't even begin to imagine. And she gets to see God face-to-face. The beauty that must radiate from His presence! One day, I'll be there, too. But not yet." Chuck tapped his fingers together, then continued. "So the way I see it, despite her suffering while she gave birth, she had a victory in the end. I could only wish I had it as good as your mom has it right now."

Jesse, his lip in a quiver, contemplated what his father said. He sensed a yielding inside, a sense that life would come together indeed.

Jesse nodded, but said nothing.

And he knew his father understood.

The past was past. Healing had arrived.

CHAPTER 50

THAT Wednesday evening, Jesse fought slight nausea as he wound through the streets of Hudson. But he knew it wasn't an aftermath of the tacos he'd eaten for dinner; no, it was psychosomatic, a nervousness that surrounded what he was about to do.

Though he found the church parking lot packed when he pulled in for the 7:30 service, he managed to locate an empty spot in the far corner. Jesse checked his watch—a few minutes late as planned. He didn't want to be noticed when he walked in.

As Jesse zipped his coat, he made his way past aisles of cars. Most of the license plates he passed contained a tag for Summit County, Hudson's location; but because Hudson sat close to the county's northern border, many members arrived from Cleveland's Cuyahoga County and other communities to the northeast and northwest. Few families seemed to travel from areas to the south, as you headed toward Akron.

Jesse snorted under his breath. He couldn't believe he'd actually come here tonight. A year ago, he never would have pictured himself entering this building again. For that matter, he hadn't stepped foot inside a church building while he'd lived out west. So, in spite of all the time he spent here as a kid— regardless of its second-home status to him back then—tonight he fought a queasy stomach and felt like an outsider. But beyond his abdominal butterflies, he found himself unemotional.

Random snow flurries, Lake Erie's finest, circled through the dark air, and Jesse tasted the flakes that melted on his lips. He inhaled the scent of smoking chimneys, where nearby households gave their fireplaces a test run for the season. And he continued to press ahead, determined not to run the other way. He and God had an appointment.

As he reached the church building, Jesse heard the sounds of beating drums and a bass guitar, whose vibrations raced in invisible currents beneath his feet. And when he opened the lobby door, the volume level doubled in his ears. He detected an air of excitement in the atmosphere, to such an extent it seemed all but tangible.

Jesse entered the auditorium, where the music could be heard at its fullest through the large amplifiers. The room was dim, like a concert setting. Toward the front, bright lights focused on the platform, where a band and singers led worship for over one thousand attendees. Not a single suit could be found in the building. Though he'd arrived feeling like an outcast, now Jesse felt invited. A party had begun and they had expected him.

He headed to the aisle on his far right and counted rows. While he didn't want anyone to notice him, he also didn't want to sit alone. As promised, Eden had saved him a seat in the tenth row from the back, at the end of the row. And as the people around him sang, no one seemed to notice him or whisper. Because the church membership had expanded during his years away, he didn't recognize half of the faces.

Her eyes closed, hands at rest upon her heart, Eden swayed to the up-tempo music and sang along. Jesse gave her a side hug to let her know he'd arrived. When she opened her eyes, she beamed a smile and mouthed hello. And then, once again, she closed her eyes to enter back into worship. Eden, focused on the one she'd come to sing to, lifted her hands in praise. She didn't make a big deal of Jesse's arrival. For that he was grateful.

Jesse removed his coat and set it on his seat as the band moved into another energetic song. Like the church's members, the band represented a broad age range. A twentysomething guy played lead guitar; a man in his sixties worked his way around the drum set. Jesse remembered the drummer from long ago, back when he had darker hair—a former hippie who had struggled through a heroin addiction prior to his Christian conversion. "I never imagined myself in a church," the man had said on one occasion. "After an addiction like that one, I'm thankful just to be alive: I'm proof-positive that God loves everyone."

In the semi-darkness, Jesse observed the sea of individuals around him, some of whom lifted their hands or clapped in worship, while others rejoiced with bursts of gladness. On a spontaneous occasion, he saw someone shout for joy or leap up and down a few times in reverence. Jesse found the twofold activity fascinating: Assembled as a group, these people worshipped together in song; yet each experienced an intimate, one-on-one worship connection with God. Each part came together as a whole.

Chuck's perspective on worship time, which came prior to his preaching segment, was that each church member should have the freedom to approach God from where they are. For some church environments, that might mean classical hymns and solemn rituals. But Chuck's church, like the preacher himself, had always been a place of expressive worship. And early on,

Chuck had taken hits from critics who misinterpreted this worship style as irreverence. But Chuck believed God took interest in *hearts* rather than red tape, and often pointed to David in ancient Israel, who, although a distinguished king, had danced and rejoiced through public streets in an expression of worship.

Jesse recalled many moments of worship like tonight's. And as it turned out, these fervent acts—the lifted hands and leaps of praise—were expressions of gratitude to God. Over the years, many of these people, like the drummer, had told their stories of deliverance. Some testified to how God had comforted them after a loss or delivered them from a drug addiction. Many had a simpler story: They had begun a normal day and by evening had given their lives to the Lord after a casual conversation with a friend.

Testimonies of recoveries and healings abounded here. For some, their answered prayers came by way of an instant miracle, while for others the road had proven long and arduous—but victorious in the end. And now, as these memories poured back into Jesse's mind, he realized these imperfect people were similar to him—shortcomings, struggles and all.

So here he stood tonight.

The lights dimmed further and the band segued into a softer, more intimate song. The claps and shouts ceased as more hands lifted. On the platform, the lead singer leaned closer to the microphone during the keyboard-driven song—a song of gratitude, a song of love. A sense of reverent passion seemed to fill the auditorium.

Jesse felt broken on the inside, like a piece of pottery shattered on a concrete floor, fragile. An acute awareness of past regrets and desperation, a heart's cry, welled up within him. In the darkness of the room, unnoticed by others, Jesse closed his

eyes and lifted his hands as though he and God were the only
ones in the room. Though he couldn't bring himself to sing,
Jesse listened. His heartbeat accelerated. Tears trickled down his
face. And Jesse soaked himself in the lyrics of hope; the chords
washed over him and massaged his heart like the touch of a
finger—God's finger. Jesse felt a cleansing occur, followed by an
acceptance, as the enormous, soothing arms of God wrapped
around him.

How long had it been since he'd felt so protected?

The band lulled into an instrumental interlude as Chuck,
dressed in jeans, approached the platform. The preacher stood
there for a while. He observed the people engaged in worship,
who whispered praise to God, the same God who had whispered comfort to Chuck himself. In reverence, the preacher
waited for the proper words. At last, in a tender voice, he spoke
through a microphone as the band continued to play behind
him at a softer volume.

"Whether you're visiting tonight and don't know God, or
whether you've been here numerous times before," the preacher
said, "I want to tell you we serve a good God here. We serve a
God who loves us unconditionally—no qualifiers, no performance measurements. And that's an assurance for each person
in this room. He loves you so much, He gave his one and only
Son, Jesus, to set you free. The Bible says that without the shed-
ding of blood, there is no forgiveness of sins. So when Jesus was
nailed to a cross two thousand years ago, your sins were nailed
there with Him—He shed His blood to cover those sins. And
He would have done it if you were the only person on earth."
Chuck paused a moment, then continued, "Jesus rose from the
dead and is alive to this day. So whatever you're going through
in your life, God sees your situation. He wants you to invite

Him into those circumstances. Whoever calls on the Lord will not be disappointed. He acknowledges you, and He delights when you acknowledge Him. People speak of the passion of the Christ; well, I have some news for you: *You* are His passion, His deep desire. If people knew how beautiful the living Jesus is, how unique He is—they would want Him."

As the music continued and the band moved into another song, Jesse abandoned himself to worship and reconnected with the Jesus he'd known as a kid.

Deep within, Jesse sensed a humble pleasure, a fresh renewal.

A thirst quenched.

CHAPTER 51

"I want to tell Drew."

Brick Oven was crowded when they met for dinner the following evening.

"Tell him what?" Caitlyn asked.

Jesse hesitated, but his resolve resurfaced again. Confident, he locked eyes with hers. "I want to tell him I'm his father."

Caitlyn hadn't expected this. In mid sip, she swallowed her iced tea. "Oh, I … oh …"

Jesse examined her eyes in an attempt to read them. "I mean, if it's all right with you," he added. "*Only* if it's okay with you."

"I suppose I'm not surprised. He's crazy about you, and you two have gotten along so far."

"Six months and counting."

Caitlyn chewed on her straw and appeared to evaluate him. "Are you sure you're ready?"

"I've weighed it in my mind over and over." Jesse took her hand in his. "He deserves a dad. We've taken that away from him long enough. I'm begging you for the chance to give it back to him."

Across the table, Caitlyn fidgeted as she listened.

Jesse continued, "There's a piece of him that aches. I've been able to help fill part of that void, but there's still a side of him that hungers—I mean, he looks for his dad in people's *eyes.*" Jesse caught her gaze. "He thinks his dad doesn't want to know him, and it hurts him inside. I don't want him to endure that any longer."

As Caitlyn seemed to warm to the concept, they pictured Drew and Jesse together. They talked about the positive long-term development that Drew might experience with a father in his life. Then Caitlyn laid out the unknowns and the risks that would accompany the decision.

She looked at Jesse, her voice a tender plea but her facial expression firm. "If we do this," she said, "you can't turn back. If you leave, you'll break his heart beyond repair. He loves you already; you've established that bond. So today, things are different than when you first came home. If you go away again ..."

Jesse clasped both of her hands in his and gave them a squeeze, gentle yet sincere. "I promise: His needs come first." He squeezed tighter. "From now on."

At first, Caitlyn didn't respond, though her eyes drilled into Jesse's, as if to search for a hint of impulse or lapse. But Jesse remained decisive. She said, "I need to know this; I need to hear it from you: *Do you love that little boy?*"

"More than life," he replied. Not a trace of hesitation.

With this, Jesse peered deep into Caitlyn's eyes and saw her struggle for an answer.

CHAPTER 52

"WE'RE going to tell him," Jesse said. "Cait and I are going to tell Drew I'm his dad."

Jesse started to chew a fingernail but caught himself. He awaited Eden's response.

Though she remained calm, a blink of her eyes revealed Eden's excitement. On the tail end of a half day of vacation, she had stopped by the church before she headed to her office. In an empty meeting room at the church building, she and Jesse ate an early lunch of burgers and fries, which she had brought with her.

"How do you feel about it?" she asked.

Jesse took a deep breath and released it in a slow exhale, the kind that comes right before you hit a button marked "Activate." He replied, "Thrilled. Nervous."

"That's understandable."

"You're the social worker; you unite families all the time. What do you think of the idea?"

"What do *you* think of the idea?" she countered.

"I believe it's the right thing. It comes from the deepest part of my soul," he said. "But once we tell him, everything will change. So the unknown is a bit frightening—not for me, but for Drew. How will he respond when he finds out I'm the guy who had never been around for him? Will he *want* a relationship now? Even though, with all my heart, I want to take this step and be a father to him—what if the shock hurts him all over again and causes him a brand new kind of anxiety? What then?"

Eden studied Jesse's nonverbal indicators.

Eden brushed salt crystals from a fry before she slid it into her mouth. She squinted as she chewed, then followed it with a sip of diet cola. "You've told me lot about Drew since you reunited with him. You've shared some of the details he's told you, many of which come from deep inside him," she said. "And to me, it's obvious the one thing that little guy has wanted most is to know his dad. He's held out hope that his dad would return."

"Yeah, I guess you're right," he said.

"You're following your heart. You're doing the right thing."

Jesse nodded, but his demeanor remained anxious.

Eden checked the time on her watch. Then, in a hasty move, she wrapped up their lunches. "Come on." She got up from her chair. "I want to take you somewhere."

"Where?"

"You'll see."

Curious, Jesse wiped his hands on a napkin and followed her out the door.

———————

When Jesse and Eden arrived at the adoption agency where she worked, she introduced her big brother to the staff, all of whom offered warm greetings. Next, Eden pointed to an internal window, a single glass pane covered by a pair of thin curtains, in the far corner of the main office. "The room's through there," she said and gave Jesse permission to observe the event that would occur. After she left for her office, Jesse indulged the staff in stories from Eden's childhood, tales they would surely use as blackmail in the future.

While in mid sentence, Jesse shifted his attention to a married couple in their mid thirties, who walked into the agency and spoke to the receptionist. The sandy-haired man attempted to contain his excitement, while his wife, her hands clasped together, radiated.

Those must be the parents, Jesse concluded.

Soon Eden walked down the hall to greet them and led them to the room on the other side of Jesse's window, where they signed some final paperwork. Then Eden left the room.

Discreet yet respectful, Jesse took occasional glances through the window. The small room had a living-room feel, complete with a sofa and loveseat, table lamps and end tables. But the couple couldn't remain seated. No doubt caught between nervousness and eager anticipation, the husband paced a while before he returned to his wife's side, where he wrapped his arm around her shoulders. She wrung her hands.

The door to the room opened again, and in walked Eden— with a tiny infant in her arms, wrapped in a blanket.

Their baby girl.

And here, the world halted for the new parents. For an endless moment, the awestruck couple stared, speechless, at their daughter. At first, Jesse noticed the couple's hesitancy: their date with destiny had arrived. After years of protracted delay, while the couple's names edged step by step to the top of an extensive waiting list—after all the home studies, the legal issues, the prospects and setbacks—the moment had arrived: a dream fulfilled.

With careful steps, the couple met Eden halfway across the room. Jesse watched as Eden laid the sleeping baby into the new mother's open arms. Both parents' eyes moistened and opened wider, as though to absorb every available detail.

Moments like this can't be bought, Jesse thought to himself. Before he knew it, he'd glued his eyes to the window pane. Although he stared straight through, no one noticed. Transfixed on the life-changing event that unfolded before his eyes, Jesse watched as the couple wept. He watched the wife's self-conscious giggle as a tear dropped from her eye onto the baby's forehead. Eden smiled, patted her on the arm, assured her it wouldn't harm the infant.

With joy Eden watched the trio. From the way Eden's face gleamed, you would think she had started these people's lives all over again.

But then again, she had.

She had just turned them into parents.

And Jesse had witnessed the transformation with his own eyes. Blown away, hand to mouth, he tried to shake his head in wonder but found himself immobile for the moment.

Here before him unfolded the gift of life. And Jesse, grateful to be alive, wouldn't throw his own life away for anything.

CHAPTER 53

THEY sat together on the sofa in Caitlyn's living room. With Drew in the middle, Caitlyn and Jesse flanked him on each side.

Jesse pivoted toward his son and said, "Your mom and I have something to tell you."

His eyes innocent, Drew peered at Jesse, while Caitlyn turned and placed her hands on her son's shoulders.

Jesse struggled for words as the moisture evaporated from his tongue. This wasn't as straightforward as he'd imagined. His racing pulse fit for a speedway, he looked down at his own hands and noticed they shook with tension.

Drew noticed too. "Are you okay?"

"Yes." Jesse feigned composure but fooled no one. He pressed his hands against his own knees for stability. "Buddy, I've had a chance to get to know you for a while …" No, wrong way to start. The minute became elastic as chewing gum, and Jesse hung midway with nothing but air beneath his feet.

He's waiting for you. Say something.

Jesse tried again. "Drew … you remember shortly after we first met, don't you? When your mom and I told you that she and I knew each other long ago, spent a lot of time together as high-school kids?"

Drew nodded. Behind Drew, Caitlyn urged Jesse forward with a nod of her own. How could she stay so poised? Jesse certainly didn't share her coolness. His brow started to bead with perspiration; he wiped it, then clenched his jaw and decided to clutch for confidence anyway. Jesse shared a bond with Drew, after all.

Jesse leaned closer, a few inches from the boy's face. He searched deep within Drew's eyes.

A puzzled look on his face, Drew asked, "What?"

"You have eyes like mine," Jesse replied, a reference to Drew's remark at Brandywine Falls.

Drew grinned. "I know."

Jesse tried again. "No, I mean, *you have my eyes.*"

At first Drew looked confused. He furrowed his eyebrows at Jesse's words—and then the words appeared to dawn on him. Drew's facial expression emptied; it transformed to a blank, bewildered stare. Almost imperceptible, Drew leaned his head back an inch.

Jesse placed his hand on Drew's knee to reassure his son. They stared straight into each other's eyes; neither flinched, neither blinked. "I'm your dad, Drew."

Drew's eyes fluttered with shock before he stopped them. He didn't say a word. Perhaps unsure how to respond, his brow furrowed again as he looked down and stared at his knees. He raised his head again and peered behind at his mother, who caught his glance and nodded to confirm the truth. She squeezed his shoulders and continued to monitor the situation.

Slowly Drew pivoted his head back toward Jesse but wouldn't make eye contact with his father. Instead, Drew stared down at his feet. Jesse couldn't blame the kid for his shock: For so many years, Drew had hoped his dad would return, only to discover his parents had excluded him from their critical secret. How else could Jesse expect him to react?

322   JOHN HERRICK

Jesse laid his hands on his son's arms in an effort to reassure him again. At this point, the boy's sense of security had to have taken a nosedive. "Drew? Buddy?"

Drew jostled his arms to shake Jesse's hands off.

Caitlyn whispered into Drew's ear. "Drew? Honey, do you feel okay?"

Drew shrugged as his face flushed pink. His lips appeared tense; he himself had tightened them. Jesse could tell Drew fought to hold back tears. And the boy still wouldn't make eye contact with him. Caitlyn closed her arms around Drew and kissed him on the head.

Jesse started to get concerned. He couldn't care less about himself—he needed to know his son was safe. "Drew?" he said in a near whisper. "Look in my eyes …"

Hesitant, Drew lifted his gaze and their eyes locked. Jesse noticed the tear that Drew fought with all his might to subdue. Jesse knew it wasn't a tear of anger, but of fright—of a helpless child in a desperate grab for a lifeline.

The kid was stronger than Jesse estimated. And yet, Jesse couldn't imagine how vulnerable Drew must have felt.

Caitlyn rubbed her son's arms but remained quiet.

Jesse knew he needed to say something but felt so unprepared himself. "I know this is a shock to you. And it's not fair for you to be put on the spot like this … this can't be easy … I—I didn't know how else to tell you."

Jesse tousled the hair on top of Drew's head, which failed to trigger a reaction. Drew looked back down toward his feet, as though his parents had betrayed him and he didn't know who to trust. Jesse heard the sound of Drew's teardrop hit his sneaker. Drew wiped his eyes, and their moisture formed a sheen on his fingers.

Jesse leaned in once again. "Drew, please say something—even if you're angry, please say something …"

But Drew continued to stare at the floor. The boy's murmur cracked as he spoke. "Why didn't you tell me before?" he asked. The question sounded like a plea. Jesse's gut constricted.

Jesse paused. At this point, he could only offer his son transparency. "I didn't feel I had any right to put you in that position while I was a stranger." No, that wasn't the whole truth. "And I was afraid, Drew."

Drew looked as if he hadn't eaten in five days but couldn't locate an appetite. Jesse knew that in a matter of minutes, his son had found himself drenched with anger, love, hurt, betrayal—a rapid influx of emotions, more than most ten-year-olds ever needed to bear.

Caitlyn wrapped her arms tight around the boy. "We don't expect anything from you," she whispered. She veered around to meet his eyes with hers. "Do you want some time to let this sink in? Maybe a few days with just you and me?"

Drew mouthed agreement as his eyes glossed over again. His mother laid a kiss on his cheek, from which a tear clung to her lip.

Drew got up and padded to his bedroom without another word. Jesse and Caitlyn listened as the door clicked shut.

In the stillness, Jesse stared at a random spot on the living-room window, one hand over his mouth. "What a horrible idea; I don't know what I was thinking. How's he *supposed* to react?"

Caitlyn laid her hand on his. "You did fine. His life just got turned upside down. He needs a little time," she said. "He's waited for you for years, Jesse—he needs his dad. Don't give up."

His elbows at rest on his knees, Jesse drew his steepled

hands to his chin. He bounced his chin on his fingertips in nervous response.

"Yeah …"

CHAPTER 54

IN concurrence with Caitlyn's suggestion, Jesse kept his distance, which gave Drew time to sort through the revelation of his father's identity. Jesse, though he kept in touch with Caitlyn each day, craved to communicate with his son and comfort him. But he realized the kid needed time to process his emotions and talk them over with his mom, the parent with whom he was more comfortable and who, at this point, seemed to remain the one aspect of the boy's life that had *not* shifted beneath his feet.

Several days later, with permission from Caitlyn to revisit anytime, Jesse stopped by their house after dinner. Caitlyn answered the door and let him in.

"Is he here?" asked Jesse.

A tranquil blink of her eyes, then Caitlyn gestured with her head toward the back of the house. "He's on the patio."

"How's he coping?"

"It's sinking in gradually. He started to ask questions." Her eyes communicated a soft, welcome glint that assured Jesse all would work out fine in time. "He's shaken, but he's open. Go talk to him."

Jesse stepped outside on that dark October evening. Beneath the porch light, he found Drew, collected, seated on a chair as he gazed at the stars. Although Drew didn't acknowledge Jesse's presence, he kept careful watch from the corner of his eye. Jesse noticed the kid wore a long-sleeved, hooded Ohio State T-shirt with its hood pulled over his head, but not a coat. Maybe his observation meant his parental instinct had kicked in. But in reality, Jesse knew he noticed only because he himself felt like cold aluminum in the chilly air.

"Your mom said I'd find you out here," Jesse said, careful to exude comfort through his tone. To help break the ice, he added a hint of humor: "Aren't you freezing?"

Drew shrugged. "It's not too bad out." He was right; it couldn't have been less than forty degrees. Jesse pulled a chair alongside Drew's and shared the backyard view. And Drew continued to watch. Jesse wondered if the boy felt more secure with his father's soothing presence a heartbeat away.

"How've you been?" Jesse pretended to be captivated by the horizon.

"Fine."

Jesse nodded but kept his eyes on the stretch before him. He folded his hands in his lap and let a quiet minute pass before he spoke again. "When I was a kid—much younger than you—I lost my mom. She didn't leave town, and it wasn't her fault she was gone; she died unexpectedly. I spent almost my whole childhood without her, wishing she could come back to me—oh, what I would've given to have her back. I never got the chance, though." Jesse looked down at his son. "I wasn't here for you, Drew. I can never make that up to you. But if you're willing to give your dad a chance, you *can* have him back. And he loves you so much."

Drew wiggled.

Jesse continued, "I'm sorry; I never wanted to lie to you. Your mom and I just wanted to protect you. You know how much I care about you and respect you."

Amid a gust of cold breeze, a vulnerable Drew wrapped himself in his own arms. "Why did you go away before I was born?"

Jesse pursed his lips. "I was selfish … I regret a lot of my choices in life."

Drew bit the inside of his cheek as if he tried to process what his father said. "What kind of choices?"

"Choices that hurt a lot of people. Decisions that wouldn't make you proud of me. Things I wish I could take back." Jesse turned toward Drew and, even though his son wouldn't look at him, bent down to his eye level anyway. The little boy trembled as a tear ran down. Jesse reached over to wipe the tear from his son's cheek—and Drew let him. When, at last, Drew met his father's eyes, Jesse added, "You are so important to me, and there's nothing—*nothing*—I wouldn't do for you."

His son quivered. Jesse's heart tore until he couldn't stand it any longer. When Jesse leaned over to pat Drew on the shoulder, Drew—to Jesse's surprise—pivoted around and hugged Jesse, his thin arms wrapped tight around his father. Drew clutched Jesse's coat with his small hands.

Drew needed his dad.

As Jesse embraced his son, he felt the boy's tremors against him between sobs. Both men cried. And for the first time, Jesse discovered what it was like to hold his son. Overwhelmed, Jesse buried his head in Drew's hair as Drew buried his face in Jesse's chest.

Drew refused to let go: He had waited a long time for this.

So Jesse continued to hold him, rock him gently. Soon he rested his cheek on top of his son's head.

"It'll all be different now," Jesse whispered. "I promise."

CHAPTER 55

JESSE surfed the Internet through a wireless connection on a laptop he'd owned since L.A. On this Tuesday lunch hour, perched on a high stool in a local café, Jesse sniffed his coat. Sure enough, the aroma of bagels and espresso beans had permeated the fabric.

Blake walked in to grab a sandwich to go. On his way out the door, he noticed Jesse and wandered over to him.

"Any juicy celebrity rumors?" Blake tapped the laptop.

Jesse peered up, then returned to his screen. "I'm on a job hunt."

"But you and your dad are still on good terms nowadays, right?"

"Of course. But it's time for me to locate something long term and stable so I can get out of Eden's way—she's overdue for that."

"Got any ideas?"

"I learned a lot about composition concepts through photography, so maybe I can find a job in a company's PR or marketing department. Even if it's entry level, it's a step forward." As Blake sipped coffee from his to-go cup, Jesse glanced up again. "Actually, there's another reason: Cait and I told Drew."

Blake's eyebrows shot upward. "That you're his dad?"

"Yeah, so I want to provide better support for him."

"That's terrific! How long have you been on the lookout for a new job?"

"Couple of weeks. Next week, I have an interview with a snack-food manufacturer in Cleveland. They plan to expand their media ads, and they consider all my years on film sets a big plus."

Blake doubled the crease at the top his takeout bag, which crunched in his grip. "Have you told your dad about Drew?"

"Not yet. It's still only you and Eden who know."

"I might be worth reconsideration. I think Chuck would understand."

"Maybe you're right. Drew should have a grandfather in his life."

Blake checked his watch. "Listen, I've gotta get back to the shop so my staffer can take his lunch break. We'll catch up later, okay?"

Blake left Jesse to his want ads. Before Jesse powered down the laptop and left the café, he located two more prospects.

———————

On the way home from work that evening, Jesse relaxed in the driver's seat. For the first time in years, his life seemed to come together, its fractures filled in and smoothed out like wet patches on a potter's vase. Jesse felt content; his confidence mounted by the day.

When his cell phone rang, he didn't notice it at first, transfixed instead on a setting sun that glowed an electric burnt orange. But he caught the call on the final ring.

"Jesse!"

She sounded distraught.

"Cait?"

"Jesse, I—"

Frantic. Scared.

Jesse heard a faint siren and the dense rumble of tires in the call's background. Wherever she was, Caitlyn was in motion. And her voice carried a slight echo. Had she called from a large vehicle?

"What's the matter?" Jesse asked.

"It's Drew ..."

Jesse tapped his finger on the steering wheel. More anxious by the split second, he waited. No further response from Caitlyn. Just sirens and tires in motion.

"What's going on? What happened to Drew? Why do I hear a siren in the background?" He waved his hand in circles, willed her to respond faster.

"We're in an ambulance," she said. "Drew's in trouble. I don't know what's wrong with him. He won't wake up!"

"Which hospital? I'll meet you there."

"St. Mark's, near Interstate 77. Do you know where it is?"

"I'm on my way."

Jesse slapped the phone shut and hung a sharp right.

PART THREE

SAVING DREW

CHAPTER 56

JESSE rushed through the automatic sliding doors of the ER and scanned the congested waiting area. He found her seated alone yet surrounded by a mass of other people who waited. Some shouted, others dozed; a couple of them held cloths against gashes on an arm or leg.

When he made his way to Caitlyn, immediately Jesse noticed her cheeks, chapped from sustained weeping. Her eyes red, arms crossed over her chest as though to secure herself, she seemed calm now. With all the chairs around her occupied, Jesse knelt down and grasped her hands. They were cool to the touch. He embraced her for a beat, and then they parted.

"How is he?"

She sniffled, ran a finger beneath her moist eye. "Much better. He regained consciousness and they stabilized him. They're getting ready to move him upstairs."

Still worried, Jesse nodded. His own symptoms started to flash through his mind, which added to his fear that Drew might face serious trouble. "What happened to him?"

"I got home from work early and started to cook dinner. Drew shot hoops outside by himself. He pushed himself hard at it, determined to perfect some sort of running shot."

"He told me it wears him out when he runs like that."

"It does—I knew I should have stopped him at first sight, but I didn't. I kept making dinner. After a while, I didn't hear

the basketball bouncing but figured he'd gotten bored with it."
Caitlyn pressed her fingers against her eyes. "Five minutes later,
I heard frantic beating on my front door. It was Ryan's dad,
from across the street—Drew was lying on the driveway. He
wouldn't move or respond. I ran outside, and sure enough, he'd
collapsed on the pavement. I couldn't wake him up."

Jesse drew her hands into his, pressed them to his mouth
as he listened.

"I was so scared—I thought he was dead." She opened her
eyes. "I checked his wrist and found he still had a pulse. Ryan's
dad had already called 911, so the paramedics were on their
way."

Though relieved to hear Drew's symptoms were different
from his own, Jesse remained concerned about his son.

"I knew I should have had his exhaustion checked out. I
didn't trust it from the beginning, but I couldn't find any other
symptoms."

Jesse kissed her hand. "He's fine now. We'll talk to the
doctor and find out what's wrong."

Four hours later, Jesse and Caitlyn watched as Drew, now
in stable condition, slept in a hospital room. Aware that Drew
loved bright surroundings, Caitlyn turned on every possible
light in case he awoke. The room was semi-private, but the
other bed was unoccupied. Jesse could hear the faint ticks of his
own wristwatch.

Much calmer now, Caitlyn stroked Drew's hair and felt his
forehead on occasion to catch any preliminary signs of a fever. A
heart monitor beeped in steady rhythm as Drew slept.

A white-lab-coated Dr. Higgins tiptoed through the door
and flipped through sheets in a manila folder. Though he

appeared in his early fifties, the man possessed the composed bedside manner of a grandfather. "How's our guy?" he asked.

"Still sleeping," Caitlyn replied.

After a quick perusal of the heart monitor's numbers and the other equipment, the doctor glanced over Drew to confirm changes hadn't occurred in the last hour. After this, he sat down with Jesse and Caitlyn at a small table in the corner of the room.

"Drew appears stable at this point. He's fortunate his head hit his arm rather than the ground when he fell," Dr. Higgins said. "I'll order additional tests for tomorrow so we can get a more conclusive picture. That will help us determine if there are other factors at play beyond exhaustion. Has Drew been hospitalized in the past?"

"No," Caitlyn said.

"And you said he's shown signs of fatigue more than once— beyond the normal rate of growing tired?"

"Yes."

"Any other symptoms you can recall?"

"No," Caitlyn said. "That's why I hesitated to look into it."

The doctor offered a compassionate smile. "That's understandable. But after today, we'll want to have anything unusual checked out, even if it's minor." One last look over Drew's record before the doctor flipped it shut. "Assuming Drew remains stable, he should be able to go home tomorrow afternoon." With a pat to Jesse's back, one dad to another, Dr. Higgins rose from the table and made his way to the door. There he glanced at the young couple again. "You can stay with him here tonight if you'd like," he said, then left the room.

Jesse and Caitlyn watched Drew sleep a while longer before Caitlyn curled up on the unoccupied bed. Jesse drifted to sleep on the sage vinyl loveseat beside Drew's bed.

The next afternoon, prior to Drew's discharge, Dr. Higgins instructed them to keep Drew in bed rest for twenty-four hours, with no heavy activity for a week. Staff would examine Drew's test results in greater detail and schedule follow-up appointments if necessary. Should further symptoms or out-of-the-ordinary events occur, Jesse and Caitlyn promised to bring Drew straight to the hospital.

Disappointed by the bed-rest scenario but too worn out to complain, Drew slept.

When evening arrived, before he headed back to Eden's house for the night, Jesse stopped by Drew's bedroom. Curtains closed and lamps turned off, the furniture looked like small, dark hills. Jesse sat on the edge of the bed and stroked Drew's hair before he realized Drew was awake.

Jesse offered a smile, still frightened on his son's behalf. "Feeling better, buddy?" he whispered.

"I'm okay."

Drew sounded thirsty, so Jesse reached nearby for Drew's glass of water, which the boy sipped before he reclined back into the pillow. Drew uttered more words before Jesse coaxed him back to sleep.

Jesse found Caitlyn on the living-room sofa and sat beside her. She drummed her fingers on her lap as she stared at Jesse.

"This whole situation makes me nervous," she said. "The mom in me says this isn't good."

"Would it help if I move in? That way, whatever comes down the pike, you won't need to face it alone."

She considered his proposal and replied, "I think it would help Drew if you live here. It would provide more stability for him; he'd have a male role model—his dad—in the house."

Jesse pulled her toward himself, kissed her on the cheek, and together they rocked.

"I'll move in this weekend," he said. He would need to strategize an explanation for when Chuck heard he'd moved out of Eden's house. Maybe he could tell Chuck he'd moved into a friend's apartment. Too tired to think about it at the moment, Jesse continued to cuddle with Caitlyn.

The pieces would come together. Right now, his son needed him, and Jesse assigned priority to that. All other issues and concerns, Chuck-related or otherwise, seemed miniscule by comparison.

CHAPTER 57

AFTER he'd examined the test results in detail, Dr. Higgins informed Jesse and Caitlyn that a more serious medical issue had come into play, which necessitated further steps. He referred Drew to a specialist, Dr. Bernstein, who kept an office at the same hospital.

Drew underwent numerous tests over the next month and grew weaker in the interim.

Afterward Dr. Bernstein requested a meeting with the parents, but without Drew.

"We've done what we can to try to determine Drew's condition," Dr. Bernstein said, "and, unfortunately, I'm concerned by the results."

"Were you able to diagnose what's wrong?" asked Jesse.

A solemn man, Dr. Bernstein peered through small glasses, his forehead crinkled. "It's a blood disorder, but it's unidentified."

"More tests are needed?"

"I mean it's unidentified, Mr. Barlow. We've ruled out all known blood disorders. At first I leaned toward a diagnosis of multiple myeloma in an early stage, but when we studied the tests further, I became less convinced because we found a low Bence Jones protein factor. We're convinced it's a less common illness, one for which we don't have an official name. We've seen a limited number of cases, primarily concentrated in industrialized countries—the United States, Britain, Ireland."

As the news soaked in, Jesse and Caitlyn sat stunned. Jesse conjured a mental picture of Drew in declining health and wondered if his son underwent internal pain. When the image became gruesome, he didn't even want to think about it any longer. Jesse wished he could take his son's pain upon himself.

The doctor continued, "As I said, the illness is unidentified. We recognize its symptoms, but we're still learning about it, still compiling data. From the few cases that exist, we know the condition progresses rapidly, and it's considered severe. But due to that limited number of cases, we don't know how to determine its severity on a per-patient basis."

Caitlyn bit her knuckle. "How could the severity vary across patients? Isn't the illness the same illness for everyone?"

"The condition ranges from treatable to fatal—but we don't yet know if the determining factor is the severity level or just a matter of catching the illness early enough for effective treatment. In the cases experts have studied, the mortality rate is greater than 50 percent."

Caitlyn turned her face away from the doctor. Jesse held her close.

"What happens next? What do we do?" Jesse asked.

"Where possible, patients received bone marrow transplants, and in those cases, doctors documented a 100-percent success rate. All of those patients survived and appear to live standard lives after recovery," Dr. Bernstein explained. "Because we are unable to predict fatality risk at the patient level, and considering Drew's young age, I recommend an aggressive approach. And as mentioned, the success rate with a bone marrow transplant runs at 100 percent."

"And what happens without a transplant?" Jesse asked.

"Fatality is more likely than not," the doctor replied.

"How much more likely?" Caitlyn chimed in.

"All factors considered, we need to regard the possibility that this is indeed fatal, and in such cases … the patient had an average of eighteen months."

Caitlyn's eyes watered. "To live?"

"To live. I'm sorry."

Restless, Caitlyn gazed around the room as if in search of respite. At last, she said, "Okay, let's do it. How soon can we move forward with a transplant?"

"Before we take that step, I want to try less invasive measures first, to see if we can hinder the progress of the disease. Based on past cases, we have at least that much time, and it could prove successful. But in a couple of months, if we haven't made progress, the bone-marrow scenario would become our best option. And if the situation unfolds that way, we can proceed with the transplant as soon as we locate a marrow match—*if* we can locate a match. To be safe, we'll begin the search process immediately."

"Where would we look?" Jesse asked.

"First we'd need to draw a sample from Drew. We can compare it to a bone-marrow-donor database. But the chances of a match decrease outside the family, plus time is of the essence. The best chances are a sibling or parent."

Jesse began to open his mouth to volunteer—but then simply nodded in agreement. He recalled his conversation with Dale in L.A.

Baer's Disease.

Don't make a blood donation—that could be fatal with the condition.

Jada's phone call—they're convinced something's wrong with Jesse.

Regardless of whether he were a perfect match, given his own symptoms and suspicions of the condition he himself faced, no one would allow Jesse to donate. Not if it meant a risk to his own life. Not even for his son's sake.

Jesse's heart wrenched for Drew.

And a wrench of heart, it appeared, was all he could do for his son. That, and hope the less invasive options proved successful—or that someone else would prove a marrow match for Drew.

CHAPTER 58

LATER that week, Jesse stopped by Eden's house for dinner, just the two of them. He had offered to cook dinner but couldn't think straight. Eden retrieved a ready-made meatloaf from the freezer, and while the microwave thawed it, they sat at the kitchen table. He relayed the details of the latest visit to Dr. Bernstein.

"Is Drew aware of what's ahead for him?" she asked.

"Cait and I told him yesterday."

"How'd he handle it?"

"As usual, he didn't say much. I don't think it's fully sunken in for him yet." Jesse put his face in his hands to relieve the pressure. "I can't stand the thought of that kid going through more tests; the kid's spirit is broken." Jesse explained the prospects of a bone marrow transplant and mentioned the best chances of a match resided with Drew's parents.

Jesse explained the marrow process as Eden watched— and then Eden eyed him closer. The stress of watching his son endure a tragedy would strike anyone as understandable, as would the pressure of how to pay the medical expenses that would mount. Even with Caitlyn's insurance, the copayments themselves would deal a hefty hit to their finances. But Jesse also forgot to maintain eye contact with Eden.

Eden's eyes narrowed. "Are you facing something yourself? Beyond Drew?"

He'd let his guard down. Jesse maintained his facial composure and guarded against other abrupt movements. He had to remain calm. "Of course not. Just worried about Drew—he's my kid."

"I think it's time you told Dad about Drew," she said, and Jesse hoped this meant she figured she'd overreacted with her question. Eden added, "It's none of my business and it's not my life, so I don't have a clue how Drew's situation must feel to you. But you're bearing this on your own shoulders, and you don't need to—not when you're surrounded by people who support you."

Jesse could sense his resilience crumble. Wary at the idea of telling Chuck the truth—though he couldn't explain why he felt that way—Jesse had to admit, the prospect appealed to him. By this time, he'd hidden Caitlyn's pregnancy for just shy of twelve years. Jesse had no reason not to tell Chuck. After all, Drew was Chuck's grandson, his flesh and blood. And it would help Drew to have the additional support.

It would be difficult to take such a step. Then again, Jesse had hidden the truth for so long, maybe it wasn't fear he battled, but stubbornness.

Jesse had denied Drew of a father. How could he deny him a grandfather too?

Jesse stalled the entire next day. His church-maintenance tasks provided a convenient excuse.

When his workday ended, he took an indirect route to Chuck's office, wound through corridors and stairwells, anything to kill time. Jesse felt nervous, a sensation reminiscent of when he'd first walked into Chuck's office months ago, but more severe this time. For today he wouldn't simply appear before his father—he would reveal a secret and admit he was a liar.

Jesse wouldn't have imagined this scenario a year ago. His greatest fear didn't rest in the revelation he would unveil, but in its aftermath. After months spent rebuilding his father's trust, today he would risk destruction of that bond. In a matter of minutes, Jesse would admit he was not who his father believed him to be; Jesse was, in actuality, a father himself.

But this step would help Drew, Jesse reminded himself. After all, Jesse felt weak, whereas Chuck's life abounded with faith. Drew needed his grandfather's prayers.

A quiet tap on the door. Chuck looked up and invited Jesse in. Jesse closed the door behind him and sat down, not at the opposite side of the desk, but beside his father, eye to eye.

Jesse inhaled and exhaled in staccato, the way he breathed amid freezing temperatures.

Chuck furrowed his eyebrows. "Are you all right? Son?"

Son. That word sounded precious to Jesse, who held new-found appreciation for its meaning and flavor.

Son: a term of love, nearness and acceptance.

"I can't do this anymore," Jesse said.

Chuck removed his reading glasses and scooted closer. "Do what?"

"I can't lie to you anymore." Jesse felt his face grow flushed and heated. "Caitlyn and I—when we were eighteen ..."

Concern washed over Chuck's face. He placed his hand on Jesse's knee. "Jess?"

"We have a son. His name is Drew."

At first, Chuck's face paled from shock; he tried to speak. Instead, he sighed and rubbed his eyes in frustration. "Jesse." And then Chuck's shoulders froze. He uncovered his eyes.

"Wait a minute. You have a child and you were gone for—are you telling me you *left* him?"

This was the part Jesse dreaded. "I didn't know she'd given birth."

"How come?"

Jesse hesitated. "We'd agreed to get an abortion—"

Chuck shook his head. Jesse was a teenager again. Jesse startled at the sound of Chuck's hands hitting his own knees in anger.

Jesse held his hands out. "She didn't go through with it. She said she couldn't do it. But I was already gone by the time she changed her mind. Listen to me." Chuck's lips tightened almost to the point of disappearance. "I've taken responsibility now."

Neither man spoke for a while.

Jesse had pierced his father with the truth. Chuck, who must have tried to determine whether to blow up or restrain himself, glared from one corner of the room to the other. Though these revelations occur, what parent *expects* a day like this to come, one in which your son tells you he got his girlfriend pregnant? At this point, Jesse could think of nothing else to do except bear his heart. So he did.

"I've been an awful person," Jesse said. His tears burned his cheeks as they rolled down. "I didn't know what else to do or where else to go, so I ran. Back then. To California. And that's the reason I came back—I ran out of steam. I couldn't ignore the guilt anymore.

"I'm a liar and a coward, Dad. I hid the pregnancy. And then, when I found out Drew was alive, I hid him from you and begged Eden not to tell. It's not her fault; it's mine." Jesse's hands and voice shuddered from lack of emotional control. His heart palpitated with thumps he swore were audible. "I'm so sorry for the pain I've put my own family through—you, Eden. And Drew. I've tried to put things together—honest, I have. But I'm too screwed up to make it happen by myself. Please forgive me for what I did to all of you. I hate myself, the person I've become."

While Jesse spoke, Chuck's glare softened, and then transitioned to a look of compassion. As Chuck drew his son into his arms, Jesse couldn't resist; he leaned into his father's shoulder. And together, the two wept.

"You're forgiven," Chuck said. "Before you say anything else—you're forgiven. I'm always here for you. I don't count against you whatever you've done wrong. I'm your dad, Jess; I love you."

They held each other until the weeping subsided and Jesse calmed.

A sense of cleansing in his chest, Jesse looked into his father's eyes. "Caitlyn and I—we're back in touch, and I'm making amends. I promise I'll be a good father like you. Drew knows I'm his dad; we're growing together. But he's in trouble. He's sick, and they don't know what it is or if he can recover. I don't know what to do for him. I'm scared—so scared. Not for me, but for Drew ..." Jesse pleaded with his eyes. "He's my son."

Chuck rocked his son, an adult yet always his child. "I know."

When they parted from their embrace, the relief felt like a morning tide, a fresh start.

A secret exposed. The darkness quenched.

They kept quiet for five minutes, or so it seemed to Jesse. He had liberated himself from the heavy burden on his soul. Even his exhales felt lighter.

At last, Chuck broke the silence. He put his hand on Jesse's knee and grinned. "So, when do I get to meet my grandson?"

CHAPTER 59

D URING one treatment session, as he waited for his son, Jesse's mind wandered.

His son's resolve fascinated him. Drew had withheld his emotion the night Jesse told him he was his father, and that self-control resurfaced during treatment. While Jesse wished Drew would communicate more, he admired the kid's inner strength.

But as the months progressed, Drew's external strength began to dissipate, due not to physical exertion but, rather, to the stress of tests and treatment. Jesse wondered if the treatment was painful. He couldn't bear to watch his son flinch, yet he refused to leave Drew's side. Because Jesse had put his permanent job search on hold and continued to work for his own father, considerable leeway ensued. So Jesse took Drew to most medical sessions.

Jesse loathed Drew's illness. He resolved to find a way to rescue his son. Somehow.

In his heart, Jesse sensed he would prove a precise match for Drew, and the bone-marrow option was the only surefire one. It would come down to that—and when it did, Jesse intended to have a strategy ready. The need for a plan, a method to hide his own suspected illness, consumed him as possibilities scurried through his mind in a stream of consciousness. But he eliminated each option for one reason or another.

His own hospital stay had occurred more than halfway

across the country, and no one here was aware of the incident. If Jesse didn't say a word, surely no one would figure it out— at least not until he had accomplished whatever he needed to. Regardless of the risk he himself faced, Jesse valued Drew's survival more.

True, Jesse's own sickness proved a stumbling block and a greater enemy than he'd anticipated. But he was confident he could defeat it, or at least downplay it.

His life for Drew's.

For Jesse, the question was no longer *if,* but *how.*

How could he mask his own internal symptoms?

Dr. Bernstein interrupted Jesse's thoughts to inform him he could take Drew home.

———————

When they arrived home before six that evening, Drew felt exhausted and wanted to sleep for the remainder of the night. Caitlyn had prepared a quick dinner, but Drew wasn't hungry. She tucked him in, they spoke for a few minutes, and she kissed him goodnight. Then Jesse made his way into Drew's darkened bedroom.

Drained from the emotional rollercoaster of recent months, Drew lay limp against the pillow. Jesse sat beside him on the bed, pulled the blanket snugger beneath the boy's chin, and kissed him on the forehead.

"Kinda rough today?" Jesse asked.

"It's been worse." Although tired, Drew's eyes remained halfway open.

"You're my champ." Jesse reached for Drew's hand, and the boy gripped him.

They listened to the heat as it billowed from the vent on

that mid-winter evening, before Drew whispered, "Do you think there's a God?"

Taken off guard, Jesse struggled not with the question itself, but with the context in which it emerged. Even though Drew was aware of the severity of his illness, Jesse grew concerned. Did his son sense imminence within?

"Yes, I do." Jesse brushed a hand through his son's hair. "Is everything okay?"

Drew shrugged. Jesse coaxed him further, and soon he heard his son sniffle in the darkness.

Jesse found Drew's other hand and held them both between his own. "What's wrong, buddy? You can talk to me."

Jesse heard a heavy swallow from Drew. "I'm afraid to die."

The words sent a dagger into Jesse's kidney. He felt Drew's hands tremble.

"You won't die," Jesse said. "I won't let that happen. I promise."

"Are you afraid to die?"

"I was," he said, "but I'm not anymore, because I know where I'll be when I die. And it will be even better than anything I've experienced." When Jesse noticed the words soothed his son, he continued. "When I was a kid, I listened to my dad talk about heaven, and he said there will be streets of gold, people from nations I've never visited, constant light. Water of life flowing from God's throne. And there's a tree of life—the Bible says its leaves are for healing. No more sickness up there. Doesn't that sound nice?"

"Mmm-hmm," said Drew, a clear attempt at boldness.

As Drew began to drift to sleep, Jesse told him, "Your grandpa lives nearby. Would you like to meet him?"

A faint, sweet smile as Drew, half conscious, nodded.

———————

Drew's favorite birthday gift that year was a grandfather.

Born in early February, Caitlyn had delivered Drew without a hitch, just overdue. Unlike the day of his birth, however, he was surrounded by loved ones today, his eleventh birthday. Eden and Blake arrived first. Before they walked inside, they stomped off clusters of powdery Ohio snow. Caitlyn led them into the living room, where she introduced them to Drew. Jesse joined them, and the three guys turned on the television to watch the Cleveland Cavaliers play in Chicago.

The doorbell rang a few minutes later and Jesse jogged over to greet Chuck, whose face couldn't have been brighter as he peered into the living room to catch an advance glimpse of his grandson.

Jesse called out to Drew and gestured for him to come over.

As the blond-haired boy approached, Chuck knelt on one knee. "Are you Drew? Happy birthday, big guy!"

Drew leaned against Jesse and offered a bashful smile.

Chuck extended his hand and they shook. "I'm Chuck."

"This is your grandfather. He's a minister."

As Chuck peered face-to-face at his first grandchild, he counted aloud the number of features that Drew and Jesse shared. And the first feature he mentioned: their green eyes.

"Jesse said you ride a motorcycle," Drew said.

Chuck laughed. "Yep, he's right about that. Are you gonna go for a ride sometime?"

Still shy, Drew said he would indeed, then bounced back over to the game on TV. But by the end of the day, Chuck had drawn Drew into a stream of conversation.

Jesse led Chuck over to Caitlyn, where Chuck hugged the

woman who, as a teenager, had made the choice that allowed him to meet his grandson today.

That day, while a birthday celebration for Drew, also carried a reunion tone for everyone else. Jesse floated around the room to take snapshots, including several of Drew with his grandfather. When the time came to slice Drew's cake, Eden borrowed Jesse's camera—after, of course, a training session from Drew—and snapped a shot of Jesse and Caitlyn, who surrounded Drew as he blew out the candles.

The picture became Jesse's immediate favorite: his first family picture of Caitlyn, Drew and himself. Later, he would print an extra copy and often hold it against his heart when no one else was around.

In this moment of honesty, Jesse treasured the scent of candle smoke, the cheers of Drew and crew as the Cavs won the game, and two more inches of snow that accumulated outside. Jesse wanted to soak in each detail.

Jesse shook his head in disbelief. To think that he nearly gave this away for a superficial relationship with Jada. Almost one year ago, he sought an abrupt end to his life in a suicide attempt. But today he wanted his life more than anything.

And then he remembered, to sacrifice his life on Drew's behalf meant a countdown of his own days and hours. This, Drew's first birthday spent with his dad, would, more likely than not, also be his last. Jesse wanted to cling to his life, but his desire to see Drew cling to life stood stronger.

Happy birthday, Drew.
From your dad.

CHAPTER 60

AS the weeks marched on, Jesse obsessed in his hunt for a method—any method—to mask his own sickness. Dr. Bernstein had exhausted their other options. Drew had given a bone-marrow sample. Caitlyn, Eden and Chuck had all undergone tests, but none of them proved a match. Jesse had concocted excuses to delay his own test but, by now, had run out of ideas. Meanwhile, the process to identify a potential match in a national donor registry continued, each day critical as Drew's life projection dwindled to twelve months.

Twelve months—with Jesse's hands still tethered and not an inkling of a plan.

On a Saturday afternoon in early March, Jesse drove to the church and sat down on the sidewalk in front of the building. His car sat solitary in the parking lot.

The sun sliced through dreary skies in a hairline fracture. Jesse shivered and shoved his hands into his pockets. With the temperature still cold in the upper thirties today, it had warmed even further earlier in the week and the snow, the bottom layer of which dated back to December, had started to melt. Along the perimeter of the sidewalk peeked splotches of green grass, jagged lines which ate their way toward the center of the lawn.

Twelve months.

Alone and riddled with angst, Jesse clenched his jaw to

release the heartbreak of watching his son suffer. Time was running out fast, slipping away beneath their feet.

Jesse had no doubt of his own Baer's Disease scenario; the symptoms had worsened since December. He could feel his body react but had, for Drew's sake, managed to conceal it. As marrow tests eliminated each family member, Jesse sensed in his gut he was Drew's final hope for a donor. His son was dying—and Jesse had no choice but to watch, unless a plan occurred to him. Soon.

Pictures of Drew flooded Jesse's mind. Not pictures of today, but of Drew's childhood without a father. His first day of kindergarten. His eighth birthday. His first unexpected basketball through a regulation-height hoop.

Then Jesse pictured the nights when Drew had questions but lacked answers. The family life Drew had been forced to forego because his dad wasn't around. It wasn't fair to the kid.

And now this.

Numbness settled in Jesse's belly as he dropped to his knees beside the lawn. In torment, Jesse screamed with all his might.

And as expected, no one heard. His voice echoed against the brick walls.

His gut wrenched, but Jesse couldn't cry anymore. Dry and empty, he fell prostrate to the ground and closed his eyes, desperate for an answer.

He lay his palms flat against a patch of moist grass. He clutched the blades and felt the damp, defrosted soil between his fingers.

Once again, Jesse sat up and fingered the cold soil. In an absentminded manner, he picked a random chunk and rubbed it between his thumb and forefinger. Jesse watched the dirt and grass particles crumble and fall to the ground. He recalled his father's sermon on a particular Sunday, when Chuck mentioned that God had formed the first man, Adam, from the dust of the earth.

The dust of the earth.

Jesse examined the soil on his hand, held it against his nose and closed his eyes. He savored the vibrancy in its scent. It smelled like life.

His heart jumped. He opened his eyes.

His fingers slowed in motion as he reached down and plucked another blade of grass. Rapt with the grasshopper-colored herb, he held it close to his face, rubbed his thumb along the specimen's smooth, lined surface.

And realized he had a plan.

CHAPTER 61

AFTER Drew's next treatment, Jesse and Caitlyn conferred with Dr. Bernstein while a nurse tended to Drew.

"I had hoped we could find an alternative, but that hasn't been the case. We haven't been able to hinder Drew's illness, so we need to move into our final option," the doctor said. He turned to Jesse. "Have you given further thought to a bone-marrow test?"

"I want to be tested," Jesse said. "But we'll need to get Drew home today. Can I set up an appointment?"

"Of course. It's a simple procedure: They'll prick your finger and collect drops of blood. If it's a match, then we'll take the next step."

Jesse's next step would occur sooner, but it wouldn't involve a finger prick.

———————

According to Jesse's research on the Internet, Baer's Disease involved a lower-than-normal count of all three blood-cell types: red blood cells, white blood cells, and platelets. Ashwaganda was an Asian herb prevalent in the areas of Sri Lanka, Pakistan and India—and it lifted all three cell types. Jesse needed to locate a product of pure Ashwaganda or, at least, one with a heavy presence of it.

Not only would the herb's presence increase his blood-cell counts, but the increase would, in turn, bring temporary relief of his symptoms as well. A nosebleed while in the doctor's office could upset his plan as much as a low cell count. And the beauty of an herb, as far as Jesse could tell, lay in its natural origin: During the test and donation phases, no one would detect the presence of a manufactured drug in his blood. After all, he figured, a multivitamin contained an assortment of natural elements. No one questioned their presence, did they? Just products of the earth. Dust to dust.

Moreover, Jesse's last recreational use of marijuana had occurred a year ago, so he didn't expect the hospital staff to discover any remnants. Thankfully, he hadn't slipped in that area during his regretful incident at Sanders's apartment.

Jesse's research also warned the Ashwaganda herb would not constitute a long-term remedy for Baer's Disease; in fact, its use could cause the condition to worsen. But Jesse already faced a fatal risk with a marrow donation—an aggravated sickness of his own was the least of his concerns.

And perhaps, in the end, staff couldn't use his donation at all if Baer's Disease would cause harm to Drew. But if Jesse never received the chance to donate, *Drew's* chance of harm appeared to stand at 100 percent through an early death. To Jesse, the logic was clear.

The overhead bell rang when Jesse entered Naturally!, but he knew Blake wouldn't greet him. Blake had plans to meet with a real-estate agent that day to look at possible site locations for his foray into expansion.

As Jesse wandered aisle by aisle, each container blended into the next. The labels looked similar, a representation of three different natural-herb companies, with details found only when he read the plain text on each label. After the first two aisles, the names congealed in a mental blur, and aside from the vitamins grouped together, he couldn't determine the layout of the store. Was it based on root herb or intended consequence?

Jesse startled when a store employee offered assistance. Before Jesse could answer, the teenager pointed at him.

"Hey, aren't you Blake's friend from L.A.? I met you months ago when you stopped by. I think you'd just gotten into town."

Jesse's heart pounced. "Yeah. You're Matt?"

"Good memory. Blake mentioned you guys went to shoot hoops that afternoon. Said he killed you on the court."

Nervous at the kid's detailed recollection, Jesse hoped a casual comment about today's visit wouldn't make its way to Blake. But Jesse remained calm so he wouldn't arouse Matt's suspicions. "I've gotten rusty when it comes to basketball, I'll admit."

"Can I help you find something?"

"Ashwaganda? Or something with a heavy amount in it?"

Matt appeared confused. He clucked his tongue and waved for Jesse to follow him. "Sure, this way." Halfway across the store, Matt led Jesse to a shelf that looked the same as the others. "We don't get many requests for that product."

"Yeah, thought I'd try it out. I'm not big on medicine."

"Something going on?"

Nosy high-school kid. Didn't Blake train his staff not to trample people's privacy? Then again, Matt saw Jesse as an acquaintance, not a passerby.

Jesse maintained his composure, played down the need. "Not a big deal. Had some nosebleeds lately and thought this might help. But for all I know, nosebleeds could just be due to humidity."

"In the middle of winter?"

Just ring up the purchase, kid. "We keep our house well

heated. My girlfriend's always cold." Casual. No big deal. Jesse willed him to hurry.

Jesse's rescue arrived in the form of a man who sought a jar of St. John's Wort. Matt processed Jesse's purchase. Relieved he'd kept his interaction with Matt and his memory to a minimum, Jesse paid cash and left the store.

As he climbed into his car, Jesse noticed his own hands shook. He had just purchased a product that could send his life into turmoil—or perhaps termination. The entire way home, his stomach churned bittersweet, the sugary sense of preserving Drew's life rinsed with an acidic foreboding of imminent death—a tug-of war between gladness of a new family versus the ache of knowing they would part again through a tragedy. Jesse didn't want to sacrifice his life and would have done anything to avoid it—but his son was in bad shape. And Jesse's love for Drew prevented him from backing down. At least this time around, his departure would benefit, rather than harm, his son. A gift.

From this point on, a slight yet relentless anxiety made its home in Jesse's gut.

When Jesse pulled into the driveway at Caitlyn's house, where he now lived, he turned off the engine and sat in the car, overwhelmed with the emotion of the end to come. Less than a year after his reunion with Caitlyn, Drew and Chuck, he would prepare his departure. Without words, Jesse would need to say good-bye in other ways. He would exhibit joy and normalcy, all while he covered the pang that soured his stomach whenever he pictured separation from his loved ones.

He'd cried a lot lately; after all, he'd been through much in the past year. But each tear was worth it—his opportunities to do so continued to diminish. And here in the car, Jesse's eyes

watered again, a short spell, and he wiped them. As soon as
he entered the house, he made a beeline for the bathroom, an
excuse to splash cold water on his eyes before Caitlyn or Drew
noticed redness from the tears.

Yes, he would suppress a lot in the weeks ahead.

But today he had another opportunity to indulge his family.

Jesse headed toward the kitchen, where he heard Caitlyn
and Drew chat. With Drew at the kitchen table engrossed in
homework, his back to the entryway, Jesse sneaked up and
squeezed a hefty hug from behind.

Surprised by the unusual entrance, Drew joked, "Are you
going psycho?"

Next Jesse proceeded to Caitlyn. In a tight embrace, he
planted a kiss on her temple.

If indeed he didn't wake up following his donation, Jesse
determined to make his final days count.

CHAPTER 62

As expected, his bone-marrow test boiled down to a finger prick and a few drops of blood. He could have undergone the test sooner but decided to wait at least a week to allow the herbs to take full effect in his system.

With each step, the end loomed closer.

When his appointment ended, he called Eden and found her schedule open, so he drove to her office to lift his spirits. They sat together behind closed doors.

"How'd the test go?" she asked.

"As simple as yours did."

"I wish I could've helped him. Hopefully you're a match."

Eden caught Jesse as he lulled into deep reflection, which he explained away as concern for his son. Jesse's preoccupation, however, had deeper roots: Jesse accepted the prospect of heaven, but the concept of a never-ending eternity—an absence of time altogether—stretched beyond his comprehension and left him with an undercurrent of apprehension.

In addition to that larger notion, Jesse's thoughts circulated around Drew's safety after the departure. But he felt confident Chuck would serve as a father figure to his grandson. Another base covered.

From the opposite side of Eden's desk, he wondered if this marked his last visit with her. Jesse fixed his gaze on his sister and offered a chapter of final words.

"I hope you know how much I appreciate you. You're the glue that's held our family together, and I'm grateful for that."

Eden bounded around the desk and hugged him. "Oh, how sweet, my big brother loves me!" She felt him tremor and noticed beads of perspiration on his forehead. "You're shaking. Are you okay?"

"I'm fine," he replied. "Nerves—it's been an emotional week."

He gave her one final hug, told her he loved her, and took in another glance of her office on his way out.

Eden studied him as he hung a left from her office. He sensed her analytical gaze, one that suggested he had left her with a lingering impression that something was awry.

CHAPTER 63

DR. Bernstein had fast-tracked Jesse's marrow test and informed Jesse his marrow was indeed a positive match. Immediately Jesse arranged his donation appointment before he had a chance to procrastinate. When he revealed the news to Drew, Jesse could see the transformation in Drew's face as relief settled in. The burden lifted from the little boy, who had worried about whether a match existed.

Things had fallen into place: His dad would take care of it.

And here Jesse sat, two weeks later, alone in the hospital waiting room in the middle of the afternoon. When he pictured a waiting room in the past, Jesse imagined a bleach-white environment, one that sparkled and smelled of disinfectant. Instead, this room resembled a hotel lobby with its fresh décor, tans and browns, and pots of coffee on a table in the corner. Instructed to fast for twelve hours, Jesse, at this moment, craved water and red meat. Drew, Caitlyn and he had indulged in a cheeseburger and fries the evening before, and it had felt like the last meal of his life. Then again, perhaps it was.

Jesse darted his eyes away from the coffee pot and replayed the prior night's memory. Beside him, a man in his fifties, a fellow nervous patient, tapped his feet and shook his leg. He turned to Jesse, and Jesse knew the man wanted to calm his own nerves with conversation. "Do you have kids?" asked the man.

"A son." At first, Jesse didn't want to talk. But on

reconsideration, he decided his own nerves could use some calm. "He's ill—severe—but they can't figure out what the illness is."

"You're waiting for him?"

"No, I'm here for a bone-marrow donation. We're a perfect match."

"What a relief." The man smiled. "You'll enjoy a nice, long life with your son."

Jesse's stomach cringed. "Yeah …"

Caitlyn promised to bring Drew to the hospital after school to greet Jesse when he awoke. Despite Jesse's attempt to dissuade them, Caitlyn insisted. He couldn't justify his hesitation and avoid her suspicion, so he prayed they would handle the outcome with peace.

During his last stint as a hospital patient—the only other time, for that matter—he'd arrived unconscious and awakened in a bed. He had no idea what to expect today. What would happen if they discovered his plan at the last moment? Jesse gritted his teeth and suppressed the thought.

Each minute that passed seemed double in length. His stomach empty, his tongue dry, the nervousness made him want to vomit. Sorrow loitered in the pit of his soul.

"Jesse Barlow."

A nurse led him down a corridor to a semi-private partition, where she instructed Jesse to empty his pockets. The nurse logged, bagged and tagged his possessions, then asked him general medical questions, the answers to which she wrote on a clipboard. Dr. Bernstein had asked the same questions a few days ago and had informed Jesse that he would waive the typical pre-surgery tests—no need to suspect health issues at such a relatively young age. Though surprised they could forego what seemed to him critical tests, Jesse had heard of its occurrence when it involved outpatient services for other patients his age.

Jesse had lied to Dr. Bernstein about his medical condition and claimed he had no health concerns, no symptoms of which he was aware. And today, he lied again to the nurse.

Most people come to the hospital to *avoid* the risk of death. No one suspected anything.

No red flags had surfaced. No one discovered the herbal presence. Eerie how simple he'd found it to sidestep the process.

The nurse left his flimsy cubicle and shut the curtain while Jesse changed into a hospital gown and slid onto the wheeled bed. Once the nurse tucked him in and treated him like royalty, she hooked up a heating tube to the bed to keep him warm. Jesse adored warmth.

Inside, his belly continued to somersault. He grew weary with sorrow as the minutes ticked away.

Another attendant greeted him, one who wrapped an elastic band around Jesse's arm and inserted an IV into his vein. Jesse shivered a bit as the burst of cold liquid sped through his bloodstream.

"Saline solution," the attendant explained. "This will help prepare you for the anesthesia."

Jesse would undergo general anesthesia and would go unconscious before death could occur. Dying in one's sleep seemed peaceful. A year ago in his apartment, Jesse had pined for peace and swallowed a bottle of pills.

The minutes continued to tick. His opportunity to turn back dissipated.

And then the anesthesiologist arrived, another nice-to-meet-you for Jesse. By now these greetings had become routine, and soon Jesse's thoughts coasted to his son's face. Then Caitlyn's. Chuck's. Eden's.

Soon another reunion would occur.

Jesse would see his mother again.

As Jesse grew woozy from the anesthesia, another attendant released the brake on his bed and wheeled it down the corridor. From a distance, Jesse could see a pair of doors that led to his destination. As his bed approached, the doors loomed larger, sixty feet away. Then fifty-nine … fifty-eight … fifty-seven …

The impact of the anesthesia struck fast. Jesse drifted toward unconsciousness and a permanent sleep. He had expected to feel a floating sensation as the drug took effect, but instead, it hit him off guard and triggered a rapid drift into oblivion.

The last thing Jesse remembered was his roll down the corridor.

Fifty feet … forty-nine … forty-eight … blackness.

———————

In the back office of his shop, Blake stared at the bookkeeping record on his computer. Matt, the hired help, wandered in and said, "Looks like we're running low on vitamin-A tablets. I've searched the storeroom but can't find any boxes."

"Next week I'll put you to work on a physical count of the entire inventory."

"Sorry I asked." Matt chuckled and started to head out of the office, then spun on his heels. "By the way, I saw that friend of yours a few weeks ago—the one from L.A."

"Oh, Jesse? Yeah, he's made the hometown rounds."

"No, I mean I saw him *here*. He came one day while you were gone."

Blake kept his eyes glued to his computer screen as he

typed. "How many times have I told you to put my messages on my desk?"

"No message. He bought something."

Blake's fingers froze. He uncrossed his legs and rested his elbows on the desk. "Bought what?"

"A container of Ashwaganda."

"Ashwaganda?"

"Yeah, it seemed odd to me, too."

"Did he say why?"

"Nosebleeds."

Blake pretended to dismiss the incident, and Matt returned to the sales floor. Blake looked over at the clock on his computer. Jesse should have arrived at the hospital by now.

Blake squinted, shook his head. Didn't Jesse realize an herb could skew the results of any tests they performed on him? It could prove downright dangerous.

Nosebleeds. Back in February, Drew had mentioned he'd witnessed a nosebleed while Jesse and Drew were out one weekend.

Blake resumed with his computer but ended

up with his arms crossed against his chest.

Jesse wouldn't concern himself about nosebleeds unless they were frequent.

Ashwaganda. It could be used to raise the levels of all three blood-cell types …

And then the color drained from Blake's face.

Blake stumbled for the phone at the corner of his desk, raced through Eden's number.

She didn't pick up. Blake jostled his hand on his knee. "Come on …" His hands slickened with sweat.

Eden picked up on the final ring before her answering machine could kick in. She didn't have a chance to say hello.

"Thank God you're there," Blake blurted. "Don't go anywhere. I'll pick you up in five minutes."

Blake arrived at Eden's house and left the engine running. He banged on Eden's front door until she arrived, her expression equal parts confusion and alarm.

"Come on!" Blake shouted, already in a sprint toward the car. "We don't have time to talk!"

Eden locked the door and ran to join him.

When she got in, Blake peeled away and headed south on Route 91. "Which hospital is Jesse at?" Blake demanded.

"St. Mark's. Why?"

"No! It'll take us thirty minutes to get there!" Blake slammed his fist against the steering wheel.

"Your face is pale! What's the matter?"

"The herbs."

"What?"

"I didn't know about it. Jesse came to my store a few weeks ago to buy herbs. I have a hunch it's a cover: I think Jesse knows something about his own health—something that otherwise would have prevented his marrow donation. And I think he wanted the herbs to mask the issue long enough to make it through the medical hurdles." Blake sped faster, veered around other vehicles, bit his lip as he approached the freeway. "I think he's risking his life for Drew. Jesse knows the consequences and did it anyway."

"You mean, he could die?"

"If he hasn't already."

Limp, Eden sank back in her seat. She looked too shocked

to say anything else; instead, she stared at the dashboard clock as the minute digit leaped by one.

Blake glanced her way. "Do you have your cell phone with you?"

"Yes." She rushed to open her purse.

"Call Chuck. Tell him to get over there."

———————

When Jesse opened his eyes to discover he'd survived the procedure, words couldn't describe the sense of relief. If not for his post-procedure weakness, he would have bounded to his feet and howled with delight. He soaked up his surroundings inside his hospital partition. Had he ever felt happier to see a bland environment rather than a bright, heavenly one?

His bandaged flesh felt sore. The staff had collected marrow from his hip bone. Groggy from the anesthesia, he peered over and found Caitlyn and Drew seated in chairs beside his bed. Jesse could hear the steady bleep of a monitor accent the periphery as a nurse shuffled behind him.

Caitlyn ran her fingers through Jesse's hair. "Welcome back, sleepyhead."

Jesse sighed under his breath in response. It was all he could muster as the anesthetic haze retreated. He managed an inkling of a smile at the corner of his mouth before he shut his eyes again.

Thirsty—his tongue had become sandstone—a nurse lured him out of reprised slumber with a plastic cup of ice water, which he quaffed within seconds. The nurse fetched another cup; Jesse consumed it along with a few graham crackers.

Minutes later, when Jesse appeared to reach near-full attentiveness, the nurse and attendants departed for a while so he could recover with his family at hand. Drew's eyes seemed glued to his father, who lay in a hospital bed for the boy's own sake.

This is what it looks like when your dad loves you, Jesse's motionless body communicated.

If asked to reach into the farthest crevices of his memory, Drew, Jesse hoped, wouldn't recall feeling as important to anybody else as he did at this moment. Even through Jesse's squinted eyes, Drew's flesh appeared to warm a notch, the tangible effect of a father's love in action.

Caitlyn bent down and whispered into Jesse's ear. "Thank you." Then she raised her voice to its regular volume so Drew could overhear as well. "You know, Drew was concerned about his dad." She rubbed her son's neck and said, "I'll be back; I want to get a bottle of water from the gift shop downstairs. You two catch up."

And she left the father and son together in the partition.

Drew gazed at Jesse's hip. The boy looked mesmerized by the bandages that covered the wound.

Though tired, Jesse could still speak. He reached out and took his son's hand. "Do you like the flimsy apartment they set up for me here?"

"Did it hurt?" asked Drew, who left Jesse's attempt at humor unnoticed.

"I don't know. I slept through it," Jesse teased. "It's a little sore, but no big deal." Jesse felt a bit short on breath. "Come here, buddy."

Drew came close to Jesse, who wrapped a weak arm around his son. They huddled together. Jesse drew his son's head closer.

Jesse pressed his cheek against Drew's head and said, "Do you know how much I love you?"

"Yes." Drew had spent his whole life without this affection

from his father. But now, Jesse could feel security emanate from Drew as his father's arm surrounded him.

"Never forget that love, buddy. I hope—"

Jesse's body lurched as a knifing pain stabbed him inside. A wince, then he grunted under his breath, tightened his lips as he tried to maintain composure. He didn't want to scare Drew.

The pain grew sharper. He winced again.

"Are you hurt?"

"No, I'm fine." Frightened, Jesse gasped for breath.

It's happening.

"Jesse?"

To Jesse's ears, Drew's voice sounded muffled. Jesse shut his eyes, endured the intense pain. He wanted to tell Drew to find a nurse but couldn't breathe.

The monitor shrieked in alarm.

Drew froze.

Jesse held him closer. He sensed his time was short.

When he located a wisp of voice, Jesse aimed his mouth toward Drew's ear. "The nurse will be on her way. I don't have much longer." With every word, Jesse felt his oxygen drain away.

Drew sobbed.

"Your mom'll need a lot of love over the next few months," Jesse struggled to whisper, "so take care of her and give her lots of hugs, okay?"

"Dad …"

"You'll be okay." Jesse pressed his head against his son and their teardrops mingled. "I love you, Drew."

"Daddy …" Drew bit his quivering lip. His face flushed red and hot tears poured from his eyes.

In an obvious panic, Drew broke away and ran into the

corridor. He screamed for the nurse, who was already a few feet from the door, a white-coated doctor behind her. Another attendant grabbed Drew and held him tight as the boy tried to break free and cling to his dad.

When they reached Jesse's bed, the monitor retreated to one long, steady tone.

———

On the first floor, Caitlyn sipped her bottled water as she left the gift shop and rounded the corner to the lobby, back toward the elevator. Behind her, the hospital's automatic-entry doors slid open as Blake and Eden ran through. When they saw Caitlyn ahead, they dashed faster and shouted.

Out of breath, Eden caught up with Caitlyn and grabbed her by the shoulders. "Where's Jesse?"

"Upstairs. Why?"

"He's in trouble."

Blake raced for the elevators. "Chuck's on his way! Hurry!"

———

From the corridor, they heard the commotion and the monotonous, foreboding tone. When Caitlyn, Eden and Blake arrived at the partition, they found Jesse surrounded by two staff members, who prepared electric paddles in a second effort to revive him.

A red-eyed Drew, his face scarlet and streaked with tears, ran to his mother and clung to her. Caitlyn held him while she stared at Jesse in alarm.

Drew tried to speak through hysterics. "Mom, he started hurting and fell asleep. They couldn't wake him up …"

Caitlyn wrapped her arms around Drew and covered his face from the sight.

Chuck, in a pant, arrived at the door, his eyes on the electric paddles. He stared at his son, a father unable to rescue his boy. "Jesse!" And the preacher fell to his knees at the foot of the bed.

EPILOGUE

LATE April the following year, Drew, now twelve years old, carried a duffel bag into his grandfather's office at the church. Alone. Seven o'clock sharp on a Saturday morning.

Chuck wrapped up some paperwork. "Hey there, champ! All packed and ready to go? It could be a twelve-hour drive with all the pit stops, you know."

"Ready. Can we go for pancakes on the way there?" Drew wore a red baseball cap, which Chuck had bought him at a sports shop in town.

Chuck laughed as he walked around the desk with a duffle bag of his own. "Sure thing." On his knees now, he stared into his grandson's eyes and still seemed astounded to see the boy alive. "You know how much your dad loved you to do what he did, don't you? He was willing to give his life for you."

With a nod, a healthy Drew smiled, his confidence in a clear boost. "Yeah."

"That's how valuable you are, big guy."

"Tell your grandpa to get a move on!" Jesse walked through the doorway, duffle bag in hand. With the other arm, he grabbed Drew in a bear hug. "Ready to go, slugger?"

"Let's go. Grandpa promised we'd eat breakfast on the way."

Chuck snorted as he packed his Bible into his duffel bag.

After the medical staff revitalized Jesse, they conducted

further tests, which confirmed the existence of Baer's Disease in him. But under a physician's guidance and a medical regimen, Jesse and his physician brought the symptoms under control. With his son safe, Jesse felt relieved to be alive.

As expected with Jesse's blood condition, staff deemed his marrow ineligible for Drew. Jesse, however, harbored no regrets, and in due time, they located a donor through the national marrow registry. Jesse wondered at the extent to which he had tried to rescue his son, regardless of the cost. Given the same scenario, would he have risked his life again? Probably so, he figured. After all, Drew was his son. Jesse loved him more than life.

But one positive result came about from the experience: Bound together by the tragedy, Jesse and Drew were inseparable nowadays.

Chuck rose to his feet again. He stared at his own son and bit his lip. Jesse returned the gaze.

Alive from the dead.

Repeatedly the preacher had told Jesse that he could break down into tears each time he recalled how the doctor revived Jesse. The play-by-play had seared itself in his mind with crystal clarity. The critical final seconds had stretched for what seemed an eternity as Chuck prayed at the foot of the bed and begged God for a miracle.

This morning, the preacher shook his head.

Prayers do get answered, his smile seemed to say.

Duffel bags in hand, the three men—three generations—walked toward the door, single file, to begin their road trip. On their way out, Chuck patted Jesse on the back. Jesse guided Drew by the shoulders. Chuck turned off the light and shut the door.

The next day at 12:05 p.m., the Indians would play the Cardinals in St. Louis. And the Barlow trio had twelfth-row seats.